MONTE COOK &
SHANNA GERMAIN

The Night Clave

A Numenera Novel

**ANGRY
ROBOT**

ANGRY ROBOT
An imprint of Watkins Media Ltd

20 Fletcher Gate,
Nottingham,
NG1 2FZ • UK

angryrobotbooks.com
twitter.com/angryrobotbooks
Touched by a star

An Angry Robot paperback original 2017

Cover by Federico Musetti
Set in Meridien by Argh! Nottingham

Distributed in the United States by Penguin Random House, Inc., New York.

US edition ISBN 978 0 85766 720 5
UK edition ISBN 978 0 85766 719 9
Ebook ISBN 978 0 85766 721 2

Printed in the United States of America

9 8 7 6 5 4 3 2 1

"A carefully woven tale that builds slowly, rewarding patient readers with revelation after revelation, building to a crescendo at the climax."
Barnes & Noble Sci-Fi & Fantasy Blog

"Despite the setting and sci-fi/fantasy blending, this novel is an intense character study of a woman trying to literally rebuild herself. The writing is lovely and borders on the poetic. Equally impressive is that despite the strange setting, language and terms, and wondrous tech, Germain grounds the world through the characters and keeps the focus on them. This is a fantastic sci-fi/fantasy novel but readers of any genre will fall deeply into Talia's story."
San Francisco Book Review

"I really enjoyed it. It is absolutely completely other worldly."
Ever the Crafter

"Readers who enjoy their fantasy and science fiction together need look no further than the mech-enhanced cast of characters in this alt-world fantasy story. Like the work of Kameron Hurley, this novel is bleak, full of tough-as-nails women willing to do what they must to survive, yet tells a universal story that many fantasy fans will relate to."
I Am Booking

"Germain's realization of Enthait is vivid, to the point that the reader can taste the dust in the air and murmurs of a living city like bees buzzing around the hive, and her ability to twist a story round history and half-dreamed memories builds the kind of novel that is tantalizingly missing just the right pieces to pull the reader in until the end."
King of Books

To those who love what they fight for
and fight for what they love.

You know you're on the right side if the people love you.
                                        – RILLENT BOURE

1. Every Death Starts With a Very Good Plan

Kyre had no guiles about their purpose here. They'd come to kill a man – not just a man, an Aeon Priest, a clave leader – and there was no way that he, not even he, with his ability to push things into ornate words and pretty boxes, could find another container to put that in.

What would it be like to see Rillent after all of this time? Not just see him, but...

"Kill," Aviend said from where she was crouched beside him. They were taking a breather, halfway up the outside slope of the crater. Every step, rubble trembled and threatened to fall, to give away their position. They'd practiced this a hundred, two hundred times. Still, pebbles shifted. Dust clouds rose beneath their feet and threatened to call attention to their movements. Slow and careful. Slow and careful. "The word you're thinking about is kill."

"Reading my mind again?" he asked.

Most of Aviend's form was wrapped in a brown and grey sleeksuit. Even her usually wild hair was tucked beneath the suit's hood. Only her face showed as she cast a glance at him. Her eyes were a deeper brown than the fabric, flecked with gold. Aviend's typical smile was a cautionary thing, only one side of her lips curving, as if her mouth was always trapped between joy and worry. The one there now was a full curve, both sides. Not comfort, but a delight to finally be doing something beyond practicing for this day.

"Nothing else to read around here," she said.

It was an old joke between them, a leftover from a younger, more innocent time. Despite what she'd tried to convince him of when they were kids, Aviend couldn't actually read his mind. Or anyone else's. She just had an uncanny knack for knowing what people were thinking. "It's in the cheekbones," she'd said once, but that had made no sense and he hadn't known whether to believe her. It was disconcerting sometimes, the way she could look at him and know what was going on in his head, but it also meant a lot of words he didn't have to say. Over the years he'd grown to appreciate that about her. Like so many other things.

"Gloaming," Aviend said, lifting her chin toward the sky spread out above and before them. "Right on time."

It was, and it was. Night was falling the way it often did over the Stere: slow, as if this was the only place in the world where the coming of the dark did not matter, where its very presence was made unnecessary by the dark-leaved woods, the neverending umbrage continually caught trunk-to-trunk. He knew without turning that behind them the endless forest had already gone to pitch, shadowbacked by its thickness and depth.

From here, clinging to the side of the rise and looking upward, the view was daunting. Day lingered, trying to keep its hold along the edges of the far-off mountains, as night slowly spread its grey and purple over the sky's pale skin like a fresh bruise. If all went according to plan, the light would stay long enough to see them to the top of the rise and disappear just when they needed it to.

There was a lot riding on the phrase "if all went according to plan". But it was a good plan, maybe even close to a perfect plan. It was also their only plan. If it succeeded, a man would be dead and they would be safely away before anyone was the wiser. If it failed...

"It won't," Aviend said. She didn't wink – it wasn't her style – but she did a thing, maybe without even realizing it, where she shifted her lips sideways and lifted a brow. It was, he thought, the same as a wink. A reminder of the secrets between them, the promise of things to come. An acknowledgment of how hard they'd worked for this very moment.

"Time," he said to her unasked question.

As one, they moved. Together they crawled up the remainder of the slope, low through the rubble, hands and knees, sometimes elbows and thighs. Staying flat. Staying tight.

They didn't talk. They didn't have to. They'd been working on this plan long enough that he couldn't remember when they hadn't. For so long, their lives – his, Aviend's, Delgha's, Thorme's – had been filled with devices, maps, time plans, and the shared dream of Rillent Boure's end. Everything – every piece of equipment, every late night of planning in the base, every risk they'd taken to learn a schedule or a secret – it all led to this moment. For good or for ill.

As Kyre climbed, he did a mental equipment check. He'd done it once before they'd left the base, but there was no such thing as too careful. He touched each object with his mind the way others might touch it with their fingers.

Obedient rope coiled at his hip. It would drop him down the inside of the crater they were climbing and then pull him back up when he was ready. He disliked the rope. Its semi-sentience made him wary, but he was not one to disregard a good tool just because its attributes made him uncomfortable.

Polarizer glasses. Lenses off. All he had to do was say the word and they'd come on. At least that's what Delgha had promised him.

Long-range launcher, strapped to his back. A gift from one of the many people they'd helped escape from Rillent's trenches.

Corrosion projectile sealed in an organic sheath, and tucked into his pocket. There was no way to keep the projectile's coating from eating away at the launcher. So the timing of removing it from the sheath, loading it, and firing it was going to be paramount. He'd done it a thousand times with a regular projectile. But they only had one of these.

The piece of equipment he didn't want, but he checked off his mental list anyway, because he always had it with him and would have it until the day he finally had to use it: a silver and red nodule on a strip of leather that looped his neck. It snagged and pulled as he moved, as if to remind him of its presence, of its purpose. The nodule was last resort. Or whatever came beyond last resort. Putting that cypher in motion meant everything had gone horribly, irrevocably wrong. He'd only come close to using it once. He hoped he'd never have to.

The small things came last. Two shortblades in the sleevesheaths on his arms, med kit, ceramic detonation cypher (because you never knew when you'd need to blow something up), the strongglass-and-steel ring that he never took off.

By the time he finished the list, they were nearly at the top. The sloped side they were climbing, the broken bits of buildings and statues and walls that shifted and tumbled beneath their feet, had once been their home. Before the kubrics. Before Rillent. Before there was even an inkling in his mind that they would plan to take another man's life in cold blood. That *he* would plan to take another man's life in cold blood. That he would become a killer. A killer, like the man he had to kill.

What luxury they'd known, before the ruin. Worrying over ghosts and small affairs and whether Aviend's mother would approve of him. It was silly and horrible and he missed it with every fiber of his being. That complex simplicity of less dark times.

Not everyone thought of what had happened as the ruin, of course. For Rillent and his pseudo-clave and his believers, everything that had happened was not the end, but the beginning. Rillent had told Kyre more than once that you knew you were on the right side if the people loved you. Rillent's people loved him, without question. Every night at the drop of dark – just a few minutes from now – they would chant his name and tell him so. They would show their gratitude for everything he'd given them, for their lives and their loves, their homes and their sustenance. Not knowing there were two people climbing up the outside of the crater who were about to take all that away from them.

As they neared the top of the ridge, Kyre smelled it, that mingling of scents that rode over each other rudely and cut each other off, like so many sentences in a conversation. Meat, fresh and rotted, sweating too hard and too long in the sun. Intercut with the sweetness of wolflilies, their honeyed rise made all the more piquant by the putrid undercoat. Rillent had the fuchsine flowers planted all over the forest, a failed attempt to disguise the stench of death.

And the scent that Kyre only knew as belonging to the

kubrics themselves, one that was more in the back of the mouth than in the pull of the nose. Shuddery, metallic, a bite of metal and stale air. It made him want to cough, or puke, or both, and so he pulled the back of his gloved hand across his mouth. The pressure against the fabric released a soft hiss of less-foul air captured from kinder places than this.

Kyre took a moment to swallow down his reaction and the fresh air that followed, then glanced at Aviend. She'd pulled the neck of her hood up over her mouth and nose, but mostly seemed focused on watching the sky intently. Any minute now.

From inside the dugout crater that was once the town of Ovinale, their childhood home, came the slinging sound of a large device powering up. A bluish light flickered hot then faded, pushing its light into the darkening sky for a blink before it went black again.

That spot of light got them moving. Silent as shadows, on their forearms and forelegs, slithering forward as much as anything, moving themselves their final few feet to the top of the rise without so much as a single shift of stone or statue.

"Steor," he whispered, and the polarizers warped his vision for a blink before they settled. Once they activated, he could barely tell the difference.

He and Aviend reached the top just as night reached them. Just as the light from below rose, blue and bright, to momentarily obscure everything but a long metal strip that jutted out from the building. Just as Rillent Boure, the man they'd come to kill, stepped out onto the raised walkway into the shine.

Next to him, Aviend's breath caught and then released in a barely audible curse.

"Don't let him see you," Kyre said. An unnecessary

caution. Even as he spoke, he could feel her pulling back slightly, lowering her body down to the ground next to him. Becoming shadow inside shadow.

Rillent believed Aviend was dead. They needed to keep it that way.

To Kyre's eyes, Rillent looked like the same man he'd been when Kyre had still believed in him. Imposing in his stride as he moved toward those gathered below him, Rillent was wrapped in a purple robe, garnished with gold, that covered and nearly concealed his thinness. He carried his long silver weapon with the loose hand of a man who understood that he was strong enough not to need it.

A broad gold wrap crossed his forehead, cleverly concealing the implant embedded at his hairline. Kyre had only seen it once – a quick glimpse of the half-buried black device that Rillent believed was the key to his power – but he knew he'd never forget it. It was that device that he and his launcher needed to focus on. In the shadows it was hard to see Rillent's features but they weren't ones that Kyre would easily forget. The broad hooked nose, the thin lips, his oddly purplish eyes.

Just behind him, the nonhuman shape of Rillent's trusted shield. Faleineir. Kyre swallowed back the acetic swell that rose in his mouth at the portentous movements of the tall, angular varjellen.

He moved his gaze elsewhere. Shadowed figures on the edges of the thin strip matched Rillent's long, sure strides. Their lights both highlit and masked, focused and diffused. One moment, Rillent's face was shone upon, visible in its every crevice and scar, its every puncture and piercing. The next, he wore a mask of cerulean shadow and smoke.

Rillent seemed small in that moment, but Kyre knew it was only because of the vastness of the structure upon which he stood. One of the five identical and ancient kubrics that had lain fallow under the forest's floor for who knew how long. Until Rillent had arrived in the Steremoss and begun to uncover them. Until Kyre had helped him do so.

The kubric rose and rose, twisted in its beauty, all leading the eye in toward the pathway upon which Rillent now strode. The structure was wide as a dozen ravage bears, end to end. As tall as a hundred men stacked head to foot, and that was just the part already dug from the earth. Who knew how far down into the earth it went, to its end? If it had an end. When he'd been inside, he'd begun to think it was endless, puncturing the very planet itself.

Who knew what original purpose these giant devices held? Or what the long-ago creators had in mind when they'd built them? He didn't. He didn't think Rillent did either, nor did Rillent care; they were merely a means to an end. A power source for his plans.

The blue light behind Rillent flickered, then streamed upward, lifting the sky from marengo to a blue shine that took away Kyre's breath. It made his nose tingle at the edge and his eyes water. He'd forgotten, even as he thought he remembered, the light's pulchritude. Even through the polarizers, the angled shape pulled at him like a drug, like an old friend, like the long gone comfort of his mother's arms. It was a call he thought he'd forgotten, but the shine forced him to remember with a sudden, uncomfortable blaze. He couldn't, for the moment, think of anything else. Couldn't see anything else. He knew that Aviend was beside him, somewhere, but he couldn't sense her presence, couldn't tell if she was calling his name.

Kyre lowered his body until it rested flat to the ground, and pressed his chin hard to the rubble. It cut and scratched, but he didn't care. It forced his head to stay upright under memory's pull of Rillent's easy promises and Kyre's own desire to believe them. Kept him from caving, the way his body ached to. His muscles strained, drove the skin and bones of his chin and throat into the edges of the debris.

Through the otherworldly din of the light, Aviend's touch came against his shoulder, a reminder of something real, something true. He didn't believe he could move into it, though he needed to. Somehow, she knew and came to him instead, and a moment later, it was the length of her pushed to him, armor and weapon and the side of her face, and her voice saying, "Aviend."

Why she said her name and not his own he didn't know, but it was the right thing. He could turn his head and see her. Her features were painted with a sheen of blue, afterimage of the device. He blinked the color away.

"Stay here," she said, pointing a finger toward her face. He did. The pull of the light called to the corners of his eyes, the movement of his blood, but he stayed. He watched the blue flicker across the row of silver piercings up her ear and touch upon the green flecks in her eyes. He stayed and breathed again when he could.

"Rougher than you anticipated," she said, her eyes flicking along his face. "Even with Delgha's lenses."

"Yes." He thought about it for a moment. Remembering the hook and tug of it set his teeth on edge. "But also, it's gotten stronger somehow, I think."

"The pull or the light?"

"Both."

"That means Rillent has gotten stronger too," she said.

Aviend was looking right at the light. He could tell by the way the blue moved between the edges of her teeth, filled in the white of her eyes. It sank into each tiny hollow of her skin and lay there, dormant and dark. And yet it didn't draw her. Didn't talk to her or ask anything of her. A wash of jealousy at her ease trembled and broke along the edges of his skin. He reminded himself that everything he'd chosen – for good or for ill – had led to this moment. And that she had pulls of her own.

"If we have to switch, we know the risks," Aviend said. "They're not... insurmountable."

"They're not good, either," he said.

Where the pull of the light beckoned to Kyre's mind, it was Rillent himself who beckoned to Aviend's. And Rillent was stronger than the light by magnitudes.

"We go as planned then," Aviend said. It wasn't a question, not really.

"We go as planned."

When Aviend's mother, Nuvinae, had been the leader of their clave and someone came to her with a problem, she was fond of saying, "You're the one who talked to the philethis. There are seventeen ways this could go, and all of them are yours." It was a sentiment he hadn't understood when he was younger – although the first time she'd said it to him directly, it shook him so hard his teeth rattled. But now he thought he might have a glimpse of what she'd meant to convey. They had opened this door. Whatever happened next was on their shoulders.

Aviend nodded, no more questions, and scooted back a bit more. She had her own job here, one that was at least as important as his – making sure that they got out of this alive.

Kyre pulled the launcher from the strap that held it to his back. It was already a long thin thing, lighter than it should have been to carry, but heavy as it needed to be when you held it steady and looked through the scope. He twisted the small key at the end, stretched it longer. It ratcheted out with a series of tiny clicks. He would have preferred to carry it on his back down the slope, leave his hands totally free, but no matter how many times they'd tried it, he couldn't get the launcher set up and loaded in time. This was the only way that guaranteed him a shot.

He didn't muse on the obvious. That he'd never killed anyone before. That he had no idea what it would be like to lift that scope to his face and see another person through it. To pull the trigger and kill a man.

Not a man. A monster. But also still a man.

He uncoiled the cable at his waist, then held the end in the air. The first time he'd tried to rappel from the obedient rope, he hadn't been sure he could trust it to hold him. Now he didn't even have to think about it. He spoke a few words to the end of it and released it into the air just at the edge of the cliff. It hung there, unmoving even when he tugged on it. The rope would hang there until he asked it to come down. He peered over the crater's lip. Down below, just where the rope ended, was a ledge, an outcropping of some once-useful piece of material that had gotten shoved into this hill with everything else. It was slick as ice, and nearly as transparent, but it was just big enough for him to stand on. Hollowed out to give him coverage from the light. And angled perfectly for Rillent's dais.

The whole interior of the crater was lit with blue, almost as daylight. It was so bright he could see the dirt and drit, the pieces of rubble, sharp and blackened, that stuck out at odd angles in the downward slope. Too bright. As it was, there was no way he could make it down without being seen. Thankfully, Rillent was a man of strict ritual and grand gestures. Precise, even. That's what they were counting on.

He glanced back at Aviend. She was crouched low, setting up the final bits of the dispatcher, twisting together a series of thin wires into a delicate and complicated pattern and threading them through a small black box. It was such a tiny device for what it could do, sending the two of them far out of reach of Rillent and his men.

Although he considered himself somewhat tech savvy, the dispatcher was one device that he couldn't quite wrap his head around. He understood what parts went where and how to operate it, but didn't understand how it worked. But sending people instantly through time and space was one concept that he was all right with not grasping. In fact, if he thought about the idea too much, it made him feel nauseous. So he mostly didn't think about it, other than as their way home once all of this was over.

When the yellow light on the side of the box blinked twice, Aviend gave him a nod. Ready.

Now they just had to wait and hope that nothing would fall. One tiny piece, cracking, and everything they'd worked for would come tumbling down.

Below them, Rillent reached the end of the walkway. He lifted his weaponless hand. Kyre couldn't see the crowd at the base of the kubric – human-sized shadows shifting in the dark – but he could hear them respond to Rillent's actions. A rising murmur of voices. Part chant, part song, part prayer. To these people, Rillent was a savior, a leader. The one who had rescued them from their lives. Listening, Kyre felt a pang of anguish for what he was about to take away from them, and then pushed it away. The security, the promises, they weren't real, no matter what the people of the Stere might think.

The rise of voices was overridden by Rillent's deep bass

tone as he began to speak. Rillent had a voice built for persuasion, a soft timbre that made you feel as though you had chosen to step off the ledge for him, that made you feel good for having done it. Kyre couldn't make out the words, but he'd heard them enough times that he could tell what they were just by Rillent's hand gestures. The intonation of the welcoming, the repetition of promises, the empty words of an Aeon Priest who'd ripped everything from them and left them with nothing but their own shadowed grief to eat.

When Rillent lifted the hand in which he held his weapon – loose grip, soft hold, so that it seemed as if it might fall down among the worshippers at his feet – Kyre felt his breath hollow out inside his chest.

The blue light blinked, and darkness overtook the crater faster than any living thing. The black came without a sound, hushing everything in its wake.

Now.

As soon as the sky blacked, Kyre took hold of the rope and began to lower himself down the inside of the crater. Closer to Rillent. Closer to the light, which would return as planned – he hoped – just as he planted his feet on the ledge. Going down, his body moved without his mind, the practice of muscles and timing. His mind went on without his body, thinking of the ledge below, the launcher, scope to eye, Rillent zooming toward him through the lens.

He'd made it the length of three hand-over-hands, barely halfway in his descent, his feet finding their first of many touch points, when he thought he heard Aviend say something from above him.

It might have been her. It might have been his own nervous mind. It might have been the Stere's ghosts, although he'd only heard them speak half a dozen times, and never in

Aviend's voice. Having slipped back from the ledge to protect herself from Rillent's eyes, Aviend was out of his sightline. He couldn't stop, not now, not when the blackout would only last a few seconds, and so he kept going, hand over hand, finding his way through the dark until he felt the ledge beneath his foot. He'd barely stepped onto the small outcropping of stronglass when the lights came back up.

Everything in his body wanted to exhale, a great last release, but there was no time for such luxuries. Rillent was already rising into the air in the wash of new light, arms raised. If you were down below, watching your god rise, it seemed a magical thing. Your savior flying above you with nothing more than the power of his mind. But Kyre had touched the box beneath the man, had inadvertently laid the foundation for that great rising, and he knew it for what it was – nothing more than a device like any other, projecting false power. Just like the one he held in his hands. Like the one around his neck.

As Rillent rose, Kyre leaned back into the side of the crater, letting the shadows of the hollow fold over him like a cloak. If Rillent looked up, he'd see Kyre, the launcher, the rope. But there was no reason for Rillent to look up. Rillent only ever looked down.

From his floating vantage point, Rillent again began to address the crowd below him. Kyre pulled the corrosive projectile from its container, grateful to see his hands unshaken. First try, he loaded the tiny synth cylinder into the launcher. He had mere seconds before the corrosion would eat away at the barrel and render both objects useless.

He lifted the launcher to his shoulder. Through the scope, he could see everything. Every fold of fabric. Every wrinkle of skin. The shape of the hidden implant at his forehead. Every seed of a lie that left Rillent's lips to fall and spread over the crowd below. A man. A monster. And what would Kyre become when he pulled the trigger, put a bullet into the brain of another human being? He would know soon enough.

Kyre put his finger to the trigger, exhaled slow and steady, a great long breath. And then he heard Aviend call his name.

Devices never talk to Aviend. She knows they talk to Delgha, whispering secrets of efficiency and repair, suggestions, even alternate uses. But she and devices have a more... cantankerous relationship. They don't tell her anything. In fact, she's pretty sure they fight her, cog and wire, out of nothing more than spite. She blames them fully for the number of times she's had to take one of their number out of the base and throw it into the woods, swearing and irate. They always work it out eventually, her and the device. But it's almost never pleasant. It's always her asking and then threatening and finally getting in there with her hands and tools and forcing.

So she fully expects the dispatcher to fight her. It has on every single trial run, so why not now, when it really matters?

But by some miracle of mechanics, it doesn't. She glides the wires through their twists and turns. Intricate. Delicate. More song than sync, and maybe that's why it works this time.

It's up and running so fast she's sure she's forgotten something, but no. Light's blinking and everything's settled. Her job's done until Kyre returns. Then she'll use the dispatcher to carry the two of them to safety.

Ready.

Blackout.

Go, she thinks.

So dark she can't see Kyre start down the rope, only hear him. He barely makes a sound but she knows his breathing, the slip of his gloves. Each soft touch of his boots to the side of the crater.

In the darkness, she lowers herself flat to the ground and pushes herself forward. When the lights come up, she wants to be able to see. Aviend had never wished ill will upon another person until Rillent entered her life. This fierce desire for a man's death is a dark retching hole in her stomach. She won't look away. But she can't watch the death. Not because of the hole, but because of Rillent's hold on her. She can't risk that. After all, that's the reason Kyre is down in the hole instead of her.

Instead, she plans to watch Kyre lift the launcher, close the gap between them. Close down Rillent.

Everything inside her spreads anger at the thought of Rillent, at the thought of his name, at the thought of what he's doing, what he will do if they don't stop him. The wolflilies they saw on their way here; not native to the Stere, spreading far and wide in the soil of Rillent's dead. She tries not to work from anger, not ever, but it's always there underneath the other parts of her, wiggling cava worms beneath a rotting log. She closes her eyes. Deep breath. In. Out. Opens her eyes again.

The light returns, spreads up the side of the cavern. Kyre's already touched down. Back to the slope, loading the launcher. She feels her breath leaving her. Acrid and damp. Like being punched in the gut by someone you love so you can throw up whatever's poisoning you.

A human-shaped shadow shifts at the bottom of the crater.

Aviend says Kyre's name out loud and regrets it before her mouth is even closed. More regret when she sees the rope still for a microsecond, as if Kyre heard her and has paused.

When the rope shivers again, showing Kyre is still on the move, she turns her attention back to what she'd seen below him. She takes a risk – ghostfell, what is she doing? – and pushes herself forward a bit more to get a better view.

Halfway up the slope, maybe not quite, below and to the right of Kyre, the shadow inches upward, momentarily hidden from the light.

At first, she'd thought it was a ghost, lost and trapped away from its home by the crater's angled slope. The ghosts of the Steremoss weren't stupid, but they had trouble navigating the world. As if their senses lived in a world where everything was just a bit different. She'd seen them bump into trees and fall into rivers. Not like they couldn't see the thing in front of them. More that they believed so strongly that it was an illusion that it wouldn't or couldn't affect them.

But this thing is no ghost. It's human. Or close enough. She wasn't sure until the lights shifted a bit, spreading their grey cast farther along the sides of the crater. Kyre talks of the lights as if they are blue, and she believes him, but to her, they are always grey. Not sky and water, but metal and stone. She's told Kyre they don't affect her, but they do. They make the edges of her head squeeze together in a dull throb that travels across her temples to the backs of her eyes and blurs her vision. It's part of the reason she'd been momentarily sure she was seeing a ghost. They're not awful for her, not as bad as for Kyre, but what she'd do to never have to look at those lights again... If someone shows up right now and makes a bargain with her, she will take it. No questions asked.

No one shows up, so she squints against the light and watches the figure. Young and scared. The way it moves is quick and light, its body made of long bones and reach. But something is holding it back, too, a lean to the side that seems to be slowing it down. Injury? Maybe. And a new one at that. This is a body still figuring out how to adjust to a broken form of movement.

So not one of Rillent's men coming for them. Which is good, but also bad. If it isn't one of Rillent's men, then what is it? And, most important, just how dangerous is its presence going to be to their plan? All it has to do is move in a way that draws the gaze of Rillent or his men, and it's no far leap for them to look a little higher and see Kyre making his way down the side of the slope. Just her luck, for a shadow to botch up eons of hard-laid plans.

For a moment, everything in her stills. Out breath. Think. Should she call Kyre back? Everything they'd worked for, broken. It's possible that he'll have time to take his shot before anyone notices him, but if not, every moment of her hesitation puts them both at risk. What were the chances that Rillent would look up and see Kyre and not know exactly who he was and what he'd come for? Less than zero, she thinks.

A sudden thought slips to her. Maybe Rillent already has looked up. Maybe he's already sending his glaives. She won't look at the Aeon Priest, can't look at him, and so she doesn't know. Flying blind.

No. She has to believe in the plan.

On the other hand... the thought isn't one she likes, but it's there, unbidden and unrelenting... the boy – she is pretty certain that it's a boy down there, based on that reckless fling of limbs and life – could be useful. It's clear he's running.

How long until someone notices he's gone? If Kyre can be quick – and she knows he can, knows he is – then they can be out before anyone notices. Rillent will have the boy hunted down. Kill him, as sure as she's pressed to this dirt. But she and Kyre will be free.

Aviend, are you willing to kill another human for this? Her mother, always, in her head. Aviend doesn't mind. It is better to have her there, questioning judgment, than to never hear her at all. And this time, her answer is easy: Yes. Yes, she is. Rillent is at stake. Everything is at stake. And she knows, in a way that she's never known before, down to bones and marrow, down to blood and breath, that they will never have another chance.

As far as she can tell, neither the boy nor Kyre have seen each other yet. Maybe they'll just pass each other by in the darkness and everything will go – almost – as planned.

Please don't screw this up, kid. She doesn't know where the kid part comes from, but there it is and it seems right so she runs with it. Don't look up. Go wherever you're going and pass us by. Dark to dark. No harm done. Mostly.

The shadow form reaches a hand, shifts upward and a little to the right. Yes. That's it, kid. Kyre will go down, and the kid will come up. Kyre will take his shot. Rillent will be dead. She doesn't let herself think any more about what will happen at the point where the kid reaches the top, because she and Kyre will be long gone by then.

Kyre's still hidden in the hollow of the ledge, not touched by it. Which is good. Which is the plan. He's closer to the edges of the lightplay than she would like, but safe. For now.

The shadow form, though, is another matter. The kid's lit up like he didn't even know there was such a thing as lights. Which is impossible, considering where he's coming from. Almost like he positioned himself dead center of the beam. Wanting to be seen. Wanting to be caught. Or just inexperienced and afraid. It's taken their team all their time and resources to put this plan in motion. What chance does a kid have, running from Rillent, without resources or a team?

She can see so much about the kid in the glare. So much she doesn't want to know. Dark outfit, complete with the hood that's pulled up tight. Sleeves and shoulders flecked with silver dust. She bets there's a black metal loop around his neck. A heatsear behind his left ear.

This kid's high-reaching hand is purple in the shine. Which means it's actually red under all the grey she sees. She pulls the zoom screen from her hood down over her eyes. Winces at what shows up in the lenses. Too close. Blood and marrow. Grisly like he pulled it from the mouth of some beast. Blood pools fast in his knuckles until it drips down the dark purpled skin to his elbow. And still he holds tight, gored fingers glued to the shifty debris. He stops, right in a spot of light so bright it blinds her to look at, even after she slips the zoom screen away.

She doesn't realize she's thinking about rooting for him until she already is.

Climb, you brehmbrained little shadow. Climb. Or you're going to get us all dead.

The kid doesn't. He stays, frozen in the light.

She would have sworn they'd covered every contingency. Light patterns. Rillent's schedule. Faleineir and the rest of his glaives. Their equipment. Her ability to get them to safety. Even Kyre's ability to actually kill a man.

But some kid pulling an escape attempt with – she's sure – any number of Rillent's men on his heels? Who could have planned for that?

A glance at Kyre shows he's got the launcher up, poised. He's on perfect time. He's not looking down. Why would he? The shadow below his feet shouldn't be there, and he has other things to focus on.

Rillent must be rising on his platform. His god box, he calls it. God, my ass, she thinks. It takes a certain kind of person to claim godhood from what is given to them by machines. And a certain kind of person to believe it. Of course, Rillent has a little help in that department, doesn't he? More of what he claims as god powers, but which are nothing of the sort.

The boy starts moving again, that lopsided lilt of a climb, and she can breathe again. All right. All right. That's a start. Now—

A guttural scream. The sound rakes the back of her neck like claws brought back from a nightmare. Her ears pulse with pain, reverberate the sound again and again into the soft spaces in her head.

Destriatch.

What are they doing here, at the kubric? Rillent always keeps them stationed along the borders of the Stere. Under Rillent's eye, the destriatch stalk the edges of the forest, claim its boundaries as theirs. As Rillent's. What could have made him call them back here, leave his borders unprotected? They don't have a plan for this, because it is an impossibility. Beyond impossibility.

Skist, kid. You really are going to get us all killed.

Another howl, to join the first. The sound makes her want to throw up and push herself off the edge at the same time. She wants to claw her ears off. And that's even before the howls rise, turn. Become song. Not song. Nothing like song. The malignity.

She's heard it before, once, but never close like this. Only from far, far off. Rillent was here, and her mother was still alive. The fearsong had made her fall to her knees. She was no small child, but her mother had scooped her up as if she was and run, so fast the branches had whipped their face and her ears. Aviend cried out, once, and her mother had nearly smothered her against her coat. It was the only time she remembered being afraid of her.

Inside the shape of the crater, the malignity resonates and grows. Amplified, the sound shatters the stab in her head and forms it anew. She can't imagine what it's like for Kyre and the boy, caught inside that hollow of sound.

Through the pain in her head, she sees a new movement. The first of the crourhounds pushes from the shadow of the kubric like it's being freshborn. The front all teeth and claws and spider eyes, wet fur oil-slicked. The middle all black metal and smoke. The tail end disappearing into nothingness. It's that empty place where the hindquarters should be that makes her feel most queasy. How can such a beast exist? Live? Hunt and murder? She doesn't know, but that's what it does. That's what it is.

Another beast pushes out of the darkness into the light. This one missing its belly. Everything else teeth and tail. Hindquarters that hunch and scrabble. Blue as Kyre's light. Not furred, but spined and spiked.

She is sure there are more coming. Rillent's army. Destriatch. Crourhounds. Black beasts of meat and machine and murder.

The first two start to scrabble up the slope. They've all gone silent. No howl. No song. Not even the rocks they stir up make noise when they fall. She sees they will be on the kid in a heartbeat. In a stride. In the opening of a maw.

Catching shadows or silence or some other thing that

should be there but is not, Kyre's head cocks, angles, carries with it the long scope. First to the beasts, then to the boy. Then, dropping the launcher, up to her.

Kyre is asking her a question that she does not have the answer to. She thought she would do anything to kill Rillent. But it turns out, she is not, as she thought, as she told her mother in her head, willing.

"Kyre," she yells, because she has no other choice, no other action that makes any sense to her. "Choose!"

At her yell, the destriatch give up their silence, scrabbling faster, screaming their song of blood.

At her yell, Rillent turns.

At her yell, everything falls away.

It's as though she's got the zoomshield down, but she knows she doesn't. She remembers once, a long time ago, years ago surely, pushing it up. Because of purple. Not this purple. This is eyes. Rillent. So close. Irises, purpled. Big as moons. Bigger than her. Eating her up. She sees wolves in his eyes. Maws of bloodied teeth. Coming. No, here already. The skin of her face breaks and burns. Gores. Holes down to her bones. To her teeth. The cold of the air through her eaten skin.

Welcome back, little one.

"Out," she means to say. "Get out of my skisting head."

He doesn't go. He never does. She knows that everything is lost. Like it was lost so long ago. When she was small. And her mother was there-not there. Ghost mother. She misses her. Rillent will take care. He will take away the black bad. Bring back her mother. She wants that, doesn't she? To see her mother again? Yes.

Over Rillent's silent voice, "Aviend. Look at me."

No. She won't. She wants the promise in the moons. She

wants one more day, one hour, one minute with her mother so she can say something important and true. Something that will not leave her with this hearthole.

"Aviend." Shaking her now, taking her away and she won't go. She won't.

But she does, and there is Kyre's face. His beautiful, not-Rillent face. His plain dark, not-Rillent eyes. Her mother falls away. The promises dissolve. The truth is here, in the broken dirt and the wolflily death cloy and the touch of Kyre's hand to her face.

"He caught me," she says. "He…"

"I know," Kyre says. He is heart incarnate and she just wants to fall into his being, see only him, until she can forget the color purple forever.

The boy is there too, behind Kyre. Hands and knees. Panting. His hand drips blood. The gash on his leg – what made him teeter his way up the slope – is giant. Gaping. "You chose," she said.

"I did," he said.

The right choice, she knows. Although it feels very much like the wrong one right now. He gives her a nod. He knows.

"How long…?" did Rillent have his hold on her? It felt like seconds and eternities, all crumbled like an egg in a dangerous hand.

"We have to go," Kyre says. "They're coming."

Not far now, the hounds, coming. Rake of nails and claw. Panting. Snarls. No more songs now. The time for singing and hunting is over. It is the time for the death and the destroy.

"Yes," she says. "You two. Take the ride." The dispatcher will only take two of them to safety.

She knows already that Kyre will say no. Not that the boy shouldn't go. They've already brought the boy onboard. And what you asked of the philethis, you took from the philethis. But he would say that Aviend should go and he should stay. That she's a liability with Rillent. Although that's not how he'd put it.

But they'd decided this already, all of them. If things went wrong, she would get Kyre out. Alone. If things went wrong, she was the contingency plan. If things went wrong, she was not supposed to leave this ledge until everything in front of her had died. Or she had.

This time, it's her choice and she's already chosen it. She turns the device. Levels them both into the machine's light.

"I'll meet you back at the base," she says. "You know I will."

It's the first promise to him she's ever risked breaking in the very telling.

And then she makes them both disappear.

As Kyre flickers out, there's movement. A small ceramic globe flies toward her. Aviend catches it, more instinct than skill. His detonation cypher.

She starts laughing. He knew she'd catch it. He knew she'd send them off without her. Probably as soon as he saved the boy, he'd known. And he'd made a backup plan. She has never loved anyone so much in her life as she loves Kyre Makara right now.

So. This is it. Her moment. She stands and fights and dies. Or she gets creative and finds a way to survive.

Aviend bobs the ceramic ball up and down in her palm. Once. Twice.

"Come on, you horrors!" she yells over the side of the crater.

Then she waits.

The destriatch climb, pack and hound, becoming one

and many, swarming up the side. They're working together, laddering over each other up the steepest parts. Un-slowing. Plowing up the incline toward her.

She resists the urge to toss the cypher right the fuck now. She waits. A few feet. A few more. Her blood thumps in her ears, echoing the hound's horrible song, their scrabble and howl.

She holds until she can taste the electricity of the closest one on her tongue. Until she can practically feel its metal and meat breath against her hand.

She lobs the detonation in the middle of them. Waits until she hears the *tck-tck* of the pre-explosion.

And then she runs like hell.

Traveling through space and time was never smooth, but this one was particularly bad. Kyre barely tossed the cypher off to Aviend before the edges of his body softened, stretched, snapped back with a whistling urgency. His knee barked on something in the dark – tree? rock? something else? He couldn't tell. He hit it hard enough that it was sure to leave a bruise, but not so hard that it felled him. His stomach flipped upside down, then righted itself with such force he felt like something in there actually dislodged.

But those things he'd come to expect. A hundred trials and you got used to losing the edges of your skin.

It was the other pain that caught him off guard. The realization of what had just happened was only beginning to settle on him, a fine-powdered dust of mistake that could choke you if you let it. They'd failed. Rillent was still standing. Not just standing, but now he knew about them. They were still out here. Still alive. Hunting him down.

And Aviend? He didn't know. They'd never fought the destriatch before. He'd seen them, of course. But only in the beginning. Once, they'd been predators. Now they were something much, much worse. They'd become what everything became beneath Rillent's hands. Death incarnate.

He'd known Aviend would send him through the dispatcher the second she told him to choose, the second he'd known what his choice would be, had to be. He'd gotten her the cypher in time, but just barely. They hadn't expected the destriatch. None of them had. Not at the kubric. So cypher or no, he wasn't sure it was enough.

It all came back to this: they'd failed. Chosen to fail, maybe, but that was still failure. Everyone's work, gone. Their one hard-fought chance, gone. All of their planning, wasted. All of their equipment, used up or lost. He'd held on to the launcher through the climb and the dispatch, but the corrosion had eaten through most of it already. There was no saving it.

And the feeling he had no box for, no pretty words to disguise it with: relief. Relief that he was not a murderer, a killer. He was just a man. Himself. Unstained by someone else's blood. Had he chosen right? Yes. No. He didn't know. Not yet. Relief, followed by guilt and fear.

Rillent had seen them. Or Aviend at least, and he hadn't just *seen* her. He'd stepped into her mind as easily as he had back in the beginning. Kyre wasn't sure which was scarier – knowing that despite all of her hard work, Aviend hadn't been able to keep him out, or knowing that Rillent now knew they still existed, that they were still alive in the world. In the woods.

They would have to face that later. First, he needed to get the boy safely to the base. Their loss was for nothing if the boy died out here. Then, he'd find Aviend. He hoped – such a bright and brutally thin hope – that she'd be back at the base waiting for him, for them. But he'd seen them, Rillent's crourhounds. He'd heard them. Felt their murderous rage, embedded and nurtured by Rillent into a palpable thing.

He would not lose Rillent and Aviend in a single night. He would not.

Next to him, the sound of twigs breaking and then a low sound of released breath. A retch, quickly followed by another, deeper and more pained. It took some getting used to, traveling via device rather than by body or beast. And then to land here, camouflaged even from yourself.

"Stay put," Kyre said in the direction of the sound. "It's just the effects of the dispatcher. We'll have light in just a-"

And there it was. Not light so much as reflection and amplification of what little light there was. But it was almost enough to see by.

Beside him, the heaving figure on hands and knees took a shaky inhale.

"Better?" Kyre asked.

A nod that didn't get a chance to finish, and then another, quieter round of retching welled up from the downed figure. Kyre's own stomach, still roiling from everything that had happened in the last few minutes, threatened to join in. He pushed it back with a press of his glove.

"Can you stand?" he asked, after it had been quiet for a few moments. "The reflector doesn't last very long, and we need to get moving."

The boy pushed himself up. He wavered and nearly fell. Kyre reached out a hand and caught him. He'd expected the boy to pull away, but he leaned in, let the help come.

The boy was something else. Not a boy at all. Not as Kyre had first thought. Just lean and hunched into himself and just young enough that he was still uncertain about where his bones belonged inside his skin. Old enough that he hadn't been born inside Rillent's trenches.

He wore the clothing of one of Rillent's trenchers though,

black on black, dusted at the shoulders and the hems with the silver-hued powder that the mortar hawks spit out. Kyre's dad had died in those colors; he would recognize them anywhere. Just like the heatsear behind his ear, which perfectly matched Kyre's.

A loop of black metal rested upon his neck and below that, a bit of leather or string that Kyre couldn't make out. He'd been overworked and underfed, from the looks of the hollows below his cheeks, for a long time.

He had a long slice along his neck that looked like it once went down slick to the bone. Recent enough, but not tonight's foray into opening skin. That he'd reserved for his hand and his leg. The hand was the worst, once, but now it had settled into a slow drip of blood that wetted the earth beside his feet. It would keep until they got back to the base.

What did worry him was the long gash running down from the outside of the boy's knee nearly to his ankle, splitting his pants and his skin, wide enough in places that the flesh around it gaped open when he moved, revealing the mottled white and pink of sinew and fresh blood. That one would need some attention, and soon.

The boy was shaking, but didn't seem scared. Relieved, Kyre thought. Surprised to have made it out alive. And likely exhausted down to his bones. Rillent did that to you. To everyone. Until he killed you.

"What are you called?" Kyre asked him, lowering his voice to softness and calm. The boy reminded him of a creature, startled awake by the light of a gun.

"Quenn." Not a note of the shake in his voice, even as his body rattled. He looked around, as if he was seeing his surroundings for the first time. They'd landed in the midforest, on the far west side of the Stere. It was the safest place they'd found for a landing – far enough from Rillent's border patrols and kubrics that they wouldn't be spotted. Far enough from the base that it wouldn't draw anyone's gaze there either. But that meant they were a hike from the base, and farther still from where Aviend was fighting for her life against a half dozen crourhounds.

But you couldn't tell from where they were standing. Here, it looked as if they were in an all-white room. Floor, ceiling, walls, even the whispering, wavering plants wore a sheen of alabaster...

...which kind of matched Quenn's eyes. Kyre thought Quenn might bolt, if he could only figure out how to get out of the illusion. The refraction was confusing, even for someone as experienced as Kyre. But it kept them from being seen. Not smelled or heard, but it was a start. One that would only last a matter of minutes.

"I don't know what's going..." Quenn's dialect was one that Kyre hadn't heard in a long time, not since he was a kid. It swallowed the second syllables of the words, turning *going* into *gong*. Northern, Kyre thought. Far away from where they were now. Far away from where he'd found himself in Rillent's trenches.

"It's a light refractor," Kyre said. He didn't know how much Quenn knew about technology, so he didn't elaborate other than to say, "It will keep us hidden from sight for a few minutes."

Quenn's eyes were still too large, too much white around the edges. He shook his hands, the injured one sending fine droplets of blood into the air.

"Quenn. Quenn, are you going to pass out? Throw up again? Take a deep breath. We've got to go and we've got to go fast, so I need to know you're with me."

After a moment, Quenn shook his head, then winced. He reached his gored hand toward his cheek, then thought better of the action, and carefully lowered his hand to his side. The lump in his throat bobbed as he swallowed before he spoke. "No." *Nah.* The dialect was tickling something in the back of Kyre's brain, but he couldn't focus on it enough to place it. He'd worry over it later.

All he could think about was Aviend. Aviend and Rillent. Aviend and the horror destriatch.

He swallowed it back and focused on the steps in front of him. Delgha had once called him unemotional, and if you knew Delgha, that was saying something. She hadn't meant it as an insult, but he hadn't been able to explain. Rillent did that to you. Taught you to keep the things you loved inside a tiny locked box that no one was allowed to look at. Because to let someone see was to let someone take it away.

"All right, Quenn, here's what's going to happen. I'm going to patch you up a bit. Enough to keep you alive…" He stopped and looked at him then. There was a lot to be learned from someone's reaction when you told them flat out they might die, even if you used nicer words.

Quenn seemed more scared than anything to hear the word "alive," as if he'd already come to terms with his inevitable death and Kyre was suddenly giving him hope. A hope that he wasn't sure he wanted. That was a low start. And a good one. It meant there was a place to go, and that place was up.

"And then we'll go from there," Kyre finished as he pulled a few tools from the pouch at his side. Talk to him. Keep him focused. "So, you've either got a brehm brain or some brehm balls, I'd say, running from Rillent. Which is it, do you think?"

Kyre was pretty sure he already knew the answer, but he wanted to know if Quenn did. He took a small glowglobe from his pouch and beckoned for Quenn to hold out his unmarred hand. "Lift this and hold it close to your leg. Left side. So I can see the..." He'd been about to say *hole*. "To patch you."

"I think the latter," Quenn said. *La'er.* "Though my sister would likely disagree." So he did know his own strengths. It was fitting together, how he'd gotten as far as he had without being killed. What he hadn't figured out yet was how he'd gotten under Rillent's boot in the first place.

"Your sister's a trencher?" More distraction for the boy, who was beginning to shake as Kyre peeled back the blood-soaked edges of the split pantleg and exposed the broken skin.

"No." His silence said there was a great deal more to that story but Kyre didn't ask it. He thought there might be time enough if Quenn wanted to tell it. It would be better if it waited until they got back to the base anyway, so everyone could hear. Stories often lost something in the retelling, he'd found. The first time was often the best.

The boy's leg was open nearly to the bone. Clean though. Seven teeth. And something straight and sharp enough to make a single, deep slice. A maiming slice. Kyre knew the shape of this wound.

"I need to fix this, Quenn, so you can travel," Kyre said. "But I'm no chiurgeon. Not by a long shot. And this is going to hurt like a mad mother ravage bear." Not as bad as that, but he wanted to prepare him.

Kyre waited until he saw understanding in Quenn's eyes, then he put his fingers to the edges of his skin. Quenn was sweatsheened, his skin slick and gritted, his muscles set tight beneath Kyre's touch.

He brought Quenn's leg forward until the glowglobe shone away the shadows of his skin. That gash deserved some of Thorme's handiwork – her tiny fingers made the cleanest stitches he'd ever seen. Kyre's own skin was testament to their artistry, in the nearly invisible seams along his shoulder. But the best he could do now was a temporary binding, to keep it clean and closed while they made their way back to the base. Then he'd turn him over to Thorme.

She was going to love that. He could already hear her, tsking her tongue loudly as she sewed, more to make a point than for any other reason. Tough love that one. But love just the same.

Taking a bit of the stretch tape from his kit, Kyre tore it into three strips, and pinched Quenn's skin together with his fingers. Quenn didn't flinch when Kyre crossed the tape, nor when he let go and everything stretched together. He made a small sound in the back of his throat, and swallowed it away before it was finished. He'd been with Rillent a long time, then, Kyre guessed. Long enough to come to expect not just death, but pain, the kind that went on without promise of an end.

The ones Rillent chose as trenchers were usually not as slight as this one; bigger, broader, hardier. But perhaps the Aeon Priest was running out of options, taking whatever labor he could. Certainly they knew he'd been speeding up the digging recently, moving at a breakneck speed. Literally. Thorme's runners had called back three fatal injuries among the trenchers just this season. In the past, fatal injuries didn't always mean fatal accidents. Trenchers took their own lives sometimes, as a means of escape. It was happening less and less, though, despite the conditions growing worse. If Rillent could find a way to enter a mind as strong as Aviend's, Kyre couldn't imagine what he could do to someone with less utter ferocity in their head.

"Better?" he asked as he finished. Quenn opened his

mouth to answer, winced as he put a bit of weight on his leg, and then nodded. "We have a true chirurgeon back at our base. She can do a much better job of fixing you up. I promise this is just temporary."

As Quenn moved, his shirt shifted. Around his neck was what Kyre hadn't been able to see before, an amulet, green and gold, a hue that matched his hazel eyes. It was a three-dimensional star built of triangles inside triangles. It only took Kyre one glance to recognize the six-pointed symbol as the one that was etched all over their base. The star of Gavani.

So the boy wore one of Gavani's stars, all of which were long rumored to have been lost or destroyed when the religion faded. He was too young to be a worshiper. His mother then? A grandparent? Or maybe a relic found in the dirt and drit and passed along without meaning. The last was most likely, as Gavani's followers had died out or given up long ago.

What weirdness was it that the very boy they'd rescued wore the pendant of the forgotten god whose temple they had taken over as their base of operations? If Kyre thought Rillent had any inkling of what they'd been doing or where they were holed up – before tonight, at least – he might have thought the boy a plant. Albeit an obvious one. But he didn't. Still, where had the boy come by it and what meaning did it have for him?

A mystery for a later time, but one that he was certain to want to ask.

For now, he asked, "Can you walk? It's a bit of a hike." Longer, and he wasn't a fan of lying, but where before he'd wanted to see what Quenn could handle, now he didn't want to overwhelm him before they'd started.

Kyre could almost see the moment when Quenn chose to shake off the shadows that were encroaching upon him.

When he looked up again, his eyes were steady. A soft, smart green. Good. They could also use more smart.

"Who are you?" he asked. "Why were you at the kubric? Do you work for Arch Boure?"

Arch Boure indeed. Kyre almost laughed, except that it was far scarier than it was funny. Rillent always did have a too-high sense of himself. Even Kyre had seen that at the beginning, and Kyre had seen so very little back then.

"I'm Kyre," he said. He debated whether to tell him who they really were, but held it back. He couldn't say why. Habit maybe. Or uneven footing. "And I can answer all of the rest of that – and any other questions you have – once we're to safety."

"You're going to take me back to him, aren't you? I know you are." The wild eyes were back. So much white. So little green. In the end, it was a good thing that Aviend was stubborn and smart enough to have sent the two of them off together. For all her strengths, Aviend wasn't that great with strangers in a panic – with most people, really. He could just imagine the two of them trapped in this illusionary box together. Aviend would already be shouting obscenities and Quenn would be running breakneck through the woods in the dark.

"Trust me. We didn't put our..." He was about to say plan. "Our lives at risk to save you just to put you back in Rillent's clutches. But we do want to ask you some questions, once your leg is fixed up. See if there's anything you know that will help us learn more about Rillent. Would that be all right?"

"You're not with him?"

"Him," said with both reverence and fear. Anger and love. But, Kyre was glad to hear, more anger and fear than the others.

"No."

Quenn lowered the glowglobe and Kyre caught a flicker of his expression in the shadows.

"You're not going to bolt, are you?" Kyre asked him. "At least not until we get your leg sewn up and give you a hot meal?"

The mention of food seemed to do Quenn in. Kyre could see it in the way his shoulders softened. He wouldn't run. At least not yet.

"Tell me who you are," he said. "Just... isn't that a fair thing to ask? I'm tired and scared and I am, honestly, a little surprised to be alive right now. So, please just tell me something, anything, that says you're not taking me back to him."

Kyre felt a stab, needlesharp, along his lower back. He hadn't meant to make him beg. He'd been aiming for efficient, not brutal.

"We're a small group..." He paused, wanting to be certain about his phrasing. He still wasn't a hundred percent sure of Quenn's story. There was a chance – so very small, but still there – that he was a spy, a plant. It had happened before. "... that has been working on a plan to..." Careful, careful. "To rebalance the power in the Stere."

"By killing him." It wasn't a question, exactly, and so Kyre chose not to answer it. They'd tried so many other ways, and none of them had worked. Killing was their last resort. "And I botched that by running away." Also not a question. Kyre let it go, waiting to see if there was more.

There was. "Right?" If nothing else, Quenn was persistent.

"It was our choice to rescue you," Kyre said. He felt like he'd said that once already, but maybe that was a false memory. Everything from the point where he'd raised the launcher to his eye until this very moment felt blurry and warped, like trees through a thick rain. And through all his attempts at calm, there was a pulsebeat in his brain. Insistent. Panicked. Aviend.

"You knew," Quenn said. "About the blackout. Just like I did." Not a rhetorical question, but one that was a gateway to the knowledge he already had locked in his brain. Kyre saw a flicker in his eyes. He was piecing an understanding together in his head.

Kyre gave him a few seconds to do so. Quenn tucked his lower lip into his teeth and stared at Kyre for a long moment. Kyre focused his impatience into something internal, a hard-pulsed heartbeat, a quickened breath. "Are you going to try again?"

"I don't know," Kyre said. "I don't know what's going to happen. I do know we need to go, though. The longer we stand here..."

The refraction's edges were already starting to waver and disappear. If they stayed here any longer, they'd be completely exposed. It was likely that nothing was out there; they were far away from both the crater and the base, not even close to any of the other kubrics. But Rillent wasn't the only thing to fear in Steremoss woods. Especially not in the dark.

"Then let's go," Quenn said.

"Stay close," Kyre cautioned. "These woods are impossible in the dark."

"I know," the boy said, and left it at that.

The suggestion to stay close was unnecessary, for it took only a few moments before they both discovered that Quenn, for all his bravado, could not walk more than a few steps without having to stop and rest. Kyre stripped off his coat and wrapped its stiff fabric tight around Quenn's leg, and then offered him a shoulder. It wasn't fast, and every slow step made Kyre's panic for Aviend ratchet one step higher. At least they were moving.

This section of the woods was long overgrown, appearing untouched. They'd worked hard to keep it that way. No trail marked their passage, and they had to weave through overhanging trees, grasping vines, and rocky outcrops. The unnamed river ran off to their left, the sound of it Kyre's main guide toward the base.

This wasn't the part of the forest they'd grown up in, he and Aviend, but now he was as familiar with it as if it had been part of his life, always. So many practice runs through here. So much wasted time and effort. And, yet, he could hear Quenn breathing beside him and knew they'd done the right thing. Made the right choice. He'd found the hardest decisions were often the easiest to live with, at least on the inside.

"Rillent has traps set in the conduits," Quenn said. "With teeth and sword."

Quenn was staring at him. This was a test that Kyre didn't know how to pass, so he told the truth. "I know," Kyre said. "I put them there for him. A long time ago."

He didn't say any more. Quenn would have to decide on his own what he thought of Kyre's choices.

They hobbled along in silence for a while.

"You really gave up the chance to kill..." Quenn was silent for so long that Kyre thought at first he'd fallen into silence or changed his mind about the question, but then he said. "Arch... Rillent to save me?" Rillent was *Rilnt*. And clearly hard for him to say.

Kyre's first response was more unkind than he meant it to be, and he was glad he didn't say it out loud. "I made a decision. I believe it was the right one."

"And that lady? The one with the mean face? Does she believe that too?"

Once, Kyre would have taken umbrage at that. Punched someone, maybe. Or at least tried to defend her with his words. But he knew if Aviend had heard Quenn say that, she would feel proud, not insulted. He hoped the two of them would have the chance to meet. "Aviend," he said. "Yes. I think she also believes it was the right one."

Quenn's footfall cracked a branch, startling a flock of aphalians in mid-feast. They went stock still for a moment, heads lit up in green and gold, chirps broadcasting their alarm.

At the sound, Quenn nearly took off. It took Kyre's quick hand on his arm to keep him steady. A moment later, the aphalians scattered, spreading brightly lit seeds from their backs as they went.

Morning always came on in the Stere like it was fighting off the night for its right to time. Fast and bright, leaving him blinking. The river off to his side bubbled with energy, growing raucous. They were getting close.

Even though he knew it was almost impossible, Kyre still felt a sliver of hope that Aviend would be at the base when they arrived. That thought alone, of her waiting there for him, was what drove him forward, what kept his feet pushing through the snagging vines and wet branches.

Quenn hadn't said anything for a few hours, but he'd stayed upright and moving ever forward. He was no longer leaning on Kyre's shoulder, but following along behind. Shock, probably. Keeping him from feeling the pain. Kyre didn't push. It was clear that he was determined not to be left behind.

As morning settled in, Kyre caught flickers of movement, purple-grey against the green of the leaves. The famous ghosts of ghost-haunted Steremoss.

As a child, Kyre had thought the apparitions his friends. His only friends, in fact, until he'd met Aviend. He'd been drawn to them, a longing that had no name, a desire to connect and make contact. He thought he'd recognized something in them, a likeness, maybe. A loneliness. A sensation of being lost. Of being in the wrong when or the wrong where.

But he was no longer a child, and he knew the ghosts for what they were – nothing more than anomalies of the earth. Empty and hollow as any other signal, explicable, alien. Not his friends at all. There were more now than when he'd been young. The earth shifting or change in energies, who knew why. He didn't look at them anymore, but they were always there in the corners of his eyes, as if begging him to once again believe in them.

He didn't comment on them and neither did Quenn. That meant Quenn had either grown up in the Stere – so used to them that he barely noticed – or that he couldn't see them at all. Some small percentage of people who lived in the Stere couldn't see the anomalies. No one seemed to know why.

They were closing in on the base when Quenn spoke for the first time in a long while.

"Mishda paal," the boy said from behind him. Not the Truth. Some other local dialect? Whatever it was, it was one that Kyre didn't know.

Kyre turned. Between him and Quenn, a tall thin shape. It was the first time he'd looked at an apparition full-on in a long time, years upon years, and he was startled to remember how human they looked. A body, a face, even an expression – this one of surprise, perhaps. He'd convinced himself long ago that the people he saw in the ghosts were a figment of his imagination, of his desire to make contact. Perhaps that was still true, but he didn't think so.

He could see Quenn through the vibrating form, his skin greyed by the vision. He was kneeling unsteadily, down on his good knee in the mud, his head lowered. He gripped his star amulet around his neck in one hand, holding it out toward the apparition. Kyre had heard of such things, those who believed that the ghosts were not ghosts, but gods, worthy of their kneel. But he'd never met anyone who believed it.

Kyre stepped forward, meaning to do what? Stop Quenn? Tell him the truth about the ghosts? But something stopped him, and he stayed his movement, letting Quenn continue in his offering.

The ghost reached out a hand – it was so clearly a hand that its very detail convinced Kyre that he was seeing things, that his mind was creating what the world had not from sleep deprivation or stress – and touched the amulet. And then both the ghost and the boy disappeared.

Quenn returned but a moment later, exactly as he'd left, looking as shaken by whatever had just transpired as Kyre felt. The ghost stayed gone, not even a flicker. In fact, there wasn't another flicker in the whole area that Kyre could see.

Kyre stepped forward, feeling a tingle of doubt as he strode through the spot where the ghost had been, but nothing happened and he was through and kneeling before Quenn without harm.

"What happened?" Quenn asked.

Well, that was an auspicious place to start, wasn't it? Kyre felt a sinking. He'd been hoping the boy would be the one to answer that.

"The ghosts have never reached for me before," Quenn said. He sounded awed.

"What did it feel like?" Kyre asked.

"Like nothing," he said. "No... More... like I went somewhere without moving."

"Like the dispatcher?"

A blank expression. Kyre tried again. "The device that brought us from the kubric to here."

"No," Quenn said. "Not like that. It was warm. Like I went to a better place," he added, as he shivered in the cool of the forest. It was chilly down here, always, but not enough that he should be shivering in the outfit that he wore. Still, he'd had a long night, and likely a longer day. Perhaps everything was just taking its toll.

Kyre had so many questions, and he missed Aviend deeply. Together, they made sense of the world, broke it apart and put it back together. He felt alone, like he was trying to fix a thing that he didn't know the purpose or even name of.

He needed to take care of Quenn first. Then Aviend. Then questions.

"We're almost back to the base," Kyre said. He wondered whether to tell him about the Gavani connection. Better not to, and allow him the moment to discover for himself. Maybe it would mean nothing. Or everything.

They'd left the river behind and he could smell the boggy peat of the swamp. There was no trail here, less so even than elsewhere. Kyre knew their direction by a tall black rock that rose unnaturally from the ground, pointing left. He stopped at the arrow's space. Home. He was so grateful to be here. He ached down to his blood. He needed sleep. He needed Aviend. And somewhere in there, he and the team would have to talk about what had happened, what to do now.

"Go ahead," he said.

Quenn stepped through Delgha's shield screen. Kyre could hear him gasp as he disappeared. He followed, nearly running into Quenn where he'd stopped. For a moment, Kyre was half in and half out of the illusory device. He wondered what he looked like. If someone was following him, did they only see half of him, or did he shimmer in and out of view, as if he too were just another ghostly vision haunting these woods?

And then Kyre was moving forward and he was through. It was as though he were seeing the base for the first time, through Quenn's eyes.

Their base, its odd metal angles overgrown and hidden, even without the shield screen to mask it. Long tendrils of green and brown wound their way across the black metal, nearly covering it, so that it seemed more like odd-shaped forest floor than anything once created for a purpose. The only unusual bit was that the vine – they called it veilvine – didn't seem to grow anywhere else in the Steremoss, at least not that he'd ever seen. Its roots dug into the hard metal as if it were soft as dirt, thriving on it without ever seeming to break the material down or apart.

It was this covering that had allowed the base to stay hidden for so long. Stepping forward, Kyre pushed back the vines to reveal a simple metal door. It had no visible handle or hinge, but in its very center was inscribed a three-dimensional star built of triangles.

It was the exact shape of the insignia on Quenn's amulet.

Behind him, Quenn drew a breath. His words were a syllabic waterfall of questions and crisscrossed excitement. "Gavani's temple? Here? It's real? But... I always thought that was just a story my mother told, of her mother and her mother's mother coming for worship. Are you...?"

So it did matter. Kyre was glad he'd allowed Quenn the moment of discovery.

Quenn looked between the star inscribed on the door and Kyre. "Are you believers?"

"Gavanites?" Kyre shook his head. "No. I didn't think there were any left. Although, perhaps your grandmother, if she's still alive?"

"No," Quenn shook his head as well. "She walks 'mong

the ghosts–" He cupped each hand to the opposite elbow, the press of the gored hand causing him to wince – "coruscates beside us. She went when I was just a boy. My parents are there too."

"May they walk," Kyre said, remembering the saying from his childhood and touching his own palms to his elbows. Saying it made him realize just how long it had been since he'd lost someone. A thing to be grateful for, surely. He didn't let himself think of Aviend, that moment of her surrounded by destriatch, bathed in blue light.

"I think I see them once in a while," Quenn said. "Walking the woods. I'd rather the ghosts than…" He didn't say Rillent's name again. He didn't need to. Kyre didn't believe that the ghosts were ghosts, but who was he to question someone else's beliefs? The promise of a loved one close at hand was not a thing to be ruined lightly.

"Come," Kyre said. "No sense standing out here when you can see the inside. Although be warned, it likely looks nothing like it did in your grandmother's day."

"It was lost long before that," he said. "According to the stories. No one in my family ever saw it. The stories, though. I feel as though I know it."

"Well, let's hope you won't be too disappointed then."

Kyre pointed to a bit of red that barely shone beneath the overlay of vine. A touch to the square revealed a small handle, barely large enough for him to hook two fingers through. He did so, and pulled. A moment later, a small *tkk* as the door popped open.

"In we go," he said. "Watch your head. There were probably other doors once, but we've never been able to find them. If they ever were there, they're long gone now. This side door, it was made for something smaller than you or I, it would seem."

Kyre reached a hand to push the hair away from his temple, revealing the thin semicircle of a scar ridged across his skin. The first time he'd entered this tunnel, he'd hit his head so hard he'd nearly passed out. And he'd bled like he didn't know – at least at that point – a person could bleed and not die. Blood and something else had run into his eyes, burning and blurring. He'd healed quickly enough, thanks to whatever miracle salve Thorme had mixed up, but he'd never again disrespected the height difference between himself and the roof.

Quenn took in the scar, then ducked his head overly low as he went through. Kyre followed, pulling the door shut behind them, knowing that the vines would slowly move over it to cover their tracks.

Inside was a long passageway, dark and tight. They could both stand, but barely. The ceiling felt like it was pressing against the top of his head. Quenn was shorter, though, safer from the claustrophobia that sometimes overrode Kyre, maybe. He hoped so, anyway.

The hallway wasn't lit, but wasn't entirely black, either. The metal itself did something to the darkness that made it easier to sense things. It wasn't light, exactly, but something else. As though he knew instinctively where the edges of his body were, the angles of the passageway. He could move through the space without touching anything, but it looked the same if he closed his eyes or left them open.

As if echoing his thoughts, Quenn asked, "Am I seeing in the dark?"

"Sort of," Kyre said. He would have elaborated, maybe, tried to explain the thing that he still couldn't quite explain to himself but at that moment, a light popped up at the far end of the tunnel, nearly blinding him. He blinked, sudden and hard, feeling bits of the night fall from his lashes onto his face.

"Kyre?" Delgha's voice, carrying down the passageway. Had she not said Aviend's name because she was already here? Because she was dead? Because... He swallowed down the reasons his mind tried to throw at him.

"It's me."

Her voice was relieved. "I saw you on the sensor." The sensor was one of Delgha's favorite devices, a screen that scanned the base's perimeter and marked any living creatures in orange as they approached. You couldn't make out much, but you could tell if it was human-shaped, or otherwise.

They reached the end of the passageway, where Delgha was lowering a small platform down. It wasn't that far of a leap up to the small room where Delgha was standing – maybe two feet. He and Aviend often jumped it, just to test their skills against each other, but it didn't feel right to do without her. Plus, honestly, he was just too exhausted, and Quenn wasn't going to be doing any leaping on that leg of his.

So he was grateful for Delgha, the platform, and being home. He climbed on as it hit their lower level, and beckoned Quenn to do the same.

In the slow way of the platform rising, soundlessly, imperceptibly, except for the way the walls shifted around you, they reached Delgha.

As the lift rose, Delgha was head-down at the panel that operated the lift, turning the switches that lifted it and locked it into place.

Delgha was everything that you could want from a tech, and a little bit more. She was smart, efficient, inventive, and, as far as Kyre could tell, completely happy to do nothing but plan and create all day.

Her long head was shaved down to the scalp. The close shear showed off her pale tattoos, elaborate rings that went around her skull, each smaller than the next, until they reached the top. There, a simple grey piercing sparked the light. She was dressed in a plain grey outfit, adorned only with a large collar made of red synth. A gift from her former husband, Lyeg, given before Rillent had taken over. Lyeg hadn't been of the clave, but he'd gone willingly into Rillent's trenches, as so many had. No one knew then just what kind of man Rillent was, or what he was capable of. He was the clave leader, and they did as he asked, unquestioning in their trust that he would lead them well, as Aviend's mother and the other leaders before her always had. The collar was the only sign of her former life that Delgha carried with her. Even the tattoos were new, one ring per year since then. She had joked once that she would have to start on her wrists soon. Her torso. Her chest. The kind of joke that was only funny because it kept you from sadness.

Kyre stepped off and waited until Quenn did the same.

"Is it done?" Delgha asked, not yet looking up.

Her question terrified him. If she hadn't heard about Rillent, it meant that she hadn't spoken to Aviend. He couldn't help but ask, "Aviend?"

In the moment of silence that followed, Kyre's heart double-beat in his chest, a capture of breath and fear that made itself known with a series of thumps against his ribcage.

Delgha looked up from the panel. "She's not with you?" she said. "I saw two... in the..."

"Skist," she said flatly, as she took in the stranger standing next to him.

Skist was right. In some small, closed part of himself, he'd nearly convinced himself that Aviend would be here, even though he knew it was next to impossible. And still. It was hard to stop the heart from dreaming up a better world.

Where in the ghostfell was Aviend? Even before he thought

it, he knew the answer. Of course he did. Plan for every contingency. That was their motto. Even their contingencies had contingencies.

"If she's not here, where is she?" Delgha asked. "I can try to scan for…"

"I know where she's going." *If she survived.* He didn't say that part. Delgha already knew it. He could see it in her face, a pained twitch beneath the calm expression.

She reached into the box on the floor next to the left panel, searching through the devices she kept at the ready. "And Rillent?"

"Alive."

"Skist." Her curse was so sharp he almost sensed it slice through her breath.

"The destriatch were there," he said.

"At the kubric? What *is* Rillent up to?" She waved away her question and handed him a small gelatinous pack, cool to the touch and moving slightly. "Answers for later. Take this. You look like you haven't eaten in a hundred years."

Kyre touched the older woman's arm briefly, by way of thanks and farewell.

"This is Quenn. Can you get him to Thorme for some patching? You, stay here please, until I return with Aviend." He said it to Quenn, but it was really for Delgha, who controlled all of the ins and outs of this place. If the boy wanted out, he'd have to convince Delgha, and Kyre wanted her to know exactly where he stood on that.

He tucked the pack into his pouch, then dropped the two feet back into the passageway. Ducking his head, he broke into a run. He knew where Aviend was going. It was just a matter of getting there while she was still alive.

The stories Aviend likes best are always of smart people in bad situations doing smart things. The ones she likes least are the ones where smart people in bad situations do stupid things.

And right now, she is living in the latter story. And she hates it.

Everything was going great – all right, not great, but good – right up until she'd reached the salt river. She'd thrown Kyre's detonation, waited until the moment it was set to go off, and then she'd run. She had no idea if she'd hurt any of the destriatch, but that wasn't the goal anyway. The explosion stunned them at least, gave her the time she desperately needed for a head start. She has a plan – she won't go back to the base, not directly, because they'll track her there. She's going to lead them off, away from both the base and Kyre's landing spot, then lose them down the length of the river. They have a jump harness at the top of Scemeri Falls that she can use to get down, loop around. Head back to the base. Be in before dawn.

It was a perfect plan. An almost perfect plan.

What she hadn't counted on was conduction.

The moment she steps into the water and the smell of salt hits her nose, she knows she's made a mistake. If it were pure water, this wouldn't be a problem. But this water is salt and sea, an inland runner of bits and pieces. It will carry electricity sure as her body will. As sure as the destriatch behind her do.

She has no choice but to keep going. Hope she makes it to the other side before they get in the water.

The beasts are coming. She hears them before she sees them. That's the way of dangerous things, she's found. Even sneaky, half-alive things like the destriatch. They make no sound with their feet or mouths, no howl or step, but she hears the black crackle of energy that roils along their fur, the metallic spittle that sizzles out that same energy as it leaps across their coned teeth. She can't tell how many or how far, but she knows they are no longer hunting for her. They have found her. They'll be at the shoreline before she can get out of the water.

She moves as slow-fast as she can through the river, trying not to make a sound or draw attention. It's hard to see the other shore, but she splashes down nearly to her waist and thinks she's about at the halfway point. In the dark, it's like navigating a room you've never been in with your eyes closed. Rocks smash into her shins. She steps and there's no bottom until her shoulders are soaked.

Her reflection shows up in the water – blued and sparked – and she knows they've arrived at the shore. She glances over her shoulder without stopping her movement and sees a long wavering line of black and cobalt crackle and spark. When they stand that close together, the electricity coming from them loops back and forth. Makes light bridges between their bodies.

If they so much as step into the water, she's as good as dead.

Run. Swim. Get out. Get out.

Every part of her body screams at her to move fast. Right now. Go. But she needs to be quiet. She needs to be unseen, unheard, unfelt. And so she does everything her body says not to.

She submerges.

What was once just water and is now the conductor of her possible death rises up and swells over her head. It's shockingly cold. Her eyes close out of instinct against the pulse of icy liquid. Here, she thinks, even as she pushes herself toward what she hopes is the far shore, is where everything ends. It's not the first time she's thought this in her life, but she figures one of these times has to be the last time. If that's the case, she almost wishes she'd killed Rillent herself. Then she could ghostfall without remorse.

At least it's peaceful under the water. She can't hear the crack and sizzle of the destriatch. Everything's stone black and blue behind her closed lids. The only sound is her breathless pulse thumping in her head, the water's pushback against her ears.

Even as she moves, even as she thinks this might become the place where she will end, she plans. If she can get to the other side without getting turned around, without attracting the attention of the destriatch, she might still be able to reach the falls. She swims. Breath pounding in her face. Her lungs beginning to talk back at her. The lack of oxygen is a quick heavy thump in her chest, an aching pain. Protest. Trading one possible death for another. Isn't that all any of them do?

Beneath her hands, pushing forward, she feels gravel. Smaller than mid-river rocks. Silt and movement. She pushes and then crawls, staying low. Hoping she's on the right side. She doesn't dare lift any part of her above the water until she has to.

Soon, she has to. It's gotten shallow enough that she feels the top of her head enter the air, reverse sinking. Her eyes.

The water drips from her lashes and clouds her vision. In her ears, from behind her, sparking and crackle. A long single sound that tells her the destriatch are still connected by their arcing energy.

She gulps air as quietly as her lungs will allow, which isn't very quiet at all, but no louder than the sound of her body floundering toward shore. The water is low here, but fast, battering at her, making every movement doubly loud. Beneath her palms, she feels mud. Sinking, wet, full of algae. She pulls herself to her feet in a single, sudden, so-loud motion and runs.

All this running away. It's not what she wants to do, who she wants to be. She wants to plan, to stand, to fight. But she runs anyway, her boots sogging, splashing water up. The sound of her feet squishing into the mud sends her a spark of hope.

Which is followed by an actual spark. The destriatch have heard her. They have entered the water. Single file. Deliberate. She wasn't outsmarting them or hiding from them. They were waiting until the moment when they were solidly connected, arc to arc to arc, and then arc to her, so they would not be diminished.

The first spark catches her heel, right through her wet boot, shivers her down to the insides of her bones. A sound rises from her, involuntary, pain-filled, pitching forward from her body as her body pitches forward at the river's edge. Heat sears up her insides. She can taste something cooking in the back of her throat. She knows it's herself, her own flesh, the second it happens. She's face down in the water, trying to push herself to her feet. Or even just to her hands and knees. But her skin feels raw and ripped. The water pops and zips around her like a million needles. Something lands like an ember on the back of her head.

The destriatch chase with deliberation. Their prey is wounded. Flailing. Edging to panic. Now is not the time for chasing. Now is the time for the slow stalk. Step to step. Closing in. The final act of this mistaken play.

Out of near-silence, the haunting howl. Starting as one, rising as one. The malignity. If the electricity doesn't kill her, this song will. It carries the sound of Rillent, this song. His weight and wish. She can already feel it, eating away at hope, at life.

Get up.

She shouts at them, raises an arm. As if she's going to scare them away. She doesn't.

Her feet, finally, touch the wet stones. Her body is still zapping her from the inside, setting her teeth against each other with each strike, but her exhale is a sigh of relief. She scrabbles, scorched palms and jittering fingers over the stones.

And then she's up and away. Dry dirt. Sticking everywhere but who cares. The river – the horrible zapping killing river is behind her, rushing somewhere else. The beasts are behind her too. Not far enough. She can hear them still coming through the water. Crackle and splash.

As she runs, she promises: she will learn how to turn their electricity back on them. In the future. For next time. Next time, she thinks again, and holds onto the idea so fiercely her fist clenches.

On the dirt, she's quieter. Even in the dark, she understands the ways of trees and paths. She grew up in these woods. They're different everywhere; they're also the same. Growth patterns, pathways, branches at eye level. She maneuvers through them, ignoring as best she can the sounds behind her. She doesn't look back. What good would it do? She can already tell they're closing in again. They are relentless. Untiring. She is exhausted. Breathing heavy. Slogging and sogging. The river bought her nothing except electrified bones, an ache at the nape of her neck.

She wishes she really could read Kyre's mind right now, know if he was unharmed, if they were making it back to the base safely. She's not worried – he's smart and savvy – but she would still like to know for sure.

Morbid thoughts. Ghost thoughts. It's not like her and that scares her. She shakes them away and focuses on her feet, her movement, the shadowshapes of trees and rocks.

The creatures are at her back, pulling up and flanking her. Think. She spins, backtracks. Always keeping the sound of the falls on her right. She's fast, but the destriatch are faster. They were designed for this forest, built to mow through it without snags or slowdown, their thick fur and electrical parts keeping them safe, keeping them fast.

So why haven't they caught her yet? They could have ripped her to shreds without so much as a hair out of place. But they are still pacing her, not closing in.

They are hoping she'll lead them to the base. They are letting her run where she wants. Rillent. Skist. She tells herself it's all right. As long as they're behind her, she can lead them away from the base. She is prey, needs to stay prey. Just not prey that actually gets caught.

The forest floor slopes beneath her feet. The squishy softness of spongemoss means she's nearly to the falls. If she can grab the jump tie – there won't be time to strap herself in, just enough to hold on – she can get across the ravine. There's no way they can follow her. Unless they can fly. And she's sure – pretty sure – that they can't. Not yet.

The hounds come through the brambles that she just left.

She can only tell because she hears wings as the millibirds take flight. The stink of flesh burning hits her nose, sinks in. Her head feels like it's full of coals. Dead bird coals.

Closer now. The sparking fills the air, so close and so loud, she flinches. Ducks her head. It almost causes her to fumble right off the rocky edge of the ravine. So many ledges in a single night. At least this one is natural. Of nature. Carved out by time and water. Not by the hands of humans bent to bondage.

A spark of blue breaks the night blanket to her left, and she swerves away. Follows the edge of the river as closely as she can without tumbling over. They can see she's tired. They must know she won't lead them to the base.

A crackle off to her left tells her the beasts are gaining, pulling up alongside her. Soon they will cut her off, narrow in on her like she's game. Which she is to them. Nothing more.

You're going to have to fight them.

Yes, yes, I know. But later.

Now.

And it's true. The one on her left is coming, full bore, not caring about nature-made or the softness of the moss. Or the cliff edge where her feet are slip-slipping in their boots. She should have had Delgha make her sticky boots, not quiet boots. The jump kit beckons. She can't see it, but she knows where it hangs. Approximately.

It's the last thing she thinks as she steps once more and goes over backward. Tumble and fall. The crackling creature howling and howling after her. It moves like gravity doesn't matter and she knows she's fucked up as she feels its teeth skim and whistle against her knee.

Mid-flight – fall, really, if she's going to be honest – she reaches for the jump kit. Hoping against hope. Her fingers catch rock, water, a branch that scratches her skin to high hell and twists her knuckle. A bit of leather. She closes her fingers on the last, braces herself for the wrench of shoulder that comes half a second later. It's impossible not to scream, and then berate herself for screaming. The pain sears up her arm.

When this is all over, if she's still alive, she's going to have to drag herself to Thorme's healing station and beg her for a patch. She's always considered herself to have a high tolerance for pain, but tonight she has reached her limit.

But she's swinging, not falling, and that's something. Both feet push off the stone outcrops, swinging her far out over the rushing river below. The jump kit is designed to take her out far enough that she can jump into the deep pool in the river's center. She can't do that now. The fallen destriatch is down there somewhere. Electrifying the water. The kit's going to have to take her to the far bank, if she hopes to get out of this.

On the near bank, she can see the destriatch, growing smaller. And then larger again as the jump kit carries her back toward them. They are doing something in the dark that she can't quite see.

Two, three times, she pushes off. Gets leverage. Her knee wrenches. Her back and shoulder. Teeth gritted so hard she's sure she'll break one.

She doesn't make it to the far bank. No amount of momentum is going to do it. The kit's not long enough to take her there. Its arc is too short. That leaves her two options. Down. Or back to where she started.

She keeps swinging, thinking, pushing. As she does so, she dips her free hand into the opening of her hip bag. Shapes and textures slip through her fingers. Round. Poking. Soft. What does she have left in her bag? Nothing nothing nothing.

For the first time ever, she has used up all of her contingency plans. She's got nothing left except herself. She can only hope that's enough.

Then, the thing she's seeking that she'd almost forgotten she had. Triangular, heavy and metallic. She pulls it out with a yell of triumph and thumbs the device. Misses. Not once but twice. Her elbow bangs against something that she is afraid is the hound tumbling near her, but is only an outcrop.

She'd packed this cypher in case she needed to use it on Rillent's glaives. Never expecting this. But here they are, and here she is.

Down is dangerous. Current-filled water. And in the dark, she can't see to aim anywhere else.

Back where she started is dangerous. The beasts are lined along the edge of the bank, as if waiting for her to decide. Or as if they already know what she will do.

She changes direction, aims for the bottom of the ravine. Not the deep pool which is surely arcing with current, but for the shore. The rocky side that she knows is there, but only by instinct. It's too dark to make out.

Her fall is silent and sure. So is her landing. Her head hits the gravel, her mouth is full of gravel. Her back twangs. She has a moment to think, "make that two patches, Thorme," and then the grey swarms in and threatens to overtake her. She lets it for the count of two heartbeats, two breaths, then she pushes it back through nothing more than force of will. If she could see, if she could figure out how to open her eyes, she knows her vision would be black at the edges, fuzzing in. She tries to fight it.

The device tumbles from her grip. She pats the area around her until she finds it, seemingly, impossibly, unbroken. She picks it up and her fingers refuse to close. She grabs it with both hands. Holds it like she's seen others hold a prayer totem, wrapping her whole hands around it, tugging it toward her.

She opens her eyes to the sound of electricity. Coming nearer. They're winding down the side of the ravine as easy as flying. "You don't have wings!" she wants to yell, but she realizes how little she understands these crackling, crazed creatures.

Devices don't talk to her, but she sometimes talks to them. "You'd better work," is all she can think to say to it. It comes out funny, because her mouth is awash with blood. She hadn't tasted it until now. Better than the meat-sizzle of her breath.

She waits until the first of the crourhounds is nearly upon her. Breath and light and mourning. Her already sensitive skin sizzles in the near-heat.

Hits the button and throws up the magnetic shield.

The rush of air past her face is loud. So is the low howl of the first hound as the magnet hits its metal parts. For a moment, it seems as if it is still coming for her. As if it will land on her and destroy her. Mouth open. Crackling black teeth, as if they've been burnt into points. Slavering. It's the one with its middle missing. Right next to her face.

And then, less slowly than it came, it begins to recede. Slow, its feet scrambling for purchase as the shield pushes it back. Her breathing is either louder than the crackling, or the shield blocks some of the noise.

The others – she can see four of them now – are coming down the shore, fast. The shield is invisible to her. She assumes it is to them as well. At least they don't seem to be slowing down. When the next two hit it, she swears she can feel the cypher shake in her hand but knows that makes no sense.

The cypher's not going to last very long. She can't sit here and wait until they all run into it. She thinks about putting it in her pocket – portable shield – but at the last second, she drops it to the ground instead. Then she pushes herself up from the muck and mud of the river bank for the second time in this long dark night.

The destriatch are stuck behind her shield. Unless they shed their metal parts somehow, she thinks it will hold them until she can get where she needs to go. The treehouse. Not because it's the safest place. It's not. She's going there because she knows it's where Kyre will look for her. And because she needs to pass out, and she refuses to do it in front of Rillent's monsters.

2. And When Everything Fails, There is Light

Kyre knew Aviend was up there, maybe dead, maybe alive, even before he began his climb into the treehouse. It wasn't an actual treehouse, but that was the best name they had for the thick metal shaft that elevatored up to the top of the treeline and landed at a small shelter. There was no sign she'd passed this way, or climbed this climb, and still he knew in his heart that she was above him. And that was breaking him. Because of the silence. There was no sound up there.

He halted at the doorway, his breath heavy as stones trying to leave his lungs. Gasping. Afraid to step forward and discover that what he feared was true. Afraid to stay still in case it wasn't and he could still make a difference.

It was her size that shook him most. Her body, curled in a corner. He'd never seen her look so small. And he'd known her when she actually was small. When they both were.

He was touching his hands to his elbows, breathing *coruscates beside us* into the air before he even realized what he was saying. She was dead, she was dead, she was–

He realized she was alive when he saw the blood bubbling up from the gash on her face. Dead bodies didn't push up blood. He thought. He hoped.

He'd never moved across a floor so quickly in his life. "Vi."

His hands and voice doing opposite things at the same time. His fingers found the med kit stashed in the corner, peeled back the seal. Inside, bearing Thorme's fingerprints, the case was filled with boosts and bandages. There were pressed nuts and water in a silver pouch. He found the health boost he wanted and pulled it out. Still full. She hadn't used any of it. Why?

Because she hadn't been able to. Because she'd been here the whole time, unable to help herself. He should have gone faster. He should have left Quenn. He should have–

"Vi, listen..." What did he want to tell her? So many things. But he was silent, focused, as he prepped the health boost, pulled back her collar. Her clothing was soaked, her skin so cold it burned his fingers to touch her. So many times he'd touched her collarbone. Never as still or frozen as it was now. It was jarring, seeing the sides of her neck coated in blood and the blackness of charr.

He pushed the needle into the bubble of her vein to release the nanotech into her body. He took her hand; it hung inside his own without life.

She didn't respond. He didn't know what that meant. He was no chiurgeon, although Thorme had taught them all the basics, just in case. This was all he knew how to do.

If Quenn were here, Kyre wondered if he would have prayed. Kyre didn't pray – he had nothing to believe in beyond science, and science required action, not prayer. He didn't even realize that he was saying "Vi," over and over as if he were invoking some ancient deity, until she said, "What?"

Her voice was quiet, shivered, and the rest of her followed suit, shuddering against him. "I'm skisting freezing," she said.

All the words were there, inside his body, but he found none of them. Instead, he wrapped his body to hers. He could feel his warmth leaving, but he didn't care. He warmed her until she stopped shivering, until she could say words without her teeth clunking together as if they might break. Until she could sit on her own and eat the nuts and drink the water.

Finally, she turned the silver pouch inside out and licked the salt from it, unabashedly. A second later, she looked at him from under tired lids. "I ate everything," she said. "I'm sorry."

He pulled the packet from his pocket and held it up.

"Thorme?" she said.

"Delgha, actually," he said. "Even our contingencies–"

"–have contingencies," she finished. The smile in her voice didn't reach her face at all. As if her very muscles were too exhausted to even try. "Let's go home."

They had no dispatcher this time. No push a button and be somewhere else. Just their feet and their willpower taking them step by slow step again through the woods.

Going home was longer than coming. Every bone in Kyre's body ached and dreamed of sleep. He was sure Aviend was worse. She'd run farther, faster through the night. The destriatch at her heels. The way they exuded the need to fear, like it was a scent, *forced* it upon you. That in itself was exhausting, never mind the running.

Never mind their failure to kill Rillent, which they hadn't talked about yet. It was the right thing to do, saving Quenn. So why did it still feel like they'd made a mistake?

They hit the ankle-deep black muck of Slisto Swamp under the high sun's filtered heat. Kyre kept one hand on the hilt of a shortblade, the other at the ready to help Aviend if she asked for it.

They hadn't seen slistoviles here in years, but that didn't mean the animate plants weren't just waiting beneath the surface for that rare bit of walking prey. Their presence did mean they were likely to have the swamp to themselves. Few living creatures chose to slog through these deathwaters. Not even Rillent's men would be keen on traipsing through this swampmuck.

"We're almost there," he said to her. She knew where they were, of course. It was just something to say, something he realized he'd gotten in the habit of saying to Quenn.

"Third time you've said that," Aviend said. Her voice was stronger than it had been just a few minutes ago, he was happy to hear. It even carried a hint of her usual snip. He'd been picking up the pace as they went along, and so far she'd kept up. They both knew that the injection he'd popped her with wasn't going to last forever. If she crumbled before they made it to the base... but this time they were really almost there. If they kept the pace, they'd make it before the boost wore off.

"Ghosts, I've never been so happy to see you bleeding as I was tonight," he said, stepping around what he at first thought was a rock and then realized was a grey-backed shelled creature of some kind. It sank into the water and disappeared without so much as a bubble.

Aviend barked a laugh, followed by a soft groan of pain, and then another laugh.

"You're horrible. I hope that when the slistoviles get you, they grow over your mouth first."

"Now that's just mean," he said.

"You're the one talking about how wonderful it is that I was bleeding."

"You know exactly what I meant."

The banter felt odd in his mouth, too light, too easy. It must have in hers too, because she fell silent in a sudden, solid way, as if shutting a door against a light. The splash of their boots filled the silence enough for a while. Dead snags rose up all around them, broken points aiming for the sky. From somewhere in the water, amphibians croaked their songs of mating or alarm or joy. But there was no sound of the destriatch. No sound of Rillent's men coming. And that was a beautiful kind of no-noise.

"Tell me about the boy?" Aviend asked a bit later, her voice so quiet it barely carried to his ears. And then, as if she needed to remind herself of the good of it, she added, "The one we saved."

As they mucked through the wet, he told her about Quenn. About how he wasn't a boy at all. About his sister. About the ghost who touched him and his grandmother and his pendant.

"Gavanites? Really?" She shook her head. "It must be weird for him, being in the base. I guess he'd say temple, wouldn't he?"

"I didn't get a chance to ask. If he's still there, I hope he can answer some things for us."

"Yeah, like how he came to be in the one place where he could screw up our long-laid plans to save the world." She winced, but he didn't think the pain was physical.

"Do you think that's what we were trying to do? Save the world?"

"Trying? Past tense? But I don't know. Don't you?"

He wasn't sure, and he didn't want to lie to her, so he said, "How long do you think the boost has?"

She didn't look at him, but her voice carried strong. "Do you want me to pretend to answer that so we can avoid the topic?"

"Yes?" Killing someone to save the world felt... an awful

lot like not saving the world at all. What did he feel about choosing to save Quenn? Mostly relief. Relief that he'd been given a way out of killing a man. But also out of the plan they'd worked so hard on for so long. Relief mingled with guilt and ran through his blood, light and heavy at the same time.

Aviend nodded, then made a small show of checking her body as she walked. "Then I'll say that it's wearing down. I've got some pain in my... everything. But mostly in the back of my head. Right... here..." She reached up and touched it gingerly, feeling around with her fingertips. "What did I do to the back of my... skisting ghostfall. What..."

He winced. He hadn't planned to mention it to her until they'd gotten back to the base. Or maybe never. She wasn't attached to many things, but she was deeply, tightly attached to her hair. Because it reminded her of her mother, he thought.

"You cut my hair? You..." She'd stopped mid-swamp, her eyes wide. Her mouth was moving but she seemed to be having trouble finding any words.

"No," he said. "I would never. But... did you get a little electricity, maybe? It looks more like a burn than a cut."

"Those beasts," she said. "Those horrible, electric, made-of-nothing, skisting brehmfilled beasts. I will kill them."

"Sure. They're horror beasts that shouldn't exist belonging to a man who..." He almost said, "killed your mother" but caught himself at the last second. It wasn't untrue, but it wasn't where this conversation needed to go. Not yet. "... wants to rule the... I don't know, Stere? World? They tried to kill you. But your hair is what makes you want to wipe them out?"

She shot him a look, one she typically reserved for devices

that were misbehaving for her. He knew her well enough to know that more swearwords would soon follow.

"Truly, you can barely tell," he said.

"I can tell. But I don't care about how it looks. That much. I care about... I don't know."

"It's just one more thing Rillent took from you without asking?"

"Yes." She was moving forward now, splashing through the swamp, loudly. He hoped there really were no slistoviles waiting under the water, because if there were she was going to wake them all. "Yes, exactly that. I just... All I had were swearwords."

He moved himself, catching up to her, no need to worry about noise now, he supposed. "I'm sorry."

"I know." She reached out and took his free hand. He knew from the strength of her fingers that it wasn't because she was falling or failing, but because she wanted to.

She misstepped and landed deep, water up to her knee, filling her boot. "Ugh. I have had enough of water to last a lifetime. I hope to never touch, smell, drink, or even see water ever again in my whole life."

"That could make spending time with you tricky," he said.

"Because I'll be dead?"

"I was thinking that you'd be stinky," he said.

"Did you see him?" she said, a moment later.

"Who?"

"Rillent. His face. He wasn't expecting us. Didn't even know we existed. I know he thought I was dead. But I think he thought you were too."

Kyre had noticed the same. "I'm pretty sure he had a moment there where he thought he was seeing both of our ghosts, come out of the forest to get him. His face..."

She mimicked Rillent for a second, made a face that was somehow both all anger and all shock. It made him laugh, even though he shouldn't, even though he knew that the very fact that Rillent had seen them, that he knew they were not just alive, but coming for him, put them both – put their whole clave – in grave danger. It felt good to laugh, even if the fear came after.

"Skist," she said. "Did we make a mistake?"

"We saved a boy's life," he said.

"To what end, for all of those others in Rillent's trenches? In the Stere? Did we sacrifice their lives for his? Was he worth it?"

They passed a grey synth tube sticking up out of the swamp. If you didn't look at it closely, it looked like just another small, broken-off stick amid a field of broken-off sticks. But the tiny, almost invisible, wiring up its side gave it away as one of Delgha's monitoring devices.

"I guess we'll find out soon," he said. "Since we're almost there."

And this time they really were.

The swamp brought them around the back of the base, almost right up to its southern wall. They splashed themselves onto dry land and followed the curve of the building around to the entrance. The third time he'd been through this tunnel since dawn, and every time it had been a completely different experience. He hoped this was the last time. He didn't think he could handle another.

"I am going to sleep so hard," Aviend said as they made their way through the tunnel, a yawn delaying the start of her next sentence. "The boost is crashing my system."

Delgha must have seen them in her scanner. She'd already sent the lift down. They rode it up, weary, silent. Touching by leaving space between them. Together through the door that felt like home, finally. On the other side, the smell of something cooking, the cool tang of reddlin spice and the warmer, sweeter scent of Thorme's special quick bread.

"Oh, but there's food," she said. "Food, then sleep?" She didn't say, "And then we wake up and figure out what the hell we're going to do now that our plan to save the world from a tyrant has broken open and we have no backup." She didn't have to. They were both thinking it. They were all thinking it.

The base's main room was big and square, four times as tall as Kyre. Broken apart only by the seemingly randomly placed strips of pellucid material that rose from the floor halfway to the ceiling. The walls were a pale grey, shined and nearly reflective, although the reflection was always distorted. More so the closer you got.

They called it the pennon, after the rows and rows of banner-like materials that floated from the high ceiling. Each bore a different creature – some vaguely familiar to Kyre, others creatures he'd never seen, and honestly never hoped to see. The colors and shapes were a mishmash, all of them clashing so wildly that they somehow melded together into something that was beautiful. He didn't know if they were the makings of whoever – whatever – might have built this structure originally, or if it was a later addition from the Gavanites, some part of their worship that he'd never heard about. Not that he knew that much about them. Bits of old stories and rumors told by nonbelievers, mostly. He'd have to ask Quenn about it. If he was still here. Part of Kyre was sure he'd gone at the first chance. The other fully expected to see him helping Thorme cook.

Off this main room, there were three doors, located midpoint on three of the five walls. One that led back out the way they'd come. One that led to a room they'd turned into a combination storage space and med room. And the last one that led to their – well, Delgha's truly – tech and planning room.

Of the various rooms in the base, this was by far his favorite, partly because of its enormity – the other rooms were clearly not made by or for humans, and they were too small or too short or oddly angled. But also because it was the place that reminded him a bit of home. Of Ovinale before Rillent. There were sleeping areas tucked between the makeshift rooms that the strips created. And a respite space filled with soft bits of furniture and the constant stream of an eternal liquidlight.

The only real decor came from the various kindnesses given by those they'd rescued from Rillent's hold over the years. Handmade blankets or wall hangings, usually spun from yol wool or crafted of local woods. Most people gave them useful things. Handmade pilgrim packs for carrying supplies. Carefully crafted clothing. Most of the furniture, too, came from those who'd stayed here a few days and then moved on. Mostly people had nothing to give, and so they gave thanks and a promise to return with something in the future. That was more than enough for Kyre, for all of them. A person alive and free was worth hundreds, thousands, of gifts.

There was a kitchen space in one corner, tucked between two of the strips. It wasn't much, but it finished the home feel for him. A portable cookstove that he and Aviend had bricked into something that resembled permanence. A couple of storage boxes topped with a makeshift counter, a table and chairs. The centerpiece was a chiller that Thorme had picked up from one of her various suppliers throughout the Stere.

This was the room where they found Thorme, already dishing up food for them. Delgha was sitting down just as they entered. The table was far bigger than the four of them needed. Once there had been more of them. This, he thought, looking at their quiet, solemn faces, was all that was left of the resistance. It wasn't much. He had to hope it was enough.

"Sit." It was a command, not an invitation. Thorme's face didn't look angry, but her stance did. She was dressed, as she always was, in the long flow of reds and greens, a toss of purple, a strand of yellow. Nearly as mismatched as the banners above them. Her long dark hair, patterned through with purple that matched her clothing, fell down her back, pulled into a loose fishbone braid that nearly swept along the floor.

The wooden bracelets, each carved by Thorme's own hand, each for some occasion or memory, most of which Kyre did not know, clickclacked as she served them wordlessly. Healer. Mother. Feeder of lost birds. That was how Thorme had once described herself to Kyre. Although that had been eons ago, it seemed. Did she still think of herself as a mother now that her children were ghostfallen? Healer, still, yes. If Quenn and the others were lost birds, then she was still that too.

"We're happy we're alive too, Thorme," Aviend said as she sat beside him. She lifted her brow at Kyre, but already had a utensil in her hand. He was starving. Famished. He would eat whatever Thorme put in front of him and happily so. Not that her food was ever bad, but it did sometimes come with a side of love so sharp and pure that it cloyed the taste.

"Hmph." Snorted through her nose, and still she set down the bread between them, followed by two bowls of stew. Tap. Tap. Wood to wood. Careful, precise.

Thorme showed her love in ire and precision, and there was nothing to be done for it, except unweave the barbed threads to remind oneself of the soft insides of her. Of which there were many.

He glanced at Aviend. She still wore the black crust that covered the edges of her face along her hairline. Her clothes were dusted with charcoal. Both things she hadn't even seemed to notice until he pointed them out to her.

He wasn't sure he'd ever seen her so beaten down. Looking at her here, half asleep over her food, her skin torn and broken, the back of her hair crimped with electricity, made all of his own sense of defeat come rushing back. They'd failed so deeply. But then she smiled at him and said his name, and he couldn't do anything but be grateful they were alive.

He knew they should talk about Rillent. About the plan gone wrong. So very, very wrong. But he wasn't ready yet. The mix of guilt and relief was still swirling, trying to settle into its place. He didn't know where it would land.

"How's Quenn?" he asked, mostly to stave off any incoming questions. The bowl's heat felt good against the palms of his hands. The stew was too hot to eat. He could tell by the steam that moistened his face, but his hunger got the best of his caution and he tried anyway. That was a mistake.

Thorme was already pulling cool water from the chiller, pouring it into a glass. Kyre lifted it quickly but gratefully, steam still rolling from his mouth.

"Nice," Aviend said. She and Thorme had joined sides against him now, laughing at his misfortune. Good. Laughter was good. Laughter meant some small part of them was still alive inside.

"You are both horrible monsters," he tried to say, but it came out jumbled with hot stew and cool water. Only making the two of them laugh all the more.

He swallowed everything down, relieved to discover that he didn't seem to have done permanent damage to the inside of his mouth, and narrowed his eyes at Aviend.

"Later," he mock-whispered.

"You…" she started.

Quenn was standing in the doorway. Or in the space between the two panels that worked as a doorway anyway. It was clear he'd been asleep, probably in one of the spaces they'd just passed. He rubbed at his face, caught the side of the dressing on his hand, and dropped it with a wince.

"What's funny?" he asked. He looked, and sounded, more like a boy than he had at any point previously. It reminded Kyre that even though he wasn't young, he was young. Or had been until Rillent got a hold of him.

"Kyre doesn't know how to eat properly," Aviend said.

"Quenn, this is the mean-faced lady," Kyre said. "You can just call her Aviend."

Aviend side-eyed Kyre, one brow arcing slightly, but it was a sign of how exhausted she was that she didn't have a quick and slicing response. "Thorme closed up your leg?"

When Quenn nodded and lifted the pantleg to show a seam of tiny glowing stitches, Aviend nodded. "She did a good job."

From across the small space, Thorme closed the chiller with a click of the door and of her tongue.

"And your hand?" Aviend asked.

He held it up and wiggled a few fingers inside a simple black bandage. "I'm grateful," Quenn said. "To all of you."

"We hope you can answer some–" Kyre started.

"Sit," Thorme interrupted, pointing her spoon at Quenn.

Already clearly well trained by Thorme in just a short amount of time, Quenn quickly took a place across the table from Kyre. He didn't reject the food Thorme put in front of him, although Kyre was pretty sure he'd probably already eaten at least once. Good. It meant he was feeling hungry, which was always a good sign. Coming out of Rillent's grip was… confusing, to say the least. And hunger was one of the first signs that you were coming back to yourself.

Aviend hadn't said anything about Rillent being in her head. Not yet. He wondered how she was processing that, if she needed time the way that he needed time.

"I thought this might be Gavani's temple," Quenn was saying, between bites. "I thought it was, because of the design on the door."

"And now?" Kyre asked. Grateful to have something to talk about that didn't involve death and failure and pain.

"I don't know. I don't think so. Unless the stories are wrong. Or unless there's another room in here that I didn't find. This doesn't look anything like what the stories say."

"What do they say?" Aviend asked. "The stories?"

Quenn lowered his head and closed his eyes. For a moment, Kyre thought he'd gone to sleep suddenly. Well, who could blame him? They'd all had a rough night.

But then Quenn started speaking. It was hushed, singsong, and in it, Quenn lost his dialect completely. Every word, every syllable was clearly enunciated, almost overly so. He was reciting something from spoken memory.

Begin and the stars shall find you.
Breathe and the stars shall know you.
Know and the stars shall enter you.
Enter and the stars shall touch you.

"My grandmother always said that before she talked about the building. I never understood what it meant, but she said it was the essence of Gavani. She always described the temple as being the shape of the sixfold star."

From beneath his shirt, he pulled the necklace that Kyre had noticed earlier to reveal a pendant. Its angles caught the light, the gold blazing bright. "Like this. But I haven't seen any rooms that look like this. So, rather, I guess what I mean to say is that I think this probably is the temple, by the marks on the door. But that the stories, as I know them, as I guess I've believed them, are not real."

Kyre shook his head. "When we came here, we were expecting a temple like that too. Old stories, rumors. The main room didn't seem very temple-like, so we thought there might be secret doors or rooms. We never found them."

"I didn't either. I looked." So maybe his disheveled expression wasn't sleep after all, but something else. Sadness. Exhaustion. Maybe a little embarrassment that he'd been searching for something in their home and hadn't found it.

"I was looking forward to seeing the starroom, most of all," Quenn said, his voice quiet.

"Starroom?" Kyre and Aviend said together, in voice and in glance. Kyre had never heard the word.

Quenn nodded. "That's the room the prayer is about. Or that's what my mom always told me. She said it…" He dug around for the words. "…made you feel connected to the stars. It must have collapsed or…" He seemed unwilling to admit that it might never have been. Kyre could understand that.

"I'm sorry," he said. "That must be disappointing."

"I'm surprised at how disappointing it is," Quenn mused. For a second, Kyre saw him as he'd be in the future. Considerate. Compassionate. Fierce. Knowing what kind of man he was going to become should have made it even easier to know they'd done the right thing. But it didn't. Not entirely.

"It's one of those things that you didn't know you wanted until you almost had it," Quenn said. "Do you know those things?"

Aviend was nodding next to him. She'd stopped eating, and he could see she was having a hard time keeping her eyes open. "All the time," she said. "All the time."

They had a lot to talk about, all of them, but Aviend was right. First sleep. And maybe one of Thorme's painkiller devices. Anodyne pinches, she called them. They tasted like scrub and hurt badly enough that you flinched just thinking of putting them on your tongue. But after that, you were out. For hours. No pain. No nothing. He didn't like it, but a thing didn't need to be likable to be necessary.

As if hearing his thoughts, Aviend yawned next to him, her jaw popping. A bit of moss fell out of her hair and landed on the table. She didn't bother to pick it up. "I'm sorry, I've forgotten your..." A sleepy, deferent wave toward the boy.

"Quenn."

"Quenn. Right. Sorry. It's been a long... something. I want to talk to you more, but I am going to drown in this fantastic food if I don't sleep soon. I get the sense that you want to go...?" She paused, let him fill the silence.

"To my..." he seemed to search around for the word he wanted, and then came up with one that didn't quite seem to be right. "Family."

"To your family. But could you stay for just a bit more? Until I catch up on some sleep and then we can talk? Just a little bit. I promise."

Quenn stirred his spoon without looking at any of them. There was still something there he hadn't said, or didn't want to say. If Aviend was less asleep at the table, she'd probably try to pull it out of him. But Kyre was patient.

Finally, Quenn nodded. "For a little bit."

She wakes up, sure she's drowned. Something's in her lungs. Black and graveled creatures. Slippery and somehow dry as stone. They dig in, a thousand spiked feet piercing her lungs. And then she's coughing. Dry and hacked air. The kind that shakes her chest with each upheaval.

So not drowned. Just dreaming of drowning. Of dying.

Hello, little one.

Those damned purple eyes. And of Rillent. She hopes only dreaming. Could he have found them, found her, already? She doesn't know. Shakes away the memory of his face.

Her lungs do hurt, though. Not as bad as before Thorme forcefed her some pill that tasted of...

"Burps and swampmuck." She realizes she's said it out loud, and is grateful that she's the only one in the room. Well, Kyre too, but he's sound asleep. One arm thrown across his face. She hopes dreaming of better things than her. Rillent's purple eyes, of course, but that's nothing new. The destriatch. Shatter and pain. And running. Always running. She hates running. More than anything. Has done enough of it for her whole lifetime.

She pushes herself from bed, careful not to jostle it too much and wake Kyre. Although by the looks of him, she could spar with the pillows while jumping on him and screaming and not have to worry about him so much as opening his eyes. That's good. He needs the rest.

She does too. So why's she up? That's the question. Thorme's pill should have knocked her out for days. Maybe it has been days. How long has she slept? A minute? A year? Something in between.

Everything aches. Pulls. Twangs, if not audibly, then visibly. She smells of scorched hair and skin, of bogs and blood. Maybe that's what woke her. Her own stench. She needs a wash, but the thought of water – any water, even the sweet cool water that comes in from the riverpipes – makes her want to retch. No washing, then. Not yet at least. She'll have to deal with her own stink. She wants to touch her hair, her no-hair, but resists. There is so much wrong. That's just the one thing that's wrong that she can actually touch. But it doesn't mean she should.

Stepping across the floor of the sleeping space jars her bones. And whatever's in her bones that feels pain. Muscles. Heart. Mostly her heart. They'd been so close. And now they are even further than they'd been before. Rillent knows they are out here. That they tried to take him down and failed. That she is still alive. She is sure of it.

Will he come for them? Of course he will. No question. The only question is when and how. They need a new plan. But before that, they need to find out Rillent's plan. What he knows. What he's going to do. She'll gather everyone in the morning. Whatever time it will be next. Make a plan together.

The pennon is mostly dark, beyond the dim glow of the liquidlights that line the walls. There's no natural light in here, so dark is as dark does. It doesn't necessarily mean it's still night outside. Although she's guessing so, since everyone else seems to be sleeping.

Everyone except for the figure inside the tech room. She can see someone pacing in there, crossing the door, a grey shadow. It's not Delgha. Delgha never paces. Clearly not Kyre, unless he suddenly awoke and raced past her in the dark to pace the floor. And Thorme never went in the tech room if she could help it. Certainly not alone. "Too cold, too sharp, not enough human."

That leaves...

"Quenn?" she asks as she nears. The thin figure inside pauses in its stride as she leans on the doorframe. She shivers from the cool air. Delgha's rigged up a system for one of the devices, which needs cooling to run, and it always makes the room seem overly chilly. "Can't sleep?"

The tech room is the smallest room in the base. Egg-shaped, with a far end that narrows in, so small that you'd nearly have to crawl to reach it. The front end, where she's leaning now, is large. Taller than three humans. Rounded. Loaded with tech. More devices than Aviend can understand or even want to. Most of this is Delgha's purview, and Aviend is usually very happy to leave it to her.

Pacing still, though the space is almost too small to hold his steps. He has to about-face every few seconds. He's barely hobbling anymore at least; Thorme did good work on his injury. It's clear he's been awake for a while. Pacing this whole time? She wonders. For so long at least that his turns have taken on a kind of dance-like flow. She doesn't think he's aware.

Quenn doesn't answer her obvious question. "Who are you?" he asks. "I mean, really?"

She sighs, the last drycough of spike-legged creatures escaping her lungs. She isn't ready for this, but she's not sure she ever will be. She's always too brash, too harsh. Never has the right words at the right time. Unless it's for Kyre. It's like she can see what someone needs so quickly. But then her response gets caught up in the netting of her brain and tangles on the way out.

"Ask me something more specific," she says. "Something I can answer easily in the dark."

"Are you the leader of this group?"

That's a valid question. But not one that's easy. Of course he wouldn't know that. Ask anyone else here and they would say yes, without hesitation, that she was the leader. Ask Aviend herself? And.

"Not really," she says. "We're more of a collaborative effort. We've been working to..." The last of the sleep is gone, but the aches remain. Haunting reminders.

"I know," he says. "Return the rightful balance of power to the Stere. Kyre said the same thing. But... by what right? I mean, I'd be happy to see anyone beyond Ar... Rillent in charge, but who are you to think you can take him down? So many have tried. So many have failed. Rillent took down Ovinale. The whole clave. He took down Arch Enpelia."

His voice is rising, getting frantic, fearful. Words pacing in time to his feet. She can see he's been in here even longer than she thought. Left alone with his own thoughts. Panicking. She wishes Kyre were here. He's so much better at this sort of thing.

She pushes her hands together. Presses the webbing between her thumb with the thumb and forefinger of her other hand. It calms her. She wishes she had a way to calm him. Yesterday, she would have. She would have said, "We won't fail. We have a plan." They don't. They *had* a plan. But that plan failed. For Quenn. Because of Quenn. There is nothing in the world that would make her say that aloud.

So she says what she can. "We won't give up," she says. For the first time since she yelled at the black beasts to move, she feels a glint, a spark, a warm glow of hope. Maybe not all is lost. Maybe they can rebuild. "We'll make a new plan and..."

The hopespark doesn't catch. It dies into blackness mid-sentence.

Quenn stops pacing. In the half light, she can see his face. His too-thin cheeks. The pendant rising and falling with his chest. He waits, unmoving, in the dark for her, until he can wait no longer. "And what?" The hope, the eagerness in his voice is so sharp it cuts her in the soft places beneath the bone.

"I don't know," she says softly. She doesn't. For the first time in such a long time, she is still and uncertain. Moving is easy. Standing here in the not-knowing is so hard.

"You said Rillent took down my mother. Did you know her?" She sees his face, the struggle beneath the skin, and realizes that he didn't know. Still doesn't know. And why should he? Ovinale's clave was large and powerful enough to extend its services beyond its own village, but not to the point where others would know family lines. "I'm Aviend Enpelia."

His stillness is stunning, filling the small room.

"Enpelia?" he says. "As in Arch Enpelia." It doesn't sound like a question, but she thinks that it is.

"Nuvinae, she..." Is? Was? She doesn't know how to talk about it, skips over the verb that defines the distance between the living and the dead. "My mother."

In a movement so fast she can't catch him, Quenn crouches in front of her. He rocks on the balls of his feet, puts his palms in his opposite elbows. He makes a small noise of pain, moving his hurt leg so. His forehead lowers so far that his voice is muffled by the bend in his throat.

"Forgive me," he says. "Arch Enpelia. I didn't know."

"No," she says. "No, no, no. That's not..." Now she really wishes Kyre were here. He'd have the boy risen and moving on to some other topic already. While she's just standing here, stuttering. Does she touch him? Yell at him? Beg him?

She puts her hand on his shoulder – he's so much bonier under his heavy cloak than she expected, and she'd expected pretty bony. Rillent really did his number. She wonders if he realizes how lucky he was to get away alive, and thinks he probably does.

"Please get up," she says, finally. "Truly. That's not what..."

She blames her loss for words on sleep deprivation and anguish, but knows it's not entirely true. There is too much pain in her depths still that makes it hard to talk about.

"My mother was an Aeon Priest and clave leader. Neither are an honor that I have held." She is surprised to find herself falling so easily back into the formal language of her upbringing. Her mother was an Aeon Priest to her core, and a leader in every bit of her skin. Try as she might, she couldn't impart her deep knowledge of the numenera to her daughter, but she'd given her the ability to at least pretend to be the latter, even if Aviend forgot it more than she remembered.

"You should be, though. Rightfully. Rillent..." There is no faltering attempt at respect this time, no pretending to believe that Rillent is true Arch. Quenn is still crouched, but raises his head toward her. It's the first time she sees him show anything akin to anger. There's a lot of it in there, behind his eyes. She wonders what else he keeps so well caged. Did he bring it with him, or learn it in Rillent's trenches?

"Come," she says. "Will you sit with me?" She holds her

hand out to him and helps him rise. There is a low bench along the back of the room, amid devices and boxes and various sundries. She slides the bits of some project of Delgha's – brainbuds, maybe? – off the bench and gestures. Sit. Tries to make it more of an invite and less of a perceived demand.

Quenn sits next to her, fiddling with his pendant. It makes a soft whoosh as the pieces of it slide around beneath his fingers. His movements are thoughtful, but given over to rote. She imagines how many times he's done this very thing with this very pendant. The innumerable number of times his fingers have slid over it. At home, and then in the trenches. And now. She's surprised Rillent didn't confiscate it. Realizes that Quenn must have kept it well hidden.

"You grew up in the Stere. You know that the passage of the leadership doesn't work that way in a clave," she says. "Lineage is for kings and queens, not Aeon Priests and claves. Rillent was appointed by the people after my mother..." *Was killed. Was killed. Was killed.* "Died.

"Besides," she adds, because she can't stand to stop talking with the word *died* the last thing on her tongue. "I'm not an Aeon Priest. Nor do I have any desire to be one. So I can't lead a clave or become Arch."

That's more than she's said about all of it in a long time. It makes her tired. But she can tell Quenn has something on his mind. And so she leans back to the wall and waits.

"How weird," he says. His voice is soft. Musing. "I expected the stories of a long-ago religion to be true, and they were not. But I never believed the stories about this. I thought they were just a falsity. Another myth that people tell themselves because they want it to be real. Like Gavani. Or like how Rillent really does just want to save us all. I never did believe the stories of Nuvinae's daughter and the Night Clave, and it turns out you're the most real of all."

Now it's her turn to be shocked into silence. She's glad she's sitting. She's not sure she would be able to stand through what he just said.

"Did Kyre tell you that? Who we are?"

It's one thing that she and Kyre had kept from their childhood. When they used to sneak down into the underground tunnels beneath the clave to hide from the boredom of everyday life. "We are the Night Clave," they'd say in unison, fingers pressed together. For a long time, she thought they'd left the name behind in the drit and dirt as teenagers. Then came Rillent. And the need for a name that showed the word clave meant something again. A collective where the numenera was used for knowledge and good. Not for power and death.

"No," he says. "Who else could you be? In the trenches and the trees, people whisper the Night Clave like a prayer. Or like a god."

"There's no such thing as gods," she says. And regrets it. Of course it's possible that after everything, Quenn still believes. Why does she say such things?

"I know," he says, surprising her. "But people need something to believe in, don't they? Why not you? Why not the Night Clave?"

He's asking if she really is the Night Clave. If they're the gods everyone believes they are. The weight of the question makes her want to cry. And run back to bed, borrow some of Kyre's dreaming bliss. And make a new plan, a perfect, unfailing plan, for destroying Rillent's power. Once and forever.

"Do you want to talk about it?" she asks instead. "Rillent, I mean?"

"Not much to tell." Whir with the pendant. He doesn't look at her. "He hooked my dad, my younger brother, into becoming trenchers. The usual promises. I begged them not to go, but..." His shrug is more in his elbows than his shoulders, but it says everything.

"When?"

He makes a show of thinking, although she's pretty sure he doesn't have to. She's thinks he knows exactly when. He's buying time so that he can speak without breaking down. She looks away, through the door into the darkness of the pennon. Gives him the moment. "Two years ago now."

"And you?"

"I went to get them back. I thought..." He trails off, shaking his head. "It doesn't matter. They're dead, both of them. Worked to... In..." His voice falls apart, a choke of anguish and anger rolled into a shuddered breath. She can tell by listening that even after everything, after Quenn had known his family had been killed at Rillent's boot, that Quenn had fallen too under Rillent's spell. That he can't forgive himself for that.

She leans against the wall, feeling the pain as the back of her head presses to the curve. It's a pain she can hold on to, and she does.

"Good men, smart men, have fallen to Rillent's power. There's no shame in that," she says. "Rillent got Kyre too, you know." It's not the kind of thing Kyre usually shares, but she thinks if he were here right now, hearing this, he'd say the same.

"But not you?" he asks.

She thinks of herself, at the side of the crater. Rillent's face in her mind, his purple eyes taking her down and down. "Not like that. Rillent and I have a... different relationship."

"I can imagine," he says. He clearly means because of her mother, but that's not it. She doesn't correct him, though. It's so complicated and she never has the words. Not even for Kyre. Not even for herself.

"You were there a long time," she says. "Kept yourself alive." It's a question, if he wants it to be.

"I needed to find my family," he answers. "I let Rillent do whatever he wanted. Did whatever he wanted me to do. The things, the things I di–" The rest of the word chokes out and dies away. He shakes himself, hard. "I learned the kubrics inside and out – they're all the same in there, every one."

"But none of them had what... who... you were looking for."

"No." The word fades away.

The silence stretches. She keeps thinking one of them will get up to go, but neither of them does. The pain in her head keeps her awake for a long while, but she's pretty sure she's dozing by the time he speaks again.

"How are you still secret?" he asks. "How does Rillent not know about you, not know you are here?"

"He does now," she says. Bites her tongue, but too late. She really should have stayed in bed. "Well, not *where* we are. Rillent doesn't care about religion or temples. Useless, as far as he's concerned."

"And that makes it the perfect place to hide," Quenn says.

"It did," she says. "But unless Rillent has suddenly reverted to a much kinder, gentler version of himself since I last spent time with him..."

A small noise of disbelief from Quenn.

"...then he will use everything he has to hunt us down and find us."

"And kill you," he says.

She doesn't disagree, although she's not certain. Rillent will kill the others, without doubt. He'll have Faleineir start, let the varjellen strip away skin and heart and mind, and then Rillent will finish it. But will he kill her? She's not sure. She thinks he'd find other purposes for her. Worse things.

"Thank you for saving me," Quenn says. "I wouldn't have made it."

I know, she thinks. It wasn't all for you, she thinks. But it was. It was for all of them. Maybe most of all for Kyre.

Instead, she says, "What now? For you, I mean?"

"Now I go back to Nalloc."

She's heard of it. Wettown, it's been called, not inappropriately. She can't remember where it is. Steremoss is a big wood. Dotted with little towns. How far from one of Rillent's kubrics? How far from his destriatch?

"You could stay and help us," but even before she completes the sentence, he's shaking his head no.

"Why? For real?" He said "family" before, in front of everyone. She wanted to see what he'd say now.

"I promised my sister I'd come home. With or without them. I'm the last one she has. She is the last one I have."

He looks at her coyly, up through his lashes, as if daring her to counter what he's about to say. "Besides, I'm no fighter."

She wants to say, "There are many ways to fight," but she will not give in to challenge when she can see he's made up his mind. He already knows that there are many ways to fight. Of course he does. And he knows too that he's a fighter. He fought himself into Rillent's hold and out of it again. The words are a way for himself to feel better about going. She doesn't begrudge him that. Nor will she take it away from him.

"When will you go?"

"Soon," he says. "I was just getting up the will to leave when you got here."

"We can go with you. See that you make it through in case Rillent has patrols."

"No," he says. "You've done enough." It sounds almost bitter, but she doesn't think he means it that way. It's hard to be in someone's debt. Especially when it's nothing you asked for. It can make monsters out of the best men. She doesn't think it will make a monster out of him.

She doesn't push for him to stay. It's not her way. She wishes it were, sometimes.

"Before you go, would you be willing to come with me first? Just for a moment? There's something I could use your help with."

He says yes, not as one who wants to say yes, she doesn't think. Maybe as one who's afraid to offend. It makes her sad. It's one of the things she despises about power, even pseudo-power like what he's giving her. It leaves so little room for people to choose what they want.

Still, she's grateful for his unquestioning acquiescence. That must have been rough under Rillent's boot. And rougher still to break from it. She thinks beneath his frailty and youth, he's got so much more strength than one would guess.

This room is Delgha's space. Of all the things scattered about the room, only one of them is truly Aviend's. The strongglass orb hanging in the air above the central table. It was her mother's, one of the few things she could salvage in the destruction. It's just big enough around that she can't wrap her hands fully about it, but she does so, as much as she can. The orb comes to life beneath her palms with a quiet whirr.

She touches a button along the top. It opens flat, still

resting on nothing. On its surface is a map of the Stere, self-lit inside the stronglass panes, drawn by two different hands. Her mother's, the artist, with her fine lettering and her exact landmarks and locations. And Aviend's, whose work is more scattershot and uncertain. Sizes and distances are all approximate. But she thinks it's a good approximation.

Beside her, Quenn gasps softly.

"I've never seen the whole woods like this before," he says. "It's so big."

How to tell him the size of the world? She can't. She doesn't even know it all herself. She puts her hand along the western edge, traces it out, off the map, for as long as her arm will reach. She knows that's still not far enough, not even near, but the comparison is good enough for the moment. "I went here once. Beyond here, to a place called Lhauric. A single city greater than all of the Stere combined."

She doesn't remember much of it. Only glimpses. She was a child, holding the hand of her mother, an Aeon Priest, a clave leader. In a place where none of that mattered. Lhauric was full of great beasts and blood sacrifice. Red and black, metal and synth. Gods that forced their believers to kill and maim and die.

She doesn't say any of this. What good would it do? Quenn knows already the desire of Rillent's power. Knows already how he aims to be a god.

"I worry that whatever Rillent is planning, it's going to stretch to there and beyond," she says.

"What *is* he planning?" Quenn asks.

"We don't know," she says. "I wish we did."

Aviend gives Quenn a few minutes to look at the map in silence. Then she says, "Where is your home? On the map. Approximately?"

He gets a nervous look in his eye. Protective. Even after all they've talked of.

"No," she says. "Not like that. We just want to know how far Rillent's reach extends. Where is safe still."

After a breath, his finger lands on the far northwestern side of the map, nearly to the forest's edge. It's not all that far from here, but it's a long way from the kubric. Damn. She'd been afraid of that. All the way, then.

"Destriatch?" she asks.

"When I'd left? Yes. Now? I don't know. He seems to be pulling them back to the kubrics."

She touches the bit of her scorched hair. "I noticed that," she says.

The question is why? She doesn't know. Something they're still missing, even after all this time and planning. Why would he pull them back? Leave an opening? He must have found something else, something stronger, that would give him protection or power. Or both.

"But that might have changed by now," Quenn adds, almost as if he's afraid that saying it might make it true.

"It might have," she agrees. Letting him go. Back to his home. His family.

His fingers running over the pendant whir, almost like the map before them. As quick as he'd moved before, he moves again. This time the star is off his neck and falling onto her palm before she can think to close it. Heavy. Both smooth and sharp.

"You need to have this," he says. "For saving me."

"I can't," she says. She means it.

"Is it easier if I say it doesn't mean anything to me anymore?" His voice is tender as a torn petal underfoot. And she realizes this isn't about her. It can't be. He needs to go, to leave the yesteryears behind, with their ghostfalls and dead gods and mortar dust. Move forward.

"Yes," she lies.

"Then it doesn't mean anything to me anymore." He lies too.

She turns the pendant over and over in her hands. Thinks about the way someone enters your life and changes it. So quickly. As fast as falling. Before you can blink. Or breathe. Or say thank you.

Begin and the stars shall find you.

By the time she slips the pendant over her head, Quenn is already walking out the door.

"Coruscates beside you," Aviend says to the empty room. He's not dead, yet he is. A part of him, at least. A part of them all dies, she thinks, after Rillent touches them.

Kyre finds her, still sitting there in the morning. She thinks she's slept, but she can't remember. Her back is cracked with bad angles, and her ass is all bone and ache.

"Vi," he says. The nickname catches her attention. He only calls her Vi when he's very, very serious. She has a vague recollection of him calling her that while she was in the treehouse. Or it might have been a dream.

He looks serious now, standing in front of her. Not catching her eye, like she's a millibird he is afraid to startle. He has sleep hair and sleep eyes, and when he fists one hand and wipes it across his sleepy lips, she thinks she might just melt right where she's sitting. "We need to talk about what happened," he said.

Rillent. He means Rillent. Who's still alive. Still enslaving people. Still working toward his horrible end. Whatever that is. She wishes she knew. The fact that she can't figure out his goal, his desire, his very purpose, lends to her feeling of not being smart enough to figure this out. To fix it.

"Or are you planning to keep hibernating in here in the dark like a ravage bear?" he asks.

It's an innocent, teasing question. And yet it's not. He's asking her if she's ready to talk. He knows her well enough. It's not that she's afraid, exactly. Or maybe it is fear, but not fear of death or the destriatch or even Rillent. But fear that she will once again believe she is prepared, planned, perfected, only to discover at the wrong moment that she is none of those things. No, it's not a fear of death, but a fear that she isn't as smart as she tells herself she is. That she will fail not just herself, but Kyre. Delgha. Thorme. Quenn. Her mother. The whole of the Stere.

They don't need to talk about it, she thinks. They were both there. They made a choice. Right or wrong, it's done. Now they need to look forward. Move forward.

No. She knows that he's right. She's avoiding things. It's not like her. That in itself makes her anxious. She can tell herself that she's protecting the base by not thinking about things, by keeping her thoughts secret from Rillent and his probing gaze.

But she can't keep him out forever. He's going to find them. When that happens, they need to have a plan. Not just a plan, but something that's already in motion.

There's something Kyre wants to say too. His face tells her. But she can't find the space inside herself to make room for it. Not yet.

"No," she says. It's the best she can do to answer all of the questions that she can feel him pouring into her. It's her most honest self, and she gives it all to him. "But I'm not ready yet. I need to… I don't know what I need."

"I'm here," he says. "When you figure it out. Or when you don't."

She stands, sleep-ached and muscle-torn, and goes to him, and inside all of the darkness and cold, he is heat and warmth and light.

A few days after Quenn left, Kyre woke to find himself alone again. Which meant Aviend had dreamed of Rillent. Or perhaps, not a dream at all. He hoped it was only that, and not reality. If that were true, then Rillent was moving faster and more aggressively than they were ready for.

He reached an arm out, found the bed chilled. She'd been awake for a while, then.

In the past, he'd have gotten up, gone to find her. But he understood her better now, her need to move after she woke, the footfalls to wipe away Rillent's hold. Rillent had never come for him that way. He hadn't needed to. Kyre had gone to him, eager to help him build a better town, a better world.

He'd tried to imagine what that might feel like, to have someone else in his head, commanding. He couldn't. Aviend saw into his head, to be sure, but that was a welcome thing, a fair connection. Not a takeover.

With Quenn here and then gone, Kyre felt the absence of the other clave members more acutely than he had in a long while. No one talked about how their group had narrowed in, gnawed itself down to the bone. It was as if they couldn't bear it, couldn't admit how skeleton they'd become.

Once, the Night Clave had been closer to a dozen. Mostly

members of the original Ovinale clave who'd followed Aviend here after her mother's death. Others had come after Rillent destroyed their towns. Still others – himself included – had only made it out from under Rillent's boot after too long beneath it.

Only two of their members had died. Others had left, had enough, changed their mind. They went elsewhere in the world, looking for a place where they could just live out their lives without the touch of men like Rillent, wherever that might be. Some went back to their families in the Stere, wanting to believe that Rillent wouldn't touch them there. That they'd be safe if they didn't make waves. He thought Quenn might be hoping for that, a little.

He understood, all too well, the pull of that. It was heavy on the best of days, and exhausting down to his marrow on others. Always fighting and failing. Always waiting to see what new thing Rillent would do, how he would stretch the sphere of normal into something misshapen and gruesome. And then convince everyone that this was better, normal, exactly what they'd agreed to, what they'd fought for.

He couldn't blame Rillent for everything, especially not his own position there. Not entirely. He'd joined him willingly at first. Believed in Rillent's vision of the Stere growing powerful, of their families being protected. Even after everyone he knew was dead or dying, Kyre had still believed. Not even when Kyre's father died beside him in the trenches, gave out under the weight of the work and the press of Rillent's impossible timeline, not even then had Kyre pulled away.

"There's no shame in wanting what Rillent was offering," Aviend said quietly, as she entered the room. She joined him in the bed, shifting to press her body to him. "He's a liar and a killer, but he's smart. He spins a world and makes you believe.

He made us all believe."

"Not you," Kyre said.

"I did," she said. "You know I did."

He did know. She'd told him the story long ago. She was the first that Rillent had come to. She said that was why she'd been the first to step away from him. He wasn't sure he believed her, but he thought she believed herself.

"Thorme put together some pilgrim packs, if you want," she said. "I think she thought we could use a task."

Thorme was right. Today, of all days, Kyre was happy to step into the pennon and see the pilgrim packs stuffed full with foods and seeds, probably medicine, cyphers, whatever other supplies Thorme had been able to scrounge up and trade for. It felt good to be hiking through the woods with a heavy pack on his back, Aviend beside him, breath and footsteps. And it felt especially good to enter the clearing and see familiar faces, faces they'd helped rescue from Rillent's hold.

They arrived at the clearing with no trouble. None of the defenses had been triggered. They'd seen or heard neither ghosts nor people. At least until that very moment.

"Aviend! Kyre!"

The man coming toward them was tall and lean. Topped by a flowering of bright white hair, limbs bending at unusual angles, he looked less like a man and more like a plant blowing in the wind. If Kyre had a favorite plant, it would be Toev Riack.

True also of Aviend, he guessed, by the way she said his name. Such rare delight on her tongue. "Toev," she said, and touched both palms to the man's cheeks by way of greeting.

"It's been too long," Toev said. He gestured toward the makeshift buildings behind him, the common area where people were cooking and working on building... something. A shed, perhaps. In the small garden nearby, a little boy hacked at the dirt with a shovel, a woman laughing beside him. There were few men. It was harder to pull men from Rillent. "Come and sit. We're making a meal. You can share it before you head back."

Kyre caught Aviend's glance, the smallest shake of her head.

"This isn't a comfort visit, I'm afraid," Kyre said. "We need to be quick. And share news."

"Ah." Toev took a moment to glance at their faces. Kyre wondered how much of the truth he saw there. Whatever it was, it was enough that he said, "Well, come and sit briefly anyway. But here, away from the others."

He guided them to a small table near the garden's fence. There wasn't much growing in the soft sod, but still an improvement. Just last year there had only been a mound of debris and stone where a small town had once stood. Now half a dozen rows of something green and blossoming were fighting for space with weeds, and a couple of umlan goats were bleating their despair at having eaten all of the shrubs within their reach.

"The garden's looking good," Kyre said. He unloaded the pack from his back and set it beside Toev, who rested his hand on the top with all the protectiveness of a parent. Toev didn't say thank you. He didn't have to; they were together in caring for these people, helping them get back on their feet. Everyone did what they could. Thanks were unnecessary in times like these.

Aviend followed suit with her pack, saying, "I believe Thorme even said something about there being a few treats in there for the young ones."

"Thorme's heart is bigger than most people's whole bodies," Toev said. Then a moment later, grinning, "As is her displeasure, should you be dumb enough to find it." His laugh was as scattered and angled as his body.

It felt good to sit in the sun and laugh about the kindnesses of the people who mattered in his life. Kyre wished, just for a moment, that they didn't have to talk about dangerous things. He would have liked to sit here longer, in this small vision of a possible future built despite Rillent, with the warmth of the sun on his face, and not feel fear for their very lives. But the shadow of Rillent's knowledge felt like a great blackness slipping across the landscape. He kept feeling like if they didn't hurry, that blackness would catch them when they weren't looking and they would drown in it. All of them.

"What's your news?" Toev asked, as if he were sensing Kyre's impatience.

Aviend had her chin on her hand, watching something in the direction of the garden. He wondered, briefly, what she was thinking. It was rare that he couldn't guess, but he noticed it happened more in the moments when she was thinking of Rillent. As though she were putting up mental blocks, allowing no one through.

Since she didn't seem likely to answer Toev, Kyre did so. "Rillent knows we're alive. Knows Aviend's alive. We don't know what that means yet, but we know it means he'll be scouting for us. For the base. Maybe even for everyone here."

They hadn't told Toev, or anyone else outside of the base, what their plans were before. Normally they gave him a heads up, enough so that he could protect the clearing should something go wrong. Kyre should have known, even as they chose not to tell him this last time, that it meant they weren't doing the right thing.

Toev's eyes were pale, a pearly blue-grey to his ivory hair. He followed Aviend's gaze, watching the goat standing on its hindlegs, stretching to reach the bottom branches of the nearest tree.

"You'll need to prepare everyone," Kyre said.

"We are always preparing," Toev said. "I'll relay the news to everyone at dinner. Is there more?"

Grateful that Toev didn't ask how Rillent knew, Kyre shook his head. "Not that we know yet. We'll send runners if we know more."

"We saved a boy, Toev," Aviend said. "Well, not a boy so much. A Gavanite."

"I knew a Gavanite once. It was long ago." He cupped an elbow into his opposite palm. "Coruscates."

"Coruscates," Kyre echoed. It seemed he'd been saying that a lot lately. After such a long absence, the word felt like sad sustenance in his mouth.

Aviend pulled the pendant from where it had been laying hidden against her skin, letting it dangle from her fingers. In the sunlight, it sparked a new color, the golden hue of fall grasses.

"He gave you this? May I?"

She nodded, and leaned toward him, moving the pendant into easy reach of his long fingers.

"It was a surprise to me, too," she said. "To all of us. He seemed attached to it."

Toev moved his fingers over it without moving the pieces of the pendant. "He must have thought you needed it," he said.

He let the pendant fall. As it swung back, Aviend caught it and tucked it beneath the fabric.

"Maybe," she said. "More, I think he might have just been

shaken up. It's hard to make good decisions when you're in shock. I'm mostly just holding it safely for him until he wants it back."

As they were talking, a woman stepped from inside one of the small buildings behind Toev, bringing water and glasses toward the table. She wore not the black of Rillent's trenchers, but the gold of his personal wards. Her suit was gold flecked with black, the heels of her boots painted with Rillent's love of purples. The clothing itself was worn but well tended, patched by careful hand.

Her hair was wildly cut at various depths, tight curls of ash and grey. Both of her index fingers were nubbed down to the knuckles, clean well-healed cuts so perfectly straight they could only have been purposeful. The way she held her hands, he knew that the wounds were old, delivered so long ago that muscles and bones no longer searched for their missing pieces.

He and Aviend exchanged glances. She wasn't one of their rescues. Had another of Rillent's wards managed to escape his grasp?

As she drew close to where they sat, Kyre saw that Rillent hadn't just taken her fingers. He'd given her something. Her left eye was hollowed out and filled with a cylinder of green metal and black glass. Black fibers extended out from the bottom of it, and then sank beneath her skin, trailing down the side of her face. Their braided surface raised her skin in a pattern that would have been beautiful if you didn't know any part of the story behind it.

At her chin line, the wires reappeared, slipping out of her skin. He could see they'd been pulled from her neck and snipped – the skin there was raw and open, not yet scabbed. Both ends of the wires dangled, one up, one down, frayed as if by a long, slow cut with a too-dull tool.

"I'm clean," she said. "Not to worry." She touched the ends of the wires, laughing. He wasn't surprised to hear that the sound was a little bit mad, but not as much as he might have thought. It was mostly rueful, and mostly sane.

"You've come from Rillent?" Aviend asked.

"Just this soon," she said. Her Truth was broken and split. Not her first language, but he couldn't place the lilt, the tongue-to-teeth sound of her *ths*. "I thank Toev."

"How did you escape?" Kyre could hear, not suspicion, not yet, in Aviend's voice, but something that mimicked his own sense of... disbelief. They trusted Toev's judgment, but something felt jangly about this.

"The kubrics go up and up," she said, matter-of-factly, setting the water jug and three mismatched glasses on the table. "Rillent only look down."

Even Aviend had to snort at that, a snort that turned into coughing laughter as she tried to take a drink.

"Thank you, Nitar," Toev said. The woman nodded and slipped away, as quiet as she'd come. Kyre watched her go. She moved with the deliberate stillness of someone who didn't want to be noticed.

"She came to you?" Kyre asked.

Toev nodded. "I had that response at first, too," he said. "But her story makes sense – she was Rillent's personal tailor for years until–"

"Until the fingers," Aviend mused.

Toev splashed water into his glass, but didn't drink. "It didn't change her skills much – she can whip together anything out of fabric that you might need – but he found someone new after that. She faded and then got out."

"How did she find you?"

"We found her, half-dead, on a hunting run. Brought her back."

They sat as long as they were able.

"We should go," Kyre said, even though he didn't want to.

"I know," Aviend said. "It's just so nice to sit here for a moment with an old friend." She touched Toev's hand, and he lifted his fingers and caught hers in a quick squeeze. "Be careful," she said. "All of you. This is going to get very bad."

It was unlike Aviend to be so sure of things going wrong, and listening to her made the hairs on the back of his neck tighten. It *was* going to get very bad, he thought, and there was no way they – not they the Night Clave, not they the survivors trying to make a life here in this clearing – there was no way any of them were ready for it.

"On your way, then," Toev said. His voice was light, but the tone didn't match his steady, sad gaze. "The young ones will appreciate the treats, I'm sure."

He didn't say anything more about Rillent or preparations, but his gaze had already gone backwards, toward the people gathered in the center of the clearing.

They left him, far quieter and more somber than when they'd arrived. They'd brought things with them that were heavier than supply packs, and they were taking them home too.

"I hate that," Aviend said as they made their way back. "I hate showing up and leaving bad news and then just, well, leaving. It feels awful."

Kyre stepped carefully over the half-buried strips of metal that crisscrossed up from the ground here. If you weren't paying attention, the mottled yellow-green bits looked like moss or fallen leaves, but they were sharp as well-honed blades. There were multihued vertical strips here and there too, that leaned and shifted side to side, even when there was no wind. It was beautiful, but deadly if you weren't careful. "He wouldn't have taken weapons, not that we have many to give."

"I know," she said. A moment later, "Something's wrong."

"With the Nitar situation?"

"Yes. Rillent is just letting people leave? No, that's not his way. The destriatch were at the kubric, and so they went after Quenn. But I don't think that's why they were there in the first place."

"Why would they be there?"

"Guarding something?" she asked. She moved lightly over the metal pattern, barely watching her feet as she went. A strip to her right shifted suddenly, nearly touching her, but she bent her body out of the way at the last moment. "Watch that one," she said. "So what were they doing? Why did Rill–"

She stopped, lifted a finger to her lips. Canted her head to the left. He heard it then. The snaps of twigs. Footfalls. Voices. Too close to have come from the clearing. Maybe some of them on their way back from hunting or...

But no. That voice. He *knew* that voice.

He lifted his hand, rested it on top of his head to make a crest. Aviend's eyes went wide.

Faleineir. Rillent's right-hand man. Out in the woods. Looking.

They went down at the same time, onto their knees in the moss. Careful to find a spot between the strips. Kyre was grateful they'd already gotten rid of the pilgrim packs. The packs were big and heavy enough that they would have made it hard to crouch, and almost impossible to stay in a still position for very long. Kyre gently moved one of the loose strips over with the tip of his blade, giving himself a little more room.

They weren't close enough to the clearing to use their pre-set defenses. Which was both good and bad. Doing so might save them, but it would also reveal the location of Toev and everyone else.

They both pulled their hoods up, slow and quiet, covering their heads. The hoods worked simply by color, a green mottle that made it harder for them to be seen. Aviend touched the side of her mouth with her thumb, tapped it twice. Kyre nodded, once, in agreement. No devices. They would wait it out, see if they could remain unheard and unseen.

It was only a couple of careful, quiet exhales before Faleineir came into view. The varjellen's skin was hued in shades of magenta and violet. A thin crest of similar colors ran down the length of its head. Bulbous yellow eyes blinked slowly in their direction. Looking at those eyes, it would be easy to mistake the varjellen as slow or dull, but Kyre knew firsthand what mind worked behind those globes.

Faleineir was the only varjellen Kyre had ever known. After meeting Faleineir, Kyre had assumed all varjellen were as ruthless and horrid as this one. He didn't know for sure that it wasn't true, but he'd long ago come to believe that Faleineir was its own special kind of hatred in a bottle. Perfectly suited to carry out Rillent's horrors without question or remorse. Faleineir was in Rillent's thrall, to be sure – there was no mistaking the metalworks beneath his neck. Rillent's handiwork – but Kyre doubted it was necessary. The varjellen seemed to want to do nothing more than everything Rillent asked of it.

Kyre resisted the urge to touch his own neck. He had no such scars. No such excuses for his behavior beneath Rillent's clever hand.

Faleineir was followed by three glaives. No one that Kyre

recognized, but clearly Rillent's. They walked with purpose, but also with attention. Eyes scanning the forest. They were looking for something. Or someone.

Aviend's quick fingers, pointing to herself and Kyre. Yes, he thought so too. The only good thing was that if Faleineir and the glaives were out here still, they hadn't already found the base. They were moving away from it, not toward. Keep going, he thought. Keep walking. As if they heard him, they did. Nearly past. Kyre allowed himself to breathe, a quiet release that he felt in his gut. If he and Aviend could just—

From behind them, the call of a child, followed by laughter. All heads turned in the direction of the clearing. All heads except Faleineir's. Varjellen had notoriously good eyesight, and horrendous hearing. One of the men filled him in, and his crested head also moved toward the direction of the sound.

Skist. So much for that plan.

Aviend's response was a silent tightening of her fist. He saw that she had something in it. She slowly opened her fingers, showing off an image module. Her face was a question.

He took it from her – he was better at aiming long distances, and this was going to be tricky. He needed to find a way to wing the module past the hunting party without drawing attention to himself. How to do that without standing or making noise was a problem.

Aviend clearly saw the problem too. She picked up a stone from the ground, turned it around in her hand, and then looked into his eyes.

He nodded. She tossed the rock up in a high arc, not caring where it landed. Kyre watched it as it crashed into a tree not far from them, but far enough away. Even the varjellen heard that. All heads turned toward the tree. In a moment, their attention would certainly be drawn toward the two of them.

Except that Kyre used the split-second of their distraction toward the tree to roll into a crouch. He hurled the module past them and over their heads, and then continued the roll until he was upright again. A twig snapped as he came down, making far too much noise.

If any of Rillent's glaives noticed the sound of Kyre's rough landing, they quickly forgot it as the module kicked in. It projected the image of a humanoid... something or other. Kyre could barely see it, but he was sure that he'd never seen anything quite like it. Probably the image of some creature familiar to the people who initially made the device, who knew how many years ago. Millennia ago. Longer.

Most importantly, however, the image came with weird sounds. Soon, it projected the illusion of the thing running away. Just like Delgha said it would. Kyre watched the men stare after it. The varjellen's voice was a harsh whisper. "Go!" The four of them bolted after the image, Faleineir bringing up the rear, looking all around, warily.

They disappeared from sight. Soon the sound of their crashing footfalls began to fade into the distance.

Kyre and Aviend waited, crouched and listening. When they heard nothing further, they slipped out of the ruins carefully, keeping watch for any sign of the hunting party. None came.

When it seemed clear they were safe, Aviend said, "That kind of thing only works once. Especially with someone like Faleineir."

"Rillent likes his people smart," Kyre said, thinking about all the people the Aeon Priest had wrapped into his hold. Smart, all of them, each in different ways. It was a testament to Rillent's power that he managed to bring so much willing intelligence to his side.

The sound of the river tumbled into his consciousness. They'd been walking toward it, he realized. When they got to the bank, Aviend dropped to one of the flat stones and held out one hand. "I know you have some kind of food in that pack of yours," she said.

He laughed as he sat beside her, then opened the small pack that hung at his side, and unwrapped a few bits of dried meat for them. Aviend set a canister of Thorme's special tea between them. They ate in silence, the sounds of the river and the forest seeming to grow up around them the longer they waited.

"Kyre," she said. "What did you want to tell me the other day? Back in Delgha's room."

He saw his hands were trembling, and he twisted them together, fingers knotted pale, until he wasn't sure he could untie them again. Trembling hands reminded him of his father. Not because his father had been old, but because he had been weak. And Kyre had been weak with him. Less weak, perhaps, than his father ever had been. He could claim that, at least. Small comfort, that, once. No comfort now.

"I feel..."

What would he say, what would he admit? He should have thought this through before he'd started talking. But if he had, he knew he wouldn't be saying any of this. He would have stayed silent and let her walk away, let her carry all of the burdens that were rightfully his.

"When Quenn showed up..."

Two starts, neither of them right. Aviend waited for him, breaking apart bits of the jerky, and letting them fall into her palm. The metal ring he'd given her, oh so many failures ago, circled loosely around her finger from the weight she'd lost.

Those were the things he noticed, sitting there, preparing

to break her heart. And his.

"I was so relieved," he said. So much for that locked box. Apparently it could tumble open at any moment, without so much as a turn of Aviend's key.

"That I didn't have to kill someone. I'm responsible for this, for our failure, for all of it. For the fact that Rillent's looking for us. That he knows you're alive." The words were tumbling out, mixing together, making no sense. He felt himself wanting to stop them, but couldn't. It was like he'd opened a portal to the truth and everything was rushing through. He didn't say the word guilt, but it was woven into every word. A mantra. His mantra now.

"No," Aviend said calmly, interjecting the word into his ramble without so much as a breath of delay. As if she'd been ready for him. She rested the bit of meat on her thigh and rubbed her hands together as if to clean them. "You aren't."

He wanted to take her in his arms, to feel the exhale of her denial against his face. It took everything he had in him to keep his face from falling, to keep himself from falling, into her promise that he'd made the right decision for the right reason. That he'd saved Quenn because it was the right thing to do and not because he'd been selfish, scared, afraid of becoming the monster. That would be the easy way out. He'd taken it before, probably more times than he could count, and he did not want to do it again.

"Kyre, I can read your mind, remember?" she said. Her words carried no joy or love. But they also carried no blame or hatred. Just the softly spoken broken pass of time and space, the weight of the knowledge of how people hurt each other all the time in the promise of doing good.

She put her palm on his thigh, and leaned into him. That movement carried all of the emotions her voice hadn't. How much effort it took for the body to fall, and yet, wasn't it what they did their whole lives? Fall before one another in pain and despair and longing and love?

"Do you remember me telling you to choose?" she said. If only he could say no, shake his head and pretend that it wasn't something that he carried with him always in his mind, like mourners carried locks of their dead lover's hair.

Aviend didn't fiddle with anything. Not the pendant. Not her too-loose ring. Not her hair. Her fingers were steady on his leg. In her stillness, she was absolutely beautiful. And so unlike herself in some ways that it made his chest tighten. She looked like her mother. She looked like a leader, like the woman who had listened to the pleas of men and women, drowning and dying and destroyed, and knew before they opened their mouths that she didn't have a way to save them.

"And do you remember what you told me when we came up with that plan?" she asked. "To kill Rillent?"

He didn't. He'd said so many things, he was sure. Some of them soft truths meant to help Aviend, some of them harsher truths meant to help himself, others just mouthfuls of stones that he had no other way to get rid of so that he could breathe again.

"That's because you said nothing. You went away for a day and when you came back, you said you were resolved."

He remembered that now. He'd gone to the valley, to his father's grave. He'd walked the town that was there no more. He'd tried to remember the world before Rillent and found himself unable. It had always been like this, he'd decided. There was no before.

"There was only after," he said. At her questioning look, he added, "That's what I decided. That's when I decided it was all right for me to kill another person."

Aviend's stillness broke finally. She arched her back and something inside Kyre's chest lifted. Like a heavy tree being pushed back up into the air.

"But you didn't," she said. Her gaze was unwavering and true.

He shook his head, unwilling or unable to see what she was trying to show him.

"Killing a man to save something? That's Rillent's way. Not ours," she said. "I wanted you to save Quenn. And you ended up saving yourself. And me. All of us."

Words were good for so many things, but not for everything. There were no words in the history of words for what he was feeling right now. No words for everything he wanted to give to her, as they sat there in the dappled shade and waited for things to be safe.

He touched the circle of her ring. Felt heartened that she did not pull away.

"What are we going to do?" he said. "How are we going to destroy Rillent once and for all?"

"I don't know," she said. "But I know that we will. I believe that we will. All of us. Together."

3. Not Everything Light is Good

The first time Rillent entered Aviend's head, she was barely more than a child. Running around the Steremoss talking to ghosts and asking her mother ridiculous questions. Hiding out in caves with Kyre and making up finger language. She hadn't known yet that she was in love with him, or even what love was, really. She certainly hadn't known fear or danger, at least not like she understood both now.

The first time Rillent came to her head, he hadn't yet arrived in Ovinale to take over the Stere. Her mother was still alive. Still head of the clave. The leader of Ovinale. Arch Enpelia. Aviend had understood so little then, although she'd of course believed that she understood all of the most important things.

She'd known her mother was the leader of the clave, but hadn't been entirely certain what that meant. She just knew it was made up of people like her mother – Aeon Priests, who understood the devices they fiddled with and who kept the town, the whole forest, safe and secure. Whose job it was to help the people in Ovinale have better lives – her mother's words, not hers.

Aviend mostly knew that it meant lots of boring meetings in Celedan Hall with people who had no interest in a young, active girl. Particularly not one who'd rather be throwing rocks into puddles than sitting still and looking at machines and saying polite things to people she didn't know.

Rillent, Rillent was never boring. Rillent came to her head in the late night when she couldn't sleep and during the sitting that went on and on and when she was supposed to be keeping still and quiet and not touching any of the very important devices. He asked her about things – about her mother, the clave, Ovinale, others – and she told him everything she knew.

Having Rillent in her head made her feel special. He'd chosen her, he told her time and again, because she was special. So special that their connection was a secret. The child that she'd been had believed everything about him. Except whether or not he was real.

When, after so much time of talking to her mind, he'd shown up at the hall in person, she'd had a shock of recognition. From her spot along the back wall, she'd watched him walk into the central greeting room, where visitors came to meet the members of the clave. Even then, he wore the purple and gold, the broad wrap of fabric across his forehead. But it was his eyes – the purple, big as moons in her mind's eye – that made her gasp out loud. I know him, she'd thought.

She'd reached to tug at her mother's sleeve, to capture her attention, to tell her everything. She still told her mother everything back then. Everything except about the man in her head with the purple eyes. Because he wasn't real. Just like the ghosts weren't really real. Like her nightmares where she was drowning weren't really real either.

But now that he was here, he was real, and that meant telling her mother.

The man from inside her head looked at her across the

space. In real here, real now. Zoomed in as though he were inside her head and not standing, flesh and blood and bone, before her.

Hello, little one, he said.

Special.

She never did lift her hand to tell her mother. Looking back, she understands that moment as the one that changed everything.

She stood still through the opening conversation and when her mother said, "And this is my daughter, Aviend," and the man she would come to know as Rillent Boure said, "It is a true pleasure to meet you," and took her wrist, she had let him and said only, using every bit of proper manners her mother had taught her, "Iadace. May your cyphers never malfunction."

Then her mother and Rillent talked about the Convergence, which Rillent said was a threat to all of the claves and all of the people the claves protected, but especially to the clave in the Stere. Rillent offered his services to help the clave protect itself. To help it gain power in preparation for what he called the coming war. She hadn't really heard much of the rest, though, because it was boring grownup stuff and mostly because she had a new secret. And secrets, she'd learned, are the loudest quietest thing there is.

Much, much later, she learned that she wasn't the only one with secrets. Rillent had secrets too. And his were far, far louder than hers.

She'd let the monster in, just to feel like she was special in a way that wasn't solely because she was the daughter of Arch Enpelia.

But of course, that was the only reason the monster had chosen her. So that he could use her to kill her mother and take over the clave. To gain power. To destroy everything she loved.

I was only a child.

But she wasn't. Not at that point. At that point, she'd been on her way to adulthood, to making almost adult choices. That weight is one she bears each day. It is hers and hers alone. She refuses to let anyone else hold it or take it from her. She holds it so tight it makes the mark of her fingernails on her palm. She holds it tight now as she watches Delgha write questions out on her board. Her handwriting is small and perfectly formed.

Why did Rillent pull the destriatch back to the kubric?
*How and when will he come for us? * – Faleineir already looking?*
What is he doing with the kubrics?
What is his final plan?
What is our new plan to stop him?

That last one gets a double underline from Delgha's careful hand.

"I'm assuming," Delgha says, as she taps her writing utensil to the last question, "that we are going to go after him again, and we're not all just going to roll over and decide to let him get away with whatever it is he's doing."

"That's a fair assessment," Kyre says. "Unless someone wants to say nay."

Thorme is seated at the bench, filling booster syringes from a mix of glass bottles of myriad colors. They're spread around her like a rainbow. Unlabeled. Aviend has no idea how she keeps them all straight. Thorme is a brilliant enigma, and that's just how they like her.

The chiurgeon doesn't respond, which is pretty much

Thorme for yes. Or at least: I'm not paying attention so go ahead without me. Thorme doesn't say much, but shortly after they'd met, Thorme did once say to Aviend, "I stay quiet so I can be the first to hear someone dying." Aviend hadn't known her very well then, and hadn't quite figured out that was not what she'd really meant to say. Now she understood that the chiurgeon had been both serious and teasing in her answer.

"I don't have any other plans," Aviend says. She's aiming for light, but can hear in her voice how she falls short. "But I'll let you know if that changes."

"Smart ass," Delgha says. But there's no actual ire in her tone. Maybe just relief. Since they failed, there's a silence and sadness around the base that is hard to move around in. It's thick and heavy. Moving forward, trying to make a new plan – that's something to hold on to. It's lightening things a little bit. Not enough.

"Kyre," Delgha says. "I know you had some qualms about the last plan." A pause. "I know we all did."

"Actually killing someone, even someone like Rillent, you mean?"

"Yes, that."

Kyre's quiet for a long time. Aviend watches his face and is grateful for what he's about to say. It's hard for him, but she knows he's been holding it inside for too long. "I've never felt such a mix of guilt and gratitude and relief and panic as when I'd realized I hadn't killed someone. That I wasn't a killer."

Aviend loops her pointer finger, taps the knuckle to his leg. Support. He nods slightly in acknowledgment. In his eyes is the same sense of relief she saw when he told her the same.

Delgha draws swirling designs on the board while she thinks. "We need to make a better plan, something less lethal this time." She doesn't sound certain of their ability to do that.

"Like tie Rillent up and throw him over the falls?" Aviend says.

"Probably still lethal."

"What if we found a new way to show the people that he isn't what he says? That he's not actually working for their benefit…" Kyre says.

They'd tried that before, had come up with a plan that exposed Rillent for what he was. They'd talked to the people. Stood by the mass graves – they called them wolf dens, for the copious amounts of wolflilies that grew above them – and reminded them of family members and loved ones who'd died.

But Rillent's hold was so strong. Too strong. People couldn't see through him for long enough to break free. Those who saw were too few, too slow to awaken. Or afraid.

"We could try to save more people," Aviend says. "More rescue missions."

"Not fast enough," Kyre says. She knows it's true, but it still stabs her gut-wise to hear it. "Rillent's power is growing. With each additional bit of the kubrics he forces the people to unearth. We can all feel it."

"And," Delgha adds, "now that Rillent knows you're alive…" Eyes to Aviend. "That we're all alive and that we're coming for him… he's not going to go easy. We've given everything away. We don't have any more cards up our sleeves."

Next to her, Kyre runs his hand over his hair, the way he thinks. He has streaks of white and silver now. Sometimes she remembers him as a child, his small face overlaid with the man she knows. It's both disconcerting to realize how old they've grown, and reassuring at the same time. Kyre is one of the few things she still has in her life. After all of this time. After all of Rillent.

Kyre glances at her. In his face is a question. Two, actually, although she can see he already knows the answer to the first one.

"Yes," she says, answering them both at once. "I think Rillent's been in my head again."

Delgha tries to hold her utensil steady, but Aviend can see the soft shake of her fingers.

"So soon?" Delgha says.

"I think so. It might be just dreams, my brain kicking stuff up after seeing him again. But I think I was awake, and it feels..." She wants to say, "like fingers reaching into my brain," but that's not quite right. It's not fingers that bore their way in. It's his damn eyes. "...It could be him," she finishes.

"Is he..." Kyre makes a gesture with his fingers. Asking questions. Digging for information.

"No," she says. "At least, not yet."

"Thorme," Delgha says, her voice question and warning both.

"I'll send my runners," Thorme says. "Find out what he's doing, if we can."

It's risky to send the runners, especially now. Right after their botched attempt at killing him. But she has to admit that it's necessary. They need to know what Rillent's next move is so they can plan theirs.

"What else can we do until then?" Aviend says. The thought of sitting around, waiting for the runners to come back with news makes her feel itchy already. For as much as she hates running away, she's never been very good at sitting still.

"Heal," Thorme says without looking up. "Eat. Prepare.

You thought last time was tough? This time is going to be tougher."

The only sound in the room – the fall of liquid as Thorme fills the final boost – says how much they all agree she's right.

It was always hard to wait for the runners to come back. They were all antsy. Aviend was the only one currently taking it out on the cards.

"Skist," she announced, nearly loud enough for the whole forest to hear. She threw her well-worn card on the table. It showed a white nest dug into the earth filled with pale bloated worms. Deathbed. Losing card. "Skist and triple skist and may the broken hounds eat all your eyes."

"What if they just eat one of my eyes?" Kyre said. "Would that satisfy?"

In response, Aviend mimicked Thorme's *hmph* to perfection, which actually drew, well, not a smile, but a bare twitch of lips, out of Thorme.

It didn't matter that Kyre's card, when he laid it down, wasn't much better than Aviend's. The deathbed card was always a loss. And the one who held it always a loser. It made him sad to see it there. Aviend so rarely lost. She was the sharpest game player he'd ever met.

"That's the third time you've pulled that card in a row," he said, as Delgha and Thorme both added their cards to the pile. Out of rote more than necessity. This wasn't a game where anyone won. It was one where someone lost. Not his favorite kind of game, but he hadn't chosen it. Delgha and Thorme had vetoed any games in which he and Aviend were on the same team, citing unfair advantages. "Are you cheating?"

"To let you win?" Aviend said. "Not on your life."

"I guess I should be glad we're not playing for shins or you'd curse me with something worse than eye-eating," Kyre said. "Do broken hounds even eat eyes?"

"They will if I cut them out and feed them to them," Aviend grumbled under her breath, and then pulled the pile of cards across the table toward her and started to shuffle them with practiced ease. Their edges were worn, but the soft synth had held its colors well over the years. The fronts were a mix of images in black and green. Their backs wore the mark of some faraway ruler. A king perhaps? Or maybe a whole kingdom? He couldn't remember. A black tiger crouched on a red banner. He'd always thought the tiger was roaring, but Thorme showed him once how it was clearly yawning, and now he couldn't unsee it.

"Not your deal," Thorme said, holding her hand out, palm up.

Loosing another stream of swearwords, this time at herself, Aviend dropped the deck into Thorme's hand and pushed herself up from the table. "Sorry," she said. "I'm not a sore loser. It's just all this waiting is making me full of swears and bugs."

"That's why we're playing," Thorme said. "Something to do with our hands while we wait." As if her hands had ever been still. If she wasn't cooking or patching, she was making something. Not devices or weapons, but softer things. Things that gave comfort instead of information. Thorme had joined the clave not by accident, but by... Kyre didn't believe in fate. But they'd needed her without even knowing they'd needed her, and she'd appeared. If there was a word for that, he didn't know what it was. Luck, perhaps. But he didn't believe in that either.

"Planning," he said aloud.

Aviend shot him a questioning look. He tapped his forehead, grinning.

"It's too dark in your mind for me right now," she said. "We should go see if the runners show up in Delgha's panel yet."

"Sit," Thorme said. She dealt the cards, setting the first one down in Aviend's spot with a deliberate snap. "We'll know when they get here."

Aviend looked like she was about to protest, but then sat, still muttering swearwords under her breath. Skist was her usual preference, probably because it had the widest range of use. But she'd taken on a new one lately – brehmbrained cypher-grabber. She uttered it now, sticking her pointer finger at the sky as she said it. Not aiming it at anyone in particular, but more generally at the situation. It probably summed up nicely what they were all thinking.

It almost made Kyre laugh, to hear her swearing across the table from him. So much better than the quiet, thoughtful Aviend they'd been sharing space with the last few days. Not that she wasn't often quiet and thoughtful, but this one had worried him. Too quiet. Too thoughtful. Usually quiet and thoughtful was followed by bursts of ideas, plans, suggestions for taking down Rillent. But this had just gone on and on. Swearing at the sky was, at least, a step in the right direction.

Delgha, too, was back in motion, after holing herself up with her machines for a few days. And she'd made him test her new device this morning, a blue nodule that was supposed to stick to the side of his jaw and allow him to talk to her long-distance. It fell off as soon as he started to talk and shattered across the floor, but at least she was working on something new.

Thorme had sent her runners off a few days ago with messages for the well. Since then, she'd mostly been cooking. "The runners will be hungry," she'd said, as if every bit of food wasn't just to give her something to do.

And Kyre? He'd fixed everything in the place that needed fixing. And a few that hadn't. The cooler in here no longer made strange bird-chip noises. He'd cleaned the inflow valves on the riverpipes. Smoothed out that jerky spot in the lift.

He hoped Thorme's runners would come back soon. He wasn't sure how much longer they could all sit there, desperately needing information and action, thinking about the dead and gone. He hadn't taken up the habit of swearing at his cards yet, but he wondered how long he'd be able to hold out.

Aviend was running the edge of her cards through a long L carved into the table. The wood was covered with names. People who'd eaten here. Passed through. Been rescued or had rescued. Others who'd never been here, but should have been. Nuvinae. Lyeg. Kyre's father.

"Kyre, your go." Thorme nodded to the cards she'd dealt him, and set the remaining stack of cards off to the side of the table.

He picked up his hand and was not at all surprised to find himself looking at three low cards and a single glowing black egg. Second Chance.

The only way to not lose with a Deathbed card was if you could also play a Second Chance card. Unless someone took it from you.

He did his best to keep his face impassive. Aviend had a knack for knowing when he had a Second Chance. Had a knack for stealing it right out of his hand.

He watched her face. She was, he thought, going to make out like she had it. Which meant that she probably had the Deathbed card and was hoping someone would take it from her. Whatever she decided to do, he'd use to his advantage.

"Two of Bills and Beaks," he said, laying down the low card face up, showing the open mouths stretched across it. "To trade for—"

The panel in the tech room started whining, a sound that Delgha claimed to have modeled after some cute young creature she'd had as a pet in her youth, but all it did was make Kyre's teeth clench.

Aviend caught his eye, her grin full and quick as she pushed herself away from the table yet again. "They're back," she said. "Let's go see what our friend Rillent is up to."

The runners were both exhausted, panting heavily at the table as the others loaded it with food and drink. Their title wasn't a misnomer; it perfectly described their jobs. Run. Deliver the message to the well. Run back. Go on with their normal lives until called again.

They were both wearing green coveralls that matched the shifting shades of the forest and they both moved – even exhausted – with the air of being faster than the body they were trapped in would allow them to go. But that's where their similarities ended.

Stiler was tall and thin. Everything about him was long – bones, hair, nose, nails. Even his voice seemed stretched too far out, low and lean, falling into the air through time.

Perem was tiny and muscled, so compact it seemed like she'd been squished in from all sides. She sat curled up, knees to her chest, making her seem even smaller.

Somehow they not only matched each other's paces, but

kept each other safe. Stiler was the messenger and Perem was the guard that ran at his side.

Kyre knew little about them other than that. They all kept it that way on purpose. Sometimes it felt odd to work so closely with someone and know so little, but he knew it was safer for everyone that way. He wasn't even sure if Stiler and Perem were their real names. It was enough of a danger that they knew where the base was and how to get inside. Not that it was a matter of them breaching that faith. More that if Rillent caught you, he made it hard, nay, nearly impossible, to keep a secret, no matter how much you might want to.

They had runners on both sides, from the base to the well, and from the well to the kubric. Kyre had never met the runners on Rillent's side. Thorme was the only one who even knew their names.

The well was not, as they sometimes made it out to be, a high-tech device or a pool of information. It was a literal well, stone-built ages ago, located half a mile or so away from the kubric. It used to serve the city of Ovinale, before Rillent had crushed it under his boot to make way for his power and the unearthing of the kubrics. Now it was Rillent's personal water source. They'd originally thought to take him out by putting poison or something into it, but they had quickly discovered it was used for others as well, and didn't want to take the risk of killing those under Rillent's thrall.

Now they used it to pass messages back and forth. "Our high-tech messaging system," they called it, laughing.

They wrote notes on small pieces of transparent sheets. The runners slid them into the chinks in the stone well. The others picked them up. Back and forth. Back and forth. It was always a two-day process, at least, since the runners from Rillent's side were sporadic and closely watched.

Two days ago, Thorme had sent Stiler and Perem out with a message to see what Rillent's plans were. When was he coming for them? How was he going to do it? Their answers would be rumors and hearsay. The runners on the other side weren't high enough up in Rillent's organization to get actual information. They listened at doors, strode through hallways as though they belonged there, gathered what clues they could and passed them along. Some of the bravest people he'd never met, when he thought about it.

Once Stiler had caught his breath, he handed Delgha a thin transparent slip. Delgha unfolded the slip and pressed the heat of her hand to one side of it. A moment later, a series of symbols appeared.

She read it in silence.

"They say Rillent's not looking for us," she said.

"But we saw them already," Kyre said. "In the woods."

Beside him, Aviend nodded. "He sent Faleineir. How can he not be looking?"

"It says he's looking for something," Delgha said. Her voice sounded as surprised as Kyre felt. "But it's not us."

"Compromised?" Aviend asked. She'd taken a look at Kyre's hand and swiped the Second Chance card from it. She was trying to stand it on end beneath one finger.

"I don't think so." Delgha glanced at the runners, who shook their heads almost in unison. They were both digging into the food, murmuring thanks to Thorme between bites and breaths.

"Read it again?" Kyre asked.

Instead, Delgha handed him the sheet. It was still warm from her skin, and the inks had not yet started to fade. They only worked once, and only while still pressed to heat. Once he took his hand and heat away, they'd slowly fade and disappear forever.

The symbols were truncated, but they always were and they all sounded correct, so it didn't seem like the runners had been compromised. Although the message still didn't make sense.

He read it aloud to the group, parsing each symbol into a word or phrase to create something akin to sentences.

"Is aware of attempt. Claimed insignificant, other than loss of trencher. Otherwise, continuing on as before. Unable to find necessary... key? code? door? More as discovered."

He looked at Delgha for help with the final and unfamiliar symbol. She looked at the sheet in his hand again and shook her head. "I'm not sure, but it might be less literal. Maybe inner circle?" She made a swimming movement with her hand. "Like slipping between two things."

"All right, something about the runners trying to get closer to Rillent or his plans then. More to come as available."

"Quenn?" Aviend said. She let the card fall to the table, face up. "He cares more about the loss of a trencher than he does about an assassination attempt? Than he does about knowing we're alive?"

"That makes no sense," Delgha said.

"Agreed." Kyre took his hand away from the slip, watched the symbols fade. "But if that's what's happening, we need to figure out why."

"Perhaps Rillent has grown a heart," Aviend said, her words sly enough that if he was anyone else, he would have thought she meant them seriously. One of the runners choked on their food.

Delgha started laughing, her whole body shaking a bit. She didn't laugh much, but when she did, it changed the very air in the room. Like everyone who breathed in her sound had to join her. And they did.

"Thank you," Delgha said, when everyone had stopped laughing long enough to breathe. "I needed that."

"Grave humor," Thorme said. Her voice quiet. Had she laughed with them? He didn't think so.

"So no new heart for Rillent. But what if this is false?" Aviend said. "Not a compromise, but a purposeful mislead. Is it possible that Rillent knows about the runners and is feeding them false information?"

They all looked at Stiler and Perem, who both shook their heads. "We'd know," Stiler said. "If Rillent tried to feed the runners information, they'd know."

Thorme nodded agreement. "They're smart," she said.

They waited until the runners were fed and rested and gone before they got down to the business of figuring things out. The less information the runners had, the safer everyone was. Thorme had them on watch, so they'd be back in a few days with any incoming information.

Until then, the group needed to get into Rillent's head.

"For as easily as he gets into mine, I wish I could get back into his," Aviend said. Then a moment later, with a small shudder, "No, honestly, I don't. It's scary in there. But it sure would help right now."

All of them had crammed into Delgha's tech room, even Thorme, although she mostly stayed leaned against the edge of the door. She said it was the tech – she wasn't a fan of their *whirrs* and *squonks* – but he thought there might be something more. She never said, but it seemed that the very room itself was part of her discomfort. She was more human-focused than on devices, so it certainly wasn't how close they had to get to each other to fit into the space. Claustrophobic? Devicephobic?

It was certainly loaded up with devices, and the back end did slope down weirdly, into such a small space that he wondered why they'd made it that way in the first place. Whoever had made this. They knew it wasn't the Gavanites. All their stories – at least the ones he'd heard – told of coming upon it in the forest. It was forest even back then, and they'd found the place by accident. So it had existed before. To what end? Impossible to know.

Although, who knew how much of the Gavanites' story was true? They'd also told of a giant room that connected you to the stars, but that seemed to be myth created out of nothing more than time and belief. So maybe it was all a falsity.

They had Aviend's floating map of the Stere open, and Delgha was pointing to various places. "So we know that Rillent had destriatch guarding the forest's edges here, here..." She ran her finger along the whole southern edge, a crooked, mangled line of trees that stretched long. "All of here. Plus various midpoints. Everywhere but the kubrics."

"But the runners say that now he's pulled the ones on the edges back and gathered them all at the main kubric. It seems to have happened right around the time of our plan."

"Did he know?" Kyre felt something shift along his insides. What if it had all been a trap, a ruse to get them to reveal themselves. What i–

"No," Delgha said. "Rillent's smart, but he never questions himself. We know that. If he believed Aviend was dead, then nothing more than her showing up at his doorstep–" Aviend snorted at that. "Would prove to him otherwise."

"So not only is he not coming after us, but he's decreasing his patrols at the same time?" Aviend fiddled with the pendant as she talked. She'd taken to spinning it much the same way that Quenn had done. It was almost as if the object asked to be touched, spun, kept in motion. "That can only mean–"

"That he's closer than we thought to completing his plan," Kyre said. He felt the thing starting to happen between the two of them. He didn't have a word for it, or at least not a good one. The closest analogy he had was when you were walking with someone, side by side, and suddenly the two of you were walking at exactly the same pace, stepping at the same time, moving as one, without intentionally doing so. That's what happened with him and Aviend, only it happened in their brains.

"Whatever that is," Aviend agreed. He didn't even think she was aware that she was smiling fully, perhaps the first time he'd seen a real smile out of her since the night on the crater's edge. "We need to figure out what that is, exactly. And soon. We need to put the final pieces together before Rillent does."

"What do we know about the kubrics?" Kyre asked. "We have notes somewhere, right?"

Delgha pointed behind Aviend. "Blue metal box, tucked into the tail end of the egg."

Aviend took the lead, moving into the back corner of the room, resting on her knees as she opened the blue metal box. "Ghosts, Delgha. How much stuff is in here?" she asked as she started sifting through it. He could see not just papers, but memory devices. Not all of them still in working condition, if he was going to guess from the tangled web Aviend pulled out of the box and held up to the light.

"Just enough," Delgha said. "And I have… Kyre, can you help me move this stuff? I've got a memory orb back here somewhere with audio notes on it, from when we were still in the clave. They might not be useful. It was before we knew much, but... remember that?"

Kyre remembered. He was still a believer then. A believer in Rillent's desire to actually do good and protect the Stere, its people. The memory made his stomach churn. Embarrassment. Fear. His own arrogant ignorance. He didn't push it away, though, as he might have done once. Instead, he let it sit for a moment, remembered through it, tried to find pride or at least a sense of comfort in how far he'd come.

"Do you think–" Kyre's question was interrupted by a sound. Something shifted overhead. Far off to the right, a different space, a different thing, clonked, loud and hard, somewhere in the sloping ceiling.

They all stopped, mid-stride. Aviend lifted herself up from her kneeling position as far as she could without hitting her head on the wall. She dropped the pendant she'd been fiddling with and put a hand to the curved ceiling.

There were no more sounds.

"Rillent?" Thorme and Delgha asked in unison. Everyone's fear now. That he was coming for them. That he was already here.

"I don't think so," Aviend said. She didn't sound sure, but Kyre agreed with her.

"It sounded mechanical," Kyre said. "Like it was coming from inside."

"Yes." Delgha had flipped on her scanner, was scrolling through the various feeds. They showed nothing but dark. If there was something out there bigger than a laak, the screen would be lit up. "Nothing out there of note," she said.

They waited. Aviend and Kyre's breathing was synced, a long pause to listen, a slow, quiet exhale. It was still quiet.

"Just something in the building?" Thorme asked.

"Maybe," Delgha said. "Maybe something that happens

all the time and we're just never here to hear it." She also sounded unsure.

"Let's keep our eyes and ears open," she added. "Just because we don't think Rillent is coming for us – right now – doesn't mean there aren't a hundred things to be wary of in the Stere."

"Two hundred, at least," Aviend said as she went back to digging through Delgha's papers and devices in search of a solution.

She started pulling papers and devices out of the box with one hand, setting them on the ground next to her. Kyre couldn't see her other hand, but he could tell she was working the pendant. He could hear it whirring softly beneath her fingertips.

He trusted Delgha's devices, but it was never bad to have a backup. Even contingencies needed contingencies. "I'll go outside and take a look, just to see if–"

The whole room lit up, a pattern of bright green symbols arcing across the curves of the ceiling. The symbols – he couldn't make them out, whether they were words or images or something else – whirred and spun across the ceiling, complex patterns that his eyes had a hard time following.

"Delgha, is that...?" He realized his hand was on his blade, poised as if he might start throwing it at a bunch of marks of light.

"No," she said.

They both looked at Aviend. She was still kneeling, but she'd dropped the papers and was staring up at the ceiling above her. The dots moved over her, the same pattern, but smaller. The whirring of her pendant grew louder, seemed to rise and rise until it took over the whole room. Kyre felt like his very bones were shaking. And yet still, it was possible to hear everything that was happening. Behind him, Thorme gasped, a soft, wet sound of surprise and wonder. Delgha's hand slid across her scanner controls as she turned, her touch falling away from the device. Even Aviend, farther away, facing away from him, could be heard as though she were standing right next to him.

His first instinct was to try to make it stop. But that was a fear instinct, and it quickly faded away into wonder. Everything rose and quickened. The lights, the noise, until Kyre's very eyeballs were vibrating. He had a hard time swallowing, as though his mouth and throat no longer lined up properly.

"It's talking," she said, and her voice was a whisper. "The pendant is talking to the room."

"Of course," he said. "Of course it is."

Why hadn't they seen it before? That the pendant wasn't just a pendant. It was a key, a way to discover… what? They'd find out soon enough, he thought. He didn't believe they could stop it now even if they wanted to.

From beside him, he sensed Delgha moving forward. "Wait," he said. He wasn't sure if she could hear him, but she stopped either way. Standing at his side. He didn't turn around, but he would have bet all the shins in the Stere that Thorme had stepped back out of the room. Not a coward, but already thinking like a chiurgeon. What if the roof fell? What if everything collapsed and she had to dig them out of the rubble? He wouldn't be surprised if she was already on her way to gather med supplies.

"Do you know what it's saying?" he asked.

Delgha, watching the lights move around the room, shook her head no. Aviend didn't respond.

"Aviend?" he said. "You all right?"

A long moment of silence from her made his breath heavy.

Her head was no longer lifted. It had fallen forward onto her chest. From here, he couldn't see her face. Only the tightness of her shoulders, the loose lean of her torso toward her knees. He was about to step forward, to go to her, when he saw her empty hand raise off the ground and press downward slightly. Wait.

"M'all right," she said a moment later. "Let's give it time. See what else it has to say."

What it had to say was a lot. High-pitched screeches and low moans. A few hard knocks that made Kyre want to cover his head and drop to his knees instinctually. He resisted, remained standing. Watching the lights on the pendant and the wall match up.

"I feel like the roof's going to fall on me," Aviend said.

"The roof's not falling," Delgha said, and Kyre was grateful for her confident dispersal of knowledge. "I think something's working like it's supposed to. Despite the noise. In fact, I'm betting the noise…"

She let her voice trail away to make room for another round of low, metallic screeches.

"I'm betting it has to do with how long it's been since this… whatever it is… happened. Not in all the years since we've been here. And, if I had to take a guess, not in a hundred? Two hundred? years prior. Maybe as many as four hun–"

"Look," Aviend said.

She said look, but meant listen. When she moved the pendant a certain way, small gestures between her fingers, they could all hear the building responding in time. As if her movements were creating sound echoes.

"It's a key," she said. "Quenn's pendant is a key."

"To what?" Delgha said.

"I am going…" Her voice falling away as she worked the

star, sliding its sides and points to various angles and then waiting to see what sound her actions would bring. "...to figure that out."

She worked a new combination, let it slide into place. Then another. Another. Kyre felt like he'd been holding his breath forever, and he forced himself to let it out, a big whoosh.

"I feel like I've–" Aviend started.

There was an audible tone, shivery and light. And then everyone in the room was silent. And so was the room.

The back end of the tech room had just soundlessly, almost faster than he could comprehend what he was seeing, irised open to reveal a tunnel. Right at the smallest point of the egg. Right in front of where Aviend was.

From behind him, Thorme's footsteps as she came back into the room. He heard the fall of her healing kit as it hit the floor.

"Calaval's eyes," she breathed.

"Agreed," Aviend said.

The tunnel was similar to the one that they used as their main entrance and exit. A little too short for most of them, the same shape, the same almost-lit material. He couldn't see the end of it from where he stood. He wondered if Aviend's view was better.

He could see that on the floor right inside the tunnel was an etching of a symbol that matched Quenn's pendant. Or perhaps it was Aviend's pendant now. Or maybe it was, and had always been, Gavani's. Just on loan to the rest of them.

Aviend glanced back at him, one brow lifted. Her face was filled with an excitement he hadn't seen on her in a while. It almost made her skin glow. It certainly made her eyes wide. The green of the pendant overshadowed her natural color and made the whites into a weird yellow-green. As he watched, it faded. Both on the ceiling and in the pendant.

"Yes?" Aviend asked. Meaning: are we dropping our planning for the moment to see what's behind this new discovery?

"It could help us in some way," Delgha said. She spoke for all of them.

Aviend was already moving into what Kyre thought of as her leadership mode. If you asked her, he bet she'd say she wasn't the leader, that the Night Clave was a cooperative effort. He didn't think it was false modesty. More that she didn't fully understand her leadership role because it came to her naturally, effortlessly.

"Kyre and I go through first," she said. "We have no idea what's at the end of that tunnel. It could be Quenn's temple, or it could be..." She brought her hands together, wiggled her fingers, exploded them out. Bigger danger than we can imagine.

She glanced at Kyre's shirtsleeves, took in the blades he always wore. Checked her hip for the small set of razor rings she typically carried.

"What else?" she said.

Delgha handed Kyre a glowglobe from her workbench. He palmed it, but didn't turn it on. Not yet. If there was something in there, he wanted to see it before it saw them.

"Delgha, how are those talkpieces you've been working on?" he asked.

"Three-quarters, sadly," she said. "Maybe less. They only work if you're facing east and I have no idea why. And even if you're facing east, sometimes they still don't work."

All right. No communication then. Another plan.

Aviend had a habit of pinching her fingers into the webbing between her opposite thumb when she was thinking deeply.

It gave him a sense of calm to watch her doing it, because it meant she was working on something in her head. And that usually meant she was solving a problem he hadn't noticed yet. Or at the very least, that a crazy idea was bubbling in there.

This time, it was solving a problem. "We're not sure yet how the door works," she said. "Quenn and I were in here before with the pendant, but it didn't open. It's possible that we weren't close enough to the door. Or that it needs to be spun in a certain way. Or worn by a certain type of person. Or a combination of all three."

He followed her logic. Not knowing how it worked meant there was a chance that they'd step inside and the door would close behind them. If the tunnel went nowhere, or if they encountered something they couldn't take on, they'd be unable to get back. It was possible there was another way out – maybe more than one – at the end of the tunnel. But possible, not probable, didn't make for great odds of survival.

He would suggest she stay here and keep the door open, but he'd known her long enough that he knew the words would be a waste. She wasn't an aggressive leader – she stepped back when she needed to – but he didn't think she was about to let this one go.

"Delgha?" she asked.

"My best guess is that once the door is open, it stays open until you ask it not to. But we don't know how to ask that of it, and I'm not all that sure my best guess is on the mark."

"So we'll want to experiment," she continued. "Understanding the risk we're choosing is that the door might shut and we can't get it to reopen. But at least we'll be on this side of it, together."

Delgha looked at each of them in turn, waiting for them to speak or give agreement in another way.

When they gave it, she said, "Let's have you start by stepping toward Kyre. We'll start with proximity."

In the end, the best they could figure was that opening the door was an action, a thing that happened purposefully. It could be undone – they didn't know how yet, but that could wait – but it wasn't likely to snap shut on them after Aviend stepped out of range. Or even if she took off the pendant.

Which she did now. She placed it on the workbench, her fingers grazing it softly for a moment.

"In case," she said. "The pendant kind of... wants to be used. It tells you how to move it. Your fingers just want to spin it."

She gave a half grin as if she'd just thought of something. "That's the first time a device has even talked to me," she said. "Delgha, that's what it's like for you all the time? They just tell you what they want you to do? I feel like I finally understand what that means."

Delgha's smile was fleeting, but heartfelt. "Something like that," she said.

"Shall we?" Aviend said to Kyre.

He stepped into the tunnel first. Aviend was the close-range fighter between the two of them, but if he could see a thing before it saw them, he could take it out. And give them time to backtrack.

He let his senses explore as they moved. Like their entrance tunnel, this one didn't have light, although it did have whatever it was that made it easier to move through. But all he could hear was his own breath, even with his mouth closed.

"I expected it to be staler in here," Aviend said as she followed him through the tunnel. "There must be some connection to the outside."

Kyre inhaled, and caught fresh air. Mingled in was a scent he almost recognized, but couldn't place. Like a sweet spice that was a neighbor to a spice he was familiar with.

"Wait. Hear that?" she asked.

He wished he could look back at her, but the tunnel was just tight enough to prevent him from turning around.

Then, the sound came through. So soft he was surprised that she'd heard it. "Something spinning? But not like the pendant. Bigger."

"Maybe. Creature? Machine?"

"Impossible to know."

They continued forward. The tunnel seemed like it was eternal, a long, straight, flat box that they were walking through without end. He knew that wasn't true; they hadn't been in here for more than a few minutes, but something about walking forward into the unknown without any light was making him lose track of time and sense.

When the tunnel ended, it did so so abruptly that he banged his hand into the dark closure. A full heavy sound echoed back through the tunnel. He pushed into the blackness, but it didn't move. Not a door, but a covering. An end cap.

He popped the glowglobe on. Whatever the walls were made of seemed to be working hard to dampen the light from the device. If anything, he found it harder to see. He ran his fingers over the material in front of him, the seams and edges, and found nothing that would give.

"I think it's the end of the line," he said.

"That's it?" Her voice carried her disappointment, unmasked. "I thought for sure we'd find... Gavani's temple. Or at least something."

"Me too," he said. "I hoped."

"I have no idea how to get out of here," she said. "I'm not

sure it's possible to turn around. My body's too big for this space. Who made this?"

"Wait," he said.

His fingers had found an indent in the side of the door. Half hidden, like the one at the outside of the base. "Wait," he said again in his excitement.

He passed the glowglobe back to Aviend without turning around. She held it over his shoulder, shifted it until the shadows were minimal.

He tucked his fingers into the indent and lifted. The material slid down into the space below, creating a perfect door. "Nice," Aviend whispered. She turned the glowglobe off, putting them back in the dark.

In silence and shadow, they moved forward out of the tunnel. He took it in bit by bit, first checking for movement, action, creatures. Anything that might come forward and show itself. Beside him, Aviend had turned as he was, doing the same.

He reached out a finger, met hers. Silent acknowledgment that there was nothing in the shadows.

And that's when he really let himself look at where they were.

The entire ceiling was transparent. Not stronglass or even regular glass but something else. Something he'd never seen before. It seemed almost invisible. More than invisible. It was somehow bringing the sky closer to them. The stars, bright and big as his fist, bigger, were giving the room its light.

Gavani's temple. The starroom. This had to be it.

"How is this not visible from the outside?" Aviend's voice was breathless. "How can we not see it from the forest? Every time we walk by?"

"I don't know," he said. "I'm not even sure where we are. I

mean, look at those stars. They don't look right."

"Not right, but beautiful. And so big. I bet if you went outside and looked up, they'd be..." She lifted her fist to the sky. The stars were bigger than it, so much bigger. "A third this size? No, much less. They'd be so small."

"What does that mean?" he mused. "Either the ceiling is making them look closer, or we *are* closer. I just can't tell which."

He didn't know much about stars, but he knew they were far away. Too far to increase in size without a huge leap through time and space.

All around the edges of the large room were devices. Large, larger than he'd ever seen. Even within Rillent's sphere. Some of them seemed to still be working, their lights or dials lit and moving. Others had gone dark, likely either from the passage of time or equipment failure.

Even so, everything about it was beautiful.

"I can't believe this whole time we've been staying in that dark, cramped space," he said.

"You told me you loved the pennon."

"Well, yes, because I didn't have anything to compare it to. If I'd known what we could have been having, I wouldn't have loved it so much."

"I don't know that I like what that says about you."

"High standards?"

"Fickle."

They stood in silence for a moment. "This is big," she said.

"Huge."

"I'm sad Quenn's not here to see this," she said. He found that he was too. Maybe someday. If they found a new way to take down Rillent. Maybe this could become something again. A temple for a new world of followers. A school. Something else that no one had thought of yet.

"We should go back and tell the others," Aviend said. "Delgha will want to take a look at all of these devices."

"We should. Soon," he said. "But let's just hold this for one moment."

She put her hand inside his. He rubbed his thumb over the angles of her knuckles, across the smooth black ring she always wore.

Together, in silence, they stood in the center of their discovery, and raised their faces to the stars.

By the time they get Delgha and Thorme through the tunnel and into the star room, the overhead view has changed. Stars are still alight everywhere above. Now they're as big as their heads. And softer, a pale golden against a blue and pink background.

"Is it morning already?" Thorme asks, her voice awed. It's a tone Aviend has never heard from her before. She's got her healing kit by two fingers. It dangles and swings in her loose hold. Aviend thinks she doesn't even remember that she brought it.

"Your guess is as good as mine," Kyre says. "Better, likely."

"I can't believe the temple was here all along," Thorme says. "Right next to us. Poor Quenn, to have missed out."

Delgha had barely glanced at the stars. For one second, maybe two. She's already fully invested in the devices lining the room. She talks without turning away from her inspection of the machines.

"I'm pretty sure that the Gavanites didn't build this," she says. "Unless the Gavanites go back a lot farther than we think. This space is old. Ancient. Whatever is more ancient than ancient."

"Can you imagine how it must have felt to be the first

people to discover this place?" Aviend asks. Her neck aches from staring upward, but she can't stop. She wants to take it all in. She feels like she's had so few things to marvel at since Rillent came. As if he sucked all of the wonder and delight from the world without her realizing it until now. The sheer beauty, the sheer untouchability of what she's looking at, makes her feel hope. A seed she'd thought was dead... only buried. Only waiting. "It might be enough to get even me to believe in a god."

Aviend walks over to Delgha, the Aeon Priest sticking her hand into an opening that looks far too much like a mouth – or something else – for Aviend's taste. She'll stick her hand in a lot of things if need be. But whatever that is might be more than she is willing to agree to unless someone's dying.

Delgha pulls her hand out. Aviend fully expects it to be covered in goo or missing entirely. But it's just her hand. The Aeon Priest doesn't wear rings – too easy to get caught on things and rip a finger clean off, she always says – but she often stains her nails and the tips of her fingers in different colors. Today, they're the shimmering opalescent of fish splashing in water.

"What do you think these are... were... for?" Aviend asks.

"I have no idea yet," Delgha says. "I've never seen anything like it."

The device – can you call it that? She's not entirely sure – closest to her looks more like a mushroom than any machine she's ever known. It has a single wide base covered in symbols and levers and panels. Some of them are round, following the curve of the base. Others stick straight out from it, as though someone inserted it in there with nothing more than the shove of a hand. The base of it is as big around as she is.

The top half is much larger. A larger, softer-looking half

globe that overshadows the base. Almost seems like it's threatening to fall over. It too is covered with myriad etchings and symbols she doesn't understand.

"These don't have the Gavani symbol," she says. "Or even any words or... well, anything that I recognize. They're not Gavani-built either, are they?"

Delgha pushes her finger against a small round bubble on the top of one device. It sinks in under pressure, releasing a soft squishy exhale. When she takes her finger away, it seems to shake itself and then quickly return to its former shape. As it does so, another bubble near the base makes a sudden popping noise.

"I don't think so. There's very little that I recognize, and even less that I understand," Delgha says. "I would venture to guess that none of this was made by humans. At least not by the humans we share this forest with. This material is... not organic. But it's emulating something organic."

"It could even be that it's been... well, living and growing here all of this time. Before the Gavanites came, before anyone came."

"Evolving machines?" Aviend tries to put those pieces together in her head. Machine and living thing, together. It's not unheard of. She's seen it before, but not like this. Nitar has an embedded eye. Rillent has a device implanted in his forehead. Not that she's even seen that. But she knows it's there.

Others that she's known have had visible cybernetic eyes or limbs, other bits of hardware embedded in their skin. Creatures, too, with machines inside them. Certainly the destriatch must be both organic and machine.

This, though, is different. Integrated. As if it were both from the beginning. Must be both to survive. It makes sense, she thinks. If you take the best of both to create a thing that is stronger, evolving. Long-lived. Adaptable. It becomes what it needs to become to survive.

"Something like that," Delgha echoes her thoughts. "Makes sense from a longevity standpoint. The organic bits are bolstered by the machine bits and vice versa. I get the sense that it's bigger than it might have been once, based on the way that it no longer fits into the wall space and how it seems to have stretched out the skin that it's wearing."

Delgha points a finger at the lines running between the devices. They are transparent and hollow, filled with a golden yellow liquid. Normally, Aviend would use the word "tubes" but they twist and twine more organically. Roots. No, vines.

Aviend touches one. It's warm and pulsing slightly. She shifts her concept again. Not roots or vines. But veins. Arteries.

So if these are its limbs – or perhaps, better, its blood system – then where is its heart?

It must be somewhere else. Somewhere they haven't seen yet. She would say there are no other doors in this room, but the pendant has taught her not to trust her eyes. She walks the perimeter of the room, slowly, twirling the pendant between her fingers. Waiting for something, anything, to happen.

Nothing does. At least not something that is her doing.

Against the far wall, Delgha is still puttering with the main bank of devices. The occasional sounds rise from them; soft squeaks or hisses that remind Aviend of creatures. Then again, Delgha makes her own noises. Sighs of frustration, but more often of delight. Her *oohs* and *ahhs* make Aviend smile, even as she walks and spins, walks and spins.

Kyre joins her on her second lap around the temple. He falls into step beside her. His gait is easy, loose, like it is when he's happy about something. Or excited maybe. The two are often entwined with him. "This is cool," he says. "But I'll admit I was hoping we'd find a hidden city or something. Maybe a luxury home with actual warm water and, I don't know, an aneen or three. Somewhere with a generous leader who shares his shins and technology with his lowly subjects."

"You want to be a farmer now?" she says. She spins the pendant. Looks for movement. "Farmer Kyre? I did not anticipate that desire bubbling out of your black brain."

"I don't know…" he says. "Maybe? There's something appealing about a life in the light."

She knows he's kidding. She's pretty sure he's kidding. But she wonders. What kind of toll is it really taking on all of them? Hiding here in the dark. Outcasts. Spies and near-assassins. The hunted even as they hunt. They're doing the right thing, the good thing, but to what end on their hearts and minds? Maybe they would be better off just leaving the Stere, going somewhere safe, leaving Rillent behind.

"No," he says, and at first she thinks he's reading her mind this time. She realizes he's just answering his own questions. "I don't really want that. I mean, I do. I want a life in the light again. But I want it here, in our home. Because we helped make it happen."

"Me too," she says. It's true. It's always been true. Even if it's tempting sometimes to believe otherwise. It's out of love, but also out of ferocity. A sense of righteousness. The Stere, Ovinale – they were hers and Kyre's, her mom's, Delgha's and Thorme's. Quenn's.

It is still theirs, even if Rillent pretends that it isn't. Even if no one but them knows it yet.

They finish the perimeter walk in silence.

"Skist," she says. "That would have made it easier, if some

fantastic new door opened and led the way. Ideally with an instruction book saying, 'Do this and you can defeat the bad guy'."

"Does that ever happen?"

"In my dream version of the world."

"Think of it this way: if it doesn't exist, then I guess at least the good thing is that Rillent can't get a hold of it."

"Fair point. It's why we keep almost everything in our brains." Not that Rillent can't access her brain, so not even that is truly safe. But she doesn't say that. Kyre doesn't either. But the edges of his jaw twitch, and she knows he's thinking it.

They make it back to Delgha, who's still poking and pressing parts of the devices. Muttering. It's mostly nonsense, but every once in a while, a clear swearword slips through.

Aviend clasps her hands behind her back. When she sees Kyre watching, she says, "So I don't touch until I know what I'm doing."

"Seems smart. You're not going to blow us up, right, Del?" Kyre teases.

"I make no promises."

"Right, remember that time when you were making that..." Kyre opens his hand toward Aviend, palm upward, asking her to give him the word he's looking for.

"Butterfly drone," Aviend says.

"Yes!" Kyre says. "A cute little thing that was supposed to fly around and take recordings, and instead it nearly blew all of our heads off."

"After you touched it," Delgha says.

"You said it wouldn't do anything."

"You weren't supposed to touch it until I said so," Delgha says, matter-of-factly. Then with an unusual bit of laughter in her voice, she says, "Speaking of which, Kyre, go touch that button over there, will you? The orangish... ah... stemish one."

"No," he says. "I don't trust you one bit, Delgha."

"This one you are supposed to touch. I think. I'm trying to make a connector to..." She's not really talking to them, and her voice trails away for a few words before it's intelligible again. "...and... power and then see if I can't get the..."

"What does it do, exactly, Del?" Kyre says.

"I'm not sure. It seems vital to the purpose of all of this stuff. But I need to hold these two tubes together..." She lifts them and Aviend sees they're foaming at the connection. A kind of interplay between the two parts that forms a circle of bubbles between them. "At the same time."

"I'll do it," Aviend says.

"Sucker," Kyre teases.

"Coward," Aviend says back.

"I think 'smart' is the word you meant to use. Or perhaps 'Man who likes to keep all his fingers'."

"That's not a word."

"Fingerkeeper."

It makes her laugh.

The button that Delgha means isn't really a button, but it's the closest word Aviend has too. It's tall and rubbery, and looks like the stem of a flower without the flower. Except an orange so bright it almost hurts her eyes. "Push, Del? Or wiggle? Or what?"

"I don't know. Try them all."

"Oh, good." She feels her face do the thing that she knows Kyre thinks of as her wink, then reaches out to touch the stem lightly at the very top. A thread of fear flows through her arm, causing her to release it before she is even sure she touched it.

"Ow," she says, even though she's not entirely sure if it hurt. Even now, her arm isn't in pain. She can't remember what it felt like, except that she didn't want to be touching it anymore. "Skist, Delgha."

"Sorry," Delgha says. She frantically twists some buttons. But the way she says it tells Aviend that she's not all that surprised by her response.

"You knew it was going to do that, didn't you?" Aviend says.

"Why do you think I asked Kyre to touch it first?"

"Delgha!" she says, just as Kyre mutters a swear under his breath. She's trying not to laugh, but the look on Kyre's face makes it almost impossible not to.

"Honestly, I hoped it would do something," Delgha says. "But I didn't know what. What did it do?"

Aviend looks for words. She can still feel the emotion in her arm, which is one of the weirdest things she's ever had to say. "It's like it made my arm afraid. Not the rest of me, but just my arm. It wanted to let go of it before I even realized I'd touched it."

"Maybe some kind of defense mechanism. That's pretty interesting. Let's try it again."

"No, thank you," Aviend says. Her arm feels... weird. Like it's ready for her to ask it to do something it doesn't want to do and it might slap her in the face.

Delgha looks up, confused. Shakes her head. "Sorry," she says.

Aviend thinks she means it more for herself than anything. Delgha forgets that they're humans, sometimes, she thinks. Sees them as machines or puzzles. Something to be solved. Used. Or at least utilized. That sounds meaner than she intends it to. Delgha doesn't mean harm. But it is disconcerting, she thinks. For all of them, even Delgha, when Delgha goes into that space.

"All right, don't touch it again," Delgha says. "But try to touch it. See if it will let you."

Aviend lifts her arm. Her fingers wiggle. She wills her hand to reach toward the button. You don't have to touch it, she thinks. Just move toward it.

A thing she never thinks about: how her hand moves when she wants it to. It just does. But now she's asking it to do so, like it's a creature separate from her body. And it is absolutely refusing. It's like it can't hear her. She feels it again, the sense that her arm is afraid. She isn't – she knows what fear feels like when it lives in her body, and this is not it. But her arm? That's something else.

"Nope," she says. She lets her arm drop and swears it floods with relief. "It's like my arm is refusing to do as I ask of it. That is the oddest sensation I've ever experienced. And I've felt some odd things in my time."

"Kyre, I hate to ask, but would you be willing to give it a try, please?" Delgha asks. "I'd like to see if it's the same for everyone. Or at least for the two people I can talk into touching the thing."

"Not particularly," he says. "But I will if you need me to. In the name of discovery, and all of that."

"In the name of discovery," Delgha agrees without looking up from her swirling bubbles and tubes.

He moves over in front of the machine. "Hey, Thorme. How come you never have to touch Delgha's stuff?"

"Chiurgeon," she says simply, pointing a thumb at her chest.

"Right," he says.

"I'd offer to hold your hand, but I'm afraid my hand would

try to punch me in the face or something after that last go," Aviend says.

"Great," Kyre says. "Let's get this over with then."

He reaches out toward the stem. Aviend holds her breath. She can feel her face scrunching up in anticipation of his response. She almost doesn't want to look, but knows it wouldn't be fair to turn away. Plus, she's a little bit curious. Will his arm be scared too? What does that look like?

He touches the stem. His fingers stay closed around it. There's no reaction.

"Nothing," he says. "It's like it's not even..."

He doesn't finish his sentence.

Delgha looks up at the same time Kyre says something that starts out as a word and ends in little more than a guttural growl. His eyes roll back to whites so slowly Aviend thinks she's imagining their movement. Blood flecks his fingertips where he's holding the stem.

He disappears. Comes back. Disappears again. Returns, shuddering.

Aviend's hand won't let her grab him, won't reach out even though she asks it to, so she body knocks him, sending him sprawling so hard he hits the floor with a thud.

"What the skist is that? Delgha?"

"I don't know. I don't know," she says. She is moving fast, shutting down the devices, quick switches and pulls.

On the floor, Kyre shakes, his feet battering the floor. The blood from his finger leaves small smears of red across the floor with every shudder of his body. He shakes so hard he's moving himself across the floor in fits and starts.

"Kyre," she says. "Kyre. Thorme, get the kit." Even though Thorme is already there. Even though she already has the kit. Is already kneeling. Aviend might be screaming. She can't tell. Her throat hurts.

By force of will, Aviend gets out of Thorme's way, lets the chiurgeon kneel beside Kyre. She stays close, trying not to hover, in case she's needed.

She's never felt so helpless. It's her role to be prepared, to plan. She can make the plan. Follow the plan. Adjust if the plan goes low-gravity. But this? She's not prepared for this.

Thorme pulls a bottle out of her healing kit. Shakes it hard, once. Aviend can feel the chill coming off the bottle as liquid inside activates. The glass starts to ice over, even as Thorme screws an injector into the lid. She turns it over, taps the inside of Kyre's arm twice, and drives the needle in.

Kyre instantly goes still as death. His eyes open, but unseeing. He's not shuddering anymore, but he doesn't seem to be breathing either.

Aviend hears herself, repeating Kyre's name and Thorme's name over and over, in an alternating, escalating call and no-response, but she can't seem to stop herself. This is what true panic feels like, she thinks. It's not your death that drives you over the edge. It's watching the death of the one you love over something stupid and having no way to stop it.

Thorme breaks the cycle with a pinch on the back of Aviend's hand. "Stop," she says calmly.

Aviend does. She inhales, and can't remember the last time that she did so. "Is he…?"

"Shhh."

In order to be quiet, Aviend has to close her eyes. She's not sure why, but she understands that as soon as she opens her eyes, she will also open her mouth. She sits with her eyes closed and her mouth closed and listens to Thorme work on the body of the man she loves and she waits. It's one of the hardest things she's ever done.

"All right," Thorme says. "He's all right."

Open your eyes, Aviend thinks. But finds she can't. Her eyes are the things that are scared now. If she stays here, in this moment, eyes closed, Kyre will have the potential to be all right forever.

She feels a hand touch hers. Opens her eyes. The whitewash of Kyre's eyes has been replaced by his normal eyes once again.

"That machine… is an asshole, Delgha," Kyre says, slow and careful. The words seem to come hard.

Delgha is kneeling beside her. Now they're all kneeling, with Kyre in the middle of them. "I'm sorry," Delgha says. "I had no idea that something like that was going to happen. I should have…" She reaches for Kyre, as if to pat his shoulder or maybe his head – Aviend isn't quite sure, but then she draws back. "I'm sorry," she says again.

"No sorries," Kyre says. "I kind of offered. Although, in the future, before you sign me up for things, you should probably… probably remember that if you accidentally kill me, Aviend will never forgive you."

Aviend laughs, because he's right and that makes it funny, but the sound scrapes her raw throat like acid.

Kyre pushes himself slowly to sit. Gives a nod to Thorme's questioning glance. "I'm all right. I feel all right." Turns to face Aviend.

"I had no idea you could scream so loud," he says to her.

"Me neither," she admits. "I'm having a bit of a hard time hearing. I'm a little worried that I burst my own eardrums."

Her hand is not afraid to reach for him. She doesn't have to ask it to move forward. It just does, as if they're already in agreement that it's the thing they want to do. He takes her fingers, wraps them in his.

He drops his voice to a mock-whisper. "In case you didn't notice, our resident Aeon Priest just tried to kill me. Perhaps we should do something about that…"

"I know, but I think we kind of need her around," Aviend says. "It's probably a risk we have to take. At least for a little while longer." It's easier to be very serious about this not-serious concern than it is to be about the fact that Kyre just collapsed on the floor in a fit.

"However," Aviend says, "you are not allowed to touch anything anymore ever again."

Delgha shifts. Scratches the back of her head. "I also hate to ask, but what did it feel like? I'm guessing not similar to Aviend's experience."

"Noo…" he says. Drawn out. Thinking. "All right, I'm going to say all of this with the caveat that I might have hit my head, because it's going to sound way out there."

Delgha merely nods. Aviend gets the sense that while devices often do unexpected things, there is nothing Delgha could hear about a machine that would actually seem unbelievable to her.

"It was as though I was somewhere else for a moment. No, as though I was supposed to go somewhere else for a moment, but I got stuck. Like trying to walk through what you thought was a door but was actually a wall. A kind of porous wall."

He shook his head. "I wish I were better at this. When I was walking back here with Quenn, something happened. Something I forgot about until just now. He paid homage to one of the ghosts and then it touched him and he disappeared. It was a blink. A second. Not even. But I saw it. And he felt it.

"This felt… kind of like that looked. Only as if it didn't work the way it was supposed to."

"Whatever it felt like, that is definitely not what you looked like," Aviend says. "You looked like you were... having a seizure." He'd really looked like he was dying, but she couldn't say that word out loud. Didn't think he needed to hear it, either.

To Delgha she says, "Do you think it's a transition device, like the transporter? It takes us somewhere else in the forest?"

"Or the world," Delgha says. "The Steremoss is big, but this thing is bigger. It might take us hundreds of miles from here. Maybe farther."

"I wonder if we can use it for..." Kyre starts.

"...Rillent," Aviend finishes. "Let's see if we can find out what this stuff actually does, how far away it might take us."

"Ideally without trying to kill me again, Aeon Priest."

"I wonder why it did that to you and not Aviend," Delgha says. "It scared her away, but tried to draw you in."

"And kill me. Don't forget that part."

"Yes. Why have two different protective devices?"

Aviend looks at the devices all around the room. Each one slightly different. Had they all started like that? Or had they all started the same, and each one had grown and changed over so much time to become the thing they were now? It was almost impossible to know. At least not until they had more time and information.

"That would mean either it was built to ward off two different kinds of enemies, or that one of those – probably the last one – isn't a defense reaction at all," Aviend says. "Maybe it was trying to send Kyre where it wanted to, but it didn't work for some reason. You said yourself, Delgha, that we don't know how old it is. Even with the dual organic and machine, certainly it could malfunction, right?"

"Yes..." Delgha's rapidly scribbling on her portable

notetaker. It's clear she's got more to write than the pace at which her hand can move.

"Just our luck, it would teleport us right into Rillent's hands."

"Well..." She's still not quite ready to put her idea into the world, but it slips into her tone of voice. Clear enough that Kyre catches it, even if the others don't. "That actually might be something we could use."

"You have a plan," he says.

"No," she admits. "It's more like I have the promise that there might be a plan again some day. It's mostly just holes right now."

He nods. "We are full of things that fill holes," he says. "Or make holes. Or are holes. I don't know what I'm saying. I guess we're all just about the holes...

"Thorme," he says. "Are you sure I'm all right? I feel like I'm talking nonsense."

"That's how I know you're all right," Thorme says. "If you were making complete and utter sense, I'd have to stick you with some more needles and force a pill or two down your throat." There is no sense of tease in her voice.

Aviend snorts back laughter. Thorme's doctoring skills have always been a million times better than her social skills.

"Hmph," Kyre says, attempting to emulate Thorme's most common addition to any conversation.

"I can hear you," Thorme says. She's waving a needle that's so long it can't possibly be designed to stick in a human body.

"Delgha?" Aviend says.

"I'm done for now," Delgha says. "I limit myself to one near-death per day. Unless it's my own. Then I get two."

A moment later, as if it pains her to admit such a thing. "I might have gotten carried away, let my excitement get ahead of my science. I need to do more research."

"All right," Aviend says. "Let's take a break from the death-by-science plan. I'm starving."

Kyre snorts at her, and she waves him away. "Shush, you. I have something I want to check on, and then dinner? I saw some of Thorme's famous dossi patties in the chiller."

Thorme narrows her eyes at famous, but doesn't disagree.

"We'll continue to make a plan, unless someone objects," she says.

No one does. Which is both good and bad. Agreeing to make a plan isn't a plan, yet, but it's a promise nonetheless. A promise that they will try again to take down Rillent. To free the Steremoss and its people. To accomplish what they'd originally set out to do. Ideally, without killing anyone in the process.

Well, what else was there? You either died trying to do good and right, probably by touching a little orange stem on an ancient machine under the guidance of your friends, or you died under the boot of a man who thought he was a god. She'd choose the former, every time. And be grateful she had the chance to choose.

Once everyone has gone back through the tunnel except her, Aviend stands before the orange stem. She wills her arm to touch it. Overcome your fear, she says to it. Or to herself. She doesn't know. Thinking about her arm as a thing separate from her is both surprisingly easy and oddly disconcerting. It would be easier if it were actually disconnected, she thinks.

It won't go. She thinks she could touch it with her other hand, some other part of her body, but this isn't about that. It's about fear. It's an emotion that she despises. It feels weak. And yet. It's there. All the time. And it has a purpose. An important one – namely, saving her life.

No matter how much she wills it, she can't make it happen. Her arm will not lift. She feels like there's a lesson there, but no matter how many times she looks up and counts the stars, she can't see it.

4. Darkness Comes Without a Gloaming

Dinner never comes. Or rather, Aviend imagines that it comes for everyone else in the Stere. Around the world. And inside the base.

But it doesn't come for her.

It's her own fault. She has to touch all the things. Poke and prod. Try to understand the things she doesn't understand.

Once she was sure that Kyre was all right – he said he was exhausted but fine, and Thorme agreed but made him lie down anyway and he went but not without some disagreement – she slipped out of the clave and went for a mindwalk.

Normally, mindwalks are the kind of thing she and Kyre do together. It's how they plan, prepare, doublecheck their contingencies. Almost every problem – from as small as their own to as big as saving the world – can be solved, or at least explored, on a mindwalk.

But she wasn't going to pull Kyre out of bed, so she goes alone. She's looking for the starroom. Or some sign of the starroom. From the outside. She knows where it is in terms of the base. Or where it should be. The temple, at least from the inside, is huge. Everything about it is bigger than seems possible. And yet, she's never seen it. She's been in that spot a hundred times, more. They all have.

She understands that it's probably not important to the mission at hand, but it's like a thorn in the padding of her thumb. She won't be able to rest until she can no longer pick at it. Until the curiosity is excised.

It seems impossible to believe that a building that size could be completely hidden from view. Unless it's underground, but then how does the ceiling work, that invisible angle to the stars? It is possible that they've been looking in the wrong spot. But she doesn't think so. From above ground, an entire temple is just missing.

How, then, had the Gavanites gotten in? That was the question that she kept coming back to. There had to be an external door. She'd been twirling the pendant as she walked, but she didn't think that was going to work again. She thought it might be designed for indoor, well, doors.

It's also possible the space is an illusion, a projection of some kind. But it would have to fool all of the senses. Not just the eyes, but the hands too. It seemed possible, but her gut told her that wasn't the case. Whatever they were looking at was real – whatever that meant, exactly – and thus it should be showing up right here, in the space that she was walking toward.

She skirts the thin space between the swamp and the base, and steps into the area, based on the angle of the base and the tunnel they went through to get to the temple, where she thinks the temple should be.

And here it is. She's so surprised she nearly falls back into the swamp. Skist. Something Delgha did in there, something they all did in there, brought the temple into view. Or maybe it just made it possible for her to see it. She's not sure. But either way, it's beautiful and ornate and just as Quenn described it.

It's all shined black. Curves and points, an ebb and flow that seems to constantly be moving. When she touches it, it's still beneath her hand, but she can feel the swirls that give it an essence of movement. It's soft like moss, but without the texture.

It takes her a moment to see the outline there. A triangle edged into the material. The color is slightly different than the rest. Grey more than black.

She touches it. As soon as she does, she regrets it. Not because anything horrible happens, but because she's still recovering from touching the last thing, and she told herself she wouldn't.

Well, too late now. In she goes.

Between one stride and the next, the dark of the doorway envelops her. Between one blink and the next, the dark becomes a shine that blinds. So bright it makes her eyes close and water in a single action. All she can see is red. Pulsing and shifting. It takes her a moment to realize that's the light through her eyelids. She can see her own blood in there. It's both fascinating and disturbing.

She thinks about dropping her zoomscreen over her eyes as a makeshift shield, but somehow knows that it won't help. She'll give it a minute standing here with her eyes closed. See if her eyes adjust.

They do. Or the light does. It's hard to tell. Either way, the pain – she thinks it's weird that light can cause pain, but she knows it does – lessens and the light softens. She peeks one eye open. And gasps.

She doesn't know where she is, but she's definitely not in the Stere anymore. It looks like a forest, though. Sort of. Things that are trees but not trees. The ground beneath her boots is sloped and slanted. She can feel it give and spring, but not like moss or earth. The light feels like sunlight. Heavier and brighter than any sunlight she's ever seen. As though it has substance. It comes in through the tops of the trees-not-trees, slanting into her face.

The trees are like the devices in the temple but also not. In her first sweeping glance, she can't articulate why this is true in either place.

When she takes another step, the air swarms around her, heavier but not oppressive. She swears she can feel the parts of the air as they bump against her skin. But there's nothing to see, and when she sweeps her hand in front of her, the sensation lessens.

There's no door behind her. No tumbling stones or water. She can't hear the millibirds either. In fact, there is almost no noise of the forest she knows here at all. It makes her feel like she doesn't have her balance. She doesn't know where the edges of her body are. She puts her hands out, but it doesn't help. They look like dangling things in her field of vision, and not something that she owns and operates.

She realizes belatedly that they also don't have any weapons in them. Which is stupid. Because who knows what's here? Wherever here is. This could be something of Rillent's, filled with traps and hounds and horrors. Or even something from an ancient species. Also filled with traps and hounds and horrors.

The thing is, all of the quiet makes her feel safe. Like, how could something horrible possibly be here when there is no sound, no noise? It doesn't make sense but it fills her with a sense of peace nonetheless.

There's a structure inside one of the treelike entities. The tree must be as big around as five of her. She can see it from where she's standing. Or at least the entrance to it. A hollow carved in the trunk – she decides to keep using tree words because she doesn't have any other words – that is shaped almost like an eye. None of this is anything she has ever seen before.

Which brings her to the question: where is she?

In an attempt to find an answer, she makes the mistake of looking down.

There is nothing beneath her feet. Glancing forward, beyond her toes, she sees the same spread of moss and grasslike plants. But when she looks down again, there is nothing. Her feet are just hanging in emptiness. She can see stars below her. Or what she thinks might be stars. They're just tiny dots in a landscape of black. Far away.

Quickly, she takes a step back to where the grass and moss were just a moment ago. Now that's gone too. Where she just stood, it's green. But where she's standing now? Nothing. An illusion? A projection? Perhaps? But she's not sure which one is real and which one is fake. She hopes it's the starview that's fake, because it makes her stomach turn to think about it, and she needs to make it at least part of the way across this structure, ideally without being sick.

She decides she will not look down. She will take a step, and she will not look down. She will look at... anything in her eyeline and above. Tree-thing. Hole in tree.

Step. With her balance off due to the lack of sound, she looks. Her foot meets the ground, and still, there is nothing beneath it but the black vastness of the stars.

"Skist," she says. There is no fire in the swearword, only resignation. Whatever she's gotten herself into this time, she is uncertain whether she will be able to get herself out.

The trees are planted in a circle. Inside them, through their thick grey trunks, she can see a transparent square plate, framed in stone and steel.

The trunks look like doorways. When she tries to step between two of them, they close in on her, squeezing inward. If she were twice as wide as she is, she thinks they would trap her passage. But this, like so much else, doesn't seem to be made for humans, and so the trunks constrict but don't touch her.

In the center of the circle is a square of transparent material, as long on each side as she is tall. The material looks similar to the temple ceiling, but the view is completely different. When she leans over it and looks down – she wants to touch it, she's oh-so-tempted to touch it, but their recent incident in the temple, and her transport here, are still very clear in her mind – she sees a swath of greens and greys. It takes her a moment to realize that it's the tops of trees. More specifically, it's the top of the Steremoss. Part of the Steremoss.

If it's a map, it seems nearly useless, as it's only looking at a single section. It's just looking at a very specific part – which section, she can't tell. There are only trees. Leaves and branches.

Something catches her eye among the leaves. A creature. Captured in a map? Except that it isn't captured. It's moving.

This isn't a map. It's a viewer. She is looking down at part of the Steremoss as it is in real life. This very moment. How, she doesn't know. But she guesses that if the ceiling of the temple can look up at the stars, then the stars can look down at the Stere.

She realizes what she's said. Pushes herself back from the viewer. Closes her eyes. Holy skist, is she really in the stars? In the sky? She needs a minute. This is big.

Bigger still because if that is true, then she's stuck here with no idea how to get home. Nope. She can't go down that route right now because she will absolutely lose it. For now, she has to assume that there is some way to get back to earth, back to Kyre and the others. That she will not die up here, trapped and alone.

All right, then. She needs a plan. First things first. Figure out what the viewer can tell her. Then figure out a plan for getting out of here. Along the way, keep an eye out for food, water, danger, and any tools she might be able to use.

She opens her eyes and pushes herself back toward the viewer. Why did whoever was using this – the Gavanites? someone else? – why did they choose this section of the forest, she wonders. What did it tell them? What were they looking for?

She watches the space for a long time. Sees movement – leaves twitch or a bird hops into view and out again. But nothing that strikes her as worth the attention. Bringing her face closer to the material doesn't help; it just makes everything fuzzy and gives her a pain behind her eyes.

Her breath fogs up the material. She reaches to wipe it away with her sleeve.

The view moves. Slips sideways at her touch to show a neighboring patch of forest. Skist. It moves. *It moves.* She tries again with her hand. This time, nothing happens.

When she touches her sleeve back to the material, it moves again. Not sideways this time, but out. Zooming back. Letting her see a larger section of the woods. She tries again, and it moves again. She's not sure yet what movements of the fabric across the material make it do what, but she is sure that it's doing something.

She pulls her jacket off and uses her blade to tear one sleeve off at the seam. It makes a glove, sort of. Makeshift. But good enough for her to experiment with. After a few more tries, she gets the hang of using her fingers and the fabric to move it.

It's backwards. Pushing up makes the view go down. Down is up. A half circle sometimes zooms the view in and sometimes out. She's not entirely sure what the difference is in the arcs she's making, but it's clear the viewer thinks she's sending it two different messages. No matter. It's close enough and soon she's got the hang of it enough to get it to do what she wants.

She zooms it out as far as she can make it – it's possible that it goes farther, but she can't figure out how and anyway she has the entire Steremoss in view now.

Looking down at this, if it's right, makes her realize how close the map is that she has, how careful her mother was in creating it, and how even her own hand-drawn additions are nearly right.

There are things missing from their map. The edges of the forest are shaped differently too. From incorrect mapping or changes over time? She's going to guess the latter, because if anything, the edges are bigger. The forest has grown outward since she was little. Of course it has.

She has a list of things she wants to try to find: the base, of course. The kubrics. The clearing. Maybe Quenn's home town. She wonders if the zoom is good enough to see people walking around. It seems likely that if she can see creatures, she can see people too.

After a few false starts, she finds the river, the falls. The treehouse is a simple black square from here. She's never thought much about the roofs of things. How different they might look from above. There are towns she knows, towns she doesn't. Dotted in clearings through the forest.

The base itself would be hidden – it's all underground, of

course it is, but now that she can see the temple, she can't unsee it. From here, it's a shimmering globe of grey. Shined and glinting as metal. She remembers that she still hasn't told Kyre and the others about it. How you can see it now, somehow. Maybe they've already figured it out. She doesn't know how much time has passed since she left the Stere but her shoulders ache with bending. The view from her walk would suggest that it's nighttime – the below was full of dark skies and stars. But the forest she's looking at is in midday, she thinks. The sun's shadows are nearly straight down. No slant.

Back to focusing. She slides the viewer around to the perimeter of the forest. Picks out a few of the kubrics, one, two, three. She zooms out and finds all five kubrics. Sees them all in a single view. They're not very big, but they carry all their power in height. Stretching up toward the sky. Toward her.

They're in the shape of the star. Not just any star, but Quenn's star. Or nearly anyway. Five points of the six. So where's the other kubric? She zooms out, but can't find it. It isn't the base, unless the base has moved wildly. Surely Rillent would have found the sixth kubric by now, would have had it dug up the way he's had the others dug up. Is that what he's looking for?

She holds the pendant over the viewer. Lowers herself until its points line up perfectly with the map. The very top, the long point that stretches above all others, points up at her.

Not at her. At this place. The pendant isn't just depicting the five kubrics. It's showing her that this place, wherever she is, is the sixth kubric. They're tied together. What does that mean? She doesn't know. They're connected, she knows that much. She feels like if she just keeps staring at the viewer, the pieces will come together in a way that she can understand.

Her stomach rumbles. She can't remember the last time she's eaten or drunk. She has a lot more questions, a lot more things she wants to see in the viewer, but she has more pressing needs for now. Food. Water. Escape. Not in that order, unless they have to be.

"Where's Aviend?" Kyre asked. It wasn't like her to miss dinner. Not showing her face for Thorme's food offerings was very un-Aviend-like.

"She went for a walk," Delgha said. "To think." Her voice showed exactly what she thought of walking around, trying to think without the use of a machine at her side.

A trickle of worry scrabbled at the back of his neck like a creature with too-long nails.

The runners had said Rillent wasn't coming, but he couldn't help but feel like they were all missing something. Something obvious and dangerous.

"I'll go see if I can find her." His voice was calm, but his throat felt dry suddenly, his tongue too big. He sometimes missed the days before all of this, when they just planned in secret, when no one knew to look for them or even that they were alive. There was some safety in that, in the before.

Too late now. And everything that was before always led to this moment of after anyway. There was no going back.

"Wait," Delgha said. "Before you also go out in the woods to think – or whatever – I've got something for you."

She held out a small silver disk on the top of her finger. Kyre hesitated.

"I promise," she said. "It won't try to kill you this time."

"I know you wouldn't mean to," he said. "But…"

"No, I don't blame you," she said. "It's just a telepathy implant."

"'Just'," he said, "and 'implant' don't go together very well."

She pressed the disk to the space behind her ear, tilting her head to show him.

And then she held out a new silver disk, identical to the other one, on the tip of her finger. "Just stick it behind your ear. It should let you talk to me while you're out there."

He took the small silver disk from her and pressed it to the side of his neck behind his ear. It prickled his skin with tiny points, and then he could feel the adhesive settle in. "Like this?" he said.

No, she said. *Like this.*

He blinked. "What… just happened?"

"Oh, it worked!"

"You sound surprised," he said.

"I try to expect the worst," she said. "I've been working on these forever. Either they weren't working, or Aviend doesn't know how to hear my mind. Maybe I should have hooked you up to one a long time ago instead. All right, now you say something to me."

"Um… like what?"

"No, not with your voice. With your mind. Think it at me."

I feel stupid doing this.

YES!

"Too loud," he said. Which sounded weird, since the room itself had been silent.

"Sorry," she said. "They've only got a few uses each. I'm not sure why. They just seem to fizzle out after a few thoughts. So don't sing into it or anything. You'll use it up."

"Delgha, have you ever heard me sing anything?"

"No," she said. "But I'm sure you've noticed that people think things in their mind all the time that they don't say out loud."

"So you can actually read my mind with this? Aviend will think you're taking her job."

"No, not really. Only when you actively send things to me. It's more like... ah... I don't have an analogy. But your thoughts are safe. Mostly. I'm pretty sure."

"I'm convinced," he said, not at all convincingly.

He slipped out through the tunnel – singing a short song to Delgha on the way, because he couldn't not – and then stepped into the woods.

She didn't say anything back in his mind, but he could hear her yelling "Stop it!" down the tunnel.

Night hadn't fallen yet in the Stere, but it was coming. Black bleeding down through the blue. It made him think of Rillent, of course. Standing, flying, on his kubric. Playing god to his people.

Kyre didn't call Aviend's name. Instead, he lifted his hands to his mouth and breathed through the careful holes between his fingers.

There was no response.

He found Aviend's tracks, knew they were recent from the sharpness of the muddy imprint. He followed them around the corner toward the edge of the swamp.

And there, in front of him, rose the temple.

It seemed as natural as if it had always been there and as foreign as he imagined it would be to come upon a city where just a moment before there had been none. The globed dome shone black, rounded edges, smooth lines. It wasn't even camouflaged. Surely it had been, though, right? They hadn't just bypassed this a hundred thousand times and not noticed it?

His mind kept trying to tell him that it was so. That they'd just walked by it and hadn't been able to see it. Which might be close to the truth. He wondered if Delgha's fiddling with the devices in the temple had caused it to appear.

Aviend's footprints were here, though. Which meant she'd seen this too. And what would she have done? Touched something, he thought. Touched whatever she wasn't supposed to have touched.

A door beckoned, grey on grey. Kyre never would have seen it, if not for Aviend's footsteps up to it. Without hesitating – Aviend might be in there – he put his hand to the flat of it and pushed. Not only did it not budge, but it seemed to push back at him. Actively resistant. It was an odd sensation, and one that he didn't expect from a door. He tried again, only to find himself getting the same result.

There were no more footsteps elsewhere. No other sign of Aviend. This door didn't seem to go to the temple, at least not the part of the temple they'd found. So that meant... what? It went somewhere else?

He remembered the feeling of touching the device before. The way it made it seem like it was trying to transport him to somewhere else. Had that happened to Aviend?

Delgha, he thought, and he hoped that she could actually hear him. *I think you should come outside. There's something you have to see.*

Aviend hasn't found food. Or water. Or an exit, for that matter. But she's found something far more interesting, if less life-sustaining.

At least I won't be bored when I die, she's decided.

At the back of the forest room where she entered – in her mind, she calls it the glade – she'd found three entryways, each with a slightly different shape. The one on the right, in the shape of a simple rectangle, leads to nothing. A tall square box that seems to go up and up but has nothing inside it.

The doorway on the right is low and wide. She'd had to kneel down to try to go through it. It's covered with a film, blue-grey and rubbery. She tried to slice through it with her blade. The rubber split and then reformed. No scar. No sign that she'd even marred its surface.

The door in the middle is a tall rectangle, topped with a series of tendrils. More animal than plant.

On the other side of it is a room. The floor is bumpy and squishes as she walks. Not like mud or dirt. Like walking across the back of a giant creature. A frog or a salamander. Mottled like skin too, a bright red and green. But not wet.

The room is shaped like a triangle, the top pointed far too high for her to reach. A three-sided pyramid.

The walls are made of firm bubbles. She pushes against them in various places. They're so soft she thinks she might have found a way out. But even with her knife, they don't burst or open in any way.

There is something inside some of them, though. Tiny bodies, she thinks. Unmoving. Of what? As soon as she sees that, she stops trying to split them open. If they're hatchlings, she doesn't want to kill them. If they're predators, she doesn't want to let them out.

She feels weird being in the room with a bunch of creatures, all waiting for... something. But this is where she found the thing and it doesn't seem to be moveable. So if she wants to look at it, it will have to be here.

The thing is a book. Or something enough like a book that she can understand how it works.

It's resting on a dais in the middle of the room. There's a kind of box that's umber and gold around the edges. Inside of that is the booklike device.

There are only two pages, if you can call them that. They're both thick as her fingers. They don't move, but if she flows her hands over them, the writing on the pages changes. She learned this mostly by accident. But now she can't stop flipping through them. She hasn't found a beginning or an end yet. Unless it's an endless circle. But none of the two pages seem alike, so she thinks that it might just be a really, really long book.

All of them are languages she doesn't know – but there seem to be many. She's no expert in languages, of course. Knows only the Truth. Doesn't even speak to machines. But she can spot the difference in how the letters are used. And some have letters that aren't really letters at all, at least not that she knows of. Every few pages, there are images interspersed with the text.

The drawings make a little more sense. Not whole sense. But enough to start piecing things together. Sometimes an image takes shape, not on the page but above it. Taking on corners and angles and depth. The kubrics show up regularly, and they always rise off the page. The temple. Even a thing that she thinks might be where she is right now – a giant star in the sky that isn't really a star, but made to look like one. Looking down on the earth.

She doesn't think about that last one too much because it makes her feel lonely and small and afraid. And she doesn't have time for lonely and small and afraid right now. She needs to figure out what this place is, what it does, and how it works so she can find her way home.

The drawings seem to imply that the kubrics are a machine. Or, rather, each is a single part of a larger machine. With the… star… she doesn't have a better word… they form a device that does…what? What does it do? And why does Rillent care?

Step back. Walk through it.

Rillent had come to the clave and taken power. Why? Because he was a power-hungry monster. No, why had he come to the clave? Because he found… bought… stole? a key – his implant – and he'd followed it here.

He'd killed Aviend's mother – denounced her as a traitor to the city – and announced himself the leader. Arch Boure.

Together, with Kyre at his side, he'd begun digging up the kubrics. Gaining power, slowly. Methodically. Getting the people to trust him and then flipping his story, his promises. Trapping them tighter and tighter like the squeeze of a cragworm.

And then… what?

She flips through the images. There. The kubrics and the star are connected via some kind of energy lines. Why? Another image, the next page and...

If she'd been holding the book, she would have dropped it. As it is, she stumbles backward. Hands up. Wincing from a pain that never comes.

The destriatch. The destriatch are on these pages. Not the same – these are full creatures. Holeless. Solid. Whatever chased her through the woods, nearly killed her, they're a smidgen of the creatures created on these pages.

But they're not killing people in these images. Not hunting. Not tracking. They're protecting. Protecting the base, their base, a whole line of them, their glorious, deadly gazes turned outward.

"Rillent is doing them wrong," she says. There's some kind of hope in that realization and she grasps it tight. She touches the black and grey drawing. Traces it with a trembling finger. "He's making them, but something's missing. What?"

This, she thinks. This place, this sixth point of the star. That's what he's missing. She thinks of the message from the well. *Unable to find key.* They thought it was the runners unable to find some way to access Rillent. But what if it actually meant Rillent was unable to find the key he needed?

What if this, this place, is the key that Rillent can't find?

Oh, skist. She understands it all.

All right, not all. But enough that it makes her feel dizzy.

Rillent has been uncovering the kubrics to gain power for himself. Not to give power to the Stere as he'd promised. Not for the people. Not even, as he professes, for the Order of Truth. For himself. Only for himself. What she, nor anyone else really understands, is how? What do the kubrics actually do? They seem to give him certain capabilities – she already knows that. He created the destriatch, for one thing. Performs other mysterious "miracles". But he keeps driving. The trenchers keep working. He keeps striving for something. But what? And for what purpose?

She doesn't know yet. But now, this book, or manual, or guide, or whatever it is, is starting to make one thing clear. Whatever he is trying to accomplish, there is a giant hole in Rillent's plan. He doesn't have the final key. That's what he's been looking for. That's why he didn't care enough to come after them. He thinks he's so close to finding it. But he's not. He's not. He's not.

Because it's right here, and he's not looking at her. Not looking up.

For the first time, Aviend feels a sense of hope and relief. And maybe even excitement. They're one step ahead of Rillent. As long as they can keep him from finding the temple and this place, they can keep him from completing his plan. Whatever horrors that might entail.

We're going to beat you, she thinks. Because we're good and right and true. But mostly because we're smarter than you are.

Well, provided she can find a way back from here. A way to warn the others. A plan is beginning to form. Better than their old one, because she knows so much more. Because she understands – maybe for the first time – Rillent. Rillent's needs. Rillent's weakness.

She'd never believed his lies about helping the Stere, but she had once thought he was accidentally corrupted by his own greed. Or by the kubrics. They pulled at Kyre, why wouldn't it make sense that they would also pull at Rillent in some way? And Rillent, she'd thought Rillent had just said yes.

But now she saw him for what he was. Evil to the core. He'd never come to the Stere with the hopes of saving it or helping it. He hadn't been corrupted by power. He had corrupted his power for his own gain. From the moment he'd arrived, he'd known what he was doing. What he was hoping to do.

He'd known the kubrics were here before he'd arrived. He'd come here, not as an envoy from the Order of Truth, but as something else. As...what? A monster. No, that was too simple. There was something else buried in her memory. Very early. Rillent's eyes, in her brain. She can't... she reaches for it, but can't quite grab it. It's slippery, and it's a place she doesn't like to look because it's dark and filled with blame and guilt and a deep-rooted fear that she is the one who brought Rillent here. Or at the very least, that she's the one who opened the door for him.

She gives up after a moment. Tells herself she can't remember. But knows that she might be lying to herself. Can't and don't want to are sometimes so closely entwined it's hard to tell them apart.

Back to problem number one. How to get out of here. The book doesn't have anything in it that seems to pertain to that. Which means that traveling back and forth was either not something that people did – but here she is, so that seems to belie that idea – or it was something they did so often and easily that there was no reason to write up anything about it.

Funny that, how one person's easy was another person's wish-for-detailed-instructions. "Thank Gavani for groups," she says. The name feels funny in her mouth, but she doesn't dislike it. She's not a believer, but sometimes it's nice to have something that's not a swearword.

She'll start back at the door where she entered. She'd pushed buttons on the way in. Although she hadn't seen buttons on this side, that didn't mean there weren't any. Another thorough look certainly wouldn't–

And then she is falling through the invisible floor. Not falling. Being pulled. Rocked, was maybe the best word she found for it. Rocked and falling down. It was bright again. Too much so to open her eyes. The red rivers of her eyelids flowed in her gaze. Backlit by sun. There is no sound. So quiet she feels like she can hear the rushing rivers of red. Her blood. Pulsing.

Darkness comes on slowly, blots out the rivers. The rocking ends. There is the sense of being touched. Not by hands, but by something else. Something that is mostly ethereal, electrical. There but not there.

She doesn't want to open her eyes. She feels suddenly sure that she is floating in space somewhere, and that these things touching her are creatures. Dead stars. The ghosts of the sky. Who knows? She can't run. She can't move. Trapped in nothing. This, she thinks with rising horror and sadness, is how she's always been afraid things will end.

Delgha saw what Kyre was seeing too, thankfully. Lately, he had moments where he was sure he was starting to lose his mind. Not unheard of. There were stories of those who'd left Rillent's side in the past coming unmoored. Losing their way. Believing they were already ghosts. Those were the only ones you heard about, though. The ones who came unmoored while still attached to Rillent *were* ghosts. Or dead anyway. Buried under the wolflilies. Unless, of course, they went crazy in a way that benefited Rillent's plan.

So he was not crazy. At least not yet, and that was good.

Delgha took one look at the temple, risen out of nothing, at the blinding outline of the star that seemed to form a door and said, "Don't touch that."

"She went through there, didn't she?" It was the kind of question Kyre was sad to have asked, because he already knew what the answer would be.

"Knowing her? Yes."

It wasn't a regular door. You could tell just by looking at it, how the light shone out around the edges of it, even though there was no visible break in the material that he could discern.

"It's possible that it's just another door that leads to the temple, the one the Gavanites spoke of." The hope in his voice was false. He was grateful Delgha didn't even try to placate him with a response.

"We need to get back inside. See what we can learn from the devices."

They didn't run – that would have implied something neither of them was ready to handle – but they moved fast through the woods and tunnels, grabbing Thorme with a shout on the way by. Kyre had a tumbling, scratching moment of panic that they would find the interior doorway to the temple closed and sealed, inoperable. But it stood as it had when they'd left, irised open into the blackness.

Without even taking a breath, Delgha half-buried herself in equipment, muttering.

Even after everything that had happened earlier, if Delgha asked him to hold something or touch something, Kyre would do it, without question. It might shock him again, pull him elsewhere, knock him to the floor. Whatever. As long as they got Aviend back from wherever the temple door had taken her.

Thorme was on standby, her med kit open on the floor. She had a boost in each hand.

The stars overhead were bright enough that they lit the whole room. As Kyre watched, the sky descended into half-darkness, a purple spread that rang a memory for him. It was gloaming. That meant Rillent was probably standing on his false riser, that in one, two, three... the kubric would go dark before blaring back into light.

The stars went out. Or nearly. Became pinpoints of barely there light, impossible to find or see if he hadn't been staring right at them.

"What is...?" Delgha said, her voice muffled from under a

now-shadowed device. He heard a clonk from somewhere in the darkness that sounded an awful lot like a soft body part against a hard machine-edge. It was followed by a hissing release of breath.

"Rillent," he said. But it wasn't quite what he meant. He was piecing it together in his head. Was Rillent drawing energy from the... stars?... to power himself? That was impossible, wasn't it?

Of course it was. But what if the stars in the temple weren't the actual stars in the sky? They already seemed much larger and brighter. What if they were just representations of something else – a way to monitor or gauge energy, maybe? But why would something here be linked to something going on with the kubrics? It made no sense. But it didn't seem like a coincidence.

Before he could put it all together, the room blazed with light. The stars were as bright as they'd been moments ago.

If it wasn't for Thorme saying, "That was odd," he might have thought he'd made it up. Or that his eyes were losing their ability to work properly.

Now that it was bright again, it was harder to put his idea to words. It seemed silly, in the light, to think that it was linked to the kubrics. Why would that be? What's the common denominator? He had no idea. "That blink? I think it times exactly to the moment the kubrics go dark."

He left the thought there, waiting to see what conclusions the others would come to.

Delgha pulled herself from under the device, wiping something off her face with the back of her hand.

"That would mean that the kubrics are linked to this temple," she said. "We knew the temple was old – far older than the Gavanites that used this place. What if it was originally not a temple, but something else?"

The same question he was asking. "The kubrics draw in energy. And this place shows the energy reserves that they store. But where's the energy that they absorb coming from in the first place?"

"That's not a technology I've ever seen," Delgha said. "But that doesn't mean it doesn't exist. I've come to believe that anything is possible."

They were all staring, heads back, at the stars, which seemed, impossibly, to be staring back. Kyre had never felt so... looked at. Like the distant past was gazing right at him.

"We need to find out the connection," he said to no one in particular.

"Guess we'd better find a way to figure out where Aviend is then and get her back," Delgha said. "We're going to need all of us to figure this out."

"What can I do?" he asked.

"Use your crazy weird ability to understand Aviend's mind to figure out where she is, while I get this device to work," Delgha said. "Besides, I'm getting close. I think."

Then a moment later, "No. No, I'm not. I don't know where she is or what this does. I'm completely flying blind here. This is ridiculous."

By her uncertainty, he could tell she was moving through the machines by instinct more than by knowledge.

But of course, instinct was bolstered by knowledge, wasn't it? Wasn't that what he and Aviend had too? A sense of things, indescribable, unscientific, that passed between them? Based on the way they knew each other so well. Their lives and secrets and moments shared. A language all their own.

So where was she? He closed his eyes and imagined her for a moment, as she must have been when she discovered the temple. The way she'd stop and take it in for only a moment before she'd put her hands against it, make sure it was real. She had to touch things in order to understand them. So she would have touched it, without hesitation, without doubt.

Where he stepped back and thought things through, she went up and put her hands against them. He thought that's why she understood him so well. She could touch him, always, and often did.

So she would have touched the temple. And the door. Would it have opened for her?

Enter and the stars shall touch you.

Yes.

He opened his eyes and found he was still looking skyward. Just above him, a single star shone with a brightness abandoned by the others. It had a reddish cast about it that the others did not. He found that if he squinted, he could almost make out its shape. Six points. Clear, where the others were squiggly pinpoints of light.

"She's up there," he said.

Delgha's head clonked the back of a machine part, the *thunk* followed by a sharp swear, as she strove to pull her head out from inside it and follow his gaze.

"She's on the roof?" she said.

"No," he said. "She's up there."

He pointed to the stars. To one star in particular.

"Well, skist," Delgha said. "How do we get up there?"

"That's your job, I think," he said. "I hope. Because I have no idea."

"Vi. Vi. Vi."

The call, like a bird, mimicking voices she knows. Echoing. Repeating. It's a loop. A trick. She refuses to answer. I know you, she thinks, even though she doesn't, and I will not go to you. In fact, she can't move. She's stuck. Pulled and pulsed and tied with invisible threats.

"Vi." This time the bird sounds like Kyre. Is it Kyre? Something takes her wrist and lifts her arm. Her palm comes to hair and skin and a ring of metal. When she opens her eyes, Kyre is smiling down at her. The biggest smile she has ever seen on him.

Behind his head, the stars are giant and red and they pulse down around them and light their way. She can hear Delgha muttering at a machine farther away.

"Kyre," she says.

"You came through like a ghost," he says.

She gets what he means. She feels like a ghost. As if she left part of herself behind on the star and it's only slowly catching up to her.

"I know..." She's hesitant to overstate. "...what Rillent's looking for. I might have a plan."

"We know where he's getting his power," Kyre says. "We

might have a plan too." He's holding her hand. She's not sure when that happened. Has he always been holding her hand and she just noticed? "So together we should be doing good."

"In mine, you don't have to kill anyone."

"In mine, you don't die."

"Let's do them both, then," she says.

That was supposed to be funny, but as the sentence ends, the part of her that felt like it was catching up to her does so. All at once. The weight of her body doubles, triples. Her bones leaden. Skull too. The floor pushes back at her, keeps her forever. She can't feel her chest rising. Somewhere there are voices. She knows they're not hers, because that would require movement and she doesn't know how to do that anymore.

Hands and faces. Thorme's fingers inside her mouth. Aviend is swallowing something, but then it comes back the other way, a gagging horror that stops her breath. She forces her lids closed against the noise and light and pain. For long minutes, she is a sinking painweight. Nothing more.

How long has passed? She doesn't know. She is still heavy, but the pain is a dull echo at the back of her skull. She opens her eyes. Everyone is looking at her.

"Well," Delgha says. "Let's not do *that* again."

She doesn't have the strength to say they *have* to do that again. That it's the very thing they have to do if they want to take Rillent down.

Later, she thinks. I'll tell her later. She sleeps.

Three days. That's how long Kyre sat at Aviend's bedside while she recovered. Thorme brought him food and promises that she was going to be fine. Delgha brought him devices to mend. Things she didn't even need fixed, but she carried them in, asking for help. He worked on them because he couldn't stand the sitting, but didn't say what he felt – that nothing he fixed mattered, because he couldn't fix the one thing that did matter.

He was working on some kind of memory drone, tiny pieces that made his fingers ache, when Aviend finally woke.

"I'm starving," she said, startling him into dropping the drone, which shattered across the floor. "And what the skist is that noise?"

She looked alive, but not yet well. Black moons rose beneath her eyes and her skin had a flatness to it, a grey tinge that worried him. So many emotions across his heart, under his skin. Words were tricky things, elusive and unforgiving. When you stopped using them, they slipped away just to teach you a lesson. "And why are you way over there?"

She reached for him and he went to her, knowing he should call Thorme. Or be worried about hurting her. Or ask her if she felt all right. But he just held her, silent, until their breathing synced and he got his heartbeat back.

Thorme didn't even tsk her tongue at him when she came in later and found them talking, Aviend telling the story of her time in the star and what she'd learned, him telling her about Rillent's power source. Thorne did do a bunch of things with Aviend's wrists and mouth and eyes and even her fingers, until Aviend said, "Stop, Thorme. Stop. I'm fine."

"You are," Thorme agreed. "But I'm the chiurgeon and you will hush."

Aviend did so, casting a sly glance at Kyre, who couldn't help it. He burst out laughing, finally earning him a customary Thorme tongue-click. Half of it was the humor. The other half was clean and utter relief.

"No outside for three days," Thorme said as she finished giving Aviend her once over. "And all of this. I'll bring you a crossel berry muffin." She set down a clear vial filled with green liquid.

"Two days," Aviend said, holding up as many fingers. "Half of this nastiness. And all of the muffins I want."

"I don't bargain with patients," Thorme said. "But I do let them out early for good behavior." She looked pointedly at the vial.

"But," Aviend said, "I know what this tastes like... Look, I'm complaining. Doesn't that mean I'm feeling–"

"Six days and no muffins," Thorme said.

"No," Aviend said. "Fine." She picked up the vial, then opened it and sneered. "Ghostfell, it's like death in a jar, Thorme. I swear it doesn't have to taste like this. You just like watching us drink this horror. Seriously, what have I done to hurt you so badly?"

"Drink it," Thorme said, "while I see how many muffins we have left."

As soon as Thorme stepped from the room, Aviend held the vial out to Kyre. He gagged softly; the smell really was putrid. What did she put in those things?

"Would you like some yummy drink, kind person?" Aviend said. "It's very tasty and yours for the low price of zero shins."

"I will do a lot for you, but that might be beyond even me."

"Kyre, please... I'm dying for muffins. I'm so hungry. Don't let her take away my muffins, Kyre."

"I'm tempted to say something about how it should teach you not to touch things, but I don't want you to extend that to me," he said.

"You're a horrible, horrible partner," she said. "The worst."

And then she tried to throw back the entire vial in a single gulp. The liquid puffed out her cheeks, and the noise that came out of her was something akin to a wild thing trying to mate in the woods. For a second, he thought she was going to spit the entire thing across the room. But somehow she swallowed it down, the swears rolling off her tongue so fast he could barely keep up with them.

"One day!" she yelled. "One day and all the muffins!"

In truth, it was two days before Aviend was out of bed and another two before she felt good enough to be up and about most of the day. Thorme kept pumping Aviend full of horrible liquids, Delgha was hovering more than usual, and by day five, it was clear that the lack of progress and the too-much hovering were starting to make everyone grumpy.

So when Kyre suggested they go to the valley, just the two of them, Aviend was nearly out the door before he'd finished the sentence. They made sure that no one saw them go. Not that Thorme would have tried to stop them – probably – but surely someone would have offered to come with them, and if there was one thing they desperately needed, it was not another hovering, worried creature at their sides. The millibirds didn't count. Nor the far-off calls of the broken hounds that stalked the river's edges.

The scent of wolflilies – honey and death – arrived before the purpled sight of them. This valley was filled with the blooms, long human-sized trenches that belied their beauty. Aviend's mom was here. Kyre's dad. Most of the rest of his family too. Or at least he thought so. Whether it was true or not didn't matter. They came either way, because someone's loved ones were here and they believed in honoring that.

No ghosts walked these channels. Coincidence, or perhaps the wolflilies kept them away.

"Or the bodies," Aviend said. "Maybe it's all the bodies."

On the way, she'd plucked a bouquet of flowers – everything except wolflilies – and the crimson and golden hues seemed to light up her face. She looked healthier now – they still didn't know what had gone wrong with their process of getting her back, although Delgha was working on it – but he no longer worried that she was going to die right in front of him.

Aviend broke the bouquet in half and held them out.

Kyre shook his head. "I apologized last time I was here," he said. "I don't even think I knew what for then. My dad would have been ashamed of me if I'd taken a man's life."

"Even a man like Rillent," Aviend agreed.

It was all right for her to say that, now that they were going to put a new plan together, one that didn't involve killing anyone.

They didn't have a plan yet, though. First, they had to figure out how to get themselves to the star and back consistently without making themselves sick. They needed more information if they were going to use their secret to take Rillent down, and the only way to get that was to travel back there.

"I almost forgot that we lived in a forest," he said. "And not just in a building with stars for a ceiling."

"It is good to be outside. Even if I'm sure that Rillent is just around every corner or there's a destriatch behind every tree. I mean, I *know* he's not coming for us. But knowing and believing aren't always the same thing."

"Don't forget slistoviles," he said. "I'm pretty sure I saw one this morning."

"You're a horrible person," she said. But she was smiling and that was good.

Shaking her head, she moved toward a mound near the end of the long line of mounds. He stopped and let her go. He'd loved Aviend's mom as his own, but she wasn't his. And there were times when you needed to be alone with someone whom you belonged to, even if that someone was dead.

Turning, he walked to the other edge of the valley. At some point Rillent had stopped even pretending to cover his deeds, laying down bodies without cover. But someone had kept up with the attempt. Here, the wolflilies were younger, their blossoms daintier. Planted not so long ago. He wondered about the person, or people, who came here to do so. Rillent's trenchers, the ones he sent out with others' bodies? Or someone who watched and waited, came here after, to give the dead some semblance of their due? He would like to thank that person for the kindness given to strangers. Such a small thing.

Far off in the trees, a soft shimmer of grey moved haltingly. Made a gesture as if to open a door that wasn't there. It was the first time he'd seen a ghost this close to the valley.

"Ready?" Aviend asked. She no longer had her bouquet; he could see its brightness resting where she'd placed it across the way.

"Yes," he said.

She followed his gaze.

"You're thinking about ghosts."

He had been, in a way.

"Real ones, or imagined?"

"What's the difference?" He meant it as serious, but it came out as a bit plucky. He was startled and surprised to hear her laugh, a quick airpush of sound.

"Ah... I don't know. It just seemed like the right thing to ask at the time."

"Then yes," he said. "Where do you think they come from?"

Aviend lifted a hand to shade her eyes and squinted into the dark of the forest. The shape there had stopped and seemed to be looking at them. It was too far away to see a face, but he swore he could see the flow of clothing as it moved.

"Do they seem..." The word he was thinking was "brighter". "More real than before?"

She sucked in her cheeks and closed her eyes, as if she was thinking. By the time she answered, the ghost was gone. Faded or disappeared or just walked away, he couldn't tell.

"I think they *are* more real than before," she said. "But why?"

To solve any problem, you have to fail one hundred times. Maybe two hundred. You have to despair and howl and have run into so many mental walls that your whole brain is a mass of bruises. At least that's how it feels to Aviend at this point.

For days, she and Delgha and Kyre have worked in near-silence on what Aviend has started calling "that horrendous beast in the hall," trying to figure out the mechanism in the starroom that will get them safely to the star and back. Everything hinges on it.

Delgha has been working diligently, fingers and brain, with Kyre and Aviend helping. And they've gotten nowhere with it. Aviend has come to hate it, even as she respects it and whatever entities created it. It's complex, furious, and infuriating. Every time they change something, it squawks and calls, panicked and alarming, its caws echoing through the entire base. And every little bit of Aviend's head.

Some parts of it are so tiny she can't possibly get her fingers in there to tweak things, so she's started using tiny bits of thick wire as extensions of her digits. Which works great until she pokes a piece in between two portables and gets back a shock that runs all the way up her arm to her shoulder and into the back of her teeth. It catches her tight for a moment, shakes her to the very insides, and then does little jumpstarts along the pulse in her neck. She hears the screamsong of the destriatch in the base of her ears.

But no, it's just the machine screaming. The screech of metal grinding into metal.

It's like her life has a theme lately, and it's all about her blood turning into a pain-carrying electrical current.

"I hate you," she says to the machine, with no small amount of untruth. She is tempted to kick it – she has good enough boots on to get away with it – but Kyre's inside it currently, and she's still vibrating from the electricity that punched through her body. Unwilling to risk that again.

"It seems to hate you too," Kyre says as he pokes his head out of one of the machine's widest openings. There's mirth in his voice. For a moment, she's pretty sure she hates him too.

"I'm glad you're taking this seriously," she says, and shakes her head as soon as her mouth closes. She didn't mean that. Working in this close proximity to the star without being able to get there makes her frustrated, and every once in a while, she gets a muscle memory of herself in here, dead weight. Unable to move or scream or breathe. It all swirls inside her in a dangerous detonation of emotions. Sometimes she forgets to keep her thumb on the safety latch. "Sorry," she says.

Kyre scoots himself out of the machine. She's pretty sure he's making the escape much more ungainly than it needs to be, strictly for her benefit. Watching one of his feet tangle around the door, followed by the rest of him, helps, but it's not quite enough to make her laugh. "Just in case you follow up on that instinct that I can see you're having about kicking it. No sorries."

She folds a loose fist and play-punches him in the chest. "Oops. That was meant for the machine. I missed."

"Oh?" he says. "You ready to take this outside? Have a little brawl?"

She laughs, and her anger slips away. What it leaves behind is exhaustion.

"Agh, can't I just go through the door again?" Her voice is embarrassingly whiny, and she shuts her mouth with a snap. Who is she to moan? Delgha's been working on this nonstop for a week. She's been here, trying to help, for a couple of hours a day.

"Sorry," she says to Delgha or Kyre or whoever else is close enough to hear it. "I know why I can't use the door again. I just… I don't even know how you do it, Delgha. I'd be throwing things and swearing hard enough to shake the walls."

"You missed that part," Delgha says, handing her a skein of wire that seems to be accidentally shaped like an egg. It's surprisingly cold. "I've already gotten it out of my system."

Delgha's hair is growing out, Aviend realizes with a start. It's the first time she's ever seen her without her head completely shaved. She had no idea that Delgha's hair was such a beautiful hue. It's the golden red of echar berries. Her piercing glints like a star in a forest sky.

The thought makes her touch the back of her own head. Her hair there is still short, tight curls, although most of the crispy bits have fallen off. If her fingers don't lie, it's still a bit of a bald spot, but at least it's a soft bald spot.

Delgha senses her staring.

"What?"

"Your…" Aviend says and for some reason she's unable to get the word "hair" out without choking up. The word catches in her throat and is only subdued by a painful swallow. It's just hair, she thinks, but as fast as the thought comes, it goes. Not true, she thinks. They're changing. They're all changing. For better or worse. And it's all because of Rillent.

As if to echo her thoughts, Delgha lowers her head, offering it to Aviend. It's the softest thing she's ever felt.

"It was time for a change," Delgha says, from beneath Aviend's hand. They stand there a moment, hand to head. It reminds Aviend of something her mother would have done, but the context is totally different, and that makes it their own.

"Oh. Oh, that's it," Delgha says. She points to the floor where she's looking. "It's right there."

Aviend drops her hand. Looks. The floor looks the same as it always does. Grey and black patterned. A material that she wasn't familiar with before, but which she's come to love. It's soft on the feet, both firm and squishy at the same time. She looks, squints her eyes. She doesn't want to tell Delgha that she can't see it, but can feel Delgha waiting for her to catch on.

"I don't…" she starts. Then she does.

It is a pattern on the floor, but it's one with purpose. She can't read it or make sense of it, but it's clear from the way that Delgha starts moving from machine to machine, adjusting things and muttering, that she can. Soon, Delgha's muttering turns from question sounds to excited sounds.

"I think… yes."

Kyre's pulled himself out of the machine and is standing next to Aviend, watching Delgha. His smile matches how Aviend feels. Bemused. Excited. Nervous.

"Get Thorme and her med bag," Delgha says. "We are ready to try this."

"Reassuring," Kyre says. But he goes to find the chiurgeon and her concoctions.

Despite Delgha's optimism and the secret floor plan, nothing happens.

The machine refuses them again and again. It takes them another day, but at least they finally figure out why.

Delgha is holding up something that is crumpled and smashed. "I think I know at least one reason why it's not doing what we want it to."

It's missing a working fist. Not a fist, really. But a part that looks like a fist, and since no one in this whole world has seen this kind of device before, Aviend imagines that no one else has given it a name. So she is naming it now and forever.

"Can we fix it?" Aviend can hammer pieces together if she has to, but Delgha's the one that machines love. They practically beg her to take them apart and put them back together. If Delgha can't fix it...

Delgha turns the broken piece around between her hands. "This is... I haven't seen this tech before. The structure is broken and I think I could fix that with the right replacements. But it would have to be something strong and straight and sharp..." She falls silent, studying the device.

"Do you have that? Something like that?"

Delgha is already lost to the inner workings of the device.

Metal in each hand. Her face about an inch away from the metal and synth and... whatever else it's made of. "No," she says. "We'd need to find it somewhere. Maybe Thorme knows someone."

"Aviend," Kyre says. "What about the relic? By the clearing? With the..." He pantomimes the long thin bits of material.

"Tomorrow's Death?" Thorme asks. "I remember that relic. Is it even still there?"

They both turn to stare at her a long moment. She pointedly ignores their unspoken questions. Thorme is always a mystery.

Finally, Aviend finds words. "I didn't know that's what it was called, but I approve," she says. "We walked by it on our way to the clearing the other day. It's where we saw..." She doesn't finish. Delgha knows who she means.

"I bet you can't go very far in the Stere without running into his glaives or his destriatch these days."

That hangs in the air a moment. No one says anything.

"It's only, what, an hour's run? Without pilgrim packs," Kyre says. "In and out."

"I'll go," Aviend says before anyone else can volunteer. "Everyone else has a job at the moment except me. And I'm faster than the rest of you." She sees Kyre about to say something. "Yes, even you. I can be back in an hour. Hour and a half tops, at full speed."

Plus, she realizes, she wants to go. Maybe needs it. She's been trapped here, and as much as she loves it here, she's feeling trapped. Caught. Stuck here with memories and feelings that she's pushing away every moment. It's exhausting. For once in her life, she actually wants to run. Find a challenge that doesn't involve an insufferable metal machine.

"It's risky," Delgha says.

"What isn't?" she says.

"She'll be fine," Kyre says. "It's the right choice."

She presses her fingers to his lips. Her grin feels huge and goofy, and she doesn't care one bit.

"What was that for?"

"Everything," she says. And she means it.

A few hours later, Aviend had come back with the pieces that Delgha hoped would fix the machine. She looked better, fresher, than she had when she left. It was as though the doing something had shaken off a layer of mental grime and dust.

"I'm starving," she said, searching through the containers in the kitchen area.

"You're always starving," Kyre said.

"Only when I'm hungry," she said. "Aha!" She lifted some tiny brown cakes covered in a towel, clearly Thorme's handiwork, and set them on the table.

"She's probably saving these for something," Kyre said.

"Probably," Aviend said, as she broke one in half and held it out to him.

The cakes were sweet and savory, heavier than they looked. Crumbs fell into the indent of the Q that was Quenn's name, recently carved into the wood. Kyre blew them away. He wished he could ask Quenn about the ghosts; did he think they were brighter now than they used to be? Or–

"You're thinking about ghosts again, aren't you?" she said. "Me too."

"I don't know if I love it or hate it when you do that."

"Let's go with love so you can tell me about it."

Kyre ran his finger around and around the Q. "Quenn said that when the ghost touched him, it was like he went somewhere without going somewhere," Kyre said. No, he had that wrong. "Like he'd traveled, but was somehow still in the same place? Something like that. He disappeared, just for a moment. Maybe it took him to the star."

"Do you think?" She licked a crumb off her finger, seemed uncertain.

"Honestly, no," he said. "But I can't think of anything else."

"Are you saying we should go touch some ghosts?" she said.

"I'm sensing a theme here… with the touching of things."

From across the table, she looked at him like she was about to make a sly remark.

"Focus," he said. "And, yes, in case you were wondering, I'm talking to both of us here."

"Touching," she said.

"Ghosts first," he said.

"What if we don't find any ghosts? Can we go right to the other stuff?"

"Yes," he said.

"Then let's go look." Aviend grinned and grabbed a couple more cakes and tucked them into her pockets. "For good luck."

"I thought you didn't *want* to find ghosts."

"Right. It's good luck for me. Not for them."

They found ghosts. Or a ghost, almost right away. It was wandering along the edge of Slisto Swamp, stepping carefully, as if trying not to get its feet wet. They *were* getting brighter, he thought, more solid. This one looked like it was wearing a cloak, and he swore he could nearly see a ring glinting on one finger.

"Just my luck," Aviend said. But her voice lifted as she said it, in excitement. "I can't believe I'm going to say this, but I think you should be the one to touch it."

"Do you?"

She nodded. "You know more about what to expect, because you saw Quenn do it. But I'll be right here with my cakes in case you need saving."

"Please tell me you have something other than a cake-weapon."

"These are so heavy. They're perfect. I'll just throw it at its head."

"It's a ghost, Aviend. Intangible energy?"

In her fist, not a cake at all, but a tiny spray canister. Sly.

"Sleep inducer," she said. "I got it from Delgha."

"Got or stole? Also, you can't put a ghost to sleep. Also, I'm starting to be a little afraid of you. Every time you open your fist, you've got some new device in there."

"It's not for them. It's for you," she said. "If the ghost tries to go somewhere with you, I can put you to sleep."

"How's that going to stop it from taking me somewhere?"

"It won't," she said. "But you'll be asleep, so you won't notice. What? It's what I had in my pocket."

"This is definitely one of our better plans." He knew that she had other things in her pockets. She always did. Despite their banter, he had no worries that if something went awry, she would kick somebody's ass until it was fixed.

He stepped forward slowly. He'd never purposefully attempted to approach a ghost before. Not even when he thought they were his friends. He'd been shyer then, he supposed. Did they spook? Run away? Get aggressive? He didn't know.

He realized he was thinking of them as human, as alive.

And that's because they looked so alive. So much like a human that it was nearly impossible to remember they were just so much energy after all. All right, then it wouldn't matter how he approached it.

He strode forward, until he was nearly within reach. The air around the figure crackled and hummed in a barely audible tune. It was bright enough that his eyes strained and watered.

The ghost reached out, but not for Kyre. It leaned down as if plucking something from the ground.

Kyre dropped to his knees in the mud and muck and lowered his head, but not his gaze. It seemed important to be able to see, even though the bright made the corners of his eyes ping with pain. "Mishda paal," he said. He wished he'd thought to ask Quenn what it meant. Too late now. Hopefully it wasn't something mean or aggressive.

Two lines of energy – definitely arms, definitely hands, definitely a ring on the middle finger – reached for Kyre.

The swamp disappeared. Reappeared. In front of him a man. Not a ghost, but an actual man, with brown eyes and a dark beard. A dark ring settled on his finger. Kyre was still in the Stere, but also not, he thought, although he couldn't place his finger on why.

"Who..." he wanted to ask, but the air was still in his chest when he found himself back in front of the ghost. A moment later, the ghost disappeared.

"You went somewhere!" Aviend was clearly trying not to shout, but her whispers were so loud she was a little hoarse. "Did you go somewhere? Where did you go? What was it like?"

"I think," he said, trying to find the words for what had just happened. "I think I went to another here."

She came over and helped him come up out of the mud

and muck. His pants were stuck to his knees, sopped with brown.

"A better here."

5. Every Death Starts with a Very Good Plan, Redux

Achieving consistent travel to and from the star has presented them with a seemingly impossible series of technical challenges. But Delgha, being Delgha, is an ace at both impossible and technical.

By the time Aviend and Kyre return from their ghost walk, Delgha's waiting at the front door for them with an eagerness and impatience that she's making no effort to hide.

"I knew I should have made you keep wearing that device, Kyre," she says. "If it wasn't for your insufferable singing. I think I've fixed the starshooter for real this time – and yes, that's what I'm going to call it, hush – and if you don't let me try it out on you both soon, I'm going to try it on myself."

"You sing?" Aviend says. She can't remember ever hearing Kyre sing.

"No," Delgha says. Her steps are fast and light, and her words are clipped with excitement. "I misspoke. Caterwauling. Mewling. Making me feel like I've got scratching larvae in my brain."

Kyre lifts his shoulder at Aviend's questions, but she knows that face. He mostly keeps his mischievous demons on the inside, but once in a while, often for Delgha's "benefit", he lets them out.

"Aviend, you wear it this time," Delgha says.

"I promise not to sing, Delgha," Kyre says, very solemnly. Too solemnly. He takes the device from her and sticks it to the side of his neck.

"Same rules apply with limited uses," Delgha says. "Use only as necessary."

Delgha instructs them both to stand in a small box she's drawn on the patterned floor. "And then you walk out of the box toward the wall."

"Let me guess," Kyre says. "And then I touch something."

"No, that's it. You just walk forward when I say so."

Kyre's glance is full of questions, as is Aviend's head, but it doesn't stop either of them from getting into Delgha's box. It's big enough for both of them, but just. They're hip to hip. Aviend can feel Kyre breathing.

"Not a bad way to travel," he says. He bumps her gently with his hip and is met with Delgha's quick, sharp, "No. Stay in the box."

It makes Aviend giggle, but she realizes it's mostly excited nervousness and she tries to force her face straight. Kyre grabs her hand, which lets her channel some of her nervousness to him instead.

"All right, you can step forward now," Delgha says.

"This is probably not going to..." Aviend starts.

And then they're gone.

Everything is different. Dark and smooth and full of noise whistling in her ears.

No, the here is not different. It's just that they've come through a different entrance. She recognizes the box she's in. The simple rectangle that led to nothing.

"Well, now we know where that leads," she says to Kyre.

Who isn't there.

She can still feel his hand in hers, can feel him breathing, sense his presence with the press of her skin. But she can't see him. Or hear him.

"Kyre?" she says. She squeezes the thing her hand is holding. It squeezes back. She knows, suddenly, that it's a creature, a monster, she has picked up on her journey here. The thing has replaced Kyre and is–

"Vi?" Nervous. From far away.

And there, she can see him on the other side of the room. Thank the skisting ghosts she can see him. It's really him. The silver streaks in his tousled hair. Brown eyes scanning the room for her.

It's him. Except that she's still holding his hand. Somehow. From way over here.

"Kyre," she says. "Kyre."

They each stay where they are for a long moment. Kyre looks at his hand. "But I can…"

"I know," she says. "How crazy is this?"

She tightens her fingers. Feels him tighten back. Sees him tighten back. Feels his laughter before she can see him laugh.

"I'm afraid to move and break the connection," he says.

"Me too." Her voice is a whisper and she doesn't know why. "We'll do it together. On three."

She counts down. He counts down. And then they both step forward one tiny step. She can't feel him anymore. At least not until she takes half a dozen more quick steps toward him and wraps her arms around his neck. Kisses him.

"I thought you were a monster," she says.

"Oh, I am," he says. "Did I forget to tell you?"

Something sounds like it crashes through the glade. Kyre's hand is on his blade before she's completely let go of him. "I think it's safe," she says. "At least, whatever they are didn't bother me last time."

"There's a forest up here," he says. She watches him wonder at it all. The forest that isn't a forest. The various doors. The weird textures. The book and the map that isn't a map. She realizes that it feels weird to have had this all to herself. She shares everything with Kyre, and not being able to share this was like being forced to have a secret. She's glad they're here. Together. Even if they have work to do. Maybe especially because they have work to do. She loves him all the time, but she thinks she might love him best when they're doing that thing that they do, together.

It doesn't take long for him to soak it all in and say, "And Delgha got us here. How do you feel?"

She checks her body. Back of head. Stomach. Lungs. Eyes. The usual places that she's come to think of as pain points. She feels fine.

"Me too," Kyre says. "What's our first step?"

"Figure out why Rillent needs this place. I mean, we know he wants power, so it has to do with that. This is the missing key. But what is it the key to? And how does he plan to use it? I think we start with what he's doing wrong."

"Wrong?" he asks.

She flips through the book to the images of the destriatch. Complete and deadly as they were the first time she saw them. "He's missing a piece of this. Knowledge? Access? Something that is keeping him from fully achieving his goals."

"If that's what they're supposed to look like, I'm glad he's missing pieces. Those would wipe out the whole forest."

She traces the edges of one with her finger. Frills and scales. Not crackling energy and half-bodies. "Right, but look at this. They're defending the base. Not attacking."

"So maybe Rillent doesn't want to make them like this,

because that would screw up his plans."

She shook her head. Rillent was never able to hold back from gaining what power he could. "I don't think he knows this is what they're supposed to do. How could he?"

"So he doesn't know what they're supposed to be and he's botching it…"

Kyre's flipping through the pages, using the same movements she'd been using a moment earlier. It's one of her favorite things about him; how quickly he grasps a thing and starts running with it. There's no one she'd rather be saving the world with.

Kyre stops on an image of the kubrics. Studies them. She stays quiet, lets his brain fill in the holes. "These aren't our kubrics," he says after a moment.

"What does that mean?" She leans back, trying to see what he's seeing.

"They're the opposite of ours… Look, if you put this image…" He moves the pages in a way she hadn't known they could move, bringing two together, like folded paper. "…with this image, you get two sets."

The image is two stars of buildings. Bridges of energy between them. This star in the middle.

"What does that mean?" She's trying to wrap her brain around it. "There's another set of kubrics somewhere in the world?"

"Not in this world," Kyre says. "I think it's transdimensional. I remember seeing something about that…" He shakes his head. "Somewhere in Rillent's possession. But I can't remember why or what it was exactly."

She understands transdimensional, thanks to listening to her mother and the other Aeon Priests. Other worlds. Held apart from this one by a barrier of light or energy or space.

Her mom had believed in these faraway places, but Aviend had never been sure if they were real or just something that people hoped were real. Wasn't that true of herself too, of the Night Clave? They were real *and* they were something that people hoped were real.

"So, two worlds." Her brain is catching up to whatever it is that Kyre and the book are trying to show her. "Two sets of kubrics. One star between them. An energy bridge that connects them all and does... something."

"Whatever it was designed to do, I'm sure it wasn't to give power to someone like Rillent."

She has a sudden, horrible thought. "Do you think there's a Rillent in the other world too?"

"Let's hope not. That's more than even we can take on, I think." Kyre leans in, runs his finger along a shimmering line. "Ghostfell."

He means it, she sees, as both the swear and as information. The shimmered line is full of ghosts. But not ghosts. They're...

"People," she says. "Kyre, what if the ghosts are people from the other world. Dimension. Place. Something."

"Are they trying to come here?" Kyre asks. "The ones we see? Is that why they're becoming solid?"

That's not quite right, but she can't wrap her mind around why. The ghosts don't act like travelers. They act like people who aren't where they expect to be. Bumping into things. Falling down cliffsides. Surprised travelers.

"No," he echoes her thoughts. "That's not right. We've been thinking that ever since Rillent started using the kubrics, the ghosts are getting more solid. But what if they already were solid?"

She sees where he's going. "So it's not that the ghosts are getting stronger. It's that the barrier is getting weaker."

"Right. It's the kubrics. They control the barrier. There's five on this side, and five in the other world."

"No," she shakes her head. It's like she can sense the pieces of the puzzle settling into each other, with almost audible clicks. "I think the star does that. The star is in the middle, and controls the whole thing."

"But even without the star to control the process, Rillent has found a way to draw power. And with Rillent drawing that power, the barriers are weakening. We're seeing into another world."

"We're seeing into another world," she echoes. "Their world."

The world that built this device? she wonders. Or was that someone else, in a different place entirely, who wanted to come here for–

All of the pieces keep on sliding together. Brain puzzle taking shape. "This isn't a star," she says. "Or it is a star, but it wasn't designed for that. It's a way to travel. Or it was. From here to there…" She snaps her fingers. "Like that. If we could master these controls fully, we could bring down the barriers instantly, build a sort of bridge, cross over, and then close it up again."

"It would take a long time to figure all that out," he says, closing his eyes. "Even with Delgha helping. Rillent would probably find this place way before then."

She's the one flipping through pages now, looking for something. The back of her brain is active but the front needs to stay busy so that it doesn't interfere with her thinking.

"But Rillent doesn't care about travel," she says. "He doesn't want to go to another dimension. He wants to rule this world, right here, right now. Not some faraway place where he can't–"

"Right." They're talking faster now, ideas humming into the air with a power of their own. "He's not traveling, he's drawing power. Like I saw in the temple that time. The stars – the lights – dimming. Rillent's got a way to use the kubrics to draw power from the other universe. Maybe it's that implant he has in his head."

She nods. Kyre's thinking is right in line with her own. She keeps flipping through the diagrams in the guidebook-thing. "But whatever he's doing, it's a half measure. His destriatch aren't complete. He's jury-rigged something, but what he really needs–"

The answer is coming to her just as Kyre says it. "Is a huge conduit. He's using the kubrics to get a trickle of power, but with this star? Complete control. Lots of energy. All the energy. He doesn't know or care that this can be used to travel to another world. Back when I was... there, he was always talking about energy. Power. As if the kubrics were big generators or something. But look at this stuff. That's not what the kubrics are at all. The whole thing is a conduit. Maybe whomever built it originally didn't even care about travel either. Maybe they just wanted a whole universe to convert to energy. Who knows?"

"He'll suck it up until there's nothing left," she says. "Would that destroy it? The other world?" She knows the answer, in her heart, and Kyre's short nod confirms it.

"Dormant for so long, under the soil," he says. "In the sky. And then we went and dug it up." She can hear the strain, sharp as a knife blade, along the edge of his words.

"Someone would have." It's true, she knows it is, but it helps her to bring the words to the light, to make them, and what they carry, more real. For once, she can't tell if her words make him feel better or worse. He's watching her hands flip the pages, not looking at her.

She finds the diagram she knew she saw earlier, does the thing that Kyre did to move the pages around. Only now does she realize its importance. It looks just like the thing that Kyre had described was hidden under Rillent's headband. His implant. And in the schematic, it's associated with the controls here in the star like it is some kind of key.

"Look, Rillent can't destroy anything yet," she says. "He might have the key, but he doesn't have this place. Or the temple. Not yet."

"Not yet." Kyre taps the image she's stopped on. She can tell he's got ideas brewing. It shows up in the tiny lift of his cheekbones. Not a smile, but a rising.

He points at the diagram right next to hers. It shows a particular connection between two kubrics. But one lies on one side of the barrier, and the second is on the other side. The key between.

"We don't have to spend all that time figuring out how the whole system works," she says, looking at the connection.

"It wouldn't matter even if we did. We don't have the key."

"Right. But if this is going to work," she says, pointing at both ends of that connection, "it's going to take both of us. On each end. At the same time."

They study the images in silence for a long moment. A plan is forming, almost tangible, a thing of its own making between them. She feels like if she reached out, she would actually be able to touch it.

"We don't know how to get there," he says. "To the other... world."

"Yes, we do." She flips the book. Points.

"The ghosts," he says. "Of course. They carry us through the barrier somehow. Or, almost."

"But I think we need a lot of them, all in one place, for it to work," Aviend says. "And that means..."

"We have to send a message to the other side and ask for help."

"Can Delgha do that, do you think?"

"If anyone can, Delgha can."

"I think we have ten-tenths of a plan," she says.

"I think it might even be better than that." He smiles with a confidence she hasn't seen in a while. It makes her heart leap, just a bit.

"Let's go tell the others," she says.

He nods, and taps the device at the side of his neck to connect with Delgha, and she swears she can hear him singing under his breath.

"The two of you are going to have to split up," Delgha said. "In order to move fast enough to make everything work. Quenn's in…" She looked at her notes.

"Nalloc," Aviend said. She lowered her finger to the map floating in the middle of the room, held it there so they could all see it. She'd updated the device, using what she remembered from the map in the star. It looked to Kyre like home, but also not.

"Right," Delgha said. "North. And Thorme's contact for the psychic lure is to the southeast, on the opposite side of the Stere border."

Now that they'd come back from the star with a great understanding of everything and the start of a plan, the team had a bustle of energy about them, a sense of purpose. Funny how closely purpose and action tied together to create hope. Or maybe it was purpose and hope that worked together to create action. Whatever it was, the room was practically buzzing with energy. It was different from before their last plan.

It was different because of the killing. Last time, their plan was to kill a person. And even though no one had said it aloud, it was like they had all understood the consequences

of that. Of using Rillent's own methods to try to take him
down. It weighed. Blacked their ability to believe in the plan.
He wondered, in the end, Quenn aside, if that was really why
it hadn't worked. Either way, he was still grateful. He was still
himself.

This plan was simple. No, it wasn't. Not in the least. It had
so many steps that he had trouble tracking them. Not because
he'd forget one, but because any one of them could go wrong
and it would all come tumbling down.

"Someone can make it to Nalloc in half a day and back,
with a quick foot pace," Delgha continued. "The south side,
though. We're going to need transport for that."

"That far," Kyre said, looking at the distance from Aviend's
finger to the base. That would take days with walking. Maybe
more, depending on the trails, or lack thereof. "Too bad the
star can't take us to other places."

"Be careful what you wish for," Aviend said, laughing.
"You don't know where we might end up."

"Fair point," he said. "What do we have for movement
devices set up?"

Delgha winced.

"That doesn't look good," he said.

"Thorme knows a supplier who knows a supplier who's
selling her–"

"Trading me," Thorme said.

"Trading her – a time dilating windrider first thing
tomorrow."

"Yes!" Aviend said. "I want to use the time dilator. I've
always wanted to try one of those."

"It's all yours," Kyre said. He had no desire to strap himself
onto one of those machines and leap forward through time
and space. He didn't mind the dispatcher so much, and he

was... all right with traveling back and forth to the star. But actually screwing around with time? That was one of his big no thank yous.

"Has to be Kyre," Thorme said.

"What? Why?" Aviend glared at him. It was mostly, he thought, in jest. "He always gets the fun stuff."

"Agreed. Why do I always get the 'fun' stuff?"

"Quenn," Thorme said.

"Thorme, every once in a while, it would be useful if you said more than four words at a time, you know."

"Oh," Aviend said. "She's right."

"What? Why?"

"Quenn might come back for you," Aviend said. "But he might not. If he's going to come back, he's going to come back for me." She winced too, as if saying that about herself didn't agree with her. It probably didn't; after Rillent, she shied way from being special.

Kyre didn't disagree with her, but he didn't like it either. "Skist. You had to find somebody at the far reaches of the world, didn't you, Thorme?"

"Yes," she said simply. He didn't want to let her make him laugh, but he found himself doing so anyway.

"Fine," he said. "I'll take a ride on the time-warping, Kyre-killing machine of doom. This is starting to feel like a theme, and it isn't one I like. Don't be surprised if I come back broken in the head or drive myself off a cliff with it."

"Try to get everything we need first, at least," Aviend said. Her voice was wrapped up in tease, but her hand had taken his, and was squeezing. She swiped her thumb to her chin once. You've got this.

"Everyone, tell me your roles again." Delgha was pointing at Aviend.

"I go get Quenn and convince him to come back with me, so he can show us how he got out of the kubric."

"And thus how we can get in," Delgha finished. "Kyre?"

"Go with Thorme to get the Kyre-killer and then ride said Kyre-killer to the far reaches of the world to get Thorme's slistovile lure." He turned to look at Thorme, who was busy writing something up on labels that she was then sticking onto vials and tubes. "Are you sure that's a good idea?"

Thorme lifted one shoulder without looking at him. "What ever is?" As if she sensed that Delgha was about to point at her and say her name, she continued. "I'm going to get the Kyre-killer–"

"Nice that that's its official name now," he said. He could feel Aviend shaking next to him as she started laughing.

"Get the Kyre-killer, go find…" Thorme glanced at Aviend and Kyre.

"Nitar," they both said in unison.

"Nitar for making disguises. Let Toev know about the plan. Get the runners running. Keep everyone alive."

"That seems about right," Delgha said. "I'll work on getting a message to the other side – if we can't make that happen, all of this is for naught. After that, I'll tackle the time trackers for Kyre and Aviend, and the rest of the cyphers."

"Those of you traipsing through the woods, take care," she added. "The runners won't be back before you need to leave, so you'll be flying blind. Rumors are that Rillent's eyes are still elsewhere."

"Makes me nervous," Aviend said. "Even though we're pretty sure he's not looking for us. Still."

Kyre squeezed her hand back as she talked. Hoped his touch helped her as much as hers did him.

"We'll all need to balance fast with quiet," Delgha said. "It's a race, but it's a race we don't want to get caught at."

"Weird to think that getting into the kubric is going to be the easy part of this plan," Aviend said. "The real question is: how do we end Rillent without also ending the Stere? Without killing off the very thing, the very people, we're trying to protect?"

It wasn't a rhetorical question, but no one answered it. No one had an answer yet. Kyre had some ideas, but most of them were tucked somewhere between a very, very long shot and absolutely untenable.

Aviend played with the pendant, round and round. "One thing we know is that Rillent's power grab is set on something far larger than the Stere," she said. "If he comes into his full power, he won't stop here, in these woods. He's going to try and keep going. If it comes to a sacrifice of those within these trees and the whole rest of the world... worlds..."

She let her words trail away. They were pointed at everyone, but Kyre knew they were for him. She was asking him what he thought. He wanted to tell her, but honestly, he didn't know. He understood the concept – sacrifice a few for the greater good. And it was fine as a concept. On the page or in your brain. But as a real-world plan? One that involved the deaths of untold people who shared this part of the world? He couldn't say yes to that. Not after everything they'd learned with Rillent.

"Trust the plan," he said. "Trust us. We'll find a way."

The time dilating windrider wasn't, it turned out, a time dilator or a windrider. At least not in any way they were expecting. Thorme's supplier had it wrong, or their supplier's supplier had it wrong. Either way, somewhere down the line, the message of what was wanted and what actually arrived had gotten miscommunicated.

What showed up at their rendezvous spot, half a mile or so away from the base, was a girl who couldn't have been more than six riding a floating skiff with a pistal engine that burped solargasses strong enough to make Kyre's eyes water. It had no seat, nothing visible to steer it with, and no matter how fast and far it went, it damn sure wasn't going to do it quietly. Forget falling off a cliff in it. He thought he'd be lucky if he could get the thing to move.

"Thorme. What. In the skist. Is that?"

"I'm not sure," she said. "Give me a moment."

Kyre had never seen Thorme work her trading magic. Did she talk a lot? Grow sweet? Use tongue-clicks and rude hand gestures? He couldn't help but pay attention just to see what kind of person she became in this element of her life.

The girl – six long blue braids hanging down her back and a mass of orange facepaint that ran down her neck and stained her shirt – was neither subtle nor quiet. She revved the engine, which kicked out a stream of bright red smoke. When she coughed in the fumes, the whole skiff shook.

He heard Thorme say something to her in a very low voice. Thorme couldn't be heard over the engine. The girl obviously couldn't hear her either, because a moment later, she turned the engine off.

"Where exactly," he heard Thorme say with quiet precision once the engine had died, "is your mother?"

"Ma's down sick with the buzzes," she said. "But she says I'm a big girl and I can deliver the equipment my own self."

Kyre had no idea what the buzzes were. Some kind of disease? Something else? Was it something that Thorme could fix? He had no idea and couldn't tell from her face.

"Your mother's an idiot," Thorme said conversationally.

Kyre felt his face change at Thorme's easy tone. He didn't laugh, but he was tempted. He thought his mouth might be hanging open.

"Yeah," the girl said, throwing her mother under the rug as easy as taking a breath. "I'm not an idiot though, right?"

"You tell me," Thorme said. "You were supposed to bring a windrider. Does this thing you're sitting on look anything like a windrider to you? It's got no wings."

"No, but–"

"This is called a skiff," Thorme said. "A windrider has wings. You should tell your mom that."

The girl chewed her lip, squinted one eye closed to look around Thorme. "Is that your boyfriend?"

"No."

"Your dad?"

"No."

"Hey! Are you her boyfriend?! My ma has a boyfriend. Is

that your boyfriend?"

Kyre looked at Thorme helplessly. What was unraveling right here, right now? Things seemed to have degraded rapidly, if he was looking at Thorme to carry the conversation back where it needed to be.

"Hush, Hern," Thorme said. "You've got a bigger mouth than a cragworm."

"What's a cragerm? Like this?" The girl opened her mouth wide, as if to prove Thorme right. Or maybe wrong. He wasn't sure. Either way, she was temporarily quiet, and that was a relief.

It didn't last long.

"I need my money," the girl said. "Mom said... Five hundred shins." He could tell by her eyes, the slide to the side, that she was lying. Whatever her mom had told her to come home with, he thought it was a great deal less than five hundred shins.

"That's not what we agreed on," Thorme said. "Your mother and me."

"Mom says yes, or no windrider."

"It's not a windrider," Thorme said. "What is it?"

"It's a skift... skifter."

"Skiff."

"Skiff!"

"Right," Thorme said. She lowered her voice, and even her body a little. Who was this person, this hustler and jiver? He realized he had no idea what Thorme had been like before she'd become part of the Night Clave. "Listen, the buzzes are very, very bad. Your mom has them big, right? Did she say that? Is she very sick?"

The girl seemed to think about this for a moment and then nodded solemnly. "She said they were bad, yeah. Too bad for

MONTE COOK & SHANNA GERMAIN   245

her to come today. She said she's all the sicks.″

"Well, she's going to need something to make her feel better. Otherwise…″ Thorme didn't say that the girl's mother might die without the medicine, but it was in her voice anyway.

The girl's eyes were very big, white eggs inside her orange-painted face.

"I can give you something for her, and we'll trade for the skiff. All right?″

Thorme pulled a long thin vial from her bag. It had a label, but Kyre couldn't read it. Neither, apparently, could the girl.

"This,″ Thorme pointed at the label, "says 'Help for the buzzes. Makes the buzzes go away and never come back'.″

She held it out to the girl. "But you'll have to walk home. My boyfriend and I are going to ride the skiff.″

Thorme actually winked at him. And he had no idea what to do with that.

"Boyfriend in the skifter!″ the girl yelled, taking the vial.

"Take that carefully all the way to your mother,″ Thorme said. "And make sure she reads the label, so she can take it properly. Yes?″

"Yes.″

"Be careful, Hern. There are things in the woods far scarier than I.″

They both watched, silently, as the girl ran away through the forest, her blue braids bouncing, one hand held high, clutching the vial. In a few short seconds, she was out of sight and out of earshot.

Kyre reached out and pushed the skiff, a gentle nudge. It floated in midair, swinging softly. "Well, at least it's not a windrider, I guess. Although this looks… well, less stable, actually.″

"It is," Thorme said, matter-of-factly. "But it will carry you where you need to go. And it's nearly impossible for it to go over a cliff, since it's got anti-gravity pinions. Probably better for our needs, actually. And we got it for a song, to be honest. Less than a song."

Kyre could feel how round his eyes were. How slack his jaw.

"What?" she said. "Do you think I can't talk, just because I don't?"

"I think…" He had no idea what he thought. "What are the buzzes anyway?"

"I have no idea," Thorme said.

He glanced at her. Her face was as expressionless as it always was, but he thought he saw a twinge of smile lines at the edges of her gaze.

"But," she continued, "if I had to guess, I'd say it's something her mother made up so that she could send her daughter out to barter for her. Pull the 'woe-is-me and look at how cute I am' trick. What I don't know is if Hern actually grabbed the wrong machine or if her mother never had the right one to begin with."

"What was in the medicine you traded it for then?"

"Medicine?" Thorme asked. "Did I say there was medicine in that vial?"

Now that he thought about it, she hadn't. He shook his head. "Good," she said. "I don't like to lie."

"What was in the vial then?"

"Berried water."

"You carry berried water in your med bag?"

"It helps with dehydration."

"But it… What did the label say then?"

"It said, 'Next time don't send your daughter to barter'."

He felt his mouth fall open a bit more and tried to close it quickly. Still, Thorme saw it.

"Sometimes you just know what people are going to do," she said. "Just like I know you're going to push this skiff back to the base, because you don't want to get on it until you absolutely have to."

"I don't know if I like this new you, Thorme," he said, even as his hand was already reaching out to grab hold of the side of the skiff and tug it along next to him.

"Not new me," she said. "More like old me."

Finally, the question he couldn't resist asking, "What did you do before you came to the Stere, Thorme? Before you were part of the Night Clave?"

Her footsteps crunched in the underbrush. "Did you ever hear of Ossam's Traveling Menagerie and Soaring Circus?"

"No," he said.

"Good," she said.

She walked beside him, and didn't say another word all the way back to the base.

Moving through the woods boldly and in broadlight is the last thing Aviend expected to be doing anytime soon. But Rillent's eyes are elsewhere and haste matters, so fast and direct is the way. It's her best chance of reaching Quenn, convincing him to help, and getting back in time.

Convincing him will be another matter. The harder of the two tasks set before her, and surely the most important. She is looking forward to telling him about the temple, though. For that alone, he might agree to come back to the base.

The ghosts are getting louder. Not noisier, but fuller. Harder to ignore. They no longer stalk the edges of her vision, but step in front of her. She swears it's purposeful, their slide and stand. She's learning to stride through them, to ignore the sensation that she swears prickles on her skin, even though Delgha said it couldn't be so.

"There's nothing actually happening," she'd said. "Now that we know that it's transdimensional energy funneling through the kubrics, we know that it doesn't have a feel or sensation. It's just because they look like people that we expect them to touch us in some way."

It's just because they look like people.

And they do. Mostly strangers, indistinguishable from

each other. Flickered faces and features. Sometimes they look like the dead. No one that she knows. Small comforts. She wonders, now that she knows, if they see her too. Is there an Aviend in the other world? Does she look like a ghost to someone over there, bumping into trees that don't exist on this side?

She runs and then walks and then runs. Somewhere in there it rains, soft and light. The wet leaves touch her as she steps through them, turning everything she wears to water and weight. This section of the forest is wetter than where she grew up or where they are stationed now. She remembers traveling through marshes and puddles, downpours that she and her mother had huddled against when they'd visited this section of the Stere. The memory is instilled so deep, rises with such force at the first gust of water-threaded wind, that she isn't surprised to realize she'd chosen a cloak with a wide, capped hood. She pulls it up, lets it take the brunt of the rain.

The town of Nalloc is also much as she'd remembered, although the last time she'd been here she was barely a girl. It's small enough, she guesses, that it has mostly passed beneath Rillent's eye. At least so far.

A few buildings cluster in a clearing. The space has been man-made purposefully, long ago, from the rigorously square shape of it. Two short streets intersect each other, cut across by worn paths. A few yol graze, their yellow wool dripping with water. They lift their heads as she draws near, but otherwise pay no mind.

Everything is wet here. You can smell it in the air, how things never get fully dry. Not the wood that the homes are built from. Not the yol and their moss-tinged wool. Not the paths or the bark or even very many eternally wet people.

One of those eternally wet individuals steps into Aviend's path just as she enters the square. The movement isn't deliberate, she doesn't think. She isn't sure it isn't a ghost at first. And then she realizes it's definitely human and her hand falls to her weapon.

They both wear hoods pulled down, walk with lowered heads. The shape is wide, nearly twice as much so as her, and moves with the slow careful step of someone of old age. Aviend sidesteps without colliding, says a low apology and moves to keep forward. She isn't sure exactly where she is heading to find Quenn, but with so few buildings, she has no worries that she will quickly track the boy down.

Provided he is still here, still alive.

"Aviend?" The voice at her back is Quenn's, although the shape is not. She can't begin to imagine what has happened to the impoverished boy she saw only a short time ago.

"Quenn?" she asks, mostly to be sure. She turns, and it is Quenn, beneath the now-pushed-back hood. Of course she would know that face anywhere. It hasn't changed. How could it possibly have? Although it seems like eons, it has not even been a full season.

"What are you doing here?" Quenn asks. He seems older, and Aviend isn't sure how she'd ever thought to call him a boy.

Something wiggles inside the large rain drape he wears, drawing her attention downward.

"Orphan," Quenn says in response to her gaze, just as a small woolen face pushes itself up out of the drape, bleating. A tiny hoof, no bigger than Aviend's thumbnail, appears a moment later. "Shhh…"

"For a moment there, I thought you'd been eating more than your fair share, to make up for your time in the trenches."

Quenn laughs – has she ever heard him laugh before? She doesn't think so. Then shakes his head, mostly at the creature, who seems determined to jump out of the protective drape and into the wet muck.

"I'd hoped..." she starts, and then shakes her own head. "Could we talk somewhere?" She wants to add "dry", but knows that is likely out of the question here. But she is shivering inside her soaked cloak, her fingers too cold to bend.

"This way," Quenn says.

She follows his lumbering, orphan-loaded gait. The waddle of him is enough to make her smile, particularly as a single hoof again makes an appearance and knocks him softly in the chin. She's glad to see that he no longer limps. His leg seems to have healed well. She bets that beneath those very wet pantlegs, Thorme's tiny crisscross of scars are barely even visible. Unless you know them as intimately as Aviend does. The imagined shape of them makes her heart hurt a little.

A building is tucked into the hollow where the grove hasn't been cleaned out, carved into the side of risen stone.

"It's more cave than building," Quenn says as he pushes open the door and leads the way into a large carved room. It is mostly hollowed from the rock, with a bit of white caulked along the edges of the walls. "But it's better than wood to keep out of the rain."

It is also, Aviend is delighted to note, surprisingly dry. And warm.

The front room has very little. A few benches and a table. A drape of a curtain – crosshatched and patched, mismatching fabrics – separates this room from another. Little else to draw the eye other than a large steel orb in the middle of the room. It has large slits in it, carved out in an ornate design. Through the design, she can see flickering orange light.

She lowers down, looks inside. A fire burns bright enough in there that she can feel the heat pushing forward to her face.

"That's ingenious," she says. It really is. Much cleaner and safer than an open fire, and she bet it cooks better than the cookstove's accidental output. Holds the heat inside, radiates it out through the metal. She'd never have thought to build such a thing. Thorme would love it.

"Rillent's is much larger," Quenn says. "More... people-sized." He doesn't look at her. She thinks about what that means for a moment. About what it means that Quenn has done. About what it means for what she is about to ask Quenn to do.

Still not looking her way, Quenn kneels and lets the creature out of his drape. The tiny yol jumps sideways with a half-kick that nearly sends it toppling. Water drips from its wool despite having been under Quenn's coat. It shakes its head and then goes toward the fire ball. Lays down near, but not too near. It has clearly been here before. It's figured out the perfect "get warm but don't burn up" ratio.

"Here, lay your wet stuff out by the fireglobe and it will dry before you leave." The "leave" isn't Quenn saying anything, like it might be with someone else. He is just stating facts. Trying to be helpful.

"Thank you," she says. Quenn strips away his wrap and she is pleased to see that he has gained some weight. He's still skinny, but he no longer looks gaunt. His cheeks are less hollowed, and his lanky frame has some fat over the muscles.

The yol lifts its head and bleats at her, quiet as a dream, when she lays down her wet coat.

"I call him Ollie," Quenn says. "And this is my sister, Vesi. She built the fireglobe."

How long the woman has been standing there, Aviend

doesn't know. She clearly came from the room behind the curtain, though. Silent. Swift. Sure. The fabric's not even moving.

From Quenn's description of his sister, his need to protect and return, she'd expected her to be younger than him, a girl even. She is neither of those things. She might be older than Aviend. More likely close to the same age. She looks like Quenn, more in the body than in the face. The coloring matches too. Where Quenn's face is pointed, all angles, hers is soft. A circle filled with other circles. Even her eyes are large and round.

Her voice, however, is angular all over. It carries the same lilt and swallow as Quenn's. Obvious as soon as she says Rillent. "It's just like Rillent's," she says. *Rilnt.* "Except we don't burn people alive in ours. We just use it for tea and such."

"Vesi," Quenn says; the word is sharp but his voice is warm.

"It's true," she says as she comes forward. "You're Aviend?"

Aviend is surprised, but not overly so. Surely Quenn's talked about them, about her, in some way. She hopes he wasn't overly effusive about the life-saving part.

She isn't sure if an answer is needed, but she gives one anyway. "I am."

"Your mother..." Vesi begins. Then stops and shakes her head. "I met Arch Enpelia once, when I was young. Quenn was just born, I think. She came here and I pulled on her sleeve. Our mother..." She glances at Quenn. Quenn just shakes his head. Aviend wonders how many times he's heard this story. A lot, she guesses. "Our mother wanted to die when I did that. Your mom, she had these beautiful earrings though. These tiny black circles, and I wanted to know if I could have them.

"She knelt down and offered them to me. Even though I had no pierce holes. Even though I was just this child, pulling on her beautiful gown. My mother wouldn't let me take them. I cried. My god, how I cried. But I'll never forget her kindness."

Aviend has never heard this story before, but she thinks that sounds like her mother. She wonders if it took place the time she remembers being here, or on another of her mother's travels. She doesn't say that in the entire time she'd known her mother, she'd only ever had or worn a single pair of earrings. A pair of tiny black circles. She'd had them in her ears when she died. Aviend had buried them with her.

"I'm glad," Aviend says. "I miss her. Thank you for sharing that story." A kindness, sharing stories of the dead, but one that makes her heart grow heavy with ache all the same.

Both Quenn and Vesi touch their hands to their elbows. "Coruscates among us," they say. Nearly in unison.

For the first time Aviend wonders about the town. Its quietness. She'd assumed it was because of the weather. But she thinks that it was more likely Rillent, and that she was wrong in her original assessment that it was too small for him to notice. Small was easy. Easy to squash. Easy to kill. She wonders how many times they've had to say such prayers over those loved and lost.

"Sit, please," Vesi says, pointing to the chairs. As Aviend does so, Vesi sets a piece of pottery, curved at the bottom, on top of the fireglobe. It's a teapot of sorts, Aviend realizes.

"Did you make that too?"

Vesi nods. "I'm good with my hands," she says. Neither humility nor pride. Merely a statement of fact. Aviend likes her already, just, she thinks, as she had liked Quenn. Family trait.

The water boils fast, and Vesi is pouring it into cups and handing them out with a speed and precision that claims ownership over the space. Perhaps over her brother too. Quenn had told her that he'd promised his sister he wouldn't leave her. That had made Aviend assume she was young and needed protection. But now she wonders what the truth is. If Vesi is running this show – and she gets the impression that might be true – she's going to have a harder time with this request. Quenn may want to help. But if she can't turn Vesi, his desire won't matter.

She takes the tea gratefully. It smells of crossel berries and fir trees. Which is nice, but it's the heat that really sinks into her. She hadn't realized how cold her hands still were until she wraps them around the mug.

Aviend had expected to talk to Quenn in private, but sees there seems to be little chance of that now. The curtains that Vesi came through are hardly doors, and to ask for privacy after Vesi's kindness seems ruder than Aviend can bear.

She is going to have to say what she needs to say here, in front of both of them. She can see no way around it. It's possible they should have sent Kyre after all.

Aviend sets down the tea. Puts her hands to her knees. Turns them palm up. It's a gesture people used in the clave, what felt like eons ago now, to show respect for the numenera. A bit of humility. A request. An offer of your hands to help and not to hurt. She doesn't know if Quenn and Vesi will recognize the gesture or even respect it, but it can't hurt to try.

Quenn's eyes flick to her fingers at the gesture. She can't read his face.

After a moment, she picks the tea back up, takes a sip to buy her a moment to think. The tea smells stronger than it tastes. In the cup, it's more water and scent than flavor. The spices must be hard to come by here. She is grateful for what they've shared with her. It seems wrong of her to ask for more. And yet, she must.

She never knows where to begin asking for things, so she just starts. She looks at Quenn and Vesi while she talks. Asking Quenn without giving tacit invitation to Vesi's involvement is surely going to get her a no answer.

"I'm going to be honest with you both. I'm here because we need your help. And you shouldn't do what I'm about to ask. It's dangerous, and it's not fair of us to ask. But we're out of options. You know we are, or I wouldn't be here." The words tumble out so fast she hasn't taken a breath, and her inhale at the end is loud in her ears.

Quenn's face doesn't change. He and Vesi share a glance, so quick she wouldn't have seen it if she wasn't a veteran of those kinds of glances with Kyre.

She feels her hopes sinking. They have a backup plan for if Quenn says no, but she doesn't like it. She's going to do everything possible not to go there. She racks her brain for the right words and can find nothing other than another earnest plea rising to her lips.

"Of course," Vesi says, as Quenn nods.

Aviend nearly drops her tea. Some sloshes on to her fingers, causing her to yelp a little. Nothing is what she expected.

"You don't even know what it is yet," Aviend says. Her voice is a weird whisper. She wants to clear her throat, dislodge whatever's in there.

"Your face," Quenn says. He and Vesi share another look, but Aviend can't follow this one at all. She's an only child, and she feels that suddenly and sharply.

Quenn's laugh isn't a laugh so much as a bark, followed by

a choking, gasping cough.

"Sorry," he says. "It's just so clear that you expected a no."

"Well... I..." She is utterly at a loss for words.

"I'll help," Quenn says. "Of course I'll help. I guess I always knew this day was coming. Even if I wasn't fully aware of it, I've been preparing for it. I didn't know what it would be, or how it would look, but I knew that I'd be returning to Rillent eventually. Either he'd come for me, or I'd have to go to him."

Somehow, Quenn's easy acceptance of it makes Aviend feel worse. She'd prepared for a fight, for rejection. She doesn't know how to respond to this... agreement, other than to lower her head toward the warmth of her tea and murmur a quiet, "Thank you."

"Give us a few minutes to pack," Quenn says.

Us? It takes a moment to sink in. Is Quenn saying that they'll both help? This wasn't in the plan. She feels like Quenn, even more so than Rillent – if in a totally different way – just keeps sending their plans up in flames. "Are you...?"

"Yes," Vesi says. "Unless you think I'm letting my baby brother go off on another adventure while he leaves me here to fend for babies – they're not human babies, at least – and live in wet socks."

Aviend sees how much she'd misjudged this situation. Quenn hadn't promised to return to his sister to protect her. He'd returned because he'd left her behind. When she'd wanted to come. Demanded to come. Aviend can begin to imagine how that conversation had gone.

She drops the lower half of her face behind her hand in a soft cough to hide her grin.

"You're welcome to join us, Vesi," she says after she has regained control. "And we certainly wouldn't be sad if you helped us build something like your fireglobe and pot. Ghosts know we could use some creature comforts where we are."

In fact, she's surprised at how comfortable she feels here. In a hollowed-out cave room, with almost no furniture. It's the way that things are arranged, she thinks. It gives the space a sense of invitation. Something she hasn't thought about in so long. Not since she'd helped her mother entertain guests in that other life.

"The fireglobe is portable," Vesi says. "We'll bring it with us."

A portable hearth, she thinks. There is something deeply reassuring, and deeply sad, about the idea.

"Ollie will have to come with us too," Vesi says. "He's not old enough to be on his own. I've already gotten Gradel..." She casts a glance at Aviend. "Our neighbor – to pull the rest of our flock in with his own."

Aviend thinks how Vesi should have been a leader. Perhaps she would have been, if not for Rillent. Leader of this town, or another.

She can no longer keep her surprise quiet. "You really were expecting me?"

"Yes," Quenn says, at the same time that Vesi says, "We were hoping for you. How could we not? Rillent isn't going to stop. Not without being forced to."

Now Aviend is *really* starting to like this woman. She's like Quenn, and yet wholly not. In fact, Quenn is shaking his head a bit, even as he kneels to fiddle with the fireglobe. There are smiles in the edges of his dimples, though. They love each other through and through, she thinks. Even after he left her here.

Vesi scoops up Ollie and unceremoniously hands him off to Aviend. Aviend feels her arms rising to take up the creature's weight even as her brain is saying, "What? No." But then he's in her arms. No longer wet, even. Just heavy and slippery with sleep.

"Just for a moment," Vesi says, almost apologetically. "Last time we tied up the fireglobe, he tried to jump into it and nearly charred all his wool off. He's adorable, but I'm not sure he's the brightest spark in the sparkbox."

Aviend looks at him. His long legs are splayed every which way. One foot twitches in half-sleep, like he's dreaming of running. His nose is a hairless pink that makes her think of baby birds. He opens one eye. The pupil is four-sided, nearly square, and endlessly black. All around that, is a pale blue, nearly grey. The eye closes. The weight grows heavier.

Aviend turns her attention back to the fireglobe. Quenn and Vesi have each taken a side. There are little handles there that she didn't see before. Quenn nods. He and Vesi pull on the handles at the same time. The globe, impossibly, crumples in on itself, all along the cuts. Growing smaller and smaller until it's a crumb of metal no larger than her fist. The handles fold up and together, making it easy to pick it up with one hand.

After all of the devices, with their tiny wires and impossible parts, the simplicity of this, the ability to see how it works, makes her happy in a way she can't explain. "That's ingenious," she says.

Vesi's face changes. At first Aviend thinks she's insulted her. But no, that's pride she sees in her cheeks. "Rillent's doesn't do that," she says. "That's my own special addition. Plus..." She taps the tiny sphere, but just quickly before pulling back. Aviend gets the impression that the center might still be quite warm. "It captures the fire ember inside here. So as soon as you open it up and give it air, it lights back up. Even in the rain."

Aviend wants to show her delight again, but she knows that kind of response quickly gets overwhelming for others. Instead she says, "Our team will certainly be glad to have it. And you."

Vesi nods, then disappears behind the curtain. She's back a moment later with two full packs. Quenn takes one from her, mock whispering, "My sister likes to be prepared." Then, "What's the plan anyway?"

She wishes she could lie to him. "We're going to the kubric," she says and then because she needs to be as clear with him as she can, "To Rillent. We need you to show us how you got out so we can get in." There's more, but she lets it go for now.

His face is nearly impassive, but there, in the folds of his eyelids and angle of his mouth, that half-hidden fire. "Are you going to take him down?"

"We're going to try."

"I'm going in with you, then," he says. "Into the kubric."

"I was hoping you'd say that."

Quenn drops his poncho back over his head and holds out his arms for Ollie. Aviend has gotten used to having him there, his warm weight like an anchor against her chest. When Quenn takes him back, she feels momentarily unsettled, like her balance is off.

"We're ready, then," Quenn says.

And that's how Aviend finds herself returning to the base with not just one, but three, well... living creatures... in tow. She doesn't realize until they're nearly back to the base that she'd completely forgotten to tell Quenn about the temple.

The skiff jumped and rocked every time Kyre asked it to do anything beyond go forward or stop. Sideways was horrible. Forget trying to go up and down. He basically had to point it in the general vicinity of where he wanted it to go, push the lever, and pray.

Except he didn't believe in praying, so he mostly just swore and shook his head. The one advantage really was the speed. He was at the edge of the Stere before he'd even really figured out how to drive the skisting thing.

It didn't help that it was built for two, and he was only one, and that made him about as effective as a butterfly in a windstorm. He was sure that Thorme had requested something smaller. It got him there, alive, so all else was forgiven.

Next, he needed to find Thorme's contact, get the psychic lure, and hightail it back to the base without killing himself.

"Look for the orange smoke," Thorme had said. As if that explained everything. Or even anything.

It turned out that it did. As soon as he left the edge of the woods – stepping out left him blinking, surprised by the flatness of the land stretching out before him – he saw the lazy, off-circle rings of smoke drifting up from a camp. The color was more red than orange, but there was nothing else dotting the lowslung landscape as far as his eyes could see.

He leaned the skiff against a tree trunk and did his mental equipment check. He was light this time, prepared for moving, fighting only if necessary. Rope, shortblades, med kit. He'd brought shins in case Thorme's contact had any cyphers other than the psychic lure. Surely if he was a trader, he'd have at least a few he'd be willing to part with.

Walking across the open landscape made Kyre feel twitchy. His skin touched nothing but air. His eyes searched for some hillock or tree or relic rising from the visage in front of him, and found none that he thought were real. The ground was hard-packed, orange-rust in color. Every step kicked up a small puff of dust that quickly colored his boots and the bottoms of his pants. It reminded him of trencher dust, not in color, but in granularity, the way it clung to itself in clumps.

The camp was a little nothing, one that was likely designed to be makeshift but ended up longterm. He could tell by the way the tent and firepit and even the man sitting there had sunk into the soil like stones. Everything was sun-faded to a wash of yellow and pale. Except the smoke rings, umber circles up into the sky.

The trader hadn't looked at him, but Kyre was pretty sure he knew that he was coming. Probably heard the skiff or him swearing as he got off it. Maybe even his footfalls.

He crossed, closer, until he was in that weird space of how close do you get to a thing before you lift your hand and call out?

He decided it was now. "Iadace," he called across the space.

Another smoke ring, fat and low. It was impossible to tell if they were coming from the fire, a pipe, the man himself, or some other, weirder origin.

For every step, another smoke. All sizes. All manner of round. Soon, he could discern the difference between orange and umber and crimson and one that had a slightly pinkish undertone. He began to feel like the rings were hypnotizing, drawing him in without letting him get closer. So many footsteps were falling. They were his, but he couldn't feel his legs moving. Just the weight of his feet, the hard pack of earth.

Just like that, Kyre was there, standing in front of the camp, the man, the smoke rings.

The man snapped his wrinkled fingers and the circles disappeared. Kyre took a breath, sudden, like he'd been forgetting. It tasted of dust and metal.

"Iadace," the man said. He had a big mouth in a small head, a surreally large grin. "Now that's a word I haven't heard in a long time."

The man was short and folded in on himself. Even his skin looked folded, crimped and ironed out and crimped again. His clothes, too, wrinkled, the fabrics rippling in and out. He sat on some kind of pale animal pelt sewn into what appeared to be a stool. It shifted as the man moved.

He looked up, and his eyes were large too, even as they moved half-closed in the glare of the slanted sun. "You must be Thorme's boy?"

It felt odd to be called a boy, and especially to be called Thorme's boy, but even as he was about to protest, Kyre saw that the man in front of him was old. Not just old. Ancient. Older than anyone he'd ever known. His face was a mass of wrinkles, half of them buried behind other wrinkles, so you couldn't even tell how many there were at first. What was once dark in his giant eyes had greyed out to the same color as his tent. Sandstone and milk. Not blind, Kyre thought, but heading that way.

"Yeeees," he said. He couldn't bring himself to actually say that he was Thorme's boy – he almost had it until he thought of her face, listening in – so he just said "Yes," again.

The man rocked forward on the stool, using one long hand to push himself up. The stool unfolded itself, gave a couple of shakes so that a snout and a tail popped out, and then ran at a breakneck speed on short, fat legs toward Kyre's feet.

He tried to sidestep, threw himself off balance, nearly stepped on the creature as it went through his legs, and finally just allowed his body to go in the direction it was already going and sat down with a plop in the dirt.

Now the man was standing and Kyre was sitting. And they were still almost eye-to-eye. Mostly because Kyre had dropped onto a dimple in the earth and the man wasn't very tall.

"Don't mind Prem," the man said. "He's just trying to get home."

"I'm here for the lure," Kyre said, with as little confusion and as much dignity as he could find. His tailbone hurt. If this wasn't such a serious situation, he'd be starting to think that Thorme had sent him on a silly laakchase.

The man had been reaching out his hand, possibly to help Kyre up. At Kyre's words, he withdrew his hand, folded it back in toward his chest and stuck it in a... pocket? Small bag? It was hard to tell.

"Thorme said you didn't need compensation..." In fact, she'd something about an old debt, unpaid, but he wasn't going to go there. "But if you need something, we can work out some kind of deal."

"No, no," the man said. He bent his head to the hand he'd pulled in, tugged something long and wiggling out of his pocket. So many legs. Kyre found his feet tucking under him and he was standing and taking a step back before he thought about it. "I'm just making sure I've got everything."

He tucked the creature back in his pocket, dusted off his hands, held one out to Kyre, realized he was already standing, and gave a nod.

"Well, then," he said. "I'm ready."

Kyre was still focused on the legs of the pocket creature. Each one a different color, he thought, and all of them slightly different. He wouldn't consider himself squeamish, not by a long shot – at least not about bugs – but that was something else.

"I'm sorry," he said. "Ready to trade?"

"Ready to go."

One of them was confused, and Kyre didn't think it was him, this time. "I'm sorry, but I just need the lure," he said. "I mean..." He was starting to calculate ways to get the man, whose name he still didn't know, back to the base. If he wanted to come, Kyre wasn't going to leave him out here in this desolate expanse. Maybe he could take the lure first and then send someone back to get him.

"Thorme's boy," the man said, putting his gnarled and thankfully bugless hand on Kyre's shoulder. "I *am* the lure."

The man reached down, grabbed a bag so much the same color of the dirt that Kyre hadn't even noticed it, and began to move toward the skiff. He was *fast*. Kyre shook his head, turned, and started after him.

"I don't..." he said. "I don't understand what's happening right now."

Just as Kyre caught up with him, the man stopped and held his hand out. The man had a handshake that felt like holding a fist of wadded fabric. It was the weirdest sensation, but not bad.

"I already told you," he said. "I'm the psychic lure. Well, the Psychic Lure, capitals, if you want to get technical. Which isn't something I care about. Most people – Thorme aside, course – call me Sil. Short for Psy-L. Get it? Exhausting carting around a three-word name now that I don't need it anymore."

Kyre got it now. He thought Thorme had sent him for a device, a cypher, something small and portable, and Thorme had instead sent him for a man. A fairly small and portable man, but still. He wondered how much of that Thorme had done on purpose, and just how much he might owe her for this little surprise.

"You can psychically lure creatures. Like the…" He'd forgotten the name. "Stool. Or the… with the legs."

"Everyone has a skill," Sil said. "It's all about what you make of it." He canted his head, and in one of the folds along his neck, Kyre caught the glint of a beetle back, iridescent in greens and golds.

"Let me guess," Kyre said. "You used to be part of something called Ossam's Traveling Menagerie and Soaring Circus?"

"However did you guess?" Sil said, laughing. "Thorme told me you were a smart boy."

Time is ticking down, faster than they want it to. Every day, Aviend fights against the need to do something *now*. It's the knowledge, the hope, burning a hole in her brain as hot as the sun. Its heat urging her to do something do something do something.

But they don't have a complete plan yet. Not quite. Not yet.

She and Kyre and Quenn are working on the plans for getting them into the kubrics and back out again. The first part is fairly easy; Quenn knows the kubrics better than they could have even hoped.

It's the getting out that is proving to be problematic. Not for her and Quenn, but for the others. All of the people Rillent's trapped inside. Which was about what they expected. Still, after all of this time, their best plan is still something that basically amounts to "run like hell."

Except run like hell isn't going to work. Their runners are telling them that not only is Rillent getting stronger, the destriatch are getting faster. More aggressive and deadly. Rillent is sucking energy from the kubrics as fast as he can and using it to his advantage. He won't hesitate to kill if he thinks he's losing.

Their only advantage right now? Rillent doesn't know they are coming for him again. She hopes.

"Let's go through the exit options one more time," Kyre says. "Maybe there's something we missed."

Quenn rises from where he's sitting in front of his map and stretches. He's less gaunt now, but still lean and lanky. When he stretches and uncurves his back, he could almost touch the ceiling. Moving through the kubric's passageways is going to be hell on him. But he hasn't once complained about the prospect of being cramped inside tiny tunnels for hours on end. With some people, Aviend might think they hadn't actually thought about the consequences of that. But Quenn, she's pretty sure, has, and has accepted it as just part of the job. It's one of the things she likes about him.

Aviend runs her finger over Quenn's map. It is meticulous in its detail, right down to the location of the switch Kyre and Aviend will each need to flip.

"Why don't I remember any of this?" Kyre asks. "Like that room there?" He pointed to a large, circular room.

"That's Rillent's room," Quenn says.

"I must have been in it…"

"Very purple. Ornate curtains."

"It's the kubric," Aviend says. "Remember? It makes you forget."

It didn't just make him forget. It makes him forget that he forgets. It's part of why he's the one they've chosen to go to the other world.

"Is that Rillent? Or the kubrics themselves that do that?" Quenn asks. He'd dropped Arch long ago, but Rillent is still *Rillnt*. The sound of his name like that makes him seem less dangerous somehow.

"It's the light," Kyre says. "It's something Rillent does with the light."

"What color are the kubrics, Quenn? Their light?" Aviend's finger traces the map as she speaks. Hits a dead end. Backtracks.

"Kind of, I don't know... greyish-black? Whatever color you'd call a stone."

"It's blue to Kyre," Aviend says.

"Blue... I can see that," Quenn says. "It's got a bit of a blue–"

"No," Kyre says. "It's *blue*." How to describe the color that he sees to someone who can't see it? She supposes it doesn't matter. What matters is understanding there's a difference.

Quenn's head knocks back a little as he takes that in. "Oh," he says. Aviend wonders if he ever swears. She's never heard him do so. "How?"

How indeed?

"Rillent has this device..." Kyre's throat jags, like his swallow caught on glass. He makes his hands wide. "Long, silver..."

"Of course," Quenn says. "He carries it all the time."

Kyre nods. "It was broken, when I met him. He gave me a whole story about how it was his father's or something, and how he'd love to have it back working someday. I couldn't have built the thing, but I knew how to fix it. It was just one of the many things I fixed for him."

"I always wondered what that did," Quenn says. "I mean, he carried it around like he didn't need it, but he never let it out of his sight."

"Several things, I think, all related to control. He used it on me to..." Kyre swallows, and the pause feels longer than it is. "...make it so the kubric pulled at me. Made it harder to leave, or think about leaving."

"And that's what makes you see the kubric as blue?" Quenn says.

"I think so. I think it uses the kubric's power. And it's fickle. I had to fix it practically every other time he used it."

"I wonder if that means it no longer works?" Aviend muses. She's still tracing the map with her fingers, finding nothing that would answer the question: how do we get everyone out without Rillent noticing?

"I'd like to say no," Kyre says. "But my skills aren't *that* unique. He surely found someone to take my place long ago."

"Is it imprinted to him, do you think, Kyre?" Aviend asks.

"No," he says. "Anyone could use it but you'd have to get it away from him. And I've never seen anyone do that."

"Yeah," she says, not ready to dismiss the idea yet, but wanting to solve the problem at hand first. "I think we're going to need a distraction. To buy Quenn enough time to get the others out."

"We can't afford more people," Kyre says.

She knows he's right. "What about some destriatch?"

Kyre seems to catch her meaning right away, although she can tell from Quenn's face that he doesn't. "That could work," he says.

"We'd have to have Delgha make a portable device," she says. "Something that I can carry with me."

Quenn's face shows he's still attempting to figure out this plan. She's about to let him off the hook and explain it when they hear a low knock against the doorframe. Nitar is standing there, holding up a slew of fabric on one arm.

"Just me," she says. "Not to worry. I have disguises for trying on."

She passes out the pieces she's been working on. Full trencher suits for Quenn and Aviend. Nitar checks the fit, murmurs, adjusts.

Then a hood for Kyre. Aviend watches as he slides it over his head and becomes… someone else. Everything but his eyes. His eyes are still his, brilliant green and warm. But the rest of him, she doesn't even recognize.

"Ghostfell," says Quenn. So he does swear. Sort of.

"Agreed," Aviend says. "I can't believe how much you don't look like you anymore."

"You can look too," Nitar says to him. She has a reflecting plate that she holds up in front of Kyre's face. It's weird to see Kyre's shock reaction on someone else's features.

"That is… good, Nitar," he says. "I wouldn't even recognize me."

"That's the plan," Aviend says. It is. There's a chance he'll meet himself in the other world. And who knows what the Kyre there is like? He could be everything Rillent wanted him to be. Aviend too. It's a hard thing to think about, themselves as Rillent-horrors, but better to be safe than sorry.

"Contingencies for contingencies," Kyre says. And his voice coming out of his not-face is weirder still.

Kyre pulls the hood down and goes back to himself. Aviend breathes a sign of relief. More disconcerting than she likes to admit, that.

Nitar holds out her hands to gather everything back. "They're perfect, Nitar. Really," Aviend says.

"Not yet," she says. "No. They will be."

For the past two weeks, the base felt full of life. More so than Kyre could remember it in a long time. Quenn and Vesi and even the tiny woolen one – Ollie – they were only three, but they talked enough for ten. Or, well, the humans did. The yol mostly ran around in little leaps and jumps, bleating. He was a pickpocket, a beggar, and a consummate eater. He was also welcome relief from the focused planning and preparations, and Kyre didn't think anyone at the base minded having him around.

Sil was... well, Sil. He went out every day to splash around in the swamp, "getting my bearings," as he put it. He'd come back in at night, exhausted, damp, and smelling bad enough that Thorme had finally kicked him out of the kitchen until he could come back at half his stench rate. Watching the two of them together was an interesting experience; neither talked about their past – even though he'd tried to get Sil to talk to him about what, possibly, Thorme could have done in a Menagerie, but Sil had held Thorme's confidence easily – but you could still see the shared experience in their language, their in-jokes, their easy banter. He wondered if he and Aviend looked like that from the outside after all of this time. He hoped so.

They'd been planning and preparing steadily for nearly two weeks, but between those moments of focus and detail, there was a sense of excitement. Joy. Hope, even. So much tentative hope. It scared him a little and buoyed him too.

Last night, Delgha had sent the message to the other side. Would they get it? Would it work? Would they come and help? There was no way to know. Not until tomorrow, when they went to the kubric. The ghosts would either be there or they wouldn't. All they could do was hope that someone on the other side – someone not Rillent or Faleineir – had heard their plea for help.

Tomorrow was the day everything would begin. The day that would change all of their lives, one way or another. Kyre looked around the pennon at all the people gathered there. All of them believing. In the plan. In the clave. In each other. He reached for Aviend's hand, found her already reaching back.

"Last chance to go through this," Delgha said from the front of the room. "If you're not ready. If you want out. If you see a hole, speak now."

No one spoke. They might, before this was all over. The plan was good, but it was not easy.

"All right, first up. Aviend, Kyre, and Quenn."

Kyre rose, aware of the eyes on him, his hand still bound to Aviend's. "We head out to the kubric midday," he said. "From there, I go to the other world's kubric and Quinn and Aviend go to this one. Aviend and I flip the switches at the same time, Aviend gets the key, and Quenn gets everyone out. Then Aviend takes the key to the star and seals the barrier forever."

"You make it sound so easy," Aviend said, laughing. "You forgot Rillent, Faleineir, the destriatch, the traps, the tunnels, not running into your evil counterpart, and the whole 'going to another world' while timing everything perfectly part."

"I've decided to skip all of the bad parts," he said, "and let you and Quenn handle them for me."

"You're a horrible person," she said.

"I know," he said.

The mood in the room was teasing excitement, but Delgha was all business. She steadfastly ignored their banter as she went through the list in front of her. "Time trackers?"

Aviend and Kyre both held theirs up. The symbols that showed on the little panels didn't actually make sense to him – they were from some language of a prior world – but they had synchronized countdown cycles. If all went according to plan, when the cycles ended, they would both throw their switches. Same time, different worlds.

"Disguises?" Check. "Cyphers?" Check. "Monoblade?" To Kyre, who nodded. "Sword nodule?" To Aviend, who also nodded.

"Good," Delgha said. "Who's up next? Rescue team?"

Toev stood, bending himself up into his full, willowy height. "We'll have runners stationed from the kubric to the clearing, to help those that Quenn frees. We've got a waystation mostly finished…" Delgha's face squinted at that, and he held up a hand reassuringly. "It will be done by tomorrow, not to worry. We'll hold everyone in there until… well, until it's either safe or it isn't, I guess."

Delgha nodded, made a note. "Base team?" she said.

Here, Thorme took the lead. Kyre was delighted to see her put on some of the showmanship he'd seen from her before. Next to him, Aviend, who clearly hadn't seen this side of her before, was cocking her head as Thorme talked.

What is this? Aviend mouthed, as Thorme stood before them and outlined a plan in far more than her usual three or four words.

He moved his hand past his mouth. *I told you.*

"We're the defense crew," Thorme was saying. "If Rillent figures out what's going on, and sends out his glaives or the destriatch, or both, to attack the base, our goal is to protect it and each other without killing anyone. Now, as the chiurgeon, I understand that may not be possible. But that's our goal."

"Vesi and Sil will be your leaders here." Thorme cast a long look at Sil. Something passed between them that Kyre couldn't read, but Sil must have been able to, because he gave her a short, sharp nod. "Listen, the slistoviles are going to scare the ghost out of you. But don't run. And don't scream. Not if you can help it.

"The destriatch are going to scare you too, and well they should," she continued. She pointed at Delgha, who picked up a device off the table next to her and held it up with both hands. "But we have your backs there, too. You know what not to do."

As if prompted, the whole room said, "Don't run. Don't scream."

"Not if you can help it," Thorme finished.

Delgha scrolled through her notes. "That's all I've got," she said. "Anyone have questions? Concerns? Reasons why this won't work?"

"Only eleven million," Aviend said. She gave Kyre that impossible wink. It got him every time. "But that's how we know we're on the right side."

When Aviend enters the temple the night before they're supposed to leave for the kubric, she finds Kyre dragging a thick mattress across the floor. She's pretty sure it's the one from their sleeping room. Not that she's looked at the mattress much lately – sleep hasn't exactly been a priority for either of them the last few days – but theirs is the largest. And this one is pretty large, even though it looks tiny in the vast expanse of this giant room.

"I'm afraid to ask," she says. "First, how you got that through the tunnel. Second, what you're doing exactly."

He gives the mattress a few shoves until it's lined up perfectly in the middle of the room. "Well you're leaving tomorrow, and I thought we should spend a night under the stars."

Kyre's not really one for sentiment. She always knows exactly how he feels about her; it's never in doubt. His love is solid and real, so much so that she feels like if she just leans back at any time, he will be there. Catching her. Or shoving her. Depending on what the situation calls for.

But dragging the mattress out under the stars isn't something she'd have expected, not in a million lifetimes.

"If I'd known this was what you were doing, I'd have worn

something different," she says.

She lifts her arms to show off her newly finished outfit, having been returned to her from Nitar complete with pulls and hidden pockets and various sheaths.

"I don't know," he says. "I like it." It is an amazing piece of work, if not exactly designed for laying under the stars.

"Not to interrupt your proposed plan..." she says.

"But you're going to interrupt my proposed plan."

"Yeah. I'm having trouble with my wristblades," she says. "Watch."

Aviend adjusts the knives at her wrists, then flicks her palms to see if they work this time. The right one pops out, pointing right at Kyre. The left one doesn't. Last time, the left one worked and the right one didn't.

"Skist," she says. "Let's hope I get to stick with infiltration and not assassination, because it doesn't appear that I'd be very good at the latter."

"You won't have to kill anyone," he says. As if by saying it hard enough he can make it come true.

"But I can if I want to, right? I mean, if I happen to come upon a purple-eyed powermonger in a dark hallway, just him and me, you're not going to be mad at me if I try to take his last breath?"

"I can think of far better reasons to be mad at you," he says. "Besides, have you ever killed anyone? I mean, on purpose?"

"Not on purpose, no," she says. She pulls her jacket off, giving the act far more attention than it probably deserves. Even with two blades in the sleeves. She doesn't want to look at Kyre. They have so few secrets.

She lets the faulty blade mechanism keep her attention for as long as she can possibly let it. Hitting the button repeatedly. It still only works about half the time. Which wouldn't be a huge deal, except that the mirror cutters are magnetized. They only work if both of them work. All or none.

"Let me see," he says.

She holds out her wrists, grateful for his touch. Not just because he's good at fixing things, but because he's Kyre.

"I don't really want to go do this without you," she says.

"I know," he says.

"We always do this kind of thing together," she says. "What if Quenn and I can't communicate? What if everything goes cockwire? What if... argh. There are just so many what ifs." She's not one for nerves, usually. She's one for doing. This thing is weird and new and she hates it, every bit.

"It's a good plan," he says. "It's your plan."

"Our plan," she says. "But what if I screwed my part of it all up? What if it's terrible?"

"Your plans are never terrible. At least not when the rest of us get done fixing them. I mean, they start out a little..." He makes a hand gesture that essentially means slistovile shit.

"You're a horror," she says. "I don't even know why I put up with you."

"Honestly, me neither," he says. "Do you want to say more about that, not on purpose bit?"

She does and she doesn't. But mostly she doesn't. Kyre isn't the kind to pester her if she says no about something, because he knows she means it. So she'd better decide for sure whether she wants to say yes or no.

"No," she says. "Maybe someday. But I don't want to talk about it now."

"Then don't," he said. "Besides, I'm pretty sure we've scraped off enough well-healed scabs for one week. What do you say?"

"I say I agree," she says. And she does. "I also say I'd like to do something on my last night here that doesn't involve blades or deaths or secrets."

"Considering that's all your next week or so is looking to be filled with, I think that's a fine request," he says. "What's your pre-infiltration pleasure?"

"I was thinking…"

He glances up from the mechanisms he's working on. When he looks at her the way he's looking at her now, she swears the edges of her brain start buzzing. Loud enough that she can actually hear them. Which, of course, is impossible. Isn't it?

Although lots of things she believed to be impossible are not anymore. So who's to say. Maybe Kyre really does make her brain buzz.

"That sounds like a fine plan to me," she says. "After you fix my blades, please."

"Fixed," he says.

She laughs. "No, they're no–" But they are. She flicks her hands and both wrist blades pop out in perfect unison. She does it again and again. "Nice," she says.

"Good incentive," he says.

He dives down on the bed, grinning at her. "Come and join me in my bed upon the stars."

"Below the stars, you mean?" She stands over him, reaching down for his raised hands.

"Above, below. What's the difference?"

"Um… everything?"

"Not when we're talking about you and me and stars."

"Your logic is faulty," she says.

"How about this then: you are above me, like the stars. But I would like you below me, like… My analogy fell apart."

"Because you were going to call me a mattress?"

He wrinkles his nose. "Yeah."

"Good choice to stop there then," she says. "Your bed might be pretty, but it's not terribly private."

"Since when do you care about things like privacy?" he asks. "Remember that time we–"

"All right," she says, laughing. "Fair point. I didn't mean people, necessarily. I meant, you know. Whatever's up there, looking down."

He tugs her down, releasing one hand so she can twist to land next to him. She falls, laughing, into the openness of his arms.

"How many years do you think the stars have been watching humanity get naked and have sex and birth babies and kill each other over petty disagreements?" he asks.

"Well, that went dark fast."

"You always say that about me."

"It's not always a compliment, you know," she says. "You don't have to sound quite so smug."

"You love me. What other reason could I possibly need to own my smugness?"

"Did someone tell you that?"

"About thinking I'm right to be smug?"

"About thinking you're right that I love you."

"Yes," he says. "Some cute girl told a cute boy that forever ago. And a hundred and forever years later, I heard it through word of mouth."

"Whose mouth?" she asks.

He doesn't answer her. He kisses her instead.

And the stars, above or below or everywhere around them, shift and shine.

They've been over the plans and over the plans. Possibly too many times by now. Still, Aviend worries that they've missed something. She dreams of hidden doorways and Rillent's eyes and falling stars.

When she wakes, the stars have gone out above them.

"We missed something," is the first thing she says. Putting it into the air means it's true.

"We'll find it," Kyre says. "You've got this. We've got this." He's not awake yet, eyes still closed, one arm across her. This is when he's his most real, honest, opened-up self. If he says a thing while he's caught in the space between sleep and wake, she knows how tender it is. How not to poke at it, but to take it like the gift of an egg. Fragile and promising.

She believes in him and in the plan and in the team. Even if she doesn't believe in herself. It's not that she thinks she'll fail – although she knows that's a possibility for all of them. This doubt is the seed of something, something that she has to carry with her until it needs to be buried. As important as her knives or her brain or her–

She knows what it is that she's missed. Such a small thing. Almost the end of her. Of everything. She finds the pendant in the drawer. Runs the pieces around between her fingers.

"Let me," Kyre says. Awake now. But still soft. Still defenseless. Such a rare moment, and she closes her eyes and holds out the pendant.

He loops it around her neck. Tightens the clasp. They stand together, touching, a long time, saying nothing. And saying everything.

When they hear Quenn's footsteps in the hallway, they let each other go. The unwinding is slow and soft. Done with the opposite of need.

Their fingers stay together even as they come apart. Make the sign. It once meant the Night Clave. Now it means that still, but also something larger, deeper. The most important things never have names, because no words are big enough to hold them.

6. Enter and the Stars Shall Touch You

They set off for the kubric together first thing in the morning. Kyre had a sense of altered déjà vu. They'd done this not so long ago, he and Aviend. There was a third person now, but that wasn't what altered it.

Then he'd felt his stomach clench and roil with the thought of what was to come, but he'd thought it excitement or purpose. Now he knew it for what it was. A sense of losing himself, of losing his moral center.

You're the one who talked to the philethis. There are seventeen ways this could go, and all of them are yours.

He'd thought he'd known what it meant, but he hadn't. Not really. What it truly meant was not just that you owned all seventeen ways, but that you had to choose one that you could live with. The choice, after all, was the hard part. Someone telling you the answer was easy. To know all the options and choose the right one? That was your challenge.

Now he felt the right answer in his bones, in the movement of his feet across the moss, in the easy banter of Aviend and Quenn before him. He felt it in the cakes Thorme had tucked into his pockets at the last second, the roughhewn skin of Delgha's stained fingers as she'd pressed them to his cheeks this morning. The right decision was in everything he did and saw and thought of, and he let the lightness of it bring him to a smile, despite the worry in his chest.

Aviend glanced back at him, shifting her lips and lifting a brow. She touched her thumb to her cheek – it was stained green, all her fingers were – and the glint of her ring caught a filter of sun though the trees.

It was still early by the time they reached the far edge of what had once been Ovinale. Where once there had been roads, houses, shops and people. Now it was a smatter of graves so old and vast that the wolflilies had made a meadow of it.

You could see the top of the kubric from here. In the day, it seemed almost plain. Powerful and huge, but nothing like the ornate device it became at night. There was no movement around it, bird or beast. No sounds or shadow. But the air breathed itself of electricity, making Kyre's hairs lift from his skin. He felt as though the world had sucked all of the air inside it and was holding its breath, deciding whether to let it out.

At the top of this tiny mound; the well. Still standing. Still doing what it was made to do. And then some – he tucked his fingers into the spot between stones where Thorme had told him, feeling around for the latch. He felt it and popped it at the same moment, and a folded bit of synth fell into his palm.

Both Aviend and Quinn looked at him expectantly. He could sense their worry, although neither of them spoke aloud.

He pressed his fingers to the back of the message, watched the symbols swim into visibility. "All plans go," he read.

"That's it?" Aviend asked.

"That's it."

"That's good, right?" Quenn asked.

"That's good," he and Aviend said together. It was. It

didn't mean that things couldn't still go cockwire, but it was reassuring to know that they hadn't yet.

They sat with their backs to the well, breaking open Thorme's muffins. Eating slower than they needed to. Drawing out the inevitable.

"I was only here a few times," Quenn said, looking across the broken landscape. "Before, I mean. There was a sweet shop or a bakery or something near here. Vesi would cry for these little buns they made shaped like seskii."

"I remember those," Aviend said. "They would bring them to the hall sometimes, for the Aeon Priests. I never wanted to eat them. They had ears! And faces."

"My sister is a savage," Quenn said.

"I don't remember that place," Kyre said. He wanted to, closed his eyes and tried to pluck that detail out of his memory, but found he couldn't.

"They used to use so much powdered sugar that it puffed around in the street like snow," Aviend said. "There was always a crowd of kids gathered around it, sticking their tongues out."

And then it was there – the memory of sugar on his lips and tongue. Powder in his eyes. The dusting of it on his clothes. He'd never gone in, never seen the rabbit buns – his family didn't buy things that way – but he remembered the stillness of standing in the street, being coated in sweetness. It made him think of Rillent's trenchers now, that fine film of dust, and he pushed the image away.

He was tempted to suggest they go over the plan one last time, but he knew there was no need. It was as good as it was ever going to get, and if they failed, there would be no contingencies for them, or the world. Not this time. Not this world or the next.

His equipment check was: map in his pocket, monoblade at his hip, glowglobe, node against his neck, Aviend and Quenn and the others in his heart. Cyphers... he nearly forgot that he had cyphers for Aviend.

Kyre scooped the devices from his pack and held them out to her. A set of small clamps, a vial of liquid, and a small orange-and-black striped pill.

"Are you sure you're going to be all right with all of these?" he asked. Delgha had warned them again and again about the risks of loading yourself up with cyphers. In overly graphic detail. He felt a bit like he was handing her danger, all wrapped in a pretty package.

"I won't have them for long," she said as she placed them carefully into already full pockets. "If everything goes according to plan."

"They're coming," Quenn said.

From across the wolflilies came the ghosts, hued by the flowers. As if their feet were stained by their passage.

A few at first, and then, behind them, more.

"I guess they got the message," Kyre said.

"They're so solid," Quenn said. "I've never seen them like that."

There were so many of them. They had asked them to come, and they came. He didn't want to be up here on the hill when they arrived. It felt too much like Rillent, holding court.

"This is where we part ways," he said. He was aiming for light, teasing, but fell short of the mark.

"It's a good plan, Kyre," she said. She emphasized good, meaning: solid and strong. Also meaning: not evil. Her confidence, so much stronger than last night, bolstered him.

"It is," he agreed.

"It's going to be amazing there," she said. "I can't wait to hear all about other-me."

He took Aviend's fingers into his own, tightened around their cold tremble. "I'm sorry you can't go," he said, because he knew her enthusiasm for his own travel was a veneer over sadness. He would have given anything to go to Ovinale, the other Ovinale, with her, together.

"Maybe when this is all over," she said. "We can go back together and see our world as it should have been."

They both knew that wasn't true. If everything went according to plan, the barrier would seal forever after he came back. If it didn't, nothing mattered anyway.

"See you in the stars," she said.

He didn't look back as he made his way down the hill. The ghosts filled the grass, a wave of people – he knew they were people now – coming toward him. He pulled the transformation hood up around his face.

With some distance between them – he didn't know what was proper and so he guessed – he went down on his knees, pressing wolflilies and dirt to his skin. The petals were dew-damp and chilled, and he shivered as he lowered his head and closed his eyes.

"Mishda paal," he said.

He thought he could hear them say it in return.

There was no sensation of someone brushing his skin or of him moving through time or space. He didn't know the moment they touched him, or the moment he left the world he was kneeling in, but he knew the moment he arrived. He could smell sweetness in the air.

He opened his eyes and closed them just as quickly. And still, the view was engraved on his eyelids, bold and bright, and would not fade. Before him, a dead city, now resurrected.

When the flickers behind his eyelids faded, and he found he couldn't bear to not see, he opened his eyes. There, the town of Ovinale spread out before him. Unruptured. Unrazed. Houses still standing. The air was filled with impossible scents – the yeasty butterspread of rolls, the pure sun-warmed sweetness of flowers, somewhere a fire smoking meat. People walking toward him or away, on their way to places as mundane as the market or their home, as if everyday life was still happening here.

It *was* still happening here. It was as though he had been transported not to another place but to another time. A time that he had dreamed of as a child. He hadn't known until this very moment what he'd thought his own future would truly look like. But this, he thought, this was exactly what he'd dreamed of.

How was this possible, this place?

He forced his legs to move, to walk down the street, following the scent of sugar, the sound of children. Startled into action by everything he was seeing. He found himself stopping at random to take something in, often something he'd utterly forgotten. People who looked familiar, but not the same as the ones he'd known, went on with their business. Some acknowledged him, a nod or a tilt of a lip. But most acted as though he was just another stranger walking down a street in a city filled with other strangers walking down a street.

He looked at the time tracker Delgha had given him. He had some time; it would take Aviend and Quenn far longer to complete their mission than it would take him to finish his. He could afford to linger, if just for a few moments.

When he reached the little bakery on the corner, he stopped there, watching the clouds of sugar puff out the door.

He pulled down his disguise hood for a moment, then walked through it slow, letting the sugar settle on his lips and tongue like sweet snow.

They could come here and stay here, he thought. Breathing sugar. He and Aviend. He could go get her, before she entered Rillent's life again, and bring her here. They could live here in this space. This place. A life in the light. A life without Rillent.

But he thought of Delgha and Thorme. Of Quenn and Vesi and even Ollie. Of those they'd rescued and those they hadn't. He thought of her saying, "It's a good plan." And he knew what their lives would be if they gave up, if they left their world to the rot and ruin of Rillent. It would follow them here, he would follow them here. In person or in their minds, and so would the dark.

He would go to the kubric as planned and realign the controls. Of course he would. He checked the time tracker again and pulled up the disguise hood. Time to go.

In the end, he arrived at the wildness at the edge of town. This band of trees and rocks, of caves and hidden spaces, where he and Aviend had so often played, it was a part of him. As much as his hair and blood and bone. It was still wild here, more so now. The forest had taken back what was its own, and so had the tall grasses. He startled something dark and bounding, which in turn startled him as it skittered toward the woods.

There was no kubric in the field.

Of all the things he'd thought might happen when he came here, that was not one of them.

But even as he looked across the flat space, unable to find what he was seeking, he knew that couldn't be true. They'd seen the bridge in the star, from kubric to kubric. It had to be here.

It took him a long time to find what he was looking for. He might have missed it completely if not for the ring of wolflilies that grew around it. Their scent, without the underlayer of death to cloy it, was softer. Pure. Honey and spice, sweet and warm. It was, he realized, the same as he'd smelled in the tunnel the first time they went through it. It was so different as to have been nearly unrecognizable then.

Inside the purple ring, the very top of the kubric where it lay still buried in the soil. As children, they'd thought it so big, such a mystery. A few feet of swirled purple and grey, so different from an ordinary stone. Looking at it now, so small, so unassuming, he felt deeply what it meant to be an adult, looking back on the child that he'd been. When there was promise in everything and nothing you loved had been razed.

If only he could take it back, that choice. Seventeen ways and what had he chosen? "Show me," Rillent had said. "Show me where you saw the stone." And Kyre had. It wasn't his fault entirely; he wasn't going to put that weight on his shoulders. Rillent had come to Ovinale knowing the kubrics were there, knowing already what he wanted and how to get it. It wasn't his fault, but it had been his doing. "I'll help you dig it up," and Kyre felt like he'd been carrying that shovel, that metal weight, since that moment. He was ready to put it down, even if that meant picking up something else in its stead.

How was this possible? This place? He knew. It was possible because in this world, Kyre had never picked up that shovel.

It almost meant that there was no way to do what he needed. The unearthed kubric had been part of their lives so long they hadn't even thought that it might not be so.

The map he carried in his pocket, detailed in Quenn's careful handwriting, utterly useless. The whole plan. Here and there. Ended.

He fell down to his knees, all at once cowed by the futility of it. The weight of too many failures. A blue and white spider strung itself from a wolflily petal to one of the points of the kubric. It made fast work of it, weaving a trap while Kyre watched, bowed by his own heartbreak. Barely a moment later, a bright yellow moth fluttered into the invisible threads. It fought frantically, nearly brilliantly, a carefully controlled escape plan that got everything unstuck bit by bit. The moth lifted, opened its wings for a grand escape, and caught the edge of its wing in another thread. That single wing edge was enough. A streak of blue and white, a quick turn of threads, and it was over.

It wasn't until the moth was wrapped and the spider back to work making repairs that Kyre broke apart. It wasn't the death or even the futility. It was the careful planning, the intelligent and cautious near-escape – all undone by a single, hidden strand. He bent his head to his knee, his hands fisted down to the soil. The sound that came from him was a growl, a thing he hadn't known he owned until this moment. He buried it in the back of his hand, and then when that wasn't enough, in the fabric over his leg. The tendons in his neck were pulled tight enough that he could feel them straining against the leather wrapped there. He wanted to pull the collar off, tear it to bits and throw it to the ground. But he still thought that he might need it someday. Sooner than later, perhaps, and he would bear its pressure until that moment came.

From behind, he heard a clatter of stones and footsteps. He wiped his face, the roughness of his sleeve hopefully scrubbing away at least some layers of dirt and wet and past. Rising, he turned to see a group of children engaged in a game that seemed to involve one child throwing a stone at a tree while the others ran in front of said tree. He couldn't tell if the goal was to hit the runners, or not hit them. Based on the number of "ows" rising from the tree space, either the thrower had very bad aim or it was the former.

A girl broke herself away from the group and came toward him. Her smile was curious and instant, her eyes a deep brown flecked with gold. She wore a green-and-white striped mourning ribbon wrapped twice around her wrist.

"Oh," she said when she got closer. She was looking at him with curiosity, but not fear. He saw she wore a pair of tiny black circles in her ears. "It's all right to still be sad. I'm sad about him too."

The moment choked him like a thread. Unseen and uncertain. He wanted to ask who *him* was, but couldn't find a way to prepare himself for any of the possible answers. It was a question he did not ask, not even to himself, because even the smallest inkling of a possible answer was too ragged around the edges to hold on to.

The girl saved him from having to make a response. "What is that?" she asked.

He looked over his shoulder at the tip of the kubric. It shone and shifted, purpled and black. It's the end of the world, he thought. Of the worlds.

"Nothing," he said.

He could see she didn't believe him. She bit the side of her lip and cocked her head as if waiting for him to tell her something closer to the truth.

When he didn't, she said, "It's part of the numer... numenera, isn't it? The one we shouldn't have dug to."

He let those words sink through his brain for a breath and then into his bones for two more. *Dug to.* Were there tunnels here, after all? Could he find them in time?

"Do you know where Celedan Hall is?" he asked.

She continued to look at him sideways, tightening up her eyes. "Everyone knows that," she said, and her words filled him with relief. "How come you don't e-member how to get there? Is it the grief?" The words came out of her mouth with such soft, adult sincerity – *the gweef* – that he nearly fell. He could feel one knee buckle, then the other. Threatening to topple him. Like dispatching, he thought, only with your heart, and he managed to stay upright.

He couldn't lie to her, but he was glad he still wore the disguise hood, could hide his emotions behind the fabric. "Yes," he said. "It is the grief."

The girl – "You can call me Niev" – took his hand as softly as anyone had ever taken it, leaving him no choice but to let her lest he break both their hearts by pulling away, and led him across the space as if he were not grieving, but blind, pointing out places he might fall or where the field floor changed to dirt and stone. "Those are the baddest boys," she told him as they passed the group of children he'd watched earlier, without even thinking about lowering her voice. "And that's the school where we learn stuff. I'm better at learning than the others, but I'm not supposed to say so. Nana says it's not nice to make people feel bad."

And then they were at the front door of the hall. He had forgotten how big the building was, how sturdy the structure. When a thing falls and crumbles to dust and lays fallow for longer than your memory can rebuild it, you start to think it must have been flimsy and small to begin with. But now, there it is, the thick moss-grown walls that he'd once carved his and Aviend's names in as a child.

Niev took two steps and stopped when their arms grew

taut between them. In the sunlight, her hair took on a softly copper hue. "Well? Aren't we going in?"

Was another Nuvinae in there? Another Aviend? Another himself? A Rillent? All of these things were possible. Probable even.

"Well?" she said again.

Well, indeed.

He got moving, not at all surprised to feel her move with him, still hand in hand.

The woman just inside the door was as regal as she'd ever been, if a bit stooped from time and age.

He knew her.

But of course, he didn't. Not this Nuvinae. Not this Arch. Her long hair was wrapped high, pulled off her forehead, the blue-grey of the gloaming. She too wore a green-and-white striped ribbon around her wrist.

"Well done, Denieva," she said to the girl, whose smile inched up toward her ears at the praise. "Come in," she said. "I don't imagine you have very much time."

If having a dead woman welcome him into a demolished hall in a razed town was not surreal enough, then seeing Aviend – not really Aviend – standing at the back of the clave's hall, robed in the blues and greys of Ovinale's Aeon Priests, certainly was. But it was fine, it was all right. Until his hand was empty and the footsteps in front of him were running toward those robes saying, "Look who I brought, Mama."

"I see," she said. And when she lifted her gaze from the girl to Kyre and smiled, it was her. Exactly her. It wasn't love he saw there, but an ache so deep he didn't think anyone had ever had words for such a thing. Even through the disguise, she saw him, knew him. She made a gesture, thumb to cheek, and a glance at the girl. *Keep your disguise on. For her.*

He knew then, who they were grieving the loss of. And he cupped his palms to his opposite elbows and learned how hard it was to say *coruscates* with so many tears at the back of his tongue.

"We're glad you're here," Aviend-not-Aviend said. "Let's get you where you need to go."

When hunting a monster, use live bait. For most monsters, Aviend supposes that live bait would be more akin to a goat or a yol. Tied up somewhere, bleating its fool head off, alerting every meat-craving creature for miles around of its whereabouts.

For this monster, the live bait is her.

Rillent had always been too sure of himself, too sure of his hold on her. His belief in his own power had always been bigger than any truth she could have told him. She will not mislead him. Much. But she will hope that all of the things she knew about him then are still true, and tenfold so.

Aviend pulls her hood up, tucking her hair back into the fabric and tightening it around her face. Everything she is wearing is hued a blue-grey-black color that sucks in light and reflects nothing back. It has no name that she knows of. It's her favorite color. She thinks at the end of this, perhaps she will name it, once and for all.

She has her blades buried against the front of each wrist. The sheaths are embedded in her very skin, a heavy and welcome heft. Metal and mesh that Delgha promised she would be able to extract once this is all done. It's a risky setup, because it leaves her no out should she need to change tactics. But it's also, she believes, necessary. She needs to act like she's walking in there with one plan, and enact another.

Kyre should be here with her. She understands why he's not, why he can't be, and there's a part of her that's grateful he's not about to re-enter the kubric, not even with her at his side. But there's a part that feels his missing weight like a hollow in her lungs.

It's Quenn's job to help everyone get out. She knows "everyone" is too lofty of a goal, but she refuses to say anything else in her mind. So everyone it is. It's her job to turn the lever and then create the distraction.

First, they have to get in without getting caught.

This thick metal wall, half dug from the earth, is that way in. Or will be soon enough.

"Ready?" she says to Quenn.

She feels him nod beside her. His breath is nervous. She wants to ease it for him, but this he needs to do himself. Her saying something is a temporary salve. It would come back to bite them when her words wear off.

Aviend can feel the cyphers in her pockets starting to interact, bouncing off each other. Nothing serious. Not yet, but cyphers are fickle creatures. They won't take long to do something stupid.

She finds the small canister in her back pocket. Metal death, Delgha calls it.

Let's hope so, she thinks as she presses down. Foam shoots out in a sudden stream, strong enough to nearly splatter back on her. She leans back, tries again. Softer. The foam covers the metal wall, spreads. If she doesn't get it just right, it won't transform a big enough space for them to get inside. If it's too big, it won't fully transform the material. That's the hard part about cyphers; it's not like you can practice with them. One and done, as Delgha always reminds them.

When the last of the foam sputters out of the can, she steps back.

"How do we know when it's ready?" Quenn asks.

She taps the once-metal with her gloved fist. Nothing happens, other than a dull thud of materials coming together.

"It's not ready," she says. After a moment, "All right, you try."

Quenn follows suit, rapping his bare knuckles lightly against the metal. If there's a thud of materials connecting, it's drowned out by the sound of metal cracking every which way, long runners that spread through the material as if it were ice or glass. She gives the center a poke, and the pieces splinter and rain down around their feet. There's a hole in the middle of the metal, big enough for them to crawl through.

"Now it's ready," she says.

Aviend goes first. She made the hole as smooth as she could, but the foam spread in jags and jigs, and there are points sharp enough to scrape off the skin. Inside, it's darker than dark, made more so by the hole that's filled with light. It smells like death and metal. Decayed yet clean.

Aviend hands Quenn the vial. Two cyphers down. "Catseyes," she said. "You'll need it in the dark. Step out of the light and drink up."

He does so without question. This trust is something Aviend has come to terms with. Quenn isn't blind-following. Even with Rillent he wasn't. And he certainly isn't with her. He tells her when she's wrong, or when she's asking something he doesn't want to do. He trusts her because she's earned it. Because she will try to keep earning it.

He's going to be their eyes.

She can hear the crinkle as Quenn pulls the map out of

his pocket. He doesn't need it – he built it, after all – but she thinks its feel is reassuring to him. The way the weight of the pendant around her neck is reassuring to her.

"This is the blast conduit," he says. "We're right where we should be."

They move forward. She wants to put her hand out, feel the wall that she knows is pressing close, touch the ceiling that is only over her head because she's crouching. But she knows already that the walls would burn her flesh, not with heat, but with chemicals, and so she keeps her hands in her pockets and crouches low and trusts Quenn in return.

"First trap," he says a moment later.

He slides back to let her through and she crouches down lower. These are the traps Rillent has placed in all the conduits. Trying to keep his people in. They're aimed the other way, which is the only thing that's making this break-in possible.

It's a good trap. She marvels at Kyre's handiwork even as she begins to dismantle the hateful thing by feel. If he hadn't walked her through the breakdown step-by-step, she would just be hammering at the thing. But she thinks of his hands, showing her how to perform the motions, and she mimics them. Smooth. Soon, they're pieces of a dangerous thing going into her pack.

When she's done, she and Quenn switch places. Stay crouched there until, from far away, they hear two chimes.

Onward until Quenn says, "Second trap." And again until he says, "Third." By the time they finish the fourth and last trap, her bag is tugging on her shoulders, sending an ache through her hips.

"Kyre did say getting in would be the easy part," she says. There's already a tiredness in her voice that she wants to pretend she can't hear.

The end of the tunnel is a big box. The sudden stretch of space makes her feel off balance. There's enough light here to see by. Three entryways. Not the same as the ones in the star, but close enough. Triangle. Tall box. Low box.

She lets the pack slide down off her shoulders and hands it to Quenn. He hoists it onto his back, letting the pieces inside settle.

Aviend points to the triangle, and they move that way side-by-side. Now that there's room and light, she casts a glance at him. Makes sure he's all right. He seems to be. Moving, having a focus. Quenn's good in those spaces.

They step into the triangle and through it, as though it were no more than a projection. It isn't, but close enough. An illusion, designed to create a sense of barrier where there is none. The ground slipslides under their feet. Aviend's stomach drops and rises. She has the sensation that everything's sinking away beneath her.

With a soft thud and a shudder, they're in a common hall. Not as common as some of the others that Quenn proposed. But still too well-used for her liking. There's a benefit to Rillent's need for control, though, and that's his need for even people to have a schedule. The chimes go off every two hours, Quenn had said. No more, no less. And that's when everyone comes through.

Aviend lifts the small tool in her hand. It bores through the metal mirror in a matter of moments. No light or heat. Just a quick circle and the middle of the mirror falls out. She catches it with a magnet glove. Pulls it toward her. The plate is heavier than they'd anticipated, the magnets in the gloves less strong against the pull. It sways, threatens to drop. Quenn reaches a hand out, steadies it. It doesn't fall. In a moment, he takes it from her. The gloves demagnetize automatically.

"You go first," he says. "I'll set the plate back up behind us."

She slides in. Slithers. It reminds her of snakes she's seen between stones. Except that snakes are not all feet and boots at the far end. They don't get their pantleg hem stuck like she does now. She tugs. The sound of her pantleg ripping is the sound of exhaustion and lack of care, and she knows it as soon as she hears it.

"Watch the bolt on the right," she says. "It's catchy."

He comes through, settles the circle back into the wall. The walls on this side are lined with reflective material too. She can see herself, slightly warped and twisted. Quenn too. He looks thinner in the sendback.

"Something's not right," Quenn says. "This wall. This door."

He stands in one place and slowly spins around, as if trying to reorient himself after a fall. "I can't put my finger on it," he says. "But something's different."

"Different how?" she asks. She's memorized almost the entire floorplan based on Quenn's map. This seems exactly like he'd told her, what her mind has written down as being right.

"All of the doors and entries and everything are correct," he says. "But I feel like I'm standing sideways. Or upside down. Can you feel that?"

She can't. She says as much. "I don't understand what you're saying. But you'd better say it fast because we need to go."

"I think we're in the wrong spot," he says. "The triangle took us somewhere else."

"How?" she says. It's a silly question, and unnecessary, with a million answers. She's come to learn that doorways rarely go where they're supposed to. The how, or even why, doesn't matter. It's the what's next that does.

"Rillent must have had it changed."

Quenn's scrolling a finger over his map. The soft press of his finger. The nervous exhale. Too fast. It's no good telling him to calm, she doesn't think. It won't help. She holds her calming sounds silent on her tongue.

"I see us," he says. "We went up instead of down. We're right where we expected to be, but much higher."

"How far up?" She hears something in the walls. The click-click of a machine, maybe, off in the distance.

"Four levels."

Four levels higher than they expected. That puts them a level below Rillent's chambers. They were supposed to start on the lowest level – get Quenn off toward the trenches to prepare the rescuees – and then she would come up here alone. Skist and skist and skist.

"All right, we need to get you back down through the–"

"Hold," he says. A pause. "Someone's coming."

She hears it too but doesn't want to. "No," she says, her voice lowering with each word. "They can't be. Every two hours. Every two chimes. We're right on time."

"Right time. Wrong floor."

Here are footsteps. Hurried, little mouse footprints. *Click-click.* Not scary on their own. Except that they're coming this way, and someone seeing them, anyone seeing them, right now, is going to break the whole thing down.

They could go back through the triangle. But that would take them down to where they started again. Maybe. Probably.

"Backup plan," she says. Contingencies for contingencies. Although she hadn't planned on using these so soon. "We disguise up, go down through the inside. Walk right past them."

The disguises might not last long enough to get Quenn out. So there's that original plan scrapped. They'll have to come up with something else.

"Trenchers shouldn't really be up here," he says.

"Neither should we."

"Fair," he agrees.

"Uniforms first," she says. She twists the threads at the side of her outfit, turning it from the no-name color into something specific. Quenn does the same. Her breath catches. He looks so much like he did the night that they rescued him.

"I never thought I'd willingly put one of these on again," he says. "Or even anything that looked like it."

She lifts her head and the wall sends her reflection back at her. She sees herself so rarely. Still, this doesn't look like her.

The black trencher's uniform suits her poorly. Too big around the middle. Too short in the legs. Deliberately so. Perfectly so. It makes her look already like someone else.

The silver mortar powder on her shoulders seems too purposeful to be believed. Not random enough. She knows that's just because she can remember Nitar putting it on, attempting to spread it as if it were random and gained over time.

Her hair is pulled back so tight it changes the shape of her eyes.

No matter. It's going to get weirder before it goes back to normal.

Once again into her pocket of dwindling cyphers to find the visage changer. Quenn uses his as she's searching, and his cypher is already doing its work, transforming him into something very much less Quenn and very much more an old man.

He's looking at the map in his hand. She doesn't think he's

looked up into the mirror-plate yet.

She'd forgotten this was a needle. "Skist."

"Need me to…?"

Rather than answer, she jabs herself in the cheek with the injector. Plunges. Hisses swearwords under her breath in an order she's never used before. She might have even repeated one or two. She might have also said Delgha's name more than once, and not to thank her. She tries to keep her voice low, so no one can possibly hear her cursing.

Her right eye starts to twitch and water. Her face feels like someone's trying to shape it like clay. With a broadsword.

"Ready," she says, when she can feel her lips – someone else's lips – again. But it isn't true, and even the word knows it. It falls from the new shape of her mouth like a piece of forgotten bread.

She goes forward anyway, but refuses to look at her new face in the mirror. She is who she is, and her outside matters to her not in the slightest. She shapes her new body, created by the fit of clothes and the feel of her face, into the movement of someone beaten down by time and effort. Submissive and broken. It's not that hard to put herself there. She's been there. Different circumstances, but close enough for body empathy.

"Behind me," Quenn says. She starts to protest, and then settles back behind him. He's right, of course. It's not Rillent who's coming – she can tell by the footsteps – but she's more recognizable, even with her face out of whack. Plus, Quenn knows where he's going, and she doesn't. That's the worst time to try to lead.

The footsteps come closer. Or they move closer to them or both. There's the sense of impending collision, of every corner being the corner where they will turn it and run into their own discovery.

When it happens, Aviend has a shock of recognition – *I know her* – but she doesn't, not really. She does recognize the small, thinned out woman in gold and purple, though the hair has gone white and the face has more yearlines written on it than it once did. One of the other members of Ovinale's former clave. A friend of her mother, once. Sulb? Suila? She can't remember the woman's name, only her once-loud laughter, a sound that had filled the hall.

The woman carries a handled box with the seal of Ovinale on it. Surely an artifact of the clave's holdings, once. Now Rillent's.

Aviend feels a fierce anger rise in her. By what right, Rillent? By what right, this once-friend of her mother's? The woman's eyes swing toward the two of them as they approach, and in them, Aviend sees not loyalty. But obedience. Fear. Defeat. This woman – Sulab, it comes to her, suddenly – is not a believer in Rillent. She's trying to stay alive, as are they all. For so many years, though. Carrying Rillent's things. His plans. Aviend lets the weight of her heart stop her breath for a moment.

Should she tell Sulab? Reveal herself and their plans? Give her hope, and a chance to escape?

No. If only because doing so would put the woman at greater risk. If Rillent were to find out that she held their secret, he would certainly do her harm.

As they near to pass, Aviend ducks her head. Outward deference. Inward hidden features. The woman inhales her breath, sending Aviend's heart fluttering to her throat, sure they've been recognized. She shifts the box – the sound was merely an exhale of the weight she carries – and they pass without so much as a word.

Quenn's eyes – even though they're not his eyes anymore under the disguise – say he thought they were caught out for sure. Hers likely say the same.

Silence ahead of them. Quenn motions with his fingers. A left-then-right jab and two fingers. Two more hallways and they will be out of this mess. They cross into the first one, then second, and then pause before the oval opening in the wall.

"Downshaft?" she whispers. When he nods, she holds out the invisibility cypher to him. Her original way out, long ago. Now his. The contingency for the contingency. Already being used.

He doesn't say no or try to talk her out of it. He pockets it with the deftness of someone who understands and adapts. It's one of the reasons she likes him.

They'll split here instead. She'll find the control room and flip the switch. Quenn will head to the trenches and get everyone ready. Then, she'll distract. He'll rescue. It's not as good of a plan as the original, but it will do.

"Stars guide you," he says.

"Guide us all."

Everything was the same, except that it definitely wasn't. It didn't take long before he no longer thought of Aviend as his-world Aviend and before he no longer thought of Nuvinae as something aged and undead.

Niev, on the other hand, that was tougher. Her mother's eyes. Her grandmother's softly regal bearing. He didn't see anything of himself in there. But he chose not to look too hard. Was seeing himself or not seeing himself the worse of those answers? Neither seemed good, and so he was thankful that everything was moving quickly enough that he didn't have to try to process any of that. Not yet.

He thought he had everything in hand, mostly, until Niev said, "Oh, and you have to meet Fall," and there was the varjellen coming through the hall draped in the same cloth as the others. The same green-and-white ribbon. Fear and confusion mingled, twisted, made Kyre want to punch or run or both.

"Iadace," the varjellen said, ducking its head slightly, the magenta and violet crest shivering in the movement.

"Fall lets me help him fix the numenera," Niev said in a low voice. "But don't tell. 'Cause he's not supposed to."

The varjellen cleared its throat, and Kyre saw the glance

between the three other adults in the room. Whatever secrets the girl thought she was keeping, it was clear that she wasn't.

But that wasn't what held his attention. It was Faleineir. Fall, Niev had said. Kyre kept searching those yellow eyes for ire or anger. For hidden ruthlessness. He found none. What had Rillent done?

"I assume you have a plan," Nuvinae said to him. "You usually do."

"You were expecting me?"

"It seemed like a possibility. Even before we got your message."

"I'm surprised the Arch on your side didn't see that as well," here-Aviend said.

He didn't reply, but she reacted as though he did. "Oh," she said. "May she walk." Hands to elbows. A soft nod.

"We should go," Nuvinae said. Ever the leader, even though she must have known, too, what he was saying. Her own demise, elsewhere.

Then it was the four of them walking back across the field that he'd just left. Such peace. Such beauty. There was no Rillent in this world, at least no Rillent who had come to Ovinale. And there was, currently, although he could not bear to ask for details, no Kyre. Other than himself.

But there *was* a tunnel. That was the important part. Even this world's Kyre had been unable to resist the draw of the kubrics.

Nuvinae filled him in on the way to the tunnel's entrance. He was glad it was her telling him the story. He didn't know if he could stand to hear this story coming from Aviend's mouth, to look at her eyes while she told it.

"We've known for a while that someone was doing

something with the kubrics' energies," Nuvinae said. "They would flicker on and off, or hum. Sometimes you would hear people talking. One voice in particular. Orating almost, near nightfall."

"The ghosts?" Kyre said.

She shook her head. "We've always had ghosts. As I'm sure you have too."

He'd wondered if they would have ghosts too. As the barrier thinned, it thinned from both directions. He nodded, thinking about his longlost friends from childhood. They'd turned out to be humans after all. Not friends, necessarily, but allies at least. Distant ones.

"This was different. Bigger, brighter. Of course, we assumed it was someone here using the kubrics. Because, well, why would we assume otherwise?"

Nuvinae laughed then, a sound of rue and hindsight mingled into knowledge. "Even when Delgha and Lyeg..." A pause, asking if he knew of whom she spoke, and when he nodded, she went on. "...created a device that let us detect that the tampering was coming from... somewhere else. I'm not sure I believed it for the longest time. It was clear they were using some kind of bridge. A conduit that reached through the barriers. We didn't tie it all together with the ghosts until, well, until your message."

He could hear Aviend and Niev walking behind them. The girl spoke softly to her mother, a voice that was becoming familiar enough to take root in his heart and slowly spread.

"I know very well who was... tampering. Do you know a man named Rillent?"

She thought for a moment and shook her head no. The whole gesture seemed so alien to him. To have to contemplate whether she'd ever heard of the man. The man who killed her. The man who Kyre thought about every day. "Another Aeon Priest, who came here years back?"

"I don't think so."

"So it's one of our own who's doing this?"

Kyre nodded.

"And you know enough about the kubrics to know what he's capable of if his plans succeed?"

He wondered if they could have learned more, faster, if they'd still had Nuvinae in their world. If they could have studied the kubrics safely without Rillent involved. "We do now." He paused to think about what he wanted to tell her. "We're not the only ones in danger now."

She just nodded. He wasn't surprised she'd known.

"We halted the digging and closed up the tunnels as soon as we realized what power they held," Arch Nuvinae said. "It seemed far riskier than what we might have gotten from it."

She didn't mean to make him feel awkward or guilty, but there it was anyway. That return to the sense that he'd been the one to make this happen.

"No," Aviend said from behind him. Ghostfell, even this Aviend could read his mind. He didn't know where to put that. "You are the one who halted it."

He glanced back at this-Aviend, who was looking straight at him, her head canted to one side. She didn't have a half smile, but a full-on brilliant one. He wondered if that openness was the result of never having had Rillent in your head. What had this-Kyre been like, he wondered. Less closed off, maybe. More willing to say what he loved without fear of losing it? He hoped so.

Niev let go of her mother's hand and bowed down to pluck a wolflily and add it to her growing bouquet. The three of them watched her in silence.

"Heartblooms," Aviend said. "Do you have those in your... Stere?"

Heartblooms. Not wolflilies. Because there were no wolf dens, no mass dead, no need for a name that covered up destruction and decay. Here, a thing could hold hope and promise in its name. He wanted that for his world too.

"Not yet," he said.

They stopped along the woods, near where the boys had been playing. Rocks littered the ground, resting on newly bent leaves. This time, Niev was quiet, holding her mother's hand instead of his.

The metal door in the dirt was hidden beneath leaves and stones. Put there deliberately, then made to look like it wasn't. All the stones, he noticed, were larger than good throwing size. Whoever built this knew about the baddest boys and their game. He wondered if it was him, and thought it probably was.

A moment later, he had an answer.

"You'll need to open it," this-Aviend said. "It was made by... for you."

Kyre knelt in the dirt for the second time today. The fingerprint key – a small black square in the metal – opened for him without hesitation. He heard a sound, the small hiccup that comes at the back of the throat when you're not ready for it, and knew it was Aviend-not-Aviend.

"I'm sorry," he said, although he was not entirely sure what he was sorrier for. Being here, alive, or his other self being dead.

He knew he couldn't ask them to come with him. Not into the tunnel. Not into his world. So he declined their offer of help and entered the tunnel alone, a glowglobe that

Nuvinae had activated following behind him like a bobbing balloon. There were stairs down, and he took them, careful and slow, leaving the light of the world behind him with each new step.

Quenn was on his own now. Just like Kyre. Just like herself.

Aviend has no trouble finding the room she needs. That, at least, is exactly where both Kyre and Quenn said it should be. She sees no one, hears no one, and is inside the room so quickly that she senses a trap. But none springs.

The device is in the center of the room, as if it's the room's reason for being. She notices that Rillent stands in the center of spaces too. Neither of these things surprise her.

On the device is the orange stem. Of course it has to be that. She steps closer, arms at her sides. No. It's not the exact same. Brown instead of green. Shaped differently enough to be a sibling. Close enough that her feet cannot be charmed forward, close enough that her arm has no interest in rising.

Overcome your fear, she thinks.

And stands before the device, unmoving. She can't do it. She looks around for something to move it with. Thinks through the stuff in her pockets. Nothing. Nothing. Nothing. She can hear the time pass in the pulse of her heartbeats, the metronome of her breath. This thing, all of this, will crumble if she doesn't move.

What is it she's afraid of? It wasn't even painful to her. Kyre touched it and almost died, but Kyre's always been a better believer. Kyre is going to have to touch it again, she realizes. In another world. The lever he's going to find will be this lever and he's going to have to touch the thing that almost killed him and if she doesn't do this, it will be his life, wasted. All their lives wasted. She has to believe in the plan.

She checks Delgha's time tracker. She imagines Kyre doing the same, if he is where he needs to be. Timing is the important thing here. She won't have to wait long. Even with the mishaps, they timed her trip here almost perfectly. She watches the device cycle down to the moment.

The moment comes.

She closes her eyes and reaches for the stem. Closes her fingers around it. Nothing happens and everything happens. This is going to work. She knows it with every heartbeat, every thump of pulse and breath. Blind, she navigates the stem, turns its purpose upside down. When she's done, and she knows it's right and true, she drops her hand away and opens her eyes. That's it. It's done.

Aviend flips the switch on her clothing – sending it back to the hidden, blue-black… crescent, she thinks, that's what this color should be called.

Now all she has to do is get to–

Two steps toward the door and a crested shadow slides into it. A moment later, the sound of fabric whooshing and then a creature stands before her, calmly folding a camouflage cloak. Where the creature's hands would be gripping the fabric, there's only the appearance of air.

"I wouldn't make that smiling face just yet, if I were you. Which of course, I am not, and glad enough for it. You look like you ghostfell ages ago and no one told you, Aviend."

"Hello, Faleineir," she says.

There's no way out of this room, other than the door he's

blocking. She stands, trembling, like a frightened bippot, outside its shell. How did it see her through her disguise, she wonders. Varjellen eyesight, maybe, but she doesn't think so. Did someone tip them off? Is Rillent already in Quenn's mind somehow? Skist, she wishes she had an answer to just one of the questions working through her brain right now.

"I'd like to say I'm surprised, finding you here," the varjellen says. It always did like to hold court – it's a place that Rillent makes for it, when Rillent's too busy or bored to do it himself – and she can see that it's leaned into it, this idea that it's usually the smartest creature in the room. "But it seems like you just can't stay away."

"You're right," she says. She reaches up and rubs the corner of her cheek, dispersing the disguise cypher. Her face returns to its normal arrangement so quickly it makes her stomach swoop. She pulls back her hood too, releases the trapped hair so that it springs around her face. "I've come for Rillent."

"Again?" Faleineir's tone says it knows that's not true. That not in one hundred years will it believe that to be true. She holds her tongue, lets the varjellen think what it wants. She won't try to convince it.

In the space of the silence, Faleineir calmly folds the camouflage cloak and tucks it into a pocket of the armor it wears. Where the fabric sticks out, it makes a hollow like a triangular wound. Everywhere else, the armor is a pale yellow, the color of shining bone. The click of Faleineir's tongue in its mouth is the sound of a dry husk crunching underfoot. "And here I thought you'd come to ask for a job. Or at the very least, to grovel and beg for forgiveness for that horrible stunt you and your clave–" So much sarcasm in that word she can almost taste it. It tastes like anger and blue-black moss and the shell of a gone-bad egg. "–pulled, trying to kill the only man who's ever loved you."

The idea that Rillent loves her, loves anything beyond himself, nearly makes her laugh out loud. Still, the words hit as they were intended, a turn in her stomach at the reminder that she'd once believed such things to be true. It's a soft turn, to be sure, little more than a cringe in her gut, but she thinks she sees a flicker of satisfaction in Faleineir's yellow eyes.

She takes a breath into the space of her chest, unmoving for the moment, to steady before she speaks.

"There was a time I would have fallen for that," she says. "But that day is long past. Surely, this isn't news to you, Faleineir. Nor to Rillent."

"No."

It's rare of Faleineir to be so short-tongued. She thinks there might be more forthcoming, as the varjellen seems to hesitate over the end of the word. But there's nothing else to fill the silence, other than the eternal sound of the machines around them, humming, humming.

She wishes, just for a moment, she'd managed to sidestep him. That she'd been a little faster, a little less obvious, a little more invisible. But clearly that's not how this was supposed to go, and so she steps into what she's been given.

"If you are here to stop me, it's probably time to get on with it," she says.

"Stop you? Not I." Faleineir doesn't laugh or smile, but it makes a sound, like nails on metal, that passes as such. "I'm quite sure that Arch Rillent will be delighted to see you, up close and in person. I hear it's been ever so long since the two of you had a proper chat.

"Well," its voice is sly in a way that its face can't ever reach. "Not *that* long."

She thinks *purpled* before she can stop herself. Rillent in her head. Opening her like a doorway.

She shakes the thought away. Faleineir steps closer, probably at the obvious distress. A spider to its grasshopper. A snake to its mouse. A slistovile to its glaive. She refuses to back away, although every instinct says go. Run. Flee.

She can't. Not now. Not this time.

Faleineir gestures ceilingward, toward the series of small black holes cut there. Each one has a glass plate across it, something behind it that beeps and moves. Through it, she can see, impossibly, a figure. Cloaked in purple and gold, staring across the expanse at them. Watching them. She's surprised to see Rillent alone. No guards. But no Quenn either. Which means he doesn't have him. If he did, he would want to show off his prize. Force her to see it.

Rillent is good at hiding his hand. Unless he already thinks he's won. And then he wants nothing more than to plunk his card down on the table and crow. Impatience is a virtue, she thinks. His impatience. Her virtue.

She just has to let him keep thinking he's winning.

The varjellen cants its head as if listening, then turns yellow eyes back to her.

"Arch Rillent says he would like you to kneel, here, in his hold, in the detritus of your broken home, so that you might more clearly see everything you've already lost. Or could lose again."

She will not kneel. She will never kneel.

Inside her pocket, her fingers pop her last cypher. Through the fabric and the skin. She can feel it whoop through her blood. Instant. Rush.

Faleineir's pre-attack shift gives away its intention. It's purposeful. It wants her to fight. Well, then.

The wrist blades are not for Faleineir. Those are her last

resort, should everything go terribly wrong. So she reaches for the obvious blade at the back of her waist. She's better with hand-to-hand than she used to be. She needs to be careful.

When Faleineir reaches for her wrist, she thinks she's ready for it. But the varjellen's reforge is good, and it's so much stronger than she expected. Varjellen can alter their physiology to better deal with the situation at hand, but they have to take some time to do it. So Faleineir was prepared for this fight. Expected it. Its grip is so tight it holds her blade inside her own grip. She tries to let the weapon fall, but can't open her fist far enough. One finger twists over the other, a knot of her skin and bones.

A single twist of the varjellen's arm – a sear of pain and the grinding of bones inside her wrist – and Aviend finds herself kneeling after all. She still has her weapon in her hand, her hand that's quickly losing feeling. Time's running out. She has to...

She kicks out her leg sideways, a movement that does something strange inside her knee. The varjellen hisses. Shifts. She takes advantage and sends her blade clattering across the floor. Not too far. Still within reach.

Faleineir looks at it as it goes, a long moment. The varjellen is smart. She knows it is. She jabs out with her elbow. Gets Faleineir's attention back on her. The hit lands on the sinewy length of its leg. Not much impact but at least the blade lies forgotten. For now.

"Up," Faleineir says.

She tries to rise, a movement that is thwarted by a stab of pain riding up through her arm and into her shoulder. Faleineir is holding her down even as it's telling her to rise. If Kyre were here, he'd have something to say about that.

She says it to herself, in Kyre's voice. Gives herself one small moment to pretend that he's at her side and that all of this is all right.

Then the varjellen is talking and wrenching. "I said to get up."

At this moment, Aviend is made for pain. She inhales it through her teeth, spits it out through her fingers. The cypher is doing its duty, and she can take it all. She will take it all. Keep coming, she thinks to the creature with its fists in her face. Watch, she thinks to Rillent. Keep coming. Don't look at the blade. Don't look at what's happening in the trenches. Don't look anywhere but my face. Keep coming.

She watches, as if from a distance, Faleineir enjoying this. She wishes she could tell it that she's hardly feeling it, that it isn't affecting her. But she will not show her hand for such small pleasure.

Despite everything that rises within her, she resists the impulse to fight. That is a game she can not win. She might be able to best Faleineir in the physical fight – might – but even with that, the varjellen will still win. For every time it gives pain, it gains pleasure. She will not give it that. Not willingly.

So she calms. Looses her muscles inside Faleineir's grip. Bows her head so that she can see the floor of this room beneath her knees and the pointed toes of Faleineir's leather boots. She wants to look away, but she will not close her eyes. This, here, is what they fight for. Their home. Their lives. Taken from them. She will not look away. She will not cry out. She will let it come.

They stay that way, silent, a long time. So long that her hitched breathing softens in his chest. So long that she begins to feel something other than the dulled pains in her arm and shoulder. The grooves of the floor pressing into the flat of her knees. The ache between her shoulder blades. The itch of the mesh inside her wrists.

"Of course..." the varjellen says. She realizes it's talking not to her, but to the Rillent inside its head. How's it feel in there, she wonders. Are you happy he's in there? Sad? Does he make you feel special? Not that she can care much right now. Her wonder is a bug-like thing, tiny and crawling, hard to hold on to. There are more pressing things. Her body losing focus, growing slippery. It's not just the cypher. She can feel blood on her teeth. Something ringing in her right ear.

She starts to look up, but finds her head forced back down by a single touch. "Stay," the varjellen says from far away. "Rillent has asked me not to kill you. Yet."

"Why?" she can't help but ask. Her tongue is big. When this stim wears off, she's going to hurt for a hundred days. Thankfully, it's got a long way to go.

"Because he thinks he might be able to find a use for you. Again. Not that you haven't already done enough to help our... cause..." Even without looking up, she can tell the varjellen is smiling. A human affectation it's clearly picked up after all this time. The pleasure in its voice for its words is so palpable, she can practically smell it. It makes her want to retch. "You were instrumental in all of this destruction, after all. All those deaths. So maybe we *should* keep you alive just to thank you for that. For all you've done for Rillent. For us."

"You know... that's not why," she says.

"No? What do you imagine the reason to be?" Faleineir says. There is anger in that voice. And... jealousy? Maybe.

She picks it apart, like the wound that she knows it is. Once, she thinks, Faleineir might have been saved. But Rillent's been in its head too long. He's eaten away at all that might have been right and true, and replaced it with darkness and hate. Not the varjellen's fault. "All that loyalty. All those years of service, and still, you're not first in Rillent's heart, are you? Are. You?" Her last words punctuated by what would be new pain, if she still felt pain.

There's a chance it might kill her. It's a small chance, but still there. She has to take it.

Faleineir's eyes are studying her. It's the most human the varjellen has ever looked. It touches something along its jawline, a flick of magenta fingers over the small bit of metal that rests there. Rillent's implant.

"Rillent says you may come and visit him now," Faleineir said. "So that he may thank you properly for your contribution.

"Stand." She doesn't have a choice, as she's pulled to her feet abruptly, a snatching, jerky movement so different from the smooth glide that had pulled her down that she has a hard time reconciling that it's from the same captor.

She looks up. Rillent is gone from the black glass. Or perhaps she just can't see him properly anymore. Her eyes are fuzzy, like she's wearing gauze across her face. She shakes her head, sending spatters. No, he's still there. Watching.

Good.

Whatever small kindness she might have seen in Faleineir's eyes is gone now. There is nothing but yellow hatred.

"Oh, and Kyre says hello," Faleineir says. "Well, not hello exactly. It's terribly hard to talk when one is almost dead, isn't it?"

Her heart goes flat inside her chest, deadens out. But no. They've made a mistake. They assumed she would come with Kyre, and they've made a mistake. If they had Quenn, if they knew about Quenn, they would have said so. Rillent never holds onto his trump card. Her heart thump-thumps back to life.

Everything's in motion. Everything's begun.

Aviend draws air in through her teeth, a burble of spit and blood. She lunges for her blade.

Faleineir seems to think she's finally, finally going to fight back. It grins, pleasure and teeth, and reaches for a weapon of its own.

She uses all her strength to lift her blade. Not toward the varjellen, but toward the sky. She slams it hard against the floor. The nodule on its length cracks like bone, splintering the blade, the floor, and, she is pretty sure, one of her actual bones. Her hand, even through the cypher's dulling, lights up with a pain that causes her to utter a sound that is somewhere between scream and cry.

The nodule releases with a crackle of electricity and char that reminds her of the destriatch. And well it should. Delgha built it from the same source. Except that Delgha is smarter than Rillent, and this works exactly as she made it to.

The creature that rises from the nodule is not crourhound. It is something else. Something new. Eight legs and teeth like motors, a mouth of blood and oil. Not solid. Not yet. It will not attack Faleineir, although she can see by the varjellen's face that it does not know this.

Faleineir reaches, as she'd hoped it would, for the alarm. The high-pitched sound rises and rises, blotting out every noise that ever was. She's almost grateful for the blood in her one ear, which brings the wail to nearly bearable.

The creature honed of metal and smoke walks by them both without a glance. It's not made for human flesh. Its mission is elsewhere. It seeks its brothers and sisters, their broken half to be made whole. She wishes it – and Quenn – ghostspeed.

Faleineir is staring after it, stunned into stillness.

This time, she doesn't run.

"Rillent," she says out loud as she looks up at the glass plates in the black holes. Mouths her words slowly so he can see. Gives him everything to look at in her face.

Rillent, she says in silence, as she opens up her mind to the man she's come for. Her headvoice is not sweet or soft. He would see through that. Her headvoice is strong and solid. It is her mother's voice. A leader's voice. Her voice, as she might have been. As she pretends to be now.

"Come and get me."

The kubric smelled the same. It felt the same, but it didn't *feel* the same. There was no tug toward it, no pull, no tangle through his memories. He didn't feel attached to the place. There was, he was grateful to admit, no emotion at least to this part of this world at all.

He had Quenn's map in his brain. Once he reoriented – entering from the west instead of the east, he could figure out where he needed to be.

Each step he took, however, he knew he'd taken before. Other-Kyre had taken before. "Me but not me," he whispered in the dim light the glowglobe shed. Was that comforting? He honestly didn't know how to feel about it. Particularly since other-Kyre was dead. If it had been someone else, he realized, he would have almost felt like he was intruding. This was another person's find. Another person's place. And it had been important to him, because he'd put that fingerprint lock at the entrance. But could he intrude into a place that had been... his?

And why was it so important? Kyre thought about how he would have reacted to the discovery of the kubrics under different circumstances. With no Rillent there, driven as he was, what would Kyre have done? What kind of man would he have become in such circumstances?

He imagined a quiet life. Studying the numenera, carefully and safely. No running about the woods being chased by glaives and hounds and all the rest. Not having the love of his life risk everything by putting herself into the hands of the worst person he had ever met. It was a nice thought, but it wasn't real. He might as well be standing in a dream world, but that didn't mean he could get caught up in dreams. Aviend – his Aviend – was in real danger. He had to finish what he'd come for and get back to her.

He turned a corner. No, wrong way. He turned back and went the other direction. Only then did he notice the change. The corridor he'd been moving down for the last few minutes had been clear and bare, so he hadn't noticed, but this new direction – the way he needed to go – had a dim quality. The walls and floors were grayer.

His finger came away with an oily residue when he ran it along the right wall. The other way had been cleaned. Other-Kyre must have scraped whatever this was away in the passages he used. Which meant he never went this way, or at least didn't do so frequently. But this was the way Kyre needed to go now. He was sure of it.

Was that good? Bad? He didn't know. He pressed further. Was the glowglobe dimmer here? No. Just his imagination.

When he became conscious that his steps had slowed to a creep, he stopped and literally shook himself. Timing was important here. He checked the time tracker. Three more cycles. He had to get in place. He hurried.

Quenn's directions led him to a closed door. Just a bit more than two cycles left. Why wouldn't it open? Skist.

He breathed. Calm down, he told himself. Other-him had never opened this door. It still had its original seal. He didn't have time for this. It was time for drastic measures. He pulled out the monoblade. Kyre had always imagined that he'd end up using this in a fight, probably with a destriatch or something equally horrible.

But no, he was going to use it to kill this door. The tube hummed when he activated the switch. There was no visible change, but when he brought it up toward the door, a slice appeared across its surface. A blade he couldn't see cut through it like a knife might cut through water. He hadn't even felt any resistance. He loved it, but there was no time to love. A few dramatic gestures later and there was a hole more than half his size in the middle of the door.

Less than two cycles. He squeezed through the hole, but kept the cypher active. Jagged metal edges of the crude hole tore his pantleg. As he watched, the tear grew dark red with his blood.

"Skist!"

Time to worry about that later. The room was simple enough. The controls he knew he had to look for were in the middle of the room, like a lectern. In the middle, a single brown stem. That had to be the one.

One cycle. He tossed the blade away. He didn't think about the warm trickle of blood running under his pantleg into his boots. He didn't think about the bad experience he'd had with a device far too much like this back in the temple. Instead, he just grabbed the control.

It was a little like playing a delicate instrument. It was simple and straightforward, but it was also complex, with a million – a billion? – different options. Just for a moment, he caught his breath and found himself swept away with the incredible power of the kubrics. They could do so much. He couldn't do it all from here, not all in this moment, but if he had time – a quiet, simple lifetime – he could have used them to work wonders.

But he didn't have that life, and for that matter neither did other-Kyre. Not now, anyway. Besides, the power here, it could change someone. It could drive you mad.

And he thought about that lock on the entrance. The one that he (other-he) had placed there. And it brought him back to the moment. Other-Kyre had known that no one should be using the kubrics. It was too much for anyone. And the last person – the very last person in the *world* – who should be using it was Rillent.

That thought drove him. It was all easy then. Turned it all backward. Everything that faced up, he turned down. Everything that was right was now left. At least that's how he visualized it. And then he was done.

He looked at the time tracker. He'd done his part. And he'd done it on time. Please, he begged no one in particular, please let Aviend be safe as she does her part. Then, and only then, did it occur to him that if everything had gone according to plan with Aviend and Quenn, he likely stood in the very spot that she did right now. Only a world away. The room that she saw was some kind of version of the one that he looked at right now. He held up his hand, wondering if he was somehow touching her. Wondering if there was a way to be a ghost there with her, or see her as a ghost with him. If he just relaxed a bit, he could perhaps fade back into her world – their world – and be by her side.

But no. No, no, no. That would ruin the entire plan. "It's a good plan, Kyre," she whispered in his head.

"Good luck, Vi," he whispered back.

He pulled up his pantleg to check the cut in his leg. It was bleeding but not deep. He'd been hurt worse. He glanced around, but didn't see the monoblade. He did, however, see a hole sliced through the floor where he'd tossed it. He stared at that a minute, and then shrugged. "What possible problem could that be?" he sighed. Well, he was confident that the blade's power would fade pretty fast. Pretty confident. He took the time to wrap his leg. It took longer to staunch the bleeding than he expected.

When he crawled back out of the room, he did so slowly and carefully this time. He didn't want to be inside the kubric when he crossed back over to his world. He needed to be outside, and well away from this whole area. That was an important part of the plan.

Getting home, he knew, would be a simple matter. He wasn't supposed to be here. It would probably be harder to stay than to go back. Even now he could feel a sort of tug in every bit of his body. Thin as the walls between the worlds were at this point, it would be fast.

Going outside meant one more look at this world that he could never have. And neither could the Kyre that belonged here. That made him feel the loss of... himself in a whole new way. He was about to close himself off from this beautiful place. This place that was everything he had always wanted the Stere to be. Neither of them could have it.

No one asked him to stay. And no one asked him not to go. In fact, no one was there at all when he came up from the tunnel back into the woods.

The only sign that someone else had been here was a single bouquet tied with a green-and-white striped ribbon. Heartblooms. Kyre left it where it sat, with just one longing look. He still had to hurry. There was more to do, and it all had to be done back on the other side.

A safe distance away from the kubric, in a spot of the

nearby woods that he recognized from his own world, he let out the breath he'd been holding. He forced himself to relax. It was easier than he had even thought. It wasn't a matter of traveling at all. Just a matter of letting go.

Rillent didn't come for Aviend, but his people did. And that, really, was her goal. Bait the trap. She doesn't think they have any idea that Quenn's here, or what he's doing. They were too busy chasing her, and the creature she'd let loose in the hallway. She needs a name for that creature too, she thinks. For all of these creatures that Delgha has made. They're not horror hounds, not destriatch. They carry too much of their maker, just as the destriatch carry too much of theirs.

She's in Rillent's room. Aviend doubts he will take long to show up, so she takes a moment to mentally sort through the situation. The room is lavishly furnished. The door is closed, but she doesn't believe it's locked. Still, she can hear voices on the other side.

So, not a prisoner then. Not yet. But not free either. She doesn't know what game this is. See if she'll try to escape and then delight in taking her down? Not his style, she doesn't think. More likely, it's a test of her loyalty. Leave it to Rillent to be self-centered enough to believe that after all of this, he still has some kind of hold over her.

Faleineir had searched her. It hadn't found the hidden blades, but it had taken everything else, as she'd expected.

The varjellen had taken the star pendant, without hesitation. Even now, it might already be in Rillent's hands.

The whole room is fabric and soft, ornate as she's come to expect from Rillent's taste. Purple curtains, woven in gold. A rug that her boots sink into, and dirty up. She's all right with this.

A little much, she thinks. Even for him. Anger flares up in her as she thinks of the rest of the people in the Stere, living in nothing. Less than nothing. Not that fabrics and pretty patterns would help them.

She sits on the overly plush chair. Sinks in. The fabric is soft as newborn yol wool. Her fingers touch it, and it feels like she imagines clouds might. It makes her feel weird and weightless. She stands up. Her instinct is to pace, but she halts it. Stands instead at the window. It's not really a window. The glass is too thick to see through, but it lets in light. She imagines what's out there. The Night Clave. The other kubrics. The star. Kyre.

The door swings open behind her. She turns her body and there is Rillent. Purples and golds. Aged in the years since she's seen him up close, but not as much as she might have expected. Or hoped.

On his forehead, the dappled device that started all of this. Rillent is not wearing the gold wrap over it, and she sees it clear for the first time. A star. Six-sided. She feels hope in her chest, a lightening of her bones.

The star glows softly. Rillent glows softly too. It's an odd visage, as if his skin has a subtle light beneath it. A power that generates its own visions. But it turns him ghostly too. More like the stumblers in the woods than a living thing.

He looks at her. Intent. Silent. His scrutiny is warm and welcoming.

For one breath, she feels as she did as a child. Wonder. Light. Special.

Exhale, and she sweeps those aside, as simple as wiping away a layer of dust.

She bows her head slightly, as much to hide her face for a moment as to show any kind of reverence. Waits for Rillent to make his opening move.

It doesn't take long.

He crosses the rug between them. His boots leave no marks that she can see.

"Have you come back to me, then?" Rillent asks.

"I was not yours before," she says evenly. Even in this, she can't agree to what he's asking. But she can't deny him either. It is a dance of small, careful steps.

"And what of your Kyre?" He whirls a bit, purposefully, so that the ends of his purpled cloak swing in a perfect arc. Still trying to show off for her, she thinks. After all this time.

"Do you practice that move?" she asks. "Or does pomp come naturally to those who would believe in nothing save their own power?"

He says nothing, as she expects. But his face changes. He gives up the illusion of care and kindness.

"I could just step in there and take everything," he says, with a wave of his hand.

"In there" means her mind, of course. That great expanse of space where Rillent could rule over her, once and for all.

"You could," she says. There is no challenge in her voice, only resignation. To challenge him would force his hand; he'd have to meet it, step in. Take over. She needs him to know that she believes he can. That she will not fight him, not because she believes in him, but because she is too exhausted, too beaten, to join him. Because where's the fun in that for him?

Rillent has never wanted the power he had to take. He wanted power given under the pretense of being given freely. By her mother. The Order of Truth. The Clave. Kyre. Quenn. Herself. Countless others.

So she gives him everything. Her acquiescence. Her demureness. Her tacit agreement. She hopes in doing so she will become boring. It's a stretch, and an unlikely one, but she sees it as her best bet.

"What are you doing here?" he asks. "Another attempt to assassinate me?"

Without taking his gaze from her, he pulls the pendant from his pocket. It's clear watching him that the device doesn't talk to him the way that it does her. His fingers can't seem to find the rhythm. They fuss with it, as one might fuss with a child they don't know what to do with. She looks at it for a long time, unwilling to drag her gaze away.

"Why do you think I'm here?" She inhales through her whole body and finds the muscles inside her skin. She makes herself at home. Sits on the wide white chair that is soft as Ollie's fur.

"Because you know I'm getting close. And you want to stop it. All in the guise of coming to me for help. Or... whatever this is."

Never let it be said that Rillent is not smart. He's always been a step ahead of her in the past. She chews her nail. Delgha painted her fingers and nails with some of her stains. They are bright green. A reminder of the Stere. Of Quenn's pendant. Of Kyre's eyes.

"So you remember where you come from and why you're doing this, even if he gets inside you," Delgha had said. "You just lift your fingers to your face and you remember the green of the forest. The green of those eyes of that wild man you love. And you remember."

It was the most human thing Delgha had ever said to her. She had cried. Bawled, truly. Giant gulping rusty tears that Delgha had wiped away with the roughest piece of fabric Aviend had ever felt.

No more tears now. Dry-eyed, she lifts her head.

"Come closer," she says. "And I'll tell you why I'm really here."

He's not stupid. He doesn't take her bait. She didn't expect him to.

Instead, she takes a step onto the thickness of the rug. Her boots leave muddy marks on the pale. He sees it as an attack, as she thought he would.

Instantly, his eyes enter the edges of her mind. Purpled. So strong, this close.

She resists him. Makes it seem hard, impossible. A true feat of mental strength. Gives him space at the edges, so that he can think he's getting a hold.

Little one, he says.

She reacts as though this means something to her. As though it matters. She has this. Looks at his purple eyes and thinks of green.

He shows her the Stere, different. Alive. The people as he'd promised. It's a beautiful thing. She wonders if this is what Kyre sees right now, in the other Stere, and then wipes it from her mind.

Maybe it is she, after all, who is the monster. Maybe Rillent is right to gather this power…

No. More manipulation. Another attack from Rillent, this one creeping along the edges of her brain like slow poison. Nearly invisible. Nearly getting in.

Skist.

She grits her teeth and turns her vision to something else. Her mother. The last time she saw her. Dressed in gold and white. She focuses in on the details. The swirl of the fabric as she moves. How it takes and leaves the light.

The light of the sun is hot and high–

No. Again, she turns back, grabs for the thread of her thought so that she may unweave it. Seeks her mother's face. Can't find it. It's been too long. She can't remember. Her mother's hands instead then. The one that grips the long blade. The other holding Aviend's hand. They are going to see the new clave member, and Aviend is afraid. She is scared, more than she's ever been scared before and she doesn't know why. She clings, pulls back. Her mother, ever torn between being a leader and a mother, falters but then continues on her path. Dragging her child toward fear.

She didn't love you.

But this is Rillent's mistake, trying that angle. Aviend bats it away as easy as batting away a falling leaf that brushes her face. Because of course her mother loved her. She does not doubt that. Never did. Never will.

A surge of hope rises through her. Rillent is fumbling now, trying anything. He has lost his way and she's going to–

Your mother loved me, though. Just as much as you.

Backstab while she was fending his forward blows and she momentarily hates herself for her overconfidence, her showing off. But it's right, because he comes back forceful. Digs in.

I must not tell him about the–

She is thinking what he wants her to think. She stops herself before she gets to the word, but not before the vision of it comes creeping into her brain. A flash of forest-not-forest, a globe, a star in the sky that could give him all the power he wants.

This is the moment where she tells Rillent everything.

The world – the worlds – kept knocking Kyre for a loop. The other world, the other people, superimposing themselves over this one. Somehow, the time he'd spent there was having some kind of lingering effects. He was neither wholly back nor wholly gone.

Getting to the other Stere had been easy. Instantaneous. Getting back stretched like a dream, pushing everything before him. He could see the base, as if through water, but it seemed unreachable, no matter how he strived. It was as though he walked through a hundred Steres, each one different from the last, shuttering past him so quickly he could barely sense. Sugar. Snow. Falling flowers. A child's laughter. Woods, silent. A burnt expanse. A place much like home.

As he drew near, it seemed as though the weird fluctuations he was experiencing were lessening considerably, but then he heard the strange noises. Noises that didn't slide through and disappear. Noises that stayed. Crashing. Clashing. Screeching.

But they weren't noises from the other worlds. They were very much noises of this one. It took him surprisingly long – too long – to recognize them.

He was home. And the base – the place their band had used all these years to hide and work – was already under attack.

She is following Rillent. Literally and figuratively. There is pain in that knowledge, in that admission of her choice. But it's done, and so she follows where he will.

Where he will go, of course, is to the base. And then to the temple. And then to the star. And there, he will destroy the barriers and suck all of the energy from that world to this one. He will become a god.

Because she has told him everything. About Gavani. About the starroom. About the star itself. The barrier. The bridges. Everything.

Each step is a reminder of a different thing she told him. She runs them through and through her mind. His eyes inside her. All the purple and purple and purple. She winces to think how he'd nearly left without her and she'd had to beg him to take her. Begged, like a child. Like the child she'd been when he'd first come to her.

"I can help you," she'd said. Because she could not stay behind.

He hadn't believed her about the temple at first. "That temple? That nothing-god? That nothing-religion? I dismissed that ages ago as nothing. Beneath nothing."

He'd probed, to find the truth, and she hadn't resisted him.

She conjured up image after image in her mind – the base and all of her friends. The temple. The pendant. The star and its strange, living interior. The device that activated the kubrics. How they'd tried to make it work and had been unable.

"The greatest treasure comes in the simplest package," he mused, apparently to himself. "I've searched for the master control for so long. One more kubric. One more ancient device... somewhere. But in the Gavani temple? But no. In a structure high above." He looked up. "Always right there, above me." He grew silent. Then, finally, he smiled. "And now I know."

After belief comes his anger, as if on cue. He hasn't changed. Not one bit. "But first," he snarls, "you should know that I will destroy all of your people. Your Kyre. Your *Night Clave*. And then I will take the last step on my long journey. So very long."

She doesn't doubt Rillent has sent Faleineir ahead with his glaives and the destriatch to do just that. Have they made it? She doesn't know. Can't ask. Rillent believes that she is broken.

She feels broken. Her pain is still receded, but she's exhausted beyond measure. Holding her chin off her chest is an effort she can barely make.

They close in on their once-hidden base, and night is already falling. She can feel her pulse come alive for the first time since they left the kubric. It beats fear. Fear. Fear in a harsh rhythm.

All around them, Rillent's glaives. Some torchlit faces she thinks she might have recognized once. So many she doesn't. All wearing Rillent's colors. His stance. His weapons and armor.

From behind her, the first wail of the destriatch. She

doesn't let it stop her steps, and she wonders when she'll start shivering. Or maybe she already is. It's impossible to tell what her body is doing. All she has left is her brain.

Rillent halts when he reaches the entrance, and she halts too. He holds his silver staff-like weapon casually. He clearly feels no fear.

Faleineir stands there, at the door. Vines ripped down. Star symbol for everyone to see.

"There's no one here," Faleineir says. Its voice says what its words don't: it could be a trap. "But we heard some strange noises in the nearby woods. We're going to go investigate."

She wishes she hated the varjellen, but she knows who Faleineir is. It is her. It is Kyre. It is Quenn. All of them, any of them, if they hadn't gotten out. Somewhere inside is the Faleineir it might have been if Rillent hadn't put his claws around the varjellen's neck.

Rillent glances back at her. She raises her face. The effort it takes. There's nothing left to resist. His eyes in her head. The star, she thinks. The star. The barriers. The bridges. The power. The power. The power.

"No, keep everyone here," he says, gripping the long weapon more tightly. "But stay alert." His impatience is telling. His desire for power is palpable. Aviend can taste it, bitter and dangerous. "We're going in."

"You lead," he says to Aviend. And, reluctantly, she does.

Released from the hold of the worlds, Kyre ran toward the sounds. He'd forgotten the pain in his leg and it caught him up, but only momentarily. His teeth ground each time his foot fell to the earth.

Through the trees Kyre saw two figures, both dressed in the garb of Rillent's glaives. One held a torch like a weapon, the other swinging a long axe at a gnarled bush. No, not a bush. A mound of decaying leaves and vines. No. A slistovile. Sil had done his work.

He pulled himself to a halt. Don't run, he thought. Don't scream.

But every instinct told him to do just that. Green leafy tendrils struck out at the glaive with the torch, and the creature opened a gigantic, horrific mouth filled with swamp sludge and teeth. The glaive screamed and ran.

Kyre didn't blame him one bit. The other glaive, clearly realizing she was alone in the dark, followed suit. The slistovile lumbered after them, but its awkward legs were meant for wading through muck, not running through the woods.

Kyre stayed where he was until he could see neither soldier nor monstrosity. But he could hear more fighting, and more screaming, all around him. Dammit. Rillent's glaives didn't deserve to die. He hoped he wasn't hearing them die.

His path now momentarily clear, he ran ahead, making his way toward the base. He came to a large clearing and saw more figures. Vesi stood on top of a broken tree stump with her own torch, shouting with surprising volume.

"These creatures won't harm you if you just surrender. Or leave. Leaving is fine too." She was taller than Kyre remembered. "You're following the words of a liar. Don't give him your life! He's not worth it. He's never been worth it."

Around her, Rillent's dark-garbed followers fled. Slistoviles, like animate piles of swamp filth, trundled after them. More frightening than murdering. Kyre saw Sil standing next to Vesi's stump. Did he really have this much control over the creatures? Kyre had thought he could just lure them.

No time. No time for this. He had to get up to the star.

Less afraid of the creatures, but still giving them a wide berth, he ran to Vesi.

"Aviend?" was all he could shout.

She paused in her shouts into the confused melee. She stared down at him from her perch, silently. Intently.

Only then did he realize he still had his disguise activated. A quick touch at his temple made it fade into a shimmer of reflecting facets.

"Kyre!" Vesi shouted.

"Aviend?" he asked again.

She shook her head. "I don't know."

He shot a glance at Sil, who casually motioned behind Kyre.

Kyre turned, and saw a lumbering mass of rotting vegetation swinging a viny tendril his way. He ducked, heart thumping up into his ears, and then sidestepped away, probably quicker than he needed to. They were just so ghosting *big*. Sil seemed to make some kind of gesture, and the slistovile ran back toward the now thoroughly routed ranks of glaives.

Kyre ran off, toward the base. The forest was a sea of confusion. Glaives running about in the near-darkness, some of them injured, all of them terrified. Frantically flickering torchlight. Slistoviles slavering and stumbling through the trees like drunken madmen looking for something to rend apart.

At the entrance, he saw Delgha and Thorme in the glow of a trio of glowglobes. They were surrounded – cornered, backs up against the door itself – by a snarling, crackling pack of destriatch. There must have been five of the things, but there might as well have been a hundred. Before he could stop himself, he reached down to where he had previously kept the monoblade on his belt. His hand swiped through nothing. Skist.

To his right, he saw another group of people. They weren't warriors. They were trenchers. Workers from the kubrics. Runners. He saw Stiler among them. They stared in fear at the destriatch at the entrance, but they didn't flee.

Next to them was a large, four-legged beast Kyre had never seen before. The way each foot connected to the ground, it seemed very solid. Sturdy. Dense. Some kind of frills and scales covered its body – it seemed familiar. It lifted its face to the sky and sang, a high, clear howl that wove its way through Kyre's bones. Not the malignity. Something else. Kinder. Beautiful.

Had Delgha's plan worked?

He turned back to his friends at the entrance. Delgha was adjusting the device that Thorme held in front of them both. In a flash, a half-formed shape appeared, and approached one of the hounds. The destriatch snarled and lunged at it.

But no, it really more like threw itself at the thing that

approached. It wasn't an attack. The destriatch and Delgha's creation collided. Limbs thrashed, electricity arced around them. The two things merged into one whole. A very solid, four-legged beast like the one over by Stiler and the others.

Once the electrical display ended, the new creature walked over by the first one and sat, relaxed but alert. The other destriatch howled and thrashed and bobbed their heads up and down, but didn't advance.

By the ghosts, the destriatch weren't threatening them. They were begging. They wanted Delgha and Thorme to do to them what they'd done to the others. They wanted the merge. They craved it. Like incomplete but living works of art, they just wanted completion.

It's a good plan, Kyre.

If it's such a great plan, he practically said aloud, then where are you? Are you here somewhere?

Kyre wanted to run up to Delgha and Thorme and ask them, but what if doing so disrupted the process in some way, or just spooked the destriatch? They were still destriatch, after all. Ravenous murder machines. He got closer, and caught Thorme's eye as Delgha worked the controls of the device yet again.

Thorme returned his gaze and shook her head, slowly.

Kyre held back. But doing so was killing little parts of himself, inside. He'd arrived late. Too late. Where was Aviend? Was the plan still in motion? Why had no one seen her?

One by one, he watched as the two of them restored each destriatch to its true form. Or, if not true, then at least complete. Each of the horrific beasts not only changed physically, but he could see the relaxation pass through them like a wave across water. It was beautiful, in its own way, if one had time to think about it.

He didn't.

When the last of the destriatch in front of them had merged with the creatures produced by the device and the way was safe, he hurried to the entrance.

"Where's Aviend?"

Delgha pursed her lips for a moment, and watched Thorme set the device down. Kyre wanted to shake her to get the answer to come out faster.

"Rillent," Delgha said. "She and Rillent went into the temple. And up to the star."

"Skist, I've got to get up there," he said. "Right now."

When they're standing amid the living things within the star, Rillent finally shows his surprise and delight. Like a mask dropping away. He seems younger somehow. There's an actual skisting sparkle in his purple eyes, like that of a child. "It's true," he says, looking at her. "All of it. Everything you told me."

For the first time, he looks around the space. He looks at Aviend. Truly looks at her. Not inside her. It's a weird sensation. He touches his palm to her cheek, and she does not flinch away. He smiles. He trusts her. "Did you give me this by your own choice?"

She needs him to keep believing her. Needs him to keep her alive. She answers, "Yes."

"Why?" he says. His answer is in his question. He has always believed she would be at his side, and now she is. "We will talk about this after."

Which means he won't just kill her now that he has what he wants. Needs. He will focus entirely on the device. Exactly what *she* wants. Needs.

Rillent turns his back to her while he stands at the device. Just like Kyre suspected, the technology here is not a stranger to him. More than any of them – even Delgha – Rillent knows what to do. This is a device he has known existed for years, and he has spent his life, others' lives, figuring out how to use it. He just couldn't find it.

And now she has led him right to it.

She stands at the viewer, which is perfectly zoomed in on the base. Rillent's people, running about. A handful of destriatch, half-formed, streaming through the woods. Searching. Searching. She can't imagine what it sounds like down there. The malignity. It makes her heart hurt, thinking about that song. She can't see Kyre.

Rillent's hands glide across the controls like a musician playing a familiar instrument. "Finally," he says softly. "I've been carrying around the key for years. It's what guided me to the Steremoss in the first place. And now you've finally shown me the lock that it opens." He runs his fingers over the implant in his head as he talks.

The key is the final piece. The final thing that Rillent himself brings to the plan.

There is glee in his voice. "The power of a universe, all for my own use." It's the voice of a predator who's been toying with its prey, but knows that now it's time to kill. And to feast.

Crystalline rods around the controls begin to pulsate. It's not something she's seen before.

When hunting a monster, use live bait, she thinks.

He hears that thought, or some of it, and turns. But it's already too late. His fingers have finished entering whatever codes he needed to. He is opening the barriers. He is destroying the other worlds. He is going to be all-powerful.

That is not what happens. Not what happens at all.

The star flickers, shudders. In the viewer, Aviend can see Rillent's glaives and the destriatch below. But now she can also see Delgha's counter-creatures, the ones who will complete the destriatch, give them what they've been lacking. She can see the slistoviles under Sil's command routing the glaives in large numbers.

All around them, the devices whir. They're doing something. They're just not doing what Rillent is expecting.

"What...?" Rillent says. He is flexing his fingers, as if he expects to feel the power in them. He is looking at his long silver weapon as if it has somehow failed him.

Aviend finds she has the strength to lift her head after all. She brings her gaze to Rillent's. "We're doing what you promised to do," she says. "We're protecting the Stere."

"But the barriers should be down... the bridge should be channeling..." His face shows that he wants to turn away from her, back toward the device, but he no longer trusts her. Which is fine. She doesn't need him to anymore.

"You raised the barriers for us," she says. "Permanently. The bridge – the conduit – is cut off for good." Somewhere, her mother's voice has found her. "We couldn't have done it without you."

She can feel her heart thumping, hard and true. Her back straightens. It won't do to underestimate him. Not now. Especially not now.

"How?" he asks.

Aviend looks around but does not let herself think about the part of the plan that's still missing. Instead, she taunts, "There's two sides of a coin. Two ends of a bridge. We didn't know how to activate it, didn't have the key, but we figured out how to turn it into a wall rather than a bridge when you did. It just took two of us, on both sides, at the same time."

He shakes his head. "No. You are mine."

"I was never yours," she says.

Rillent raises his weapon. Aviend raises her fist. It is all she has left to raise. She will not kneel. She will not cower. This is the end of ends, and she will meet it as she promised herself she would.

"I will kill you," Rillent says with a sudden calm coldness.

She nods. She has prepared for this moment. Killing is what Rillent does. Of course it would come down to this. She trusts Kyre and their entire clave, but most of all herself. She is the contingency plan. She opens her fist just as Rillent throws his weapon.

The hardest thing Kyre would ever have to do was watch Aviend die in front of him.

Fortunately, he didn't have to.

Rillent's weapon flew true across the room, suddenly crackling with dire energy. But Aviend's tiny device in her palm created an energy field that not only stopped the weapon, but held it in place, its pointed, blade-like tip inches from her face.

As soon as he could move after transmitting himself to the star, Kyre stepped forward. Pain in his leg ignored. His regular blade in his hand. He would have preferred the monoblade. Dammit.

Rillent saw him arrive. "You," Rillent said. It wasn't a word. Anger incarnate. Hatred. And, maybe, fear. Rillent had no weapon. He had no power to draw from. He was trapped here without a way out. That knowledge was beginning to show in his face, in the hold of his body.

"Us," Aviend and Kyre said at the same time. They moved together, to stand side by side. Kyre shot Aviend an "I'm glad you're still alive" look. Aviend gave him a tiny "I'm glad you came back to me" smile. She looked nearly ghostfallen – he didn't want to think of what had happened to her in the kubric – but she was here and alive and standing next to him.

"Let us help you," Kyre said. He didn't know what he meant by that exactly, but he needed to offer something. Rillent was backed up to the devices, both hands up. His wide eyes said he understood that he was cornered, in trouble. Had Rillent ever been in this position before? Kyre doubted it. Who knew how he would react?

"No," Rillent said. He flexed one hand wide, twining his fingers over the others, giving a tug. The sizzling field holding his weapon dissipated like so much fluff from a seed pod in the wind. The silver staff glided through the air back to his waiting grasp. The weapon made a soft thud as it landed against his palm.

"Skist," Kyre whispered. They hadn't known that he could do that.

Aviend's wristblades were suddenly in her hands, her hidden sheaths doing their job. She stepped forward, but not before Rillent's weapon left his hand again, blazing with danger. This time, however, its target was Kyre.

Aviend could move like a bolt of lightning at times, and this was one of those times. Kyre barely had time to think about all she'd been through that day. How was she still standing, let alone moving like that? She lunged at the projectile, clearly intending to throw herself in front of it. Any other day, and she would have succeeded. And died. But that day, her body was clearly pushed further than it had been before. Her blindingly fast move was not blinding enough. She struck the weapon's shaft with her shoulder. Energy blazed. Aviend cried out. The weapon still flew.

But the force of her body had knocked it a bit askew. Just a bit. But enough. Rather than impaling Kyre's chest, it sliced through the meat of his upper arm.

Kyre dropped to his knees, blade clattering to the floor. Aviend lay on the ground just a few feet away. Pain burned down his arm. It was as though lightning had shot from each finger. All he could see was purple. He fell forward onto his face, his chin hitting the floor hard enough to knock his teeth together.

The weapon returned to Rillent through the air yet again. "You are children poking your fingers into an adult's concerns," he said through clenched teeth that might have been a smile on anyone else. "Yes, your little plan worked. You got me to strengthen the barrier, stopped the main transfer of energy. But the kubrics have been activated for years, filling with energy. I've been able to siphon a modicum of that off during that time, but here? I can access all of it, now that you've given me this place. You may have kept me from becoming the god of two worlds, but I'll still be the god of one."

Despair settled into Kyre's bones, emotional pain on top of the physical ones that already held him to the floor. He could see Aviend's face, caught her expression. She hadn't known that either.

"I've devoted my life to this pursuit. Did you really think you could understand these systems better than I?" Rillent's hands were once again gliding across the controls. Adroit. Almost lazy. Showing off. "Perhaps you should have become an Aeon Priest after all, Nuvinae's daughter. Perhaps then you could have understood enough to actually take me down."

Oh, Kyre thought. After all this time, all that headspace, Rillent still didn't know Aviend very well. Already, Kyre could feel her moving in response to Rillent's words, coming toward him.

He thought he heard her say, "Contingencies within

contingencies." He felt her fingers along his skin, and then the cool edge of her wristblade as she sliced through the leather around his neck. She was shaking. She'd absorbed most of the weapon's energies. She placed the device in his good hand, and then slumped against him. She looked small and broken as that day in the treehouse, what felt like so long ago. But he could feel her, fast and shallow breaths, alive.

He lay on the ground, gathering himself. She'd put it in his hand. There had to be some last ounce of strength in him. For the Stere. For both Steres. For his friends. For redemption.

In his hand, the cypher weighed less than it ever had around his neck. It felt like nothing. Carrying it all this time. For what? He'd thought for himself, in case he ever got to that place, that place where he couldn't resist Rillent's commands. But now he knew that he'd carried it for this moment.

The energy disruptor could disrupt anything – living or mechanical – but only for a mere moment. Maybe it would be enough. He thumbed the dial on the back. One direction was for organic disruption, the other for mechanical. He carefully moved the dial to the mechanical side.

A pulse of translucent energy spread instantly through the weird chamber. Everything went dark.

Near him, Aviend made no move or sound. Kyre struggled to his feet. At least the pain in his arm would keep him from thinking about his leg. He staggered in the darkness toward where he knew Rillent to be. What was his plan? Throttle him? Knock him unconscious? He'd dropped his last weapon somewhere.

Kyre stepped forward, silent and slow in the dark. Somewhere in front of him, Rillent would be there, working the controls, trying to bring them back. He'd have that bladed staff-thing of his. Kyre tensed, ready to launch himself at the man as soon as he saw him. The only advantage he had was surprise.

Lights started flickering back on. More lights. Where was Rillent? Kyre saw the controls returning to power, but–

Rillent was on the floor, right in front of him. Rillent shuddered and writhed, both hands clutching his forehead. His silver weapon lay on the ground by his feet.

As power fully restored itself in the star's inner chamber, Kyre stared down at the man who had destroyed so much of the world he loved. He was convulsing. His eyes were pulled tight. His fingers digging at the front of his forehead.

Skist. The energy disruptor hadn't just affected numenera in the star. It had affected Rillent's implant as well. It was just a moment, a mere moment of disruption, but it must have done something horrible inside Rillent's head. The implant must have been more than a key. It must have been rooted deep in the man's brain. And now it was killing him.

The whole time, Kyre had been wearing that thing around his neck. The whole time, he had possessed the means to kill Rillent.

He went down on his knees – pains of his body forgotten – trying to pull Rillent's hands from the device, trying to hold him steady. He didn't know what else to do. Kyre could hear Aviend climbing to her feet, coming to stand beside Rillent's writhing body.

"He's going to die," he said.

"Good." Her reply was quick. Instinctual. Sharper than he'd ever heard her.

He didn't know what to do. It wasn't as if he forgot everything that had happened over the years. The lies. The intimidation. The graves. The wolflilies. But he'd seen a different world. A place where things had gone differently. Better. Someone, somewhere, made another choice, and it made all the difference. But there were still choices to make. Any one of those choices could make a different world. And everyone made choices like that every day.

But he really was only interested in one choice at the moment.

This choice.

Choose, the philethis said.

He stopped trying to move Rillent's fingers away; their hold was too tight, riveting with every shudder. Kyre put his hands on Rillent's shoulders, tried to hold his quivering body still with the weight of his own. "If we take him, now, we can get him to Thorme. She can help him."

Aviend, the person he loved more than he thought possible, looked at him as if he were mad. But only for a moment. She knew him. She knew him better than anyone else ever could. She understood.

"You skisting brehmhearted fool," she said. "Let's go."

There is no Rillent. Not really. Oh, the tall man walks among them, his purple eyes staring out beneath the horrific scars that cover the front and top of his head. He stares blankly at the forest when they take him out on walks. Delgha says the names of plants and animals in an effort to teach him to talk again.

But it's not Rillent. Not the man who lorded over the Steremoss for these many years. Maybe, just maybe, he will recover a bit. Have an opportunity to make some new choices of his own. But for now, they will look after him.

"We rescue people," Kyre had said to the others when they brought him back to the base. "It's what we do."

"You're too kind," Aviend says practically every day, motioning with her chin toward Kyre's now-useless arm. "Way too kind." But she says it with a bit of a smile. And more than a bit of affection. Way more.

Rillent's glaives had surrendered quickly or fled. The destriatch, now complete and whole, scattered into the woods to live natural lives as hunters, but not murderers. One, they now keep as a guardian. Kyre wants to name it Barber, but Aviend doesn't think that's funny at all. Well, maybe a little.

Quenn, emboldened by how many people he'd got out of

the kubric before it sealed, took Kyre's words to heart. "We save people." It was hard to see past the glow of satisfaction in his face in those early days as he helped return all of the trenchers and workers back to their homes. It would take months to get everyone adequately settled, but Quenn and Vesi are up for it.

"I've seen another you," Kyre tells Aviend. "Another Stere. I know there are many possibilities. Many paths. We thought maybe that other world had no Rillent. But what if it did, but he was just different? What if he'd made other choices? Taken another path?"

Aviend sees the wisdom of it. It's a deep, profound sort of wisdom. But that doesn't mean she likes it. She remembers too well who he was to ever completely accept who he might become. At least, that's how it feels now.

It could be years before Rillent can talk, and Thorme's confident that he won't be the same man. Too much damage. But Kyre does what he can to make him comfortable. Almost like a child, they'll raise him as one of their own. Help him make the right choices. Maybe in that future, Aviend will be able to look him in the eye.

Maybe.

It will take those years to repair the damage that's been wrought. The kubrics, now sealed, can just be buried again, perhaps. The town can be rebuilt. These are challenges she can focus on. And with Kyre at her side, she knows they'll succeed.

She doesn't ask him about that other world. He tries to get everyone to call wolflilies heartblooms, but she never asks why. She knows he saw things there that spoke to his heart. She knows that sealing that world away forever caused him a lot more pain than she had been expecting. She sees him sometimes, looking out at the forest, hoping to see ghosts that are never there anymore.

Heartblooms has a nice ring to it. As does Delgha's idea for starting up a new clave. Vesi's first in line to join. She's as eager and capable as Aviend is tired. Someday, she'll be ready to lead.

People in the Steremoss seem interested in Gavani again, and why not? Delgha's convinced the star has more secrets and wonders to reveal, and she's probably right. But for now, it's enough to lay in the warm grass amid the... heartblooms with her love and look up at the star and all the other stars and wonder if they all hold mysteries like the one they discovered.

And it's enough to just wonder, and not know.

ACKNOWLEDGMENTS & INSPIRATIONS

We owe a huge debt of gratitude to the No Name Writers' Group – Erin Evans, Rhiannon Held, Corry Lee-Boehm, Kate Marshall, and Susan J Morris – for their feedback, insight, and time. A big thank you to Federico Musetti and his fabulous cover and to John Petersen for capturing the characters so beautifully. And to all of the wonderful people at Monte Cook Games: you're our Night Clave, and we'll fight beside you every step of the way.

Monte and Shanna

ABOUT THE AUTHORS

MONTE COOK has worked as a professional writer for more than 20 years. As a fiction writer, he has published numerous short stories and two novels. As a comic book writer, he has written a limited series for Marvel Comics called *Monte Cook's Ptolus: City by the Spire*, as well as some shorter work. As a non-fiction writer, he has published the wry but informative *The Skeptic's Guide to Conspiracies*.

His work, however, as a game designer, is likely most notable. Since 1988, he has written hundreds of tabletop roleplaying game books and articles, and won numerous awards. Monte is likely best known for *Dungeons & Dragons 3rd Edition*, which he co-designed with Jonathan Tweet and Skip Williams. In 2001, he started his own game design studio, Malhavoc Press, and published such notable and award-winning products as *Ptolus*, *Arcana Evolved*, and the *Book of Eldritch Might* series. As a freelance game designer, he designed HeroClix and *Monte Cook's World of Darkness*, and he has worked on the *Pathfinder RPG*, the Marvel Comics massively multiplayer online game, and numerous other games and related projects. He is the designer of *Numenera*.

montecookgames.com • *twitter.com/montejcook*

SHANNA GERMAIN is the creative director for *Numenera* and *The Strange*. An award-winning writer and editor, her poems, essays, stories, novellas, and articles have been widely published in places like *Apex Magazine*, *Best American Erotica*, *Best Bondage Erotica*, *Best Lesbian Romance*, *Lightspeed*, *Salon* and more. She has garnered a variety of awards for her work, including a Pushcart Prize nomination, the Rauxa Prize for Erotic Poetry, and the C Hamilton Bailey Poetry Fellowship.

Her most recent books include *The Lure of Dangerous Women* (Wayzgoose Press, 2012), *Leather Bound* (HarperCollins, 2013), and *As Kinky As You Wanna Be* (Cleis Press, 2014).

shannagermain.com • *twitter.com/shannagermain*

THERE HAVE BEEN EIGHT PREVIOUS WORLDS

Each world stretched across vast millennia of time. Each played host to a race whose civilizations rose to supremacy but eventually died or scattered, disappeared or transcended. During the time each world flourished, those that ruled it spoke to the stars, reengineered their physical bodies, and mastered form and essence, all in their own unique ways.

Each left behind... *remnants*.

The people of the new world—the Ninth World — sometimes call these remnants magic, and who are we to say they're wrong? But most give a unique name to the legacies of the nigh-unimaginable past. They call them...

Explore the Ninth World in the Numenera roleplaying game from Monte Cook Games.

www.numenera.com